The Wind In The Pylons

Gareth Lovett Jones is a photographer and author whose past work includes a novel, *Valley With A Bright Cloud*; *English Country Lanes*, a cyclist's eye-view of the countryside; and *The Wildwood*, an exploration of British ancient woodlands. His photographs also appear in Richard Mabey's *Flora Britannica*. He is currently working on a photographic exhibition on the subject of veteran yew trees. He lives on the Oxfordshire/Berkshire border by the reach of the Thames where Kenneth Grahame made his final home.

David —
Aren't you writing a book
about the weasels ??

The Wind In The Pylons

Adventures of the Mole In Weaselworld

Gareth Lovett Jones

Volume I

All the best,

Gareth

HILLTOP

Hilltop Publishing Limited

First published in the United Kingdom in 2003
by Hilltop Publishing Limited
PO Box 429
Aylesbury
Buckinghamshire HP18 9XY.
U.K.
www.hilltoppublishing.co.uk

All characters in this novel are fictitious and any resemblance to weasels, living
or dead, is purely coincidental.

ISBN 0 9536850 2 0

Cover Illustration by Judy Hammond
Book Design by Judy Stocker
Typeset in 11½pt Centaur by Avocet Typeset, Chilton, Aylesbury, Bucks.
Printed and bound by Biddles Ltd, Guildford and Kings Lynn

"Beyond the Wild Wood comes the Wide World", said the Rat. *"And that's something that doesn't matter, either to you or me. I've never been there, and I'm never going, nor you either, if you've got any sense at all. Don't ever refer to it again, please!"*

Kenneth Grahame
The Wind In The Willows

PART ONE

The Tardy Mr Mole

CONTENTS

PART ONE

The Tardy Mr. Mole

But at my back I alwaies hear
Times winged Motor hurrying near . . .
Marvole

CHAPTER ONE

EXIT MOLE, STAGE RIGHT

It was another year in the Valley. Above ground the Spring had announced its intentions, and in the Wild Wood the dog's mercury was dancing anew between the oaks and hollies like a throng of tiny pixillated ballerinas. Along the hedge-banks the celandines were turning from yellow balls to yellow cups, and everywhere the buds of sappy plants were thrust up skywards, plumped and sheened with promise.

There was not an animal who had not felt the change. The wrens perched among the dense white snow-blooms of the earliest cherry plums, singing as if they meant it; the otters twisted and twined along their crystal sub-aqueous paths with fresh vigour in their sinews; the rabbits, the shrews and the voles rose just a little earlier each day to greet the sunrise, every whisker-set atwitch with a distinctly vernal rhythm. And the moles, to an animal ...

... The moles, to an animal—it goes almost without saying—*spring-cleaned.*

Whitewashing is a contemplative business, and as he slopped and slapped his way around his little kitchen that fine March day the Mole had fallen to musing. Five years had gone by already, he thought (five years!—he could hardly believe it) since the battle of Toad Hall in which he, the Mole, had played his own small part, fighting to win back the big house from those rascally weasels' clutches. Some of the simpler animals—young hedgehogs and field-mice in particular—still occasionally stood by their doors to salute him as he went past. "It's the famous Mr Mole!" he would hear them whisper, "'E of the Great Battle Of Toad Hall! A terrible, terrible fighter 'e is—felled seven ferrets with a single blow!"

And the Mole would smile, and nod modestly, and pass on by, quietly amused at the way his humble prowess had been exaggerated.

"I 'eard it wuz ten *stoats!*" some other hoarse small voice would breathe as he walked on.

"It wuz *weasels!* Twelve of 'em!"

"It wuz *stoats!*"

"— Ferrets!"

"— Weasels!"

"— Stoats, stoats, stoats, stoats, stoats!"

Five years! The Mole still found it hard to believe. In those years, to be sure, he had had more than a few other scrapes and adventures worthy of the name. And he had seen and learned new things and—perhaps—become just a bit more of a mole of the world than once he was; a mole, at least, of that little, local, down-country world every last blade of grass of which he knew and loved as home. Why, couldn't he almost row well by now? He could hardly remember the last time he had fallen backward at the rowlocks, or splashed Ratty absolutely in the face. Nowadays, most of his oar-strokes cut the *water*.

And he was content. He was happy. Happy? Of course he was! He could answer all his own small needs with a bit of effort, and work wasn't something he had ever been afraid of. (He dipped his half-forgotten brush.) And he and his friends—his good, true, ever-loyal friends—they had had such times together, O, such jolly, jolly times. The picnics! All those waterside feasts, lolling in the whispering shade of their favourite willow-trees. The boating trips! All those glorious long and lazy summer days on the river with Ratty and Toad! What *could* be more perfect?

But if anyone had ever asked him—and no one ever had— he would have to have said that nothing since had *quite* come up to the excitement of the Battle Days. Had it, though? It wasn't ... (he slapped) ... was it? ... (he slopped) so much that he hoped for another Great Adventure ... (slap) ... obviously—(slop) ... as that ... well ...

The Mole stood back from the slight curve of the wall, brush in hand. "O, dash it all, though!" he said out loud. "An animal has to be honest!" (The paint ran down, or up, his arm.) "No, Mole, no. You would *not* say no to another Great Adventure, certainly you wouldn't, not if one happened to come knocking on your door. O ... blow!" (He fumbled for a rag.) "It's all over my elbow!" (He rinsed his fur in the sink, staring blankly.)

The real problem, thought the Mole, as he donned a work glove only to find a finger holed, the real problem was that one fiddly little job did always seem to lead a fellow straight on into another, still fiddlier little job he hadn't previously dreamed of. It did rather seem as though such little jobs might take a certain pleasure in inventing themselves—as if they might have some secret, inexplicable plan to be legion just to keep a mole from great adventures. Why, hadn't he only this morning scrubbed down the inside of his onion-cupboard, and then carefully brushed out last year's tea-dust from his tea-chest (using a paintbrush for the corners) only to find the cuckoo clock in the most urgent need of a clean? And hadn't the teaspoons contrived to get themselves shockingly disarrayed inside their drawer, and hadn't he packed them all away again (with not a single handle overlapping) only to see his old metal cruet-holder suddenly sitting there in front of him turquoise with verdigris, so that it had to be polished and polished in all its fiddly-faddly-this-way-and-that-way-and-try-again-in-the-corners-because-they're-not-really-done-yet-faddly-fiddliness?

And if an adventure didn't happen to come knocking on an animal's door, thought the Mole, well then, what could he do about it? Should he go out searching, on the lookout for adventures that hadn't happened yet? Should he pin an advertisement to some much passed tree trunk? "Mr Mole, of the Battle Of Toad Hall, seeks new exploits. Modest strategic-combat skills only. All enquiries to Mole End, in writing please"?

Such thoughts were still drifting through his head as he reached the end of his kitchen where the big old broom-cupboard stood. Now, this heavy old oak cabinet had sat in just the same spot through all the years since the Mole had inherited Mole End from his great uncle Warpmold. Every year past since he could remember, he had whitewashed around it as best he could manage, but somehow—just where he had to touch in around the edges—there was always an uneven line of paint that showed up ever afterwards.

The Mole paused again. He squinted. He stroked his chin, in deepest reluctance. He considered deeply. He put his paws on his hips. And then he snorted out loud in disgust.

"O, bother!" he said. "O blow, O *blow*! It's just no good, Mole, is it?—Really, you can't leave it like that any more! You'll have to move it this time—you'll just have to."

So saying, he grasped the back edge of the cabinet as best he could and tugged. After a moment, gruntingly, he tugged again, and then again, until at last the boulderous object consented to release its age-old grip on the floor and scrape outwards far enough to give him space to work. But in this space—stretching with an unpleasant sticky clothiness—he found the dust-whitened cobwebs of uncounted dynasties of spiders.

The appalled Mole felt urgently behind him for his broom, but hardly had he begun his flicking and twisting before he stopped once more, peering in disbelief into the deepest area of shadow. For there, waist-high behind the cobwebs, he saw a hole. A tunnel-shaped—yes, a most suspiciously tunnel-shaped—hole.

Could that be where that draught has always come from? he wondered. Was it possible that for all the years he had been at Mole End he had had a back door as well as a front one? Well, he would have to find out—and immediately too, let the whitewash complain as it may! A humming kind of excitement was already building in him as he took off his overalls. An urging point of curiosity had set his nose-tip aquiver and his little heart was beating with a distinctive thump that said, in almost as many words, "But this may be it, Mole! This may be what you've been hoping for!" No doubt about it, up this tunnel he would go, just as soon as the broom-cupboard had agreed to let him round it.

He was not greatly surprised, three minutes later, to see that the passage ahead of him was in less than first class condition. It began by climbing very gently through the familiar gravelly river-valley soils, and in some places nearest the entrance it had all but collapsed. But the Mole's prowess as an excavator soon got him round each obstacle he came to. He scrabbled and scrooged *ad lib* where he did not merely scratch and scrape; and as he got further on and the infalls became more challenging, he fell to squiggling and squoggling, with now and then a deft application of the squeezle or the squoozle. Minutes passed as he worked on, and more on top of them, so that he began to lose count of time altogether. But there was the passage running on ahead of him, drawing him along it as surely as if he had been a small boat on a swollen stream.

"On we go!" he breathed patiently. "ON we go!"

Gradually, though, the Mole felt his first urgings of excitement and expectation being pushed aside, as if by the faintest suggestion of unease. The further he went now, the more he wanted to be finished. The thought even once entered his head that he might be better off turning back and forgetting all about it.

But it was already too late for that. The line of the tunnel rose abruptly upwards for the distance of a few feet, and with a scattering of loose soil and pebbles the Mole found himself out, and done, and standing foursquare in the daylight.

As always it took the Mole a good half minute to adjust to the sudden brilliance—although the day was cloudy, so that he did not need to screw up his eyes quite so tightly as if the sun had been out. But even before he could look about him easily, he knew for certain that something was wrong. He sniffed the air, wrinkling up his nose in instant distaste. There was a smell about—several smells, in fact, but one in partic-ular that stood out: acrid, sharp, almost like that of a salt wind blowing off a seaweedy sea, yet seeming to the Mole's sensitive nose not of Nature at all. Straight away his eyes began to itch. And there was too a strange, awesome sound, such as he had never heard before nor could possibly have imagined. It was like a great continuous exhalation, or rumbling, or combination of the two, in which pulses of whining also grew and then dimmed, grew and then dimmed. Somehow it seemed far away and close by, all at the same time.

"O, but where *am* I?" he thought to himself, half out loud. "What can have *happened*?"

As his vision adjusted, so he began to look about him more keenly. And the first thing that struck him, like a hammer blow, was how little there was to see, and how utterly, utterly strange what he *could* see was. Through his own front door he would come straight up into a grassy meadow, close by a hedge whose neat rounded shape was always, by late March, dazzlingly patterned over with the tiny white blooms of the blackthorn. There was a great old oak—not in the hedge, but standing by it—whose arm-like twisted roots had been gnawed and then polished by the oily wool of resting sheep. Yet no such landmarks existed here. Instead, next to him, he found an odd, ugly little short grey post. It had a broad head bearing a door of some kind, embossed with the letters LI-OO192-PX. It made a low, slow and continuous ticking, like a grandfather clock in the very last moments before it runs down. A few yards behind this object stood a series of broken fragments of hawthorn and elder, growing in a line along a very low bank with wide gaps between them. Far away to the south, in the direction of what ought to have been his everyday entrance, there stood a big dead tree.

The ground itself was mossed, with blackened stumps of some crop of long ago sticking up from it as if it might once have been plough-land, then abandoned. A line of tall posts made of a crude looking grey-white material ran across it as far as an unmade road. Beyond this, to the Mole's left, stretched a ploughed field so huge that anything that lay beyond it might as well have been in the next county. On this vast space, made toy-like by distance, a strange yellow machine was slowly moving. Behind it, what looked like a white mist swirled out, impossibly, in a row of Catherine-wheeling shapes. The wind was blowing from just this direction.

The Mole hugged himself in anxiety, so startled by the sense of invisible danger all about him that he could not even move back towards the tunnel exit. "Something terrible—O, *terrible*—has happened here!" he whispered. Yet where *was* "here"? And how had he arrived in it?

"I must go back," he said, summoning the courage to make a move.

But just as he was about to take a step he saw a great grey vehicle with immensely fat, ridged tyres bouncing towards him over the rough ground. It was loaded with rolls of what looked like wire, and its engine made a monstrous grating-whining-growl of such a violence as he had never before heard nor imagined. Seeing this great beast come on directly at him, or so it seemed, what could any mole have done but turn and run from it? He ran in the direction of the unmade road, and within seconds the thing stood between him and the tunnel exit.

When he reached the track, still in a panic, the Mole hurried on along it. The animals that jumped down from the vehicle—a very rough-looking rabbit and, bizarrely, a couple of stoats—showed not the slightest interest in him, but the Mole was not about to go back and have a chat with them. Instead, puffing nervously, he trotted on towards a distant point where there was at least some hopeful sign of over-hanging vegetation.

"This is not the adventure I wanted!" he whispered. A hundred yards further on, negotiating a large pothole filled with a crumbling black material and pieces of old brick, he said the same thing again, a little louder and rather more petu-lantly. Here isolated hawthorns stood a hundred yards apart from one another, trimmed flat across their tops as if at the hand of some lunatic of tidiness. These gradually increased in number until a quarter of a mile later the track was lined continuously along one side with blackthorn bushes—as the Mole might have expected—but grown out, and in curiously full bloom. Beyond and above the foam of tiny flowerets the Mole could also see the rearing grey-green tops of a series of shed-like *things*, once again inconceivably immense. They were built of deeply ridged materials, wholly unfamiliar to him, and had about them the look and feel of structures thrown up in preparation for a war.

Words were written in towering letters across each of these great null artificial cliff-faces: one, in lemon-yellow, read BRAWSCHE. The one next to it—and it took the Mole nearly a minute to reach it—was made in letters that seemed, astoundingly, to be illuminated from the inside. This said

KANSAS HOMEKARE. Underneath, a flatter, unlit sign read KATCH OUR KRAZY PRICES!!! Beyond this was a very high fence made of some super-heavy-duty criss-cross wire and here, on another sign, were the words UNIVERSAL BREAKDOWN.

"Dear me," said the Mole. "O! Dear, dear me! I seem to have come up in Kansas." He noticed that the sinister breathing-roar, or roaring-breath, ever present in the atmosphere, was much louder here than it had sounded at the tunnel exit. It reached towards him through the leafless branches of a thicket to his right almost as if it were a part of them.

The Mole went on along the track, which by now had a deep screen of hazels and thorns on either side. Under them lay discarded objects: a rusted child's bicycle of an odd design, its frame bent into a sad banana-shape, a rotting mattress in which seedlings had taken root, and ahead, where a bollard bisected the path, a scattering of strange little metal cylinders covered in garishly coloured letters. JILT, read one, ZUPP another, and there, and there, and then again there, were the words POKE-A-POLAR.

Finally the Mole emerged from the shrubs into another open space. But this was a space with buildings—or at least, structures—strewn about in such incomprehensible chaos and ugliness that at first he could only cover his eyes with his paws and hope that when he removed them he might be looking at something else entirely. The strategy did not work. One vastly distended grey-blue shed lumped upward into the sky beyond the next vastly distended grey-blue shed, elbowing at one another for room in a tangling mayhem of smooth, black hard roads whose very surfaces seemed alien to him. Between all this and the spot where the Mole now stood there stretched an acreage of land big enough to support three small farms complete with livestock, cereals, roots and clover: on it stood hundreds upon hundreds of absurd, blob-like wheeled contraptions. To his great credit—despite his anxiety—it did not take the Mole very long to identify these last-mentioned objects as some strangely distorted, sealed-in species of motor-car.

One stretch of road passed near where he stood, and this was full almost to capacity with a very slow-moving queue of the same contraptions—a weary-looking animal slumped dimly at the wheel of each—going in to the expanse, whilst in the other direction an equally solid line of the things flowed out. Between these excitements ran narrow borders of straggling shrubs generously littered about with a mix of little metal cylinders and things resembling large white tumblers. And above all of this reared more wall-size letters illuminating phrases of blank opacity such as CARPET-PLANET, MISSISSIPPI CHICKEN BAKES (Mississippi? thought the Mole), PARADISE OF SUEDE, and LOUISIANA LIZARD-LOUNGES ("Ah!—O? Er.. *Louisiana*?"). Another sign at the road-edge announced, THIS WAY TO THE UTOPIA PARK TRADE NURTURY. Beneath it lay a ragged six-foot twist of what looked like old cardboard, and just behind it a series of flapping banners that one after another repeated a proposition the Mole comforted himself he knew to be nonsense: *SAVE* WHILE YOU SPEND!

Beyond the giant sheds, cranes were moving, slowly shifting immense square-shaped loads. And beyond these the sky itself seemed to have been scored across with drooping lines suspended from three-armed tapering metal skeletons as if to fence it out altogether.

Well: what could even the most stalwart and level-headed of animals have done in circumstances such as these? Was the Mole to go over into that looming horror-scape, knock amiably on one of the inching contraptions' windows and ask the animal inside for directions? Directions to where? In any case, many of the drivers looked like weasels, or if not weasels proper ... But the Mole instantly dismissed the thought as too difficult. He turned helplessly in the opposite direction and there, dim and blue in the hazy cloud-lit distances, he could just make out a line of wooded hills. There was—wasn't there?—something faintly familiar about their shape, something sufficient, anyway, to make him hope that if he could possibly get to them he might find someone, some approachable animal of his own kind, to whom he might turn for help.

So he hurried off, trying as best he could not to give the impression he was afraid. He followed a long smooth-topped pavement as it curved slowly up beneath a bank of littered grass. But when eventually he crested this slight rise, fear or no fear, he stopped dead in his non-existent tracks. For here, spreading below him like the worst dyspeptic nightmare ever suffered by a top-scale Titan, lay the dread source of that atmospheric breathing-roar, now deafening in its intensity: a "road" of such vast dimensions that even as the Mole gawped in amazement at it, he found his sense of distance and scale dizzyingly undermined.

Why, the thing had to be wider than a river—fifty yards, at least. Wider than *the* River—no, but that was impossible! Yet there it was in front of him. And on this impossible thing— in three seemingly marble-smooth channels leading west, and curving away to the edge of the world, and three seemingly marble-smooth channels leading east, and curving away to the world's other edge—there flowed two unbroken rivers of blobs, squashed blobs, angular-squashed blobs, great shoe-boxes with snouts, and pantechnicons the size of freight carriages crazily freed from their rails. All were moving at speeds so high that the Mole was quite unable to adjust his vision to the sight of them.

"Where *are* they all going?" he thought, whispering the words out loud just after he thought them. "Where *are* they all *going*? Why aren't they all back at *home*?"

He looked away, reaching out to a grey metal barrier for

support, but even as he did so he understood how the noise was generated: each missile made its own contribution as it passed, its tyres roaring along the surface of the road as if the air itself was being ripped and tattered. And the air seemed barely air at all. To the Mole—whose nostrils and lungs had rarely been exposed to anything worse than a double dose of meadowsweet pollen—it seemed as if he were being poisoned. He pulled out his spotted cotton handkerchief and clutched it tightly to his face.

The torrential road was bridged, not twenty yards from him, by a great three-channelled oval around which further blob-flows pulsed, much like rowboats in a maelstrom. But the Mole saw that to follow this upper route any sane animal would need to be inside (and thus capable of controlling) one of those urgently-whisking machines. To attempt the crossing on foot would mean running across first one flow of projectiles as it came up from the river-road on a spur, and then across another as it descended on the far side.

He stared desperately about him: to his left was a bramble-bank, hung over with what looked like ragged sheets of some opaquely shining substance (another unappealing unknown) and, just as puzzling, a number of little grey-silver and oddly patterned 'wheels'. To his right stood signs bearing meaningless arrows and white chevrons on black backgrounds, a huge blue board indicating LONDON in one direction, SWINDON AND THE WEST in the other. Here too the sky was scratched across with wires, and around the bridge-oval there stood a series of lights on very tall, thin posts, which glowed a dull crimson against the gradually darkening sky.

The Mole gazed out beyond all this, towards the line of distant hills. A suggestion of woods and fields on them gave him the faintest sense of hope. Like it or not, he thought, he had no choice: to reach them he would have to get across this chasm somehow. He walked as close as he could to the first ramp of exit, and stood on a grey cracked pavement next to a grey flaking rail, watching the perpetual stream of contraptions as they climbed the ramp to pass him. There they came: a white one, another white one, a red one, another red one ... another red one ...

Every so often, with a little self-urging "Oo!" he began a movement, as if to cross, but each time he did so his feet failed to leave their starting-post. At one moment the contraption build-up on the oval was almost dense enough to stem the flow, but the moment quickly passed.

Then, at last, there in the distance, he saw a space coming. After that mini-blob of acidic puce, leaving the flow—just *there*—there was a space. He could do it there—he could!

"I will ... I will ..." muttered the Mole into his handkerchief, pattering his little feet on the spot as he did so.

The blob of vile pucidity was bulleting towards him, very hard on the tail of the last of the preceding flow. "Soon, soon, soon—NOW!" shouted the Mole to himself. But ... O, how long was that space? ... *Another* Thing was coming now, there, at the back end of it, even faster than all the others. There it was, and there, and there, still far off but closer, closer ...

"*Come on*, Mole!" groaned the Mole. "*COME on!*" Then, with the most heroically fearsome yell of his tribal war-cry— "A Mole! A Mole!"—that he could muster, he hurled himself full in the path of the oncoming vehicle.

There was a long and high-pitched squeal, and what seemed no more than a second later the front of the machine had thumped into the running Mole, flipping him over and over its top towards the slope of its windscreen, whence in another second or so he had fallen away again to the ground. Dazed, his head spinning, and with a dull pain now running all along his left leg and haunch, the Mole saw a door flung open, and an irate animal throwing aside some kind of curved device which, oddly, he seemed to have been pressing to his face.

"You MORON! You CRETIN!—I—you—you Cranially-Very-Very-Seriously-Under-Furnished-Individual!!" shrieked the animal, jumping out and performing a little jig of rage next to his vehicle, his fists clenched high above his head. "If you want to KILL yourself, ALL you've got to do is jump off THERE!" (With trembling hand and finger he pointed towards the bridge.) "Much more effective, you know! Much more choice!" But then—in what seemed to the dazed Mole no more than the twitch of a whiskered nose—this furious individual gained control of himself and fell silent. He glanced about, just a little furtively, at the passing vehicles, then bent down to the prostrate Mole. "Are you badly hurt?" he asked.

"I have a pain," answered the Mole.

"Here, come on," said the driver. "Can you walk? Get in the car. Come on—quickly—quick, quick, quick, if you're all right—get in the blasted car!"

One or two of the vehicles leaving the great road had slowed down in passing, their windows opening as they drew closer. The Mole's demolisher-turned-helper addressed the first of these, and then shouted down to the next, "No, it's all right. Nothing serious, ha, ha! We can cope. Fine … fine … Thank you, thank you. We'll see to it …"

Seconds thereafter, the Mole found himself inside the standing projectile. The strange rounded door had been slammed, the other animal was back at the steering wheel, and the "car" (which was black, and very much of the "larger squashed" school of blobs) had rejoined the unending flow, curving swiftly away around one segment of the great grey oval and then leaving by another, rather less busy, four-lane road.

The Mole examined his leg and side. Like all animals he knew instinctively how to take an impact as best he could, and he had had enough falls in his time to be able to recognise a break in a bone at once. He would be all right, he realised, barring a big bruise or two.

"Damn!" said the driver—shockingly, of course, to the Mole, who was in the habit of blocking his ears to bad language. "Damn, damn, damn, *damn!* I mean, I ask, perhaps I shouldn't, but I do, I do ask—Do I need this? Do I *need* this— NOW?!" He appeared to be talking to the roof of his "car". Then once again, with a visible effort, he managed to calm himself. "How do you feel?" he asked the Mole, almost temperately now.

"I shall be all right, thank you very much," answered the Mole. "Nothing broken."

"AAAAHHH!" cried the driver. "Tail-crushing suede-pate! Get your long pointed nose out of my exhaust-pipe! ... Sorry. Sorry. There are just so many of these animals! You see how they drive? GET OFF MY BLASTED TAIL, PANDAMMIT!!"

The Mole turned hesitantly to where the curve of the driver's thumb was indicating—behind him—and sure enough, the rear window of the "car" seemed now to be almost completely filled: what filled it was super-squashed, rage-red, and waxed as a witch's apple. It was being driven by a sharp young weasel possessed of a very severe, flattened fur-cut not dissimilar in shape to the horizontal thorns the Mole had first passed on the track. He noted with deep puzzlement that this animal was wearing bulbous, goggle-like dark glasses, even as the dusk was darkening into night outside. He must have weak eyes, thought the Mole. Perhaps that is why he drives so close.

"Not going fast enough for him, am I?" fumed the Mole's combustible companion. "OK!—OK! This'll show the nasty little pile of weevil-poo!" The black vehicle immediately began to lose speed, and the Mole looked behind to see the follower shift instantly to one side and then pass on ahead at such terrifying velocity it seemed the machine he was in had ceased to move at all. As it did so there was an exchange of curious and, to the Mole, quite indecipherable paw signals between the two drivers.

"How do you like that, squire? Drive into a wall, why don't you? Thrusting young tail-crusher!"

The Mole's companion was, as it happened, a water rat. He was dressed in a pinstripe suit of the finest cloth and cut, and his tie was of a sober dark maroon and bore the simple *imprimatur* of what might have been some long-established school. On his left wrist glowed a large and slightly ostentatious-looking watch, held in place by a strap made of narrow metal pieces. He was perhaps a few years the Mole's senior, and to his passenger's observing eye he looked unusually tired, almost as if the tiredness had been under his fur so long that now it never left him.

The "car" turned off another maelstrom of metal into something that almost resembled a normal road. A handful of mature oaks stood at intervals along one side of it, punctuating the length of a continuous flint-and-brick wall that could (to the Mole's eyes) only indicate the presence of parkland. But as the "car" began to accelerate along this relative backwater, so the Mole's heart also began to drub in terror: the oaks were soon shifting past at a speed such as he had never seen, and the patterning of the wall quickly disappeared into a blur. And there ahead now he saw the lights of another machine which was, it seemed, coming straight towards them.

"O-o-o-o-O!" cried the Mole, jumping from his seat and urgently trying to scrooge his way to safety beneath the carpet.

"What *are* you doing?" demanded the Rat. "And *why* haven't you got your seat belt on?" He looked away at the road as the oncoming vehicle completed its overtaking, then glanced back at his odd little passenger. "For that matter… Look, get up, for the love of… It's all right, get up! Put the seat belt *on, please.*"

"… The what belt?"

"What do you mean, the what belt?—The seat belt, the SEATT—beltt!"

"See-ta … —belt …?" echoed the Mole dimly, groping

around him rather as if he had been sitting in the shallow end of a swimming pool.

The Rat stared, brief but caustic. "You cannot mean to tell me ..." He paused, snorted, looked again, a little more penetratingly this time. "You're not ON something, are you?"

Naturally, at such a question, and though still in mid-grope, the Mole looked down to establish whether he was on something or not. "I don't think so," he replied. "Er ... I am on this very nice seat, of course," he added, hoping to avoid any trace of ambiguity.

"What kind of a gastropod *polyp*—?" the Rat began. "—And anyway, what—I mean—why are you dressed like that? Are you a film extra, or something?"

The Mole adjusted his black velvet smoking-jacket, clearing his throat as he did so. "I dress like this because I feel it suits my character, Mr. Rat," he answered, not without dignity.

The driver sighed. "The name is Rette. R-E-T-T-E. Gordon *R*. Rette. Since we are on the subject."

"Mole," returned the Mole. "Pleased to make your acquaintance. O-O-O-o-o-o-O. I'm really very sorry to mention it, but do we ... have to go so fast?"

"This isn't fast! Good grief! I'm only DOING fifty-five! I *was* late *before* you hurled yourself in front of me, as it happens!"

At this point another "car" turned out of a side road one hundred yards ahead, occupying that portion of the route along which, quite reasonably, Mr. Rette had been intending to conduct his own vehicle at the speed just mentioned. With a cry of unbridled terror the Mole once more dived scratchingly at the floor-covering; Mr. Rette jammed his foot on the brake; and the intruder was avoided, but also instantly thereafter very closely followed, since its driver—an elderly and rather tiny female dormouse whose head was barely above the level of her steering wheel—evidently had no intention of moving at any speed faster than twenty-four miles per hour.

"These animals SHOULD NOT BE ON THE ROAD!" fulminated the Rat. "Did you *see* that? Did you ... Ah. Mr. Mole ... Mr. Mole?—*Do* get up, please! Just stay on the seat—please! *Did* you see it? Straight out in front of me? Not even the *hint* of a signal? No, we don't exist, do we, Grandma? It's all a dream, isn't it, dear: you're really sitting at home, aren't you, reading *Females' Own*?" He raised both paws from the wheel in an expansive gesture of despair. "Look at her, bumbling on at the speed of a stale prawn cocktail. Great crested grebes! The car will fall apart with age before she gets there!"

Not at all liking the strange sweet fug that hovered in the region of the "car's" carpet (or for that matter any of the other, entirely non-natural smells that emanated from every part of the machine), the Mole decided he would have to try remaining in a seated position.

"What—um—what kind of a machine *is* this?" he asked. After all, he thought, sooner or later he would have to find out something.

The Rat darted him a supercilious and unbelieving glance. "It's a Blumenduft S-Class, of course," he answered, much as if he had been talking to a young child. "A BPW.—GET OUT OF MY WINDSCREEN, madam! Co-o-o-ommme O-O-O-ONNN!! With the 400XX Turboid Vectro-Vacillator."

"Ah," said the Mole. "Are they—" (he gestured loosely towards the stream of oncoming traffic) "—um—are they all Beepeedoubleyous?"

"What—*what*—? What can the animal mean? —What *can* you mean? *All* BPWs? Will someone tell me what the mammal means? Of course they aren't! Where do you live normally, Canis Major? Talpa Minor?"

"Well—um ..." persisted the Mole, trying to ignore this

unanswerable query. "It stands for something, then, I suppose, Peebeedoubleyou?"

"B—P—W! Further out than Talpa Minor, obviously! Yes, of *course* it stands for something. Of course it stands for something. It stands" (and here Mr Rette pursed his lips and sighed the sigh of tragedy) for "Beddoytsarm-Purzönen-Vargun."

"Ah," said the Mole. "That's not English, I suppose."

"Poltroon! Wollock!" barked the Rat at an overtaker whose "car" was for that moment headed straight towards them at some middling-to-average fraction of lightning speed. The Mole blanched beneath his fur, grasping his seat in renewed but noiseless terror.

"Of course it isn't English," said Mr Rette eventually.

"And—er—how—I mean—does it have—um—an engine or anything?" (Here the Rat turned briefly to the Mole, disbelief writ large upon his gaze.) "I mean, I can't hear one ..." (Here the Rat turned away from the Mole and shook his head, offering nothing by way of a reply. Disbelief remained large upon his gaze, and there was something of a silence.)

"Um—Mr Rette ...?" said the Mole. "*Is* this—I know it may seem rather an odd question but, er—this *is* England, here, is it? I mean—it's not Kansas, or anything, for example?"

A rather more concentrated form of disbelief settled on the Rat's features. "You *are* on something! Aren't you? I knew it. I *knew* it! Oh, how could this have happened to me, now, of all days and months? What is it that I did?" he demanded, his eyes once again rolling up towards the roof-lining of his vehicle. "What ... *what?*"

The Mole squirmed about, thoroughly feeling the area of his seat under his tail in case there was something there, other than his tail. Then, helplessly, he looked back at the driver.

The next time he spoke it was out of instinct. "It is England, then," he said flatly. "Oh, *why* did I come up out of my hole that way?"

"Your *hole*?" echoed Mr Rette disgustedly. "Surely you can't be one of *those* animals? But then—why not? Why not? Why not that as well?"

The Mole had no idea what was meant by this, and did not feel he could easily ask.

"Now, look," said Mr Rette evenly. "Mr. Mole. You have just thrown yourself in front of my car. You don't have to tell me why. I'm not at all interested, I'm afraid. The accident was not my fault—obviously, since it wasn't an accident at all. Accidents only happen when people *don't* want to be hit by cars. I'm sure you must agree with that. And you do not appear to be badly hurt, as you said yourself just now. But since I ran into you, I will make it my responsibility to have you checked over. If there is anything wrong—anything caused by the accident—non-accident (I shall not pay for your forthcoming tonsil operation, and so on, I hope that is understood) then I will look after it, and we will part ways, no further questions asked. As it is Friday now," (Friday? thought the Mole) "you will have to wait till Monday for that. You'll have to see the Company doctor. I'll, er—oh, *damn*-damn-damn-damn-damn!—I'll put you up in the meantime, won't I? Of course I will, of course I will ... You had no other plans, I assume, other than being dead?"

"Um ... no. Not really. And, well—that's most awfully kind of you," responded the Mole, adding, "I was trying to get to the hills, you see."

"Ah," said Mr Rette. After a moment he spoke again to the elegant roof-lining of his "car". "*Why-y*? *Why-y* do these things happen?"

The dusk light had almost disappeared by the time the black BedeutsamPersonenWagen arrived at a centreless straggle of shops and pubs where traffic coming from all directions queued to get itself round a series of circular white lumps that had been placed, as if deliberately to hold it up, right at the middle of each junction. It then passed under a railway arch (Ah! A railway! thought the Mole) and then over a river bridge (O! A river!) where, on the far side, Mr Rette stopped at a small booth and wordlessly handed what appeared to be a toll to a plump and miserable-looking hedgehog in a holed pullover. (The Mole stared at the toll-booth, which from its brickwork he guessed to be quite new, puzzling.)

Here there was another village with a long, straight street some three hundred yards long, much of which seemed to be lined with high flint and brick walls. The Rat rapidly achieved pattern-blurring speed along it, braked at the top end, and swerved into a narrower side road. The first part of this was lined with parked "cars", so reducing the negotiable width to little more than that of the BPW. The Rat had just begun to conduct his vehicle along this channel when the headlights of another vehicle appeared at the far end.

"Well STOP, Pandamn you!" shouted Mr Rette.

But the headlights grew relentlessly larger. Nor did Mr Rette himself slow down. The result of this, not surprisingly, was that the BPW met the oncoming machine at a point roughly half way along the bottleneck. Mr Rette made a low growling sound—a rather disturbing sound, the Mole felt, to be heard to issue from the vocal chords of a water rat—cursed colourfully, and began to reverse back to the wider reach from which he had just started. The headlights followed him closely, and when there was enough space for the two "cars" to pass, the oncoming driver (a young female stoat, beetroot beneath her fur with self-righteous rage) leaned through her open window and shrieked, "What kind of driving do you call *that*, you terebellid worm?" With a dreadful crunching, roaring and wailing of engine parts, she then disappeared from view.

Mr Rette gripped the steering wheel and twisted his trembling paws clawingly and scrapingly around it. A voice that seemed to emanate less from his throat than his solar plexus growled, "I'll pulverize the animal! I'll throttle her with her own tail! I'll grind her brood into paté and feed them to her grey-haired elders! I'll ... I'll ... Nggghhh ... Sorry ... Sorry. Control yourself now, Rette. Come on, mal—Control ... control ..." He hit the steering wheel, perhaps rather harder than he had intended. "But I mean, great black-backed gnat-catchers! Where do they keep coming from?—WHERE?"

The Mole was far too shocked at the tone of this outburst to manage a reply, even assuming he had had anything useful to say, which he did not.

"My eyeballs ache," said Mr Rette morosely, but to himself, as he slipped the "car" back into gear.

After this they were soon in open country once more, travelling along what looked to the Mole suspiciously like a proper lane. Even so, it was not long before buildings began to appear on the right-hand side, most of them barely visible beyond high wooden fences and other barriers. They were sited on low ground, and with one exception their roofs were flat, so that at first the Mole believed they might be approaching another enclave of sheds. But it was here, after all, that his companion's house was located.

Passing along some fifty yards of a high beech hedge (itself backed by an even higher wooden fence with a barbed-wire topping), the BPW pulled into a semicircular recess. The gate here was large and made of metal twisted into would-be ornamental curlicues, and hung on tall brick posts capped by white-painted eagles. It all looked as if it might have been an entrance to a Big House, yet at the same time none of it was quite large enough, and the shapes were all wrong, and the space itself was cramped.

Out of nowhere a very bright light flashed on, and the Mole jumped. He saw that the curve of the entrance was itself flanked by tall metal posts, on top of each of which sat a curious, complex-looking device bearing a circular glass aperture fixed in a small turret. A large sign on one side of the gate read:

```
┌─────────────────────────────────────┐
│ ┌─────────────────────────────────┐ │
│ │        SECURITY CAMERAS         │ │
│ │        In use at all times      │ │
│ │                                 │ │
│ │          NO PARKING             │ │
│ │          Private Verge          │ │
│ └─────────────────────────────────┘ │
└─────────────────────────────────────┘
```

SECURITY CAMERAS

In use at all times

NO PARKING

Private Verge

Another read, "Mail in gate box, please". A much smaller one on the opposite side read, "Kennylands". Another read, "No Salesmen or Travellers. Thank you." Another read, "To Communicate With Occupants, Press This Button And WAIT".

The Rat flicked one of the seemingly hundreds of switches in the vicinity of his steering wheel and the gates swung open before them (the Mole jumped) as if at the paws of invisible spirits, without the slightest sign of animal assistance.

Mr Rette was just trying to explain the use of the "car's" door handle to the Mole when a female Water Rat hurried out of a porch in the building facing them. She was dressed in a tight, pillar-box red jacket with unsettling right-angled shoulders, and when she got nearer the Mole was struck by the boldness of her eyes, which were darkly outlined against arcs of lurid pale lilac.

"Hello, darling," she said, a hint of irritation in her voice. "Heavy traffic again?"

"Y—"

"Yes, well, look, no time, sorry. If I don't get to the village hall in four minutes flat I won't be able to deliver my piece."

"Wh—?" said Mr Rette. "It's THAT button, there! Pull it UP. UP!"

"It's the Burglary-Displacement Techniques meeting. You

do remember, don't you? I only told you about it this morning!"

"Oh, y—"

"Of course, if they'd only keep them in *jail* for longer, and punish them *properly* so that they didn't ever want to do it again, we wouldn't have to do all this in the first place, would we? Have you heard the latest figures? Mr Worthesmole told me this morning. Would you believe it—one hundred and fifty three break-ins last year, in the two parishes alone?"

"Outrageous ... outrageous," responded the Rat throatily, shaking his head as he stepped towards his wife.

"OK, look ... Justin hasn't eaten yet, needless to say. Burgerz-n-chips in freezer. There's a salad too if you can get any of it into him. There's *duck en daube* for you, if you want that. Have you eaten? Or that asparagus *crespelle*. Eight minutes in microwave. And there's *crème brulée*. Though of course you'd have to torch it yourself."

Left to his own scrabbling devices, the Mole had just succeeded in releasing himself from the padded, claustral interior of the BPW, and was breathing the cool air of the outside world again with relief and relative pleasure. Whilst the two Water Rats were running through their hurried exchanges he walked a pace or two, noting that the high fence was invisible from here, as it was lined inside by yet another barrier: a dark phalanx of very tall, funereal-looking, dense-leaved conifers of a type wholly unfamiliar to him.

By a process of elimination—since there were no other buildings in the enclosure—the Mole deduced that the structure facing him must be Mr Rette's house. This said, though, he was really quite hard-pressed to recognise it as a house at all. It appeared to consist almost entirely of blank walls, and was built out of bricks whose bilious colouring strongly suggested the droppings of wood pigeons on a damson-heavy diet. The smoothly black-tiled roof had been continued down one side almost to the level of the door, and the single visible window was both very long and very thin, like an arrow-slit with glazing. The garden was entirely laid to grass interspersed with shrubs, apart from areas comprising large grey paving-blocks, or gravel exactly the colour of tinned red salmon. Other than one tiny area raised on bricks, there were no flowerbeds.

"Er, darling ..." said Mrs Rette very quietly, though not so quietly that the Mole did not hear her, "who is that funny little mole? And what is he wearing? Has he been in a play, or something?"

"Ummmm—" responded her husband, raising a paw to grip the bridge of his nose. After this, introductions were made. "A—er, business colleague," explained the Rat, removing his briefcase from the BPW as he did so. "With us till Monday, dearest, ha, ha. Sorry to spring it on you like this again. I know I promised, I know, I know! Tell you about it later—go on—go on, if you're late!"

The Mole's first impression of the interior of the Rette home was that it was as hot and parched as a cornfield in the light of a midday harvest sun. The two animals had entered the house by way of a wide, plain, carpeted hallway leading on to a long white-painted corridor. Mr Rette did not seem to notice the heat at all, but for his guest it was overpowering almost immediately. In under thirty seconds the Mole's sense of decorum had been shattered and—shocked at himself—he undid his top shirt button under his tie.

Doors, some of them ajar, led off the corridor to a series of rooms. From one of these came a frenetic, high-pitched, plunketty-plinketty-plonketting, in which the same few bars of music (if that was what it was) were repeated over and over again. Mr Rette put his head round this door and said, "Hello, Scrunchkin. Homework? All of it? Sure? Bed, now—three quarters of an hour. OK?"

Round the next door he also put his head. From beyond emanated a crazed cackling, screaming and thumping which alternated with short bursts of equally crazed orchestral music. "Homework?" demanded Mr Rette again of this cacophony. "*All* of it, Pooplet? Well done, well done! Three quarters of an hour—bed. Yes ... yes! All right?" He turned to the Mole as they continued on: "It's Solveig's night off—ha, ha, of course it is, of course it is!—Ah, Solveig, yes—the nanny. Oh—my son, Justin. Er ... Mr. Mole."

They had now entered what Mr Rette called the "kitchen", which to the Mole seemed a place both fabulous and slightly threatening all at once. Bizarre glossy-looking devices stood along its walls, some humming, some vibrating, some whirring; even those that were completely still seemed latent with sinister life. The room was, in pure mole terms, something between two and three storeys high: four tall, narrow windows of multicoloured glass gave it the look of a place where food might be worshipped instead of eaten.

At the centre of all this stood a distinctly portly young rat, clutching a crimson-coloured can in one hand. He was wearing what looked to the Mole like a large labourer's shift inscribed with the words THIS IS NOT A TEE SHIRT, which reached generously to just above the knee. Under this he sported what could have been either very long shorts, or very short long trousers: these reached to half way down his furry calves. He had no shoes on, and his socks, in keeping with the rest of his dress, had wormed their way half off his feet and flapped against the floor as he stepped over to shake paws. Over his head he wore a woollen garment that might have been designed at the same factory that made his socks: this came to just above his eyebrows.

"Pleased to meet you, Mr Mole," he said politely. "I've just finished the new syst for the school, Dad," he told his father, pride in his voice. "They'll never get in to this one."

"That's good," responded the older rat. "Well done. Have you eaten?"

"Sort of. I just had a family-size block of chocolate

hazelnut ice cream and a couple of Knikkers on the way home from school—oop."

"You did *what*, Justin?! Great bat-nacked blackcatch … Great cat-blacked … Er …"

"I bidd't bead to *zay* dat," averred the bulbous youth, now wide-eyed and with one hand clamped hard across his mouth.

"I bet you didn't!" responded his father. "No! *I* bet. We will *discuss* this *later*, Justin.—Got it?"

"Well I was hungry, Dad," whined Mr Rette's offspring. "They don't feed you properly at school." He was already half way through the door, but turned back beaming to ask, "Great whats, was that?" After that, he was gone.

The Mole realised his first impression of the house had been mistaken. On its rear and garden sides the "walls" seemed to consist mostly of glass. There were windows stretching from floor to ceiling in every room, and as none of them had their curtains drawn, the black of the night outside now pressed softly and disturbingly at the glass.

Mr Rette began to rummage in a distracted way inside the top of what looked to the Mole like a great white cupboard that had been pushed over on to its back.

"Where is the er …?" he said. "Can you look in the fridge, Mr Mole?"

"The … er …?"

"The fridge. Right by you. There, there!—The *fridge*! Oh Pan unknot my thrice-spliced tail! Never mind!" As he spoke the Rat stepped over and pulled open the door of another huge white cupboard that had not yet been pushed over on to its back, and the Mole gasped as he looked into it. Coldness seemed to flow out from it and it was jammed, absolutely jammed full from top to bottom, with food of all kinds— some of it very peculiarly wrapped, no doubt, but still recognisable as food. Had the Mole not rather lost his appetite as a result of his recent experiences, his mouth would certainly have been watering at the sight of all the pictures of delicious-looking dishes on the packets. There was a three-quarters-finished salmon; there, some chicken pieces (one of them half eaten); there, a tilted plate of cheeses (the softest of which were leaking very slowly sideways on to the underside of a bowl of spaghetti) and a partly carved-up ham. Yet (he sniffed) amongst this cornucopia, something—several things, perhaps—was not entirely fresh.

"Do you think I might possibly have a glass of water, Mr Rette?" he asked.

"Help yourself," replied the rummaging Rat. But when he turned and saw the Mole holding a glass beneath a tap he added, "Oh, don't drink *that* stuff! The filter's off. There—there's a bottle—have that, please!"

Confused no less than ever, the Mole squinted where his host had nodded and saw a tall bottle shaped like a sausage-balloon. It was labelled "NAIAD OF THE CHURNET Purest Spring Water. From the Heart Of The English Peak District". So that was where he had come out! (Had he?) "Is this… is this the—er—Peak District, by any chance, Mr Rette?"

"Yes, I think it comes from there," said the Rat, his head still deep inside the cold cupboard. "Ah! Here it is after all. Looking for the wrong label again, silly me. Would you …" He turned and took a deep breath. "Would you like to have a seat?"

The Mole went through to where his host had gestured, entering a long room where the house roof doubled as a sloping ceiling. Here, huge sofas and armchairs covered in mustard- or rust-coloured leather sat well apart from one another on a thick saxe-blue carpet, looking as mustard- or rust-coloured whales might have done floating half-submerged on a saxe-blue sea. Out of habit he nosed about for something to read, but there was only one book in evidence. It was rather discouragingly entitled *The Vole Who Mistook His Girlfriend For A Bidet*, and was in such shiny-new condition he didn't think he ought to open it. Under it was a magazine sporting a pretty picture of a sheep in an orchard, and the words "COUNTRY DWELLING. When you're a Country Beast at heart". The only other printed material he could find was a road atlas "showing major routes".

"You don't mind duck, I hope?" shouted the Water Rat from the kitchen.

"... Duck?" muttered the Mole, turning. "O, that is very kind of you, Mr Rette, but—I don't think I'll eat anything tonight, if you don't mind." He sat very tentatively on one of the vast chairs, sinking several inches downwards into its copious leathern softness as if into the belly of an amoeba.

The Rat paused in his busying, and looked through at him. Perhaps the faintest flicker of concern might have been seen to pass across his face. "Oh, well. Will you have a drink, then?" he asked, coming towards the door.

"Ummmm ... Ummmm ... Might I possibly have a cup of cocoa, Mr Rette? I'd like that."

"Cocoa," echoed the Rat unexcitedly. "Er ... cocoa ... I'm sure we ... the children's shelf will ... Er ... Perhaps—would you like me to show you to your room? I could bring it to you there, in a minute, if you like?"

So the Mole was led to a room at the end of the long corridor, thankfully distant from the unabating twin concerts of sound in a frenzy.

"There's a receiver in there, of course," said Mr Rette. "And a labsite, if you need one—but, ha, ha, what am I saying? You've got all your own facilities, but if you'd like to use the spa bath—or the power shower—or the gym, you probably won't want that, will you? But feel free, Mr Mole, won't you? All in that direction. Just—there. Everything's made up in here but I'm afraid the—er—" (He tugged at a set of dramatically ruched, horribly shiny pink-and-yellow curtains bunched high above the wide plate window)—these curtains won't close at the moment. The auto mechanism is jammed.

Infuriating when you've not long ago paid one thousand and ninety-nine pounds per unit, plus B.A.T. We have been on to Zipp-O-Swhitt, of course, but like all these companies they are much better at installing and vanishing than at fixing the things when they fail. Do you mind? No, good. I'll—er—you'll probably need a dressing gown—I think there's one in here, actually—yes, even some slippers, good heavens, where did they come from? Oh—one other thing—don't go outside after eleven or you'll set all the alarms off. Right—well—good night. I hope you—er—feel better in the morning."

Ten minutes later the Mole's host returned in a slightly less distracted state bearing a mug of cocoa and a piece of curiously-scented sponge cake. Drinking the cocoa made the Mole feel even hotter, but he was unable to get the one vertical slot of glass at the side of the great pane open: the arm was firmly held down by a mysterious cubic metal clip.

But after half an hour of lying nearly baked alive under a great floaty thing-in-a-sheet that was more like a feather bed than an eiderdown, and of opening his eyes every thirty seconds to see the moon glaring down at him from above the ominous shrubberies of the garden, he withdrew, first to the shadows of the floor behind the bed and then, in desperation, to the inside of a long cupboard where the air seemed just a little cooler. Having lined the base of this with the floaty thing he closed the door on himself as best he could.

Surely, he thought out of nowhere, he *couldn't* have said one thousand and ninety-nine pounds ...?

A few minutes later, thankfully, the Mole fell into a deep sleep in which he remained, undisturbed, for the rest of the night.

CHAPTER TWO

TEMPUS EVANESCIT

The Mole was woken by what sounded very much like
someone riding on a bicycle. For a few moments he dozed on,
half-dreaming he was out on the open road and that, if he
didn't get out of the way very quickly, a large and unpleasant
animal with more than its fair share of fangs would pedal
straight over him. Then, with a jerk and a small cry, he opened
his eyes, discovered himself pressed hard up against the inside
of the wardrobe and so—after a moment's deep confusion in
which he imagined he was *still* dreaming—recollected where
he was. He clambered out into the room, blinking aghast at
the sunlight that now flooded every inch of it, and saw that
the door to the corridor had not been shut properly, and had
swung open a few inches in the night.

On the far side of the corridor Mrs Rette could just be
made out through a crack in her own bedroom door. And
indeed she *was* pedalling, though on a machine that could only
have passed for a bicycle if anyone had seen fit to equip it with
a pair of wheels. (The Mole put out of his mind all questions
as to why she might want to bicycle around her bedroom.) His
hostess was wearing something after the fashion of a bathing
costume, except that it covered all of her legs and feet and

arms, and was patterned in zig-zag bands of shiny black and gold.

"That's the way it's going to go in the future," she was saying. "Brigadier Leas-Tweezle is quite right, you know, Gordon. He had all the documentation with him too. Illustrating how they do it in the U.S. Secure villages, you see. What other answer is there?"

"So, how do you do it, then?" Mr Rette's rather more muffled voice was heard to say. "Put up ten-thousand-volt electric fences around the 'village envelope'?"

"Oh," responded his wife breathlessly, "I don't think it needs to be quite that uncivilised, dear. But if they can't wall them in properly in the prisons, we'll just have to wall them out, won't we? It's fairly obvious."

"So—what? Gum-chewing guards in peaked caps and reflekta-shaydes, toting sub-machine-guns?"

"Be—sensible—Gordon!" between-puffed Mrs Rette. "One or two security staff—yes, probably. But I don't think we have to copy the style of the uniforms. We can be a *bit* British about it."

"Ah—well then. Busbies with reflekta-shaydes? Castellated turrets at the fence corners? Or would moats with palisades be enough? Boiling oil? That's a thought, you know! There could be a big new market—"

The Mole did not quite follow the thread of this exchange, which is to understate a little, and in any case he did not feel he should be listening and withdrew to wash his whiskers. Even so, when he emerged again from his dumbfoundingly large private bathroom, he was unable to prevent himself hearing the next part of his hosts' conversation.

"... You mean to tell me you just brought him here straight off the *street*?" Mrs Rette was demanding. (She still had not moved an inch, the Mole noted.)

"The road surface is more precise."

"But, Gordon ... Why couldn't you have sorted it out on

the spot, there and then? He's not hurt, is he?"

"Janet," said Mr Rette firmly. "It was an ACCIDENT—or rather, a *non*-accident—on the CLEARWAY. Can you imagine the complications if the police had showed up? And how can you ever know with these things? All right, the idiot jumped straight in front of the car,"—and here Mr Rette lowered his voice slightly—"but what would have happened if I had left him there?—Not that I would have done. It would have been followed up, wouldn't it? He might have sued me. For bumping into him as he intended. Or for not bumping into him in quite the right style. You can't trust anyone nowadays. Manic-depressives least of all."

"If you'd left straight away—"

"Yes, yes, yes!" retorted Mr Rette in a more strangulated tone. "That old argument, isn't it, darling? 'Why can't you be just that bit more of a selfish swine, Gordon? Why can't you trample on everyone all the time for a change instead of only for 99 per cent of it? Why can't you ever quite achieve the zenith of one hundred per cent rottenness—that peak to which we should all aspire?'"

"I did not say that, Gordon!—Really!"

There was a certain coolness in the atmosphere, if not the air itself, over breakfast. But both Water Rat and wife were perfectly polite to the Mole and the conversation stayed, mostly unconfusingly, within the realm of what one did and did not eat at such a meal and when one did it, and what one ate for breakfast on holiday, and the ridiculousness of French breakfasts and the awfulness of their marmalade, and what one ate in the mornings when one was in a hurry to get to work, as opposed to those when one was not.

The Mole's everyday healthy appetite had returned overnight and after he had polished off a good-sized plate of eggs, bacon, black pudding and bubble-and-squeak (all fried up *extempore*, and with a certain pleasurable flourish, by Mr Rette), he ate every piece of toast and marmalade (or toast and honey) he was offered. Justin Rette and his two brown-to-blonde-furred little sisters Verity and Victoria, who were twins, watched the Mole's continuing consumption, long after they had finished themselves, with professional astonishment.

Afterwards Mr Rette made it clear to the Mole that he would have to entertain himself for the rest of the day, since every minute of his own time was already set aside for work.

"O—well—perhaps I might go for a little walk," said the Mole, completely forgetting where he was and what he might have to walk through.

Justin was still in the kitchen (today wearing a shift inscribed "THIS MAY BE A TEE SHIRT" with underneath, in very much smaller letters, "depending on your point of view"), and so the Mole asked him if he would like to join him. Polite as he was in his reply, Justin looked distinctly bored at this suggestion. "I don't think I will, thank you, Mr Mole," he said, twisting his tail round one paw. "'Fraid I've got some work to do too, today."

Mr Rette explained (or more precisely, tried to explain) the workings of the various catches, bells and switches on the Mole's route to the outside world. Just as he was closing the front door behind him, he leaned towards him. "Sorry I was so ratty yesterday," he said. "Been a bit of a trying day, you know. And it isn't every day you mow somebody down on a Clearway slipway." He sniffed. "Whatever the reason."

"Think nothing of it, I'm sure, Mr Rette," said the Mole warmly. "You've been most kind."

But as he stepped out into the big plain garden the Mole could not help but sigh, and sigh again. O! he thought— if only you *were* Ratty, Mr Rette! He pictured his dear good old friend, in his little riverside home, its parlour aglow with candlelight and the flames of a simple log fire, and thought of all the fine times he had had there with him through the years. Miserably he wondered if he should ever see Ratty, or Toad, or any of his other friends again. Wandering over the grass between one widely-spaced thickset shrub and another, he saw ahead of him a great white boat, as new to him in its massiveness and sweeping lines and silvery-metallic shininess and sheer tub-thumping, trombone-blowing brashness as any of the other objects in this awful stretch of country. It was moored at the end of the garden. So there it was: Mr Rette's, too, was a riverside residence.

The Mole approached this river and looked at it. Several other bulging and bulky barques were floating, moored and silent, on the far bank, blocking off much of his view of the fields beyond. Between two such boats he could see a wire fence, and on part of this a ragged shiny black bag of some kind was caught, flapping and rattling against itself in the strong March wind. Next to it was a pile of rubble. The Mole stared into the grey water, watching the eddies. He looked downstream, studying the vagaries of the river-edge, his eye resting for a moment on a tiny patch of reeds.

Could this be ...? he thought, but got no further with it, driven from reflection by the sensitivity of his nose. What *was* that dreadful smell, which he had noticed almost immediately he stepped outside? Here at the riverbank it was quite overwhelming: a sweet, choking, sickly scent, not dissimilar to some of the smells he had smelled in his bathroom, but far less pleasant. It rose to him off the water, died away, intensified once more. He stepped back a few paces, still staring downstream, and looked away. How could he even have thought it, he wondered. How could *this* be the River?

Having negotiated the entrance gate (it was easy enough getting out, he found) the Mole began to wander aimlessly up the road outside. The sense of danger that had been in the air all about him at his first emergence was far less strong today. Yet it was still here, as unsettling as a continuous whisper. He paused a moment then stooped to touch the smooth road surface, seeing how cleverly the gravel had been bound together with tar, itself ironed out in places into flat black "pools". "That is something," he said to himself. "Well, you know, it is. It might be rather nice, riding a bicycle on something as smooth as this …"

He glanced up at the steep field pasture opposite the house, a place where he might have expected to see sheep and a sward so closely nibbled that it showed up the shape of the hill beneath. What he found there instead was an impenetrable zone of waist-high vegetation, dotted with thorns and thickly awash at the edges with nettles. He was puzzled too by the scrappily hedged banks along the lane, where at roughly thirty-yard intervals the grass had been somehow rubbed away to leave long scoops of bare earth, some of them smooth, some driven into ugly thick ridges.

But he did not have to wait much longer before light was thrown on this particular puzzle. From both directions now there came the sound of engines and, looking round, the Mole saw a "car" (or as he decided to think of it today, a *motor*) not very far behind him, and knew that there must be another up ahead.

"O-o-o-o-o!" he said. "O-o-o-o-O!" He scrabbled up a bank as high as he could get, holding on to a low branch, then watched the two *motors* as they rushed towards one another, both apparently bent on smashing their respective ways onward. At what seemed to him like the very last second both machines swung around one another with a great roaring of engines, half-climbing the banks, each tilting over on a stretch of eroded earth. In the next ten minutes or so, this same train of events—distant engine sound, scrabbling mole issuing muted sounds of terror, near head-on crash, last-minute swerving deviations into steeply-angled dirt—was repeated enough times to convince the morning stroller that the "lane" he was following was far from the quiet backwater he had first imagined it.

Eventually the Mole turned into what proved to be a genuinely quiet, dead-end lane leading back down in the direction of the river. Here ahead he saw another cluster of houses, which had about them every sign of spanking-brand-newness. Indeed—judging by the hammering, whistling, and occasional crash that came to him through open windows—two at least were still under construction. A board above a broken hedge read:

Walking on past this, the Mole came quickly to an old, green-painted gate in a hedge that opened on to what had been—perhaps not so very long ago—a garden path. He paused. He walked on a few paces, and then he paused again. He went back to the gate. He looked at it more closely. He squinted up at the "period character cottage" sitting, as it did, high atop a steep bank now copiously dumped over with earth and rubble.

"O! ... No ..." said the Mole. "No, but this can't *be*. It can't—it *can't!*"

He went up to the old gate, leaning askew and useless on one hinge, and touched it. Then, against all further argument, he realised where he was.

As the Mole had known it, this cottage had stood at the

head of a steeply sloping garden—for him, in summer, one of the sights of the Riverside, a good way off from his own patch, but a place he passed occasionally on his longer walks. Here rows of phlox, love-in-a-mist, and sweet peas trained up twine on old hazel frames had alternated with neat rows of vegetables, while clumps of red hot pokers and a sweep of lily-of-the-valley stood against the top hedge. A wallflower-lined brick path had climbed the slope to a simple, rose-covered porch set in a front whose old bricks were mellowed to the colour of pale orange sand.

The Mole did not know the hedgehogs who lived there well, but more than once when one of them had been working in the garden he had rested a paw on that old green gate—yes, that very gate—and exchanged a few words. And now—

Now everything, *everything*, was changed! And … he could hardly bear to think about it … when *was* now? The garden and the old brick path were completely buried under soil and rubble from the gutted building, the plain plank door had been replaced by a horribly panelled, fan-lighted object, and worst of all, the old leaded panes with their multiform reflections of sky and ground and leaves were gone. In their place a set of grotesque sheet-glass gaps, thickly encased in lumping whitestuff "frames" of astonishing crudity, stared back at him like big blind eyes.

Most delightful of all to the Mole in this place had been the small orchard that occupied the high land just behind the house. The view of it, coming up the lane from the River— yes, he thought, with rapidly sinking heart, *the* River—had been quite wonderful in April, the old sloping tiled roof perfectly framed by a dense white cloud of blossom. All of this was gone now, and in its place stood four large new buildings—half stately homes, half dolls' houses, each with its own diminutive portico—jammed together with barely room to get between them in what had been a playground for poor animals' children and grazing for goats and a donkey.

The Mole walked on down the lane past a gravelled recess resembling a very small quarry, gouged out of the lower part of the garden. Here now stood a great fat *motor* in the shoebox-with-snout style, so big it could have reached the cottage roof-line. On the fabric covering a spare wheel at its rear—for reasons that could not at the moment greatly excite the Mole's curiosity—was printed the outline of a trotting hippopotamus.

You've got to go back, thought the Mole to himself. You must—you *must*! Right now—no dithering, Mole! No prevarication! You *have* to be sure.

Gathering together such wits as he could muster, he retraced his steps to the busy top lane. From here, he knew (he thought he knew) less than an hour's walking would get him back to where he had started yesterday.

"O, Great-Uncle Warpmold," he muttered under his breath. "I do hope you can see me now!"

In less than fifteen minutes the Mole was crossing the river at one of the weir bridges, and here the sickly smell raged up at him from the rim of descending water like the stalest breath of the most foul-mouthed dragon in the history of creation. At the river-edge, wherever tree roots stuck out into the water or there was a stand of reeds, a ridged yellow scum had gathered, pulsing on the current like a crushed pigskin. As he passed by, some of this matter tore itself away from a willow root and rode off on the current, breaking into a kaleidoscopic pattern as it did so.

It took the Mole five minutes to pluck up enough courage to cross a busy two-lane *motor* route—at a place that was unfamiliar and horribly familiar all at once—but eventually there was a lull long enough to let even so timid a pedestrian through. After this he joined an un-tarred, silent bridleway running south through the familiar and horribly unfamiliar countryside.

So briskly did he walk that within half an hour of starting out he was already in the stretch of country where he thought the tunnel rose, finding his way along the edge of a huge and rolling plough-land. He clutched his handkerchief to his nose again since, today as yesterday, a huge yellow machine was slowly tracking its way here. The Mole could see now that the peculiar Catherine-wheeling mist-shapes emanated from devices on a very long bar attached to the machine's rear end.

As he got closer to the spot itself the Mole's steps gradually slowed. For in the short time since his emergence, all the rough ground around his tunnel exit had been fenced in. He made himself walk on, and never mind the danger, until he came up to the tall wire fence itself. Beyond it, that same rough-looking rabbit in overalls, and one of the stoats, were busy screwing up another board with words on it. This one read:

Site Of Your New

THRIFTACENTA

YOUR Drive-In Savings
Start Here –
SOON!

Gripping the grid of wire with both paws, the Mole stared desperately through it towards the tunnel exit, and his heart—already pretty well sunk to submarine depths—dropped through a crack in the ocean floor. The exit—the former exit—and all the land around it for fifty yards in every direction was now covered with an expanse of great lumping grey building-blocks, to which more were being crane-loaded by the minute from the back of a gigantic lorry.

The Mole wandered on, limp-armed, following the potholed track to the point where the enclosure ended. Here stood the dead tree he had noticed yesterday, stark and black against the ridges of a cloudy sky. Without knowing why, he found himself trudging down towards it over the corrugated, mossy ground with its blackened plant-ends. And when he reached it there was no further room for doubt.

It is a common fear amongst moles—some have even been known to dream about it, from time to time—that one day they may emerge from their homes in quite the wrong place. Unimaginably worse, though, is the notion that they may come up one day not just in the wrong place, but in the wrong world. The Mole had never quite forgotten his Great Uncle Warpmold joking with him when he was a child about the possibility of time tunnels, and telling him how a mole had to be very careful, whenever he did it, *exactly* which way he left his burrow. He could almost see him now, laughing wheezily to himself at the idea, tears of inexplicable amusement forming at the corners of his eyes, perhaps even glancing over towards the big old broom cupboard that had stood in just the same place then as now—or rather, the Mole corrected himself, as *then*.

This dead tree, here—it *was*, it *had been*, the great old oak that stood at his own tunnel entrance. He knew its shape so well he could have drawn it blindfolded. He could even see the residual wounds in the bark on its roots left by the gnawing of long-vanished sheep. But his entrance—*his* entrance, with its little front door and "Mole End" painted in Gothic letters over the bell-pull at the side—and his small garden in its low box hedge—these were quite, quite gone. The ground itself was invisible here, hidden under a wide area of stained, hard grey stuff out of the cracks in which, here and there, a stripling shrub was growing.

The Mole sat heavily under the dead oak, staring out at the wasteland before him; then he turned his head to look back past the long fenced zone to the prairie void beyond. This— *this*—had been his home country, every willow-lined ditch, every blossom-hung nook, every tiny hedged-in paddock of which he had known and loved as a part of himself. He remembered the meadow that had been here at his very feet, with its copious splashings of pale yellow cowslips, its dottings of purple where orchids lurked amongst the long grasses—above all, the magical sight of the nodding check-ered heads of the snakes-head fritillaries spreading out across it in May from one thick hedgerow to the next.

"They destroyed my Valley," cried the Mole, pressing his paws together in helpless grief. "They destroyed my *Valley*." He breathed in deeply, struggling to stifle the sobs he had known were inevitable since the moment he stood by the broken cottage gate. Even as the tears rose stinging in his eyes, the air smelled strange to him.

Ragged bits of newspaper blew scraping over the blank grey-stuff podium in front of him. One of them was just a torn first page, half covered by huge letters reading MICE GIRLS GET TO No. 1!!! and a picture of a group of grin-ning and peculiarly-clad mouse females. PICTURES—SEE PAGES 4, 5, 6, 10, 12-15, 18 AND BACK COVER read another big caption. In a tiny box at the bottom of the sheet he read, "North Pole Melting? Figures Questioned By Slyde Institute".

Bigger sheets from another paper (it was called *The Defiant*) lay on both sides of his feet, all of them torn across the top. One bore the fragment of a date: 8th February 199–. Not knowing why, the Mole turned and re-turned the big damp sheets, finding headlines that seemed to make his own worst fears seem trivial: "70 per cent of World's Bird Populations In

Decline"; "Fuel Lobby Scuppers Climate Negotiations"; "Half Of World's Forests Already Gone". But he was too upset to read further.

His gaze drifted across the bold, strange designs of the advertisements. Many of these were for *motors* and one in particular—it occupied a whole page and was printed in colour—fixed his unthinking gaze. This showed a brilliant yellow blob in a super-squashed configuration, the front end of which had been made in a shape like a devouring mouth seen from a very low angle, as if from the eyes of a fallen pedestrian in the split second before he was run over, eaten, or both. "The Harakiru *Ballisto*", read the caption. "Fire the gun. Ride the bullet. The trigger's there right under your foot. Hey mal. Use it."

At the paper's limp back end the Mole came to the Appointments Pages. He stared on at them and, despite everything, words and phrases began to slip through the curtain of misery clouding his perception. He saw "State-of-the-Art-Technology", and somewhere near it "GROWTH!" Lower down, words told him: "You are credible. You are charismatic. You have a mission to succeed in World Financial Markets. You are innovative. You are robustly confident. You have at least ten years on the NP blade-edge."

Not far away "Challenging Corporate Strategy And Development Opportunities" slipped in and out of focus, as did "Tomorrow a Quantum Leap in Research and Marketing", and "Technology Without Frontiers!" and "Drive and Energy" and "Leadership Capabilities", "Dynamic Career Progression", "Expansion", "Progress", "Growth", "Expansion", "Growth", "EXPLOSIVE GROWTH!" …

At the bottom of the last sheet one image in particular fixed the Mole's null gaze. It pictured two young weasels dressed in business suits, the one bookish-looking with horn-rims, the other neat-furcut and sporty. Both toted small black cases and—for reasons inexplicable—both were leaping a high-jump bar. At any other time in his life the Mole would have laughed at it until he was rolling in the long grass. Yet as he puzzled over this picture now he began to wonder. *Was* it funny? Could it have some other purpose? These besuited high-jumpers were, after all, jumping in the most deadly earnest. Weren't they jumping *credibly*? Weren't they jumping *charismatically*? Weren't they jumping *with robust confidence*, as if with a *mission to succeed*? Was this, perhaps, a '*Quantum Leap*', an outward bound of '*Technology Without Frontiers*', a great leap forward to *Expansion, Progress, Explosive Growth*? No doubt about it: these young weasels jumped to win, though for what prize exactly it was beyond the Mole to say.

An hour or so later, the still disconsolate Mole found himself walking on alongside the row of riverside houses at the end of which he knew lay the relative security of "Kennylands" and the Rette family. Each of these houses must be meant to be desirable, he reasoned vaguely: they were all fairly new and set in large areas of ground. Yet each of them was, he saw, just as hideous in its own fashion as his hosts'. They were mostly built of a bland fawn-yellow brick with logic-defying flat rooves covered in gravel, and resembled nothing more than a set of great misshapen cardboard boxes waiting to be stacked. Crudely made twists of white-painted but rusting wrought iron and "gates" of bulbous tubular piping were the only attempts at decoration.

He was just about to press the button marked "Press This Button" at the "Kennylands" entrance when to his dismay the gate swung open of its own accord and Mrs Rette emerged high above him in a big, glistening shoebox-with-snout. This bulged at every point much as a pig might do after being comprehensively and neatly stung by hornets, and had a strange, translucent metallic sheen in turquoise. The Mole noticed the words "Range Crusher" on the snout.

"Are you coming in, Mr Mole?" asked Mrs Rette, looking down on the top of his head. "Oh. Hang on then. I'm just going to get the girls. Won't be more than a couple of minutes."

The gates closed behind her and the big vehicle roared the length of three gardens, paused, turned, and then disappeared. A very short time later it reappeared bearing its minuscule two-piece cargo.

"You can walk to the door?" Mrs Rette asked, smiling, when she reached the Mole. Was she joking? he wondered vaguely. There was no way of telling. "O, thank you very much, yes," he replied. One has to be polite, he thought, following the shoebox for the last thirty feet of its journey. Even when everything else is lost.

Inside, the Mole caught a brief glimpse of Mr Rette through what he took to be his study door. The animal was sitting, rather round-shouldered, in a patterned pullover that gave him a passing resemblance to an outsize bumble-bee. He was facing a long desk on which were arranged a number of box-like objects or small open cases containing mysteriously glowing windows. Looking into one of these—inside it, somehow, a map of the world was visible—he tapped quietly away at a register of little grey keys. The window in the box on his right was filled with columns and lines and tiny figures, while over to his left another quietly sighing machine was disgorging a sheet of paper, as if by magic, out of a long dark slot. The Mole was instantly troubled by the nature of these objects. Beyond the glow he also seemed to detect a continuous and disturbing flicker.

Entering the living room behind the two little rats, the Mole observed it clearly for the first time. Mr Rette must surely be no ordinary animal. The place was so long and high, the windows so large and vacant, the sofas so vast, all the other furnishings such dauntingly fine antiques. And how strange the trees looked there, silently blowing beyond the glass. For just one moment he imagined himself back in his tiny home, sitting by the fire turning a worn collar on a shirt.

Victoria sat down opposite him, coughing wheezily. Then Verity coughed. Then both girls coughed. "O, do you have a cold?" asked the Mole sympathetically. "No," answered both little rats together. "We have *assma*," they said proudly. "When I cough, she coughs," said Verity. "And when *I* cough, *she* coughs," said Victoria. They laughed, and coughed, and laughed again as if, really, *assma* might be quite fun to suffer from.

"Would you like to watch anything, Mr Mole?" asked Mrs Rette, indicating what appeared to be a very much larger, black version of the glowing window-boxes he had just glimpsed. "O, er … no—thank you," he replied carefully, wondering at the same time what exactly he might have been able to do with a map of the world and a column of figures, even if he had been able to look at them comfortably. He noticed that his hostess was now wearing a knee-length peacock-and-lime-green dress with a sheen on it not dissimilar to that of the paintwork of her car.

"Did you have a nice time at Belette's?" asked Mrs Rette of her tiny daughters.

"Ye-es!" said Verity, as if she might have answered this question more than once before. She was now half-sunk in the squeaking folds of the sofa also occupied by the Mole. "Spesh'ly when we sat on her and pulled her pigtail. Oop." The child covered her small furry mouth with a paw and exchanged a series of deeply puzzled glances with her sister.

"*Did* you now?" responded Mrs Rette. "*And* you boast about it! Wicked girl!"

"*We* want to watch a Viddy-O!" squealed Victoria, in what might or might not have been a diversionary tactic.

"In your own rooms," responded her mother emphatically. "We have ten televisions," she told the Mole. "I think, counting the broken ones in the garage, it's probably more now. And they still want to watch their videos in here".

"We want to watch *Incinerator Two*," demanded Verity challengingly, and coughed.

"You can't. You know you're not old enough."

Robovole!

"You CAN'T. Here—this is all right," said Mrs Rette, picking up a black object that might have been a book. On it the Mole saw the words "Honey, I Microwaved The Cat". "... I think," added Mrs Rette.

The girls disappeared with the object, and their mother—apparently concerned that her guest should be seen to be doing something—pointed out the local paper to him. Seeing its title, "The Riverbanker", the Mole felt bucked enough to ask, "I suppose riverbankers—um—like you and Mr Rette—know the country here awfully well ...?"

"Oh, we're not really local," said Mrs Rette quickly. "We've been here less than two years, actually. Before that we were in Dubai. And then—all over the place, you know. I'm from Watford, originally. And Gordon's from Dorking."

"Do you go on the River ... the river—much?"

"Very rarely, really. We have a boat, of course—you probably saw it. We usually make a trip once a year, in the summer, for a week. Gordon's not very good on board ship, I'm afraid." She put her hand on her stomach. "No sea legs, you know. Or river legs, or whatever it is.—Well, I hope you don't mind, Mr Mole. One or two things to do, you know!"

"No—O—no," responded the Mole warmly, picking up the paper. On the second page he found a headline that read: "SWANS HIT BY MYSTERY DISEASE—Bacterial Sludge The Cause?" He did not read further. In his present state of mind he could not have borne more bad news. Instead—to keep his now departed hostess happy—he once again leafed vague-eyed through the forty-odd pages of the advertisements that were, in fact, the essence of the paper. There again was that familiar phrase, *Paradise Of Suede*. It was located, the Mole saw, at the Meadowside Trading Estate, only two minutes' drive from junction 13A of the C4.

Just as before, there was something in the picture itself that fixed the Mole's gaze—some quality, or lack of it. Here he saw two animals—a slim male ferret in a cardigan and slacks, and a slim female ferret also, curiously, in a cardigan and slacks of a different colour. They were lying back against a sofa the size of a small dog-cart, on surfaces firmly swaddled in an acreage of bilge-coloured suede.

"At last!" read a bubble emanating from the female's mouth. "The *Suede Experience* I have always dreamed of!" There was a semblance of rapturous fulfilment on her face. "And at SO LITTLE COST!" read another bubble whose tail originated near the fine pointed teeth of the male. "Thank you— THANK YOU—PARADISE OF SUEDE!" His face too was fulsomely smiling, as though he now had everything he could ever have wished from life, and more besides.

And yet, thought the Mole, his senses suddenly prickling and sharpening, it was fake—false—bogus! It was pretence, you could *see* they were pretending. Really, it was so obvious it was embarrassing. What kind of world is this, he wondered, as troubled by the idea now as if he had a bite to scratch, where animals will sham like this and expect it to be thought true?

"Would you like a Poke, Mr Mole?" said a voice hesitantly.

"I beg your pardon?"

"A Poke?" repeated Justin, who had that moment stepped into the room from the kitchen. He held up a small crimson-coloured can, on which the Mole could just make out a design showing a small hedgehog poking a very large polar bear in the stomach. "A Poke-A-Polar? ... We've got Zupp if you'd prefer it."

"O, a *drink!*" said the Mole. "O, yes, that's jolly kind of you, Master Rette."

"D'you want it in a glass?"

What other possibilities were there? the Mole wondered. In a cup, perhaps? "Ummm ... yes, please ..."

Justin returned in seconds bearing a tray on which there stood a long narrow glass containing a brown liquid with hundreds of little bubbles in it. The Mole noticed that the youth's shift had changed colour again, and now read THIS *IS* A TEE SHIRT, under which was printed "Definitely!" in much smaller letters. Under this, in letters so small they were invisible from any distance, was another sentence: "At least, I think it is". Looking, even closer, the Mole found a pinprick line reading "What do you think? Tell me Thursday".

"I see you're reading my tee shirt," said Justin, pleased.

"Yes, I'm fond of reading," answered the Mole, blinking. He took a sip of his drink, and his eyes watered as all but the very last iota of politeness drained from him in the effort to swallow what was now inside his mouth. Was he drinking sugared perfume? Furniture polish and treacle? Liquid carbolic soap with jam? Horse-toothpaste? Some even beastlier combination of all four?

"Don't you like it?" asked Justin disbelievingly.

"Agh ..." gasped the Mole, fumbling for a response. "It's most unusual ..."

"I'll get you something else if you like."

"No, no! Thank you! This is—just—er—ga—huh—splendid."

"Anyone'd think you'd never had one before."

"Well, Justin.—Um—"

"Don't call him *Justin!*" squeaked a little voice. "His name is Shapeless!" The voice emanated from behind a half-open door, and was followed by a round of giggling.

"Excuse me," said Justin confidentially "I must just go and tickle my little sister."

"Shape-less, Shape-less!" squeaked the voice, but as the young rat began to move towards the door there was a high-pitched squeal, and then the sound of pattering feet.

"I've just scagged out a mausoletion syst for the school exams records," said the young Water Rat, his face flushing with enthusiasm.

"O! How interesting," responded the Mole as if in comprehension.

"Would you like to see it?" continued Justin after a moment. He seemed rather surprised at the Mole's attentiveness.

"Er ... ah ... Yes, please, of course I would."

"Are you into ShiftaShunt, by any chance?" urged Justin, bright-eyed.

The Mole opened his mouth like a goldfish, but no words came out of it. He had understood "Are you ..." and "by any chance?" to mean that in the best of all possible worlds he might have been expected to answer a question—keenly expected, too. But "into" had thrown him completely, never mind the rest. They did speak English here, he thought; but there also seemed to be times when they didn't.

"Well, I'm *in* your house," he managed eventually, patting the sofa in confirmation.

"Ah," responded the young rat. "Yes. You are. Yes, er ... well, would you like to come through, then?"

"Shape-less, Shape-less!" squeaked two little voices from behind another door as they walked down the long corridor. Beyond them the Mole could hear the crashing sounds of what he thought might be an orchestra; then there came the shriek of violins and a high-pitched scream; then a duet of coughing.

"O! O dear!" cried the Mole.

"Don't worry," said Justin. "They're always watching that kind of stuff. Can't do them any harm, 'cos THEY HAVEN'T GOT ANY BRAINS TO DAMAGE!" he added, very loudly.

"They must have awfully big bedrooms," said the Mole.

"Er, ye-es," responded Justin, as if not really wanting to understand what he might have meant. "Well, here we are."

The Mole was surprised (though why should he be surprised? he thought) to find that the young Water Rat's room resembled nothing so much as a slightly larger version of his father's study. True, it had a bed in it, but otherwise there was little to see except for a series of shelves and tables on which were littered three differently-sized and glowing window-boxes with a fourth, glowless and in pieces, surrounded by strange, patterned shiny bits and tools. A cupboard door standing ajar revealed an uncountable number of other similar objects, stacked anyhow with bits hanging out from them: most of these were coloured cream. On the shelves also stood two identical combinations of letters, numbers and other symbols arranged on sets of little embossed grey squares, and a variety of other similarly shaped or coloured devices. Scattered around all this were several tangled wire clusters and some very thick magazines with titles such as *IC PerFORM*, *Sonar The Salmon*, *Komputatek*, *Nybe Master*, *Ultitote* and *LabySkimma Futures*.

"This is where I drape," said Justin, with a shy little flourish. "When I'm not at school, of course."

"My!" said the Mole.

There was a short pause, after which Justin prompted, "—You were going to say ...?"

"Um—O. Was I?" said, the Mole.

"*Your* ...?" said Justin, waving his paws demonstratively.

"My ...?" echoed the Mole, in goldfish mode.

"Er ... Oh, it doesn't matter."

Being a bit of a water-colourist himself now and then, the Mole was immediately drawn to one of the few elements of the room with which he felt at all at home, a series of line drawings done on fine graph paper which were pinned to the wall above the longer of the tables. One of these was of a sheep with a funny face, another of a plant in a pot (it might just have been a geranium, he thought), a third a fish of no identifiable species. The Mole did not wish to think unkind thoughts, even less speak them, but he could hardly miss the fact that these inert outlines had no connection with anything living.

"Oh, don't look at *those!*" said the young water rat, embarrassed. "I did them on an old Knackmaker RembroPak, centuries ago. Last year, anyway."

A little further along the same wall, the Mole couldn't avoid seeing a large and no less crudely realised silhouette of a wild cat holding a knife in an upraised arm, threatening the outline of a quailing rabbit. Bold letters at the bottom of this read: WATCH OUT!! THERE'S A PSYCHOCATH ABOUT!

"Just an old joke," said the artist dismissively.

"Heh-heh, yes," responded the Mole, straining all available faculties to find the humour in it. Justin turned to one of the glowing screens. "I'm just trying to wize in a new track utility here to grease-up the instax in this tecton. Ingressing is *a problem* if you can't remember where you've ledged your dedidats. I mean, even when you've got your instax colleced, you have to be able to keep thinking of notchers that make sense."

— O! I had not realised! thought the Mole sadly. The poor, poor young lad …

"I tried XPW Zapptrak but on a 666PU with only 8 vastonybes of RIR and a nearly full iris, one bad move and it's stickaphut. Smasheroony. It's *pantagrunybes* you've got to have now, you know. Pantagrunybes! So that's it, you see, and we've just ended up with an Elephant."

"What a nice view you have from here," said the Mole.

"Yes. And *that*," (Justin nodded to the lightless window box upon which by chance the Mole happened to be resting a paw) "—I'm lofting the wombweave on that one. It didn't have kasement. But it's tricky because I'm also trying to wize in a new set of PTMs and you have to have the right gappers to get legiyoke, 'specially if you're trying to pharse in some

Snoodean logic at the same time."

"Erm?" said the Mole, in the high falsetto of extreme hopelessness. Not wishing to hurt the boy, he leaned in closer to one of the screens, feigning attention of the mildest kind. Immediately, however, he wished that he hadn't. For here he found a chart made out of numerals, words and hieroglyphs no less opaque in meaning than it was clear and glowing in form. And there was something about the screen itself—some kind of fizzing almost-tension, either in it or in the air about it, or both—that made him uneasy to be near it.

"Erm …?" said the Mole again. (He was still right at the top of his range.)

The faint sound of many violins and a soft melodious sobbing-whimper drifted into the room from the hall beyond. "Oh no! Mum's put the piped music on again!" groaned Justin. "Why she insists on listening to Mally Bunnisad all the time I can *not* tell you." He got up and closed the door. "I mean—*Mally Bunnisad*? Embarrassing, parents."

The Mole remained fixed in front of the glowing screen in something resembling snake-induced paralysis. There was nothing he would have liked better than to see the device transform itself into a teapot in a well-padded cosy, about which no other comment would have been needed than "Would you like another cup?" (To which he would certainly have added, "I think I'll have one myself, too.")

The mesmerising chart appeared thus:

Zaribathon for NAP: Olliej — nap: wizzrite (instaks) (Gyropile)

Instak	Chop	Eyebulb	Dyno	Polywaff	Mootoid	Postbax	Applikat	Lockout	Cabinet	Lifeboy

Recipe		
	Qnq wizzm/hitheres	
Inside	5913	daemon % mar 8 mar	Andy's postbak READMENICE
Outside	5914	daemon % mar 8 mar	Arkoff 1ist Laby. services lists
Upside	5915	J. Woozakandy 1/2 mar 9	KompuThrall Archive a.c. ingress? (lock2)
Downside	5916	Autosugar % neolid	Avocado M.I. address? Wayzin/wayzout
Labyrinth	5917	witgirl bloomskaya % well	trove sourcing/source sources
	5918	Ollie Joblonski % warnho	Kompuroutes/ NUMO v. da./DET Laby.

From: Justin <Rette@yeehah.com>   To: Ollie <olliej@efl.com>

Ollie

It's possible to hithere with KompuThrall aheadhaves via either BF Wizzrite PRQ/X or MNS thresholds.

KompuThrall have also written a NUMO valet/donor twixtode (pushpak) for AN wizzems – this allows AN wiz or Los Ang aheadhaves to ingress KompuThrall without the need for a threshold.

The DET/PE wombweave will give you more Labyrinth ingress/outgress. You can send and receive over a tecton without the need for any Labyvoid cabling.

Hey, 'mal – glaciate!

Justin Shape

Some muscle of curiosity within him clenched, forcing him against the odds to form a question.

"But ..." he said. "Um, well, that is—you may think I'm a bit of a silly ass, but—" (He took a deep breath)"—what exactly do you, erumm, *do* ... *with* ... this—these?"

Justin goldfished slowly back across the room. He looked at the Mole, then at the window-box, then at the wall, then back at the Mole. His eyes remained as wide as his mouth. "You really don't know, do you?" he said. "You're not joking."

"I've been out of the country for O—years and years," the Mole extemporized. "Exploring the—um—the Belgian Congo. Very jungly, you know."

"The *Belgian* Congo?" echoed Justin, no less puzzled than he had been. "Is that why you dress like that?"

"Yes—yes. No time to change into a shift yet."

"You're funny, Mr Mole."

"O. Thank you.—You can call me Mole, if you like."

"... What do you *do* with it?" said the young rat to himself, concentrating, much as an animal of the Mole's era might have concentrated if he had suddenly been asked, "What do you *do* with this 'chair'?" "Well, you see—Mole," he said in a moment, "it's DSR, right? Never heard of it? Dedidat Stowage-and-Recoupage? It's TK. How about TK? TechnoKnow ... No?—No. The Labyrinth? You don't know about the *Labyrinth*?—Never *heard* of it? Never heard about Grazing The Lab? Wow. Never heard of Labgrazers, then, Labsprinters? *Wow!* Must be some jungle."

"Very thick," said the Mole.

"This is quite a challenge," said Justin, placing a paw on one temple. "You see ... it's a dedidabank. It's for instaking.—No, simple, Rette, simple! It's where you keep— I mean, we don't exactly use the word, but—facts?"

"O!—*Facts* ..."

"Yes—facts, I suppose. Facts, really. Knowledge, right? You could call it that, if you really had to. You ... er ... well, you *log* things. You put things down. Make lists."

"O. Like shopping lists?—Sardines, and so on?"

"Yes … You could. That's one part of it. Look—here, see?" (He tapped away at the grid of letters.) "I've logged my comics collection."

Another chart materialized on the screen. "It's changed!" exclaimed the Mole, marvelling.

"Er … yes. I made it change, right?" said Justin. "See, here? I've insta—er—logged them seven ways, OK? By title-oblique-number, here; by artist, here; by writer, here; by inker, here; by which heroes appear in any given issue, here; by which baddies appear, here; and, when they appear first, that's important, here; and by the kinds of battles they fight, here; oh, and who wins, of course. You have to describe them a *bit*. I don't actually read comics much any more, but I keep getting them so's I can, er, log them. *Mothman*, mostly. There isn't anything that can't be logged."

"Um, well—and what do you do with the list, once you've got it?" asked the Mole, bucked that he might have grasped something.

"Well you *store* it, of course. On the flippiquoit. On the—on one of these." Justin held up a flat, shiny, circular object not wildly dissimilar to the things the Mole had seen in the long grass by the giant road, but much smaller.
"On one of *those*?" he repeated, descending back into the Well of Incomprehension.

"Yes—yes! It's all—Um …" (Justin paused a moment, thinking.) "Was there any electricity, by any chance, in the Belgian jungle?" he asked inspirationally.

"There may have been," responded the Mole cautiously. "But if there was, I didn't try it."

"Ah," said Justin. "Well, I suppose we shouldn't get too technical, then. Never mind how it works, exactly. But it is … ooh … clever, right? It's as if you had huge amounts of storage space all hidden away so that you can't actually see it.

It's there, but not, sort of, there in person? It's as if you had a great library—I mean, libraries are deeply unglacial nowadays, libraries are on the way out, but never mind—a library, or the shelf space waiting for it—huge, huge numbers of shelves, right? And on them you can instak—store, you know—whatever you want. All the paperwork in your life, except without any need for paper."

The Mole did have an old volume of *The Chums' Yearbook* in which he kept an occasional diary. Now and then he might sit down to write a few lines in it, in recollection of his happiest days; and he always kept his few small household bills pinned conspicuously on a spike on the kitchen dresser until he had settled them. Otherwise, though, he was not specially known as a user of paper, so he did not find it at all easy to understand why a machine might be necessary to store such items for him, even if the words could materialize as if by magic in a window.

"I don't know how you've lived without one!" said Justin marvellingly. "I mean, you know—even in the jungle."

Then Mr Rette poked his head around the door. "Justin, have you done your workout?" he demanded.

"No, Dad, I just went in there and rolled the weights around with my foot for ten minutes. Oop."

"I believe you, and I'm impressed by your frankness and honesty. But it's not the same as *doing* it, is it?! *Why* do we have a gym, I ask myself, when none of my children ever use it?"

"You don't use it yourself most of the time."

"I don't have the time, most of the time! And in any case, I am a rat of slender proportions."

"Ha!"

"JUST DO IT, O.K.?" The door closed.

"Why did I say that? Why did I *say* that?" muttered Justin. "I'm famous around the world for my honesty, of course. But that was ridiculous." He stared at the wall in confusion. "—Anyway! The other great thing about TK—one of them,

you know—is that you can use it to get dedi—er—facts—
out. You feed in one of these," (and here he inserted a small,
hard envelope into a slot) "and there it is. Info on just about
anything, up there on the screen."

Another ruled and gridded arrangement of words and
hieroglyphs appeared in the window-box, in which one title
was bolder than the rest: "THE MAGE PF/O9 THRALL
WORKSHOP SEGMENT 74: Ingressing The Labyrinth
From Seelines Basic."

"In a few years," waxed the young rat, "everything is going
to be on there. Everything you ever imagine wanting to know,
right? A great global-cyclopaedia, the whole of Animal
Knowledge, *and* with moving pictures." (Moving pictures?
thought the Mole, but did not ask.) "Once it's all in there, us
kids won't need teachers any more. We won't need schools—
yaay! We won't need to know anything, personally. All we'll
have to do is tap those keys. Anything you want to know—
it'll be in there waiting for you. Memory? Forget memory!—
'Course, we will have to remember how to tap those keys. (It'd
be a bit sad if you forgot that.) And you see, Mole, in any
case—you'd have to do it a bit yourself, probably, to understand this—but it isn't really *finding* stuff that matters. What
matters is the search. No, it's true. It's what we aheadhaves say
now, right? *The Medial is the Message!*"

The Mole pondered these revolutionary thoughts as best
he could. "But, could you learn—" (He waved his arms about
in search of an example) "— O, I don't know, could you find
out from it how to row a boat when you've lost a rowlock? Or,
what spot to choose on the riverbank if you were wanting to
catch a trout for supper? Or ... how to tell when the weather
was about to change, or when the earth was warm enough to
put your potatoes in?"

"You could find all of that. If you wanted to," answered
Justin, unenthusiastic. "Like I said, there's nothing that won't
be covered. Even archival stuff."

"But," persisted his visitor, "I mean, to do it. To *do* it, out *there*." He pointed vaguely to beyond the silent shrubberies.

"Well I don't know, Mole," responded Justin dubiously. "I mean—why bother? Why go out there when there's so much more to find in *here*? When the Labyrinth is brinkwide, and all the last wize-ins are down solid, anyone will be able to ingress anything from anywhere. *Anywhen!* And all my best mates are on it—yay, Wired-In Wizers, Worldwide! Ollie here," (and he pointed to the first window the Mole had looked at) "— see, he's in L.A."

"Oh!" said the Mole brightly, relieved at the sudden near accessibility of the subject. "And what sort of chap is he?"

"Clever ..." answered Justin, vaguely. He stared hard at the screen bearing his friend's name.

"Do you have jolly times together?"

"Yes, sure. We polywaff about on wizzrite," said Justin. "Talk about the Labyrinth, you know? ... equipment? ... what you can do with different wombweaves? ... thralls ... systs ... what you're going to be able to do when you've got pantagrunybes. (And no kidding, Mole—that's coming!)"

"But you don't ever, well ... go for a picnic together?" suggested the Mole, hopeful in a watery kind of a way.

"Who with—Ollie?" asked Justin, astounded. "Oh, no! We don't *meet*. I thought I said. We've never *met*. He's in America!"

"You mean, you've never met him at all?" asked the Mole, equally incredulous.

"No.—No."

"But then, well, how can you be friends?"

"I told you. It's the Labyrinth! That's where friends are now, right? Or will be. Out there in Labyvoid. I mean, here, you know." Justin tapped the box lightly with his round plump paw. "Here. There *and* here. Here *and*—there."

The Mole looked about the room, at the plain cream of its walls, its expanse of sheet glass, the carpet, the bed, the table-loads of boxes, bits and wires, and wondered what to say.

"— I mean, this is the future, Mole!" said Justin, and as he spoke he seemed to possess a gravity far beyond his years. "I know animals always say that, but this is where we're all going. It's just a matter of time, really. Ollie's on the Lab. I'm on the Lab. We're the aheadhaves, OK. But sooner or later everyone else is going to be on there too. The biggest party ever—see? And once it's really started, no kidding, it's never going to stop. People who don't have TK?—they won't exist. They won't *exist*."

The Mole tried as best he might to conjure a picture of a world in which, every day, every animal would be seated at a table in just such a room as this, gazing at a glowing box-window as if it were the only thing in life worth having. He tried very hard indeed. But he could not do it.

CHAPTER THREE

HEART OF THE RAG AND BONE SHOP

Monday came as Mondays must, and Gordon R. Rette woke his guest with a mug of strong tea at a time which even the morning-loving Mole felt mildly to be unreasonable.

"I'll leave it on the floor here," said the Rat, making no comment on his guest's re-encampment.

The cotton-wool-in-milk of a thickish fog, with the black of night still lurking beyond it, pressed against the bedroom's naked window-wall and it took the Mole nearly ten minutes to persuade himself that it really was time to get up.

"... All right?!" said Mr Rette briskly, returning to check on his charge's level of consciousness. Though he still looked rather tired, all the Rat's earlier heaviness was now banished: the air around him seemed to be positively crackling with energy and focus. "We will get you in for your check-up this morning," he said, "after which—I'll show you the way around when we get there—well, the day is yours, Mr Mole. I shall not want to be disturbed—I hope you'll understand. And if you need a lift to where we first—er—met, assuming everything is O.K.—it's yours."

"Ththank you very muthch," responded the Mole clothily.

Any deeper implications of this plan had been entirely lost on him.

Twenty minutes later, after a shovelling-race of a breakfast, the two animals stepped out into the first barely perceptible dilution of blackness in which the dawn might be hovering. A dazzling light came on out of nowhere (the Mole jumped), the garage door rose up without any sign of animal assistance (the Mole jumped), and Mr Rette walked over towards his *motor*. As he did so a dazzling light came on in his neighbour's front garden (the Mole jumped), and another Water Rat, dressed almost identically to Mr Rette, walked towards his own garage, just visible over the intervening wall. Though both animals came within a few yards of one another, neither acknowledged the other's presence. The neighbour's garage door rose up. The Mole jumped.

It was a very cold morning—almost cold enough for snow, thought the Mole—and through it the strong March wind was blowing its customary winter afterword: "*Remember me!*" For a moment, in his imagination, the Mole paid his dues to the dying season: winter, above all, demanded an animal's respect. A few of the preceding autumn's leaves were suddenly gusted out from some place of shelter that had kept them dry, bouncing and scraping noisily towards him across the grey paving blocks.

"Not *more* fog!" muttered the Rat as the gates closed behind them. "I am *so* fed up with these lousy driving conditions!"

"Don't you—um—get on with your neighbour?" asked the Mole, after a couple of minutes' travelling.

"I don't get on with him and I don't not get on with him," answered Mr Rette with mayoral dignity. There was a long silence, after which he added, "*I* don't know. The mal must have some defect in his peripheral vision, or something. That's the nicest way I can put it. He's perfectly all right if you walk straight up to him in the street. But when he's out in his garden, the world appears to end somewhere about a foot from his whisker-tips. I just got fed up with standing there with a big damp smile on my face waiting to say 'Good morning, Ronald.' You do, after the first year or so."

The tollbooth was still closed as they approached the river-bridge and they went straight over. "Now we get through without hold-ups," breathed Mr Rette. "No senescent snails, no flat-topped tail-crushers, no rage-crazed stoats. Paradise! If it was like this all the time, life might almost be worth living."

By the river everything was reduced to a series of dark-on-dark silhouettes, with the *motor's* fog-light cutting a low path that picked out details of the roadside in preternatural shining detail. Passing over the bridge on their right were the first rail-commuters, outlines all. Weasel followed rat followed weasel in a metronomic rhythm and at almost equal distances, each carrying a small rectangular case in just the same way. Most of these figures walked in the centre of the pavement, but some hugged the bridge parapet, whilst one or two of the most reckless chancers balanced their way along the kerbstones. They looked to the Mole like a line from some hybrid military platoon, so nearly regular were their movements.

"The 5.47ers, you see," said Gordon Rette. "Or is it 5.48 now? They keep changing the timetable, but only ever by a minute at a time. Got to keep them on their toes, eh?"

"What—um—what work *do* you do, Mr Rette?" asked the Mole.

"Do you really want to know, Mr Mole?"

Mr Mole did really want to know, and said so.

The Water Rat sighed. "I'm a Re-Engineer. A De-Stratifier, if you're with me? A Reasonablization mal. I do, in fact, head the Global Corporate Degirthing Committee for Toad Transoceanic and Mollusk (Holdings) A.L.C."

"Ah …"

"It is a great responsibility. I fire people. In a nutshell. I have a career in career-termination. I am a Field Marshal of Letting-Go."

"O—well, um—" (the Mole grasped aloud for a convincing question) "— do you enjoy your work?"

"*Enjoy it? ENJOY IT?*" retorted the Rat warmly, and as if to a challenge (though needless to say none had been intended). "*Enjoying* it is neither here nor there!—Look, Mr Mole, I don't know anything about you. I don't know who you are or where you come from, but in the real world—the world I live in— you're either In Here, or you're Out There. It's every mal for himself nowadays, and I'm not saying I like it. But if you're In Here, you've just got to keep that rubber on the road and hang in there on that scoring side like the up-to-the-wire slam-dunk hard-ball-slapper you always knew you were, or you won't stay In for long! Bullish, Mr Mole. Always bullish! That's the name of the game today."

"... Bullish?" echoed the Mole, wondering if he might have been given some advice in husbandry.

"Yes, blastsquashit, *bullish!*" said the Rat in an even louder voice, his whiskers flicking with suppressed emotion. "I didn't choose to do this job, you know—it doesn't ever work like that. I'm a pharmacognosicist by training as a matter of fact. Oh yes. I thought my research would change the world when I was that much younger. But you have to understand—with all the technological changes that are going on, and the way that companies have grown at the edges over the last few years—there's an urgent need for Reasonablization. And if you run the hit list, you stand a chance of staying off it. *Quod A-Rat Demonstrandum.*"

"'Fraid I don't know anything about that kind of thing ..."

"Well then, here's your chance to learn something!" responded Mr Rette, as if from some high lectern. "The way I look at it, Mr Mole, I do most of these animals quite a big favour, firing them. Did you know this country now has the highest stress-at-work rate in Europe outside of San Marino?—You know? Animals *die* of it! They come in to work, take off their overcoats, and keel over at their desks.

One minute they're there on the phone, the next, whomp, they're going out on a stretcher. Everyone's petrified of losing their jobs, for obvious reasons. Some of them don't even dare to go out to lunch for fear their job is gone when they get back."

Mr Rette waved one arm dramatically across the windscreen as he spoke, and the tip of his tail twitched feverishly behind his seat. "Which very often it is, of course. So when they work, they overwork. They stay late. Some animals at T.T. even keep camp-beds and primus-stoves under their desks. They never *leave* work. It's always been a roach-race, obviously. But now—believe me—it's a *roach*-race. The poor beasts stay there—I mean, you know, it is pathetic—trying to catch up with things that are always running later than the day before. There is no catching up! They just don't get it. Companies, you see ..."

Mr Rette paused a moment, running a paw across his forehead. "Companies say, 'Yes, we will pay you—and yes, some of you we will pay quite generously—to work for us. But once you are with us, Sweetie, you are *ours*. For as long as it takes. And you'll never know how long that's going to be.' Well, I save them from that—the ones I destratify. The long brown envelope, on the desk, first thing in the morning—that's tricky, with the animals who sleep there, but we're developing a technique. And there it is: freedom. An end to stress. Of course, there are problems in being Out. A collapse of the financial profile to the horizontal is one that often gets mentioned."

"The whole position sounds—well—rather bad," averred the Mole cautiously.

"It *is* rather bad! It *is* rather bad!" shouted the Water Rat, almost bouncing in his seat, as if the very caution of the Mole's response had roused him. "Nowadays, in the jobs market, animals are no better than used cars. It's true! Soon as they're out of that saleroom—or university, as some still call it—soon as they hit the road, bang! They've depreciated. And it's all downhill from there. All companies want is that first fresh work-season, when mals have guts and go and don't care too much about what they do or why they do it. They want that energy, and all of it focused into *them*. All right, a few tough cases we do tend to keep, for so long as they go on fighting, but mostly—" Mr Rette turned a paw over as if to feel for rain.

"Do you ever …?" The Mole paused, wondering if it was sensible to go further. "Do you ever feel sorry for them? When you fire them?"

"I don't have *time* to feel sorry!" exploded Mr Rette again, thumping one of his well-groomed paws on his black steering wheel in time with "time" and "sorry". "Believe me, Mr Mole. *I know*. You *can not* fight what's going on. We're all just the tiniest, most insignificant parts of it. It's very tough, but the tailline is: a rat has got to earn a living."

After about two miles they came out of the fog into the now convincing beginnings of a grey dawn. With a little grunt of satisfaction the Rat opened the throttle, and the Mole (whom he personally had belted in to his seat before they left) uttered a barely audible moan and closed his eyes. At first the road seemed completely deserted, but this was pure illusion. No more than a minute later a *motor* was to be seen racing from the opposite direction, its headlights on full beam (Mr Rette tentatively suggested the driver might think of dipping them). Then another *motor*, travelling even faster than the BedeutsamPersonenWagen, came up behind them, following closely. In a moment more it had overtaken. It was four and a half minutes to six. The morning rush had begun.

Despite himself, the Mole could not help opening his eyes every once in a while. Mr Rette's homiletic comments on the skills of his fellow-drivers were enough in themselves to have this effect, and it is a strong instinct in every animal to have its eyes open at the moment when it meets its doom. So it did not take him long to see where they must be headed, and when he caught sight of the great oval bridge ahead—with its ring of orange lights gleaming against a faintly streaked grey-blue eastern sky like some incomplete scale-model of the Milky Way—his moans moved well into audible range.

"What *is* the matter now?" demanded Mr Rette. "Will you stop that? I have to concentrate!"

"O-oo-o-oo-ooo-ooo!" answered the Mole, a paw clamped over either eye.

The Water Rat turned a little in his seat, studying his passenger, and allowed himself a brief and, it has to be said, slightly cynical snort of amusement. After which, like the worldly animal he was, he shook his head and dismissed the matter from his thoughts.

For the next forty minutes or so the BPW made pretty steady progress along the Clearway into London. Of this journey the Mole saw only the most fragmentary details: the fur-whitening sight of a pair of monstrously-tyred, *motor*-high red wheels whisking impossibly onwards-but-backwards on his left—a seemingly endless ribboning of clumped metal that looked as if it might have been thrown down overnight by spay-thumbed giants; long stretches of verge made up of brown littered earth or patches of brown dead grasses. Odd small conical objects, vast blue signs, hulking grey walls and over-bridges of blundering hideousness jumped into his vision at any moment when his paws came down, and each minute that passed the grey speckled road racing backwards under the bonnet was more densely populated by other metal-packaged users. But the faces of the occupants, in the flashes when he saw them, registered not one trace of the unbridled terror he expected. He saw nothing except an unexcited, slightly weary blankness, almost as if all this might somehow be *normal* to them.

Eventually, the Mole felt the *motor* beginning to lose speed, at first gently, then very rapidly. He heard Mr Rette's voice cry, "No?! ... Pandammit—no?!! It is six thirty-*six*! It is *six thirty-six* ... It *can't* be blocked *yet!*"

Another few moments, and the BPW had slowed to such a speed that it no longer seemed to be moving at all. This was too much for the Mole's curiosity. Over a period of about half a minute he gradually unclamped his paws, only to find that they were now sitting in a queue of *motors*, vans and pantechnicons in the outside of three lanes that were very, very slowly being reduced to two where the road climbed up, half a mile ahead. Sleet was falling now, each drop spreading on the windscreen before the wipers cleared it. Almost all the *motors* had their lights on and the three strands curved up and away into the blurry distance like some procession of the faithful bearing red lanterns behind them on their journey east.

"There is no escape," said Mr Rette, speaking now in a low and far less energetic voice. "Only a year ago you could get up at five fifty-five and get straight along here, *and* in, without a hitch. Then—almost overnight, it seemed—it got like this. So you get up at four fifty-five and lo, all the rest of them are doing the same. If you got up at three fifty-five they'd be after you a few weeks later. It's only a matter of time before all of us will be driving in immediately we have driven out. Or sleeping at the office. Those of us who don't already do that."

The Mole had never been to London. He did enjoy a rather woolly, pastel-shaded mental picture of it, gleaned from other animals' descriptions and from one or two pictures he had seen in books. He imagined it as a rather elegant, spacious place made up of large parks and harmonious eighteenth-century terraces with long sash windows and decorous shell-porches, all delicately scrolled about with railings. No such London was quite in evidence here. Instead, still, there was the Great Road, now climbing away from the ground to run along a raised and snaking grey ramp. Scattered below on both sides lay an incoherent mix of fractured rows of nineteenth century villas, garages, big industrial sheds, and blank grey-black spaces dotted with posts and signs.

And ahead of them now—as the queue of *motors* crawled

its patient-impatient way up and along the ramp—the Mole saw rearing out of this chaos a handful of the most phantasmagoric towering structures, some of which looked as if they might be made entirely from glass. He cowered down into his imitation velvet seat as the BPW drew closer to the first such monster, fearing that at any moment it might break free from its moorings and stagger thunderously towards him, spraying ragged, slicing sheets in all directions. He could hardly look at it: how could *anything* be so huge? Yet it glided slowly by; and nothing happened.

"— Can't imagine what all this office space will be used for," said Mr Rette, mostly to himself. "Once everyone's been got rid of. Carpet bowls? … Clock golf?"

Now another quadrate glass-face—this one still under construction—was looming up towards them on the right, even higher, even longer, with a hundred thousand—no, two hundred thousand!—inert slot-like windows, each of them dully burnished with a sinister coppery sheen. They raked away to some point just this side of infinity, held together in a frame of lumping, knobbled black-grey stuff that must come filthy from the factory. The topmost stories of the prodigy were hidden under a gimcrack roof of scaffolding and tin sheeting, giving it the absurd-but-not-funny look of a shanty as built by a Brobdingnagian. From this, curtains of some creamy translucent material rippled and bulbed out in the strong wind, the sleet white-striping the sky around them, revealing in each pulse terrible gulfs of darkness beneath.

"Don't animals put up buildings to be jolly any more?" wondered the Mole to himself, in a very small voice.

"'Jolly'?" came the Water Rat's dry echo. "'Jolly' is a rather old-fashioned word, isn't it, Mr. Mole?"

"… Well, you know, to cheer you up a bit?"

One eyebrow cuttingly raised, Mr Rette made no reply. Then he pointed ahead to where the two lanes of traffic were competing to filter into one, and an intense blue light flashed

in a dizzying pulse. "You see?" he said. "That's all it takes."
When they reached the spot five minutes later, the Mole saw
two *motors* that had somehow got crushed nastily together
against the long grey barrier. A hulking truck with a crane on
it was reversing up towards them, and various uniformed
animals waved and gestured.

But the crawling did not end there. Another ten minutes in
first gear brought Mr Rette's vast-cubic-capacity *motor* gently
down again to ground level, and an area slightly more recognisable to the Mole as some part of a city, though not any city
he would have wished to visit. Here rubbish lay all along the
gutters, and the pavements themselves looked cracked and
stained. They turned their inching way into a seedy-looking
shopping street where many animals were hurrying, the ordinary and the strange together. Several went by whose species
and even gender were not wholly clear—slumping creatures in
ugly, tight blue-cloth trousers, some of them with fur showing
at the knees.

"... Why aren't we *moving* yet?!" demanded Mr Rette of the
noncommittal roof-lining.

In the darkened doorways of abandoned or still-closed
shops, the Mole caught sight of what at first he took to be
piles of old rags, blankets, and boxes. But then he saw two
booted feet protruding here, an arm raised there, and then a
grubby, mat-furred face. Further along one such individual
was seated on his bedding, his feet stuck well out into the
stream of walkers. A tin plate lay on the pavement next to
him, and he played a battered violin.

"Are there *beggars* here?" asked the Mole, astonished.

"Of course there are," answered Mr Rette wearily. "All my
own work, you know," he added a moment later, his whiskers
drooping ambiguously. "— Just a little joke, ha, ha. T.T.
departees all receive very generous settlements.—Fairly
generous. None of them sink *that* far." He nodded towards
another grimy bundle, unrecognisable as animal in the murk

of a *PanoKleansorama* doorway. "At least—I don't think they do." He glanced back, grunted, and looked away again in silence, his whisker level unrecovered.

Now a young and very skinny-looking hare was splashing along right by them in the wet gutter. He was dressed in some kind of shiny, holed overcoat, and had a dark little woollen hat pulled down hard over his ears. His feet were shod with—to the Mole's eye—grotesquely ugly-looking shoes covered in lurid chevrons, stripes and lettering that might (he guessed wildly) once have had some kind of sporting purpose. The right sole was parted from its upper, causing the wearer to limp, and he half-ran with a distracted, ineffectual urgency, his arms both crushed up to his chest and quite oblivious of the crowd, as though he had to get somewhere as a matter of life and death. Yet he was covering the ground at little more than walking speed, flap-footing along in the saddest imitation of how a hare should run.

"But—we did not have beggars!" said the Mole, mostly to himself. "*Did* we? How can it be like this here—now?"

This thought process was sharply interrupted by the sound of a horn ahead; and whoever was pressing on it kept it pressed. Over the glossy *motor* roofs with their curved reflections of the buildings they were crawling past, the Mole saw a smartly dressed weasel jump out of a *motor* and rush back to the vehicle behind him. He began to hammer on the driver's window and yell, loudly enough for his voice to be audible through the BPW windscreen. Within seconds the quarrel had become a fist-fight through the now opened window, and the Mole looked on in shame as the standing weasel lunged forwards, saw-teeth bared, trying to bite the seated animal's nose. A moment later both animals were rolling on the ground, thumping and clawing at one another, this snout in these gnashers, that snout in those. Then Mr Rette's queue began to move on again.

"I really have no idea why these animals get so excited,"

opined the Rat, blithely smug. He looked down on the two snarling, pummelling citizens as he glided past them. "Dear, dear, dear. Appalling, isn't it? CLOs, the lot of them. And we are told this is a civilised country!"

The queue slowed once more to a halt, and stayed put. "D-a-a-a-amn!" growled Mr Retté, his nonchalance evaporating quicker than dew on a hot tin bonnet. "Blat-blacked, blak-blatted—" With trembling intemperate fingers he reached out to push one of the thousand-and-one buttons by his steering wheel, and the Mole jerked himself half way out of his seat belt as a crystal clear animal voice *spoke* from somewhere directly in front of him—or was it to one side of him? Or both?—No, no, impossible! There was an animal—there!—there beneath the windscreen!

"AND it's netblock in central London yet again, I'm afraid," said this impossible voice, which might perhaps have had some trace of Welsh in it. Far from being fazed by his plight, its owner went on with ebullient humour—relish, even: "We've got Inspector Paul Warren of the Megalopolitan Police on the line, I believe. Inspector Warren! Nothing moving out there again, we hear!"

"Yes, good morning," said another trapped voice (!!how could two animals be trapped in there!?)—a more appropriately mournful voice this time, whose owner sounded as if he were minding every P and Q, perhaps in the hope of being released more quickly. "I'm afraid I do not have very much of hope to offer the travelling public this morning. We have had a series of hold-ups around the capital, the worst in the vicinity of London West One, where unfortunately a postal-delivery bicycle shed its load in Wardour Street at six-oh-five a.m. Traffic is at present moving very slowly, if at all, throughout the whole of Westminster and the western end of the City. The situation is one of complete street-stroke, I'm afraid."

"... Where ...?" enquired the Mole in a tiny voice, pointing at the dashboard, and then the door, his little eyes staring.

"Pandammit—PanDAMMIT!" cursed the Rat, completely ignoring him. He gripped his steering wheel, lowered his forehead to it, and uttered a long, low, unashamedly ursine growl. The driver of the car to the rear sounded his horn briefly. "And you can keep your trap shut too!" he yelled, flailing an arm behind him. "Abject little bumper-nuzzler! Look!— Look! —" (and here he gesticulated rhetorically at the metal perspective ahead) "what difference is it going to make, you subnormal sludge-maggot?!"

For another twenty minutes or more, the BPW maintained its unassuming place in the great spreading paralysis of traffic-flow—inching, footing, occasionally even yarding, but mostly inching, its way onward. At every junction both tongue-tied mole and tongue-loose rat would stare hungrily up side-streets for some inkling of free space and a chance to move. But each vista was just as jammed as the last, roof beyond roof, boot beyond boot, away and away to the first visible bend. Many drivers were now making their own contributions to a growing improvisatory fanfare for horns whose performers may well have stretched from Ealing in the west to Bethnal Green in the remote east, from Hampstead in the far north to Herne Hill in the deep, deep south.

Several times, Mr Rette cut suddenly and desperately to the left or right, making what even his passenger could tell were the most extreme deviations from any route aimed towards a single point of the compass.

"And now we're here!" the Rat would wail at intervals. "I don't WANT to be here! WHY are we *here*? ... Please? ... Please?"

During the next long moment of absolute stasis, the rear door of the *motor* ahead of them opened. An arm protruded beyond it holding what was, quite uninterpretably otherwise, a small child's potty. This it tilted into the gutter in the 'pour' position.

"Oh, *really*," said Mr Rette in a tortured voice. "Really! This is just *too much!*—We are never going to get there! We are *never* going to get there!" he bawled, grasping at the air above the steering wheel much as if he wished to strangle it. Then "— Come on!" he said. "We're walking!"

In what seemed the merest splinter of a second he had swerved the BPW into a gap in a line of parked vehicles—this created by another *motor* which had just pushed out in front of him.

Leaping to the pavement, the Water Rat snatched his small case. Breathing "Deracitel ... Deracitel ...", he grabbed another item and then began to jam coins into the side of a grey lollipop-shaped bollard with a face on it. Then he was whisking off the Mole's seat belt ("Why *you* can't do this I do not know!") and pulling him bodily out of the machine.

"Come *on!*" he shouted, already twenty feet ahead of the profoundly disorientated Mole. "You do know how to walk, I take it?"

A moment later the Mole was at his side. "O.K.," muttered Mr Rette to himself in the low, collected voice of the field tactician. "Tube, no good from here—have to change, twice—Circle Line—no, no! Rush hour—queues—taxis out, obvious reason—helicopters?—no—so—Oxford Street ... Holborn ... Lincoln's Inn ... Chancery ... umm ... Ludgate Hill ... Mansion ... We can do it. Half an hour. Sprint, Mr Mole, sprint! Please!!"

The Mole fumbled urgently in his pockets for his handkerchief as he walked and pattered on. "This air is just *awful*," he moaned to himself. "Poison, poison!" Even with his face covered he could still smell and even taste whatever it was that floated all but visibly around him.

The pavements of Oxford Street were already getting busy and, rush or no rush, the Mole was vividly aware of the strangeness of the thronging stream, which seemed to grow in density the further they moved through it. Every animal was dressed completely differently from every other, adding (if that was possible) to his sense of chaos. In his day—the day before the day before yesterday—if a mole was dressed in a black velvet smoking-jacket, it *meant* something. But here it seemed there was either a limitless possibility for meaning—in which case there was no meaning—or, of course, there was no meaning in the first place. True, a few of the older female pedestrians were smartly and even becomingly dressed (and some of them, he noticed, spoke in foreign languages). But these few were all but lost in an unending current of peculiarity in which straw-blonde girl dormice minced along in little creased scraps of cloth as if it were summer on the beach, not sleet-weather March, and hedgehogs with their manes tweaked out into luminescent spikes alternated with young ferrets in fur-compressing shiny trousers that outlined the unmuscled boniness of their shanks. There seemed a grimness, a joylessness, on almost every face.

Here now came a ferret wearing glasses whose curved lenses supplanted eyes altogether with pulled-thin miniature reflections of other passers-by. There beyond came a shrew of dirigible vastness, the front face of her marquee-like shift inscribed with the words THE AMERICAN EXPERIENCE. Here came a group of rabbits, pavement-wide, staring ahead at all who walked towards them with a beetle-browed resentment—as though they might happily pummel any one of them into an unconscious furry heap, no reasons known nor asked.

One of these, though quite young, the Mole noticed, was losing his fur in patches, and the lowest part of his head-fur was twisted into thin, oily little strands that flicked along his collar as he glared about him in search of something new to hate. Another (and he was the first of many) wore a cap with a kind of duck's-beak brim long enough to shade out an equatorial sun at its zenith—useful, certainly, had the sun ever shown a sign of penetrating the roof of cloud above the buildings, and had he not been wearing it backwards.

"A Mole! A Mole!" groaned the Mole to himself, still struggling heroically to keep up his resolve—no, but more seriously than that, his very sense of who he was in this inhospitable place. "A Mole!—A Mole!—A Mole!"

Only moments later a ghastly wailing-choking sound, as of some wounded or bereaved animal, burst out at them from the dazzling glassy depths of a clothes shop. A drubbing drumbeat followed, and then the wailing continued in even greater agonies of desolation.

"O!" cried the public-spirited Mole. "An animal is in pain!" Without a thought for his own safety he hurled himself inside the store, penetrating it by way of a channel of bold-checked jackets on shiny chromium-plated rails. "Where is that wounded animal?" he demanded of a fat rabbit holding a clipboard. "She needs our help. Speak up now, do!"

But Mr Rette—nearly speechless with a heady mix of rage and incredulity—was right behind him. "You vapour-headed excavator!" he exploded, plucking at his case-handle in exasperation. "It's the MUSIC!"

"... music ...?" echoed the Mole vaguely, looking all around him with an unfocused gaze. "... What ... music ...?"

The walls and ceiling of the shop thumped, the air thumped, the clothes on their shining rails thumped, and then again the wailing-weasel-girl-voice skirled about them like the cry of a banshee risen grieving from its stony lair on a midnight moor.

"No!" retorted the Mole boldly, determined not to be put off. "Mr Rette, that animal is in DISTRESS!"

The plump assistant stood with his clipboard dangling from one limp paw, his nose twitching in double-time with amazement. "Please ignore him," said the Rat hoarsely, attempting a grin his lips would not agree to. "He's—er— been having a spot of trouble lately. Bit of a breakdown—you know. It's *music*, I tell you!—Come ON!" With this he grabbed the Mole firmly by the sleeve and began to tow him backwards out of the store.

"O, no ... No ... But the poor, poor creature!" cried the Mole, all his courtly instincts to the fore now and still urging him to act. "— How can we leave her here in such a plight?"

"There isn't anyone to *leave*, you bean-brained burk!" yelled his incensed companion.

The Mole stared around the shop, doing his best to locate the wounded, bereaved or dying girl. But since there was no one else in evidence besides the chubby cony and an infinity of reflections of same, he had little choice except to acquiesce.

"... But I heard her ..." he mumbled, half a minute later, by which time he and Mr Rette, still tugging, were two hundred yards further down the street.

"How fat some of these animals are," observed the Mole, another minute later. "... And how thin some of the others are," he added.

To neither remark did Mr Rette respond except perhaps by walking even faster. Not that this did him very much good. Another fifty yards on, and now in a quiet side-street, they saw ahead a young water vole, hunched on the steps of a recess-doorway and heavily draped in a collection of worn-out jackets and coats. As they drew closer to him, Mr Rette looked everywhere but towards him: it was rather as if lamp posts, waste-bins and paving-blocks had suddenly become worthy of his deepest and most enquiring scrutiny. The Mole, for his part, stared at the animal in blank sympathy and disbelief.

"G'unny chaaaynge?" whined the Vole. His fur was matted, the Mole saw, and his eyes looked slightly glazed.

Resisting the force of Mr Rette's tugs, the Mole skidded to a halt. "O, but the poor, poor animal," he breathed, to himself. Never before in his life had he heard a voice quite so weedy, so ground-down, so *ill*-sounding, not even amongst the ranks of the poorest hedgehogs. "Mr Rette, we must help him. —We must! It is our duty."

"THERE IS NO TIME!" spumed the Rat.

But to the Mole it was unthinkable not to try to help a fellow-animal in need. It would have gone against his deepest instincts simply to walk on now. "Why are you here?" he asked the Vole. "— No, we *must*," he said firmly, again resisting Mr Rette's attempts to drag him on. "Can't you go home?"

"Bit difficult when you ain't got one," said the Vole sardonically, breaking into a wheezy, compulsive, hacking cough. (Mr Rette turned quickly away, covering his mouth.)

"You haven't got one?" said the Mole. "You haven't got a *home*? O but that's awful! Terrible—terrible." Yet even as he spoke he was also thinking, how could he help him, after all? An animal with no burrow of his own has scant hospitality to offer. "Pan watch out for you, Vole," he said sadly.

The young animal looked up at him with his deep-set eyes, briefly surprised out of his cocoon of separateness by the strength of feeling displayed by this passer-by who had not yet passed. "Pan watch out for you, mal," he replied wearily, looking up the street as he did so.

"Ohhh!!" exclaimed the Rat, fumbling in his pockets, whence he produced a note. "Here!" He flung the money at the sunken Vole. "Sorry! Goodbye! COME ON, Mr Mole. Please!"

The Mole still did not move. Reaching for his purse, he emptied its somewhat outdated contents into the homeless animal's paw. But at that point the Rat got a proper purchase on him.

"How can animals live like that?" said the Mole to himself, replacing his handkerchief over his mouth at much the same time that Mr Rette removed his hand from his own, "And how can they live—here? In *this*?" By now the thing in the air seemed positively to be gripping the sides of his throat; his mouth tasted of metal, and his eyes were itching again.

The remains of this uneasy journey between London W1 and London EC2 is perhaps best left undescribed, except to mention that as the Rat hauled and yanked his recalcitrant companion on across Holborn and into the western skirts of the City of London, the Mole found it more and more necessary to shade his eyes against any glimpse of what was rearing up next to the pavements he was being tugged along. By the last stages of the walk any sense of orientation he might have clung on to until then was completely overwhelmed by the screaming up-thrust of ever more gigantic structures, brutally vying with one another as if to blank out the light of day itself. The Mole began to wonder if the poor stunned mullet-brains with their duck's-beak caps might not be a lot more astute than their looks suggested. These caps could only have been made, he reasoned, so as to shut out the sight of windows and walls ascending, against all he knew of Nature, into places where no wall or window should ever go or be.

At last, moist-browed and damp under their collars, the two animals drew close to what even the Mole could not avoid seeing was a Gog amongst Magogs—A Gargantua amongst Pantagruels—a truly Himalayan display of corporate *haute couture*: the World Headquarters of Mr Rette's employers, Toad Transoceanic and Mollusk (Holdings) A.L.C., rearing, as it did, above the very Heart of Bigness and completely blocking out all view of the sky beyond from each of the roads that approached it.

This building was not merely vast. Unlike everything else around it, which conformed to the standard of grit-grey-on-black (or sometimes, more challengingly, grit-black-on-grey), the Toad Transoceanic building was done all in shades of terracotta and blotched pinks and whites and fawns. It was clad in close on three-quarters of a square mile of polished Serravezza marble, rising in a chasmic E-shape around a courtyard-front adorned with fountains. At its remote top the building broke into a series of caps and crests resembling the roofs of some medieval city, and indeed one part of the structure here had been given tall, very thin windows in a bogo-Gothic style, lending it a strange resemblance to the Lady Chapel of a Cathedral, grabbed from its normal resting place and craned up into the sky. The immense entrance doors—each a limpid megalith of sea-green glass—were framed on either side by skeletal, nightmarish sculptures of horses, the one mirroring the other in the midst of a threatening, hoof-flailing rear. Yet, with their blocky forms and angularity of muscle-shape, they resembled less horses than machines.

"Blast oh blast oh *blast*," grumbled Mr Rette to himself, looking at the throng of animals beyond the doors, then at the Mole (in mid-jump) as the doors glid-slid apart in front of them. "Oh squash oh blast oh squash! The whole point was to get here early.—Yes, ah, morning, Cedric. This gent'mal's—er, yes—with me, yes. A pass in my name— Degirthing, yes ... Well today? ... Good ... Notsobad ... No ... No, ha, ha, we're not going to fire you today, Cedric ... No ... *Why* does he always ask me that?"

Now attired with a floppy little badge inscribed "MR MOLE. To See: Mr G.R. Rette, Dept. of Degirthing", the Mole moved forwards into a cavernous hall no less marbled and shining in its way (though done in creams and bronzes and bits of black) than the exterior. He looked about him with all the open-mouthed curiosity of a true country animal, amazed at the quietly echoing size of the place, through which many individuals were moving in a rapt and concentrated first-thing business-hush, not a single one of them seeming to notice what engulfed them.

"Right, Mr Mole," said Mr Rette decisively. "This way." He steered the unsteady Mole at speed towards the entrance to a side-corridor, and this they had very nearly reached when a loud voice some distance to their rear broke through the sounds of faintly echoing feet and muted conversation.

"Gordon!" the voice cried. "Want to SEE you!"

"No-o-o-o ..." wheezed the Water Rat through lips of board-like stiffness. "Not W-T! No, please, please, *no* ..."

Yet, automatically—like an animal about to give himself up to an armed patrol and knowing the fate that awaited him—Mr Rette turned back towards the lobby. Like a skater not one hundred per cent in control of his blades, the Mole turned with him.

<hr>

An ebullient, impeccably dressed and slightly pink-cheeked toad was striding toward them above the blur of his own reflection in the gleaming marble floor. Seeking to match him in his speed, Mr Rette pulled the Mole forward with him, muttering as he did so, "No, wait for me here.—No ... No! ... Too late ... Just don't say ... Oh! Don't open your *mouth*. Got that? Morning, ha, ha, W-T."

"Morning, Gordon. Just wanted to lock-in with you a moment on that Bhopal Plastics degirth. How's it coming, a.t.p.?"

"A.t.p., W-T."

"Going-forward?"

"Going-forward, W-T! Going-forward, going-*forward-going*-forward."

"Good, good. Oh, and the Bahrain plant? Yes? Excellent. Just remind me now, what is that, seventeen hundred jobs in all?"

"Sixteen hundred and seventy-eight," responded Mr Rette, speaking very quickly now, "with fringe variance of ten per cent, interim-enhanced, hands-on, hands-off, and of course marginal both sides the line." The Mole saw a change come over the Water Rat as he mouthed these opacities: an indefinable but disturbing sharpness seemed to bite down into his

features like a mask settling into the face that wore it, and his
tail became strangely straight.

"Fine. Good morning." The Toad angled himself towards
the Mole, though barely looking at him.

The Mole could not *not* return a greeting. "Proud, I'b sure,"
he responded, as well as he might with mouth three-quarters
closed.

The Toad was about to speak again, but paused, his previously general gaze settling on the visitor with a slightly more
focused interest. "This gentmal is with you, Gordon? Ah, but
of course he is. Splendid period smoking jacket."

"MmO—thadkyoum," gritted the Mole once more.

The Toad glanced briefly towards Mr Rette with just a
trace of puzzlement, then lost all hint of interpretable expression. "Oh, and Gordon," he said, "that destat in the
Preservatives Wing? No problems there I presume?"

"Smooth as mink, W-T! In the meat safe Thursday p.m.,
snapshut Friday. Stiff-in-the-box by end of next week latest;
ashes-on-the-roses at least fourteen days pre-April Five."

"Good-good! Fire-and-fire, Gordon, fire-and-fire! Only
way on to a rampant future, eh? Any of the old desk-durables
worth hanging on to there?"

"A pawful, W-T. Though there are a couple of other individuals I thought we might keep as ..." (and here—over and
above any dampness that might have been there in the first
place—a heavy sweat broke out on the fur of the Rat's furred
and furrowed brow) "... er, ha ... What I meant to say is that
there are two animals there who I have known for many years,
not proactively vicious, exactly, but pretty competent, you
know. I ... er ... ggh ... thought we'd keep them on, ah—
anyway. I ... hoped to slip them through without anyone
noticing. It seemed reasonable, given the numbers we are let-
going. ... What? ... What?! ... I, ha, ha ... didn't think ..."

The Rat's voice trailed off, as if the words he had just
spoken had left him speechless. He stared ahead now, much as

if a large sheet of pink Serravezza marble had just dropped on his foot, and he was very keen not to make a thing of it. Mysteriously, the sharp-nosed and unsettling quality in his face had completely vanished.

"... Interesting, Gordon," said the Toad, his eyes fixed on Mr Rette in a gaze of deepest curiosity. "*Extraordinarily* interesting! Ahh ..." He turned elegantly to the Mole, scrutinizing him and the very air about him as if checking the direction of the wind. "Perhaps you should introduce us?"

"Yes, yes. Ha.—Yes. Mr ... Mole: Mr Wyvern-Toad, Director of—All This."

"... And you are *from*, Mr Mole?" enquired the Toad, moving a little closer to him as he spoke.

"— Ab I?" answered the Mole, talking now in a very low, grumbling kind of a voice. "O, yef.—I do beg your pardob. I'b frob the Riverside."

"The arts complex? An actor, then."

"O—you know—only at Yuletide."

There was the briefest pause as Mr Wyvern-Toad weighed up this piece of information. He had perhaps been hoping for rather more detail, but did not get it. It's strange you should be feeling so charitable today, Gordon," he said, almost garrulously now, to the pale and visibly trembling Rat. "Since I myself am also feeling fairly charitable, so far as I myself am concerned. And nothing new in that, eh? Ha, ha! After all, it isn't as if the conglomerate can't stand one a piffling little *emolumentum redux* now and then without too much grief. Don't you think?"

"I—I—"

The Toad himself was now staring helplessly at Mr Rette, his protuberant eyes expressive of some heretofore unknown extreme—some outer limit—of entrepreneurial horror. "What on earth—?" Then immediately, and no less chattily than before, he went on "I mean, really, you know, one does periodically have to re-gild the plumbing on one's yachts, eh?

The sheikhs expect it, dear boy! The sheikhs do expect it! We'll be doing it the usual way—via my Directorship of the PAM Coatings subsidiary—a mere bagatelle, as I said, two point five million or thereabouts. Ha, ha, er, ha. Ha. Stuff it in one of one's Guernsey creamers—you know—pending the next-round of divi- er—divi ... dends ..."

The Water-Rat returned the Toad's pallid, lock-jawed stare with a look of sub-entrepreneurial horror of his own. An exchange took place between rat's eyes (huge and haunted) and toad's eyes (bulbous with wholly unaccustomed angst) in which something—something for which neither yet had words—was recognised between them.

"Gordon ..." said Mr Wyvern-Toad in a moment, as the ripples on his forehead began to subside. "You have a meeting at—what? Half an hour's time? Could you spare ten minutes? *Would* you mind?"

So saying, the Toad—in his new-today suit, virtually identical to Mr Rette's, barring the style of his tie and one small pearl adorning the tie-pin—glided across the shining floor towards a lift doorway. "We'll go up top," he said. "Well out of range of any long-distance ear-pricking, eh?"

The Mole wondered why they were standing silently for so long in such a small room. He wondered too at the bell-like chime that preceded both the closing and the reopening of the doors. And when they stepped out again not into the great echoing hall they had just left but into a relatively narrow, quiet, carpeted corridor—the Mole wondered yet a third time, more greatly still. For to his right now he found another window-wall, and beyond this he could see nothing at all but the sky and the hulking tips of a panorama of unthinkable collosi. Disbelievingly, he moved just a little closer to the glass, only to find that the street had been pulled from under him and lay now at least a thousand seconds' worth of futile fluttering and flapping-armed descent below. Despite himself (for he was still on best behaviour) he uttered a low moan of abject funkdom and grabbed Mr Rette very tightly by the briefcase-elbow.

"Let go of me," grarled the Rat under his breath, trying, but also failing, to shake him off.

Mr Wyvern-Toad ran a hand lightly over his fine green pate and, looking slightly bored, held up a small card in front of him. Large doors parted and the three animals walked forward into another lofty space all done in calming Wedgwood blues and greys. Ahead of them a pale gold, two-hundred-foot-long beech table stretched away to a high podium on which another much shorter table stood at right angles to the first. A curving range of long and very narrow windows with lancet tops ran up to the height of four conventional storeys: the Mole saw that, as in the Rettes' kitchen, they had patterns of coloured glass set in them. Well at least they shut out that awful, awful drop, he thought, relaxing just a little.

"Shall we go up to the High Table?" suggested Mr Wyvern-Toad. Once they had reached it they took seats at one end, the Toad draping his jacket over his own. "All right, Gordon," he said. "Your time is precious, and I'm sure you have a busy day ahead as usual. But ... we have something on our hands, do we not? And it is sufficiently intriguing to merit, I think—what, now—a small experiment? But the question is, of course, what experiment should that be?"

The still-poleaxed Rat opened his mouth in search of words, but nothing emerged from it except a short, would-be dignified, but in fact undignified and slightly choking "Aaggh ..."

"An experiment," repeated Mr Wyvern-Toad, tapping the end of his nose. "Yes, good enough. Let's try this. You don't mind being guinea-pig? As it were? No, of course not. Will you answer me a question, please?—Though we will want a series of answers, if I'm anywhere near the mark. What are—and, Gordon, pay attention to my phrasing, won't you?—what are the *unwritten* rules of the Company?"

Gordon Rette stared round-eyed at his boss, but did not speak.

"Come on now, Gordon. You know the answers better than anyone, and I know you do.—Oh, er, Mr Mole—let's see ... Would you mind sitting just a little closer to him? To humour me, to humour me! If you don't mind."

The Water Rat breathed in deeply. "W-T," he said in a stricken tone. "The unwritten rules are also the unspoken rules. *That is one* of the rules. We don't ... you know! We just don't discuss this ... Except in moments of the most critically netherpostworthy—*ex*-postworthy—misjudgement."

"So you don't want to tell me, Gordon?—Yes? Is that right? You'd really prefer not to discuss it, but something ... *something* here ... is going to make you tell me anyway. Isn't it though? All right—"

"There is only one spoken rule, W-T," temporised the Rat, tugging nervously at his tail in schoolboy fashion. "And that is: *The-interests-of-the-shareholders-are-paramount.*"

"Oh, we all know that, Gordon!" grinned the Toad disparagingly. "Move up a little closer, will you, Mr—er ... Mole ... Come on now, Rette. I can take it. The *unwritten* rules."

"Nothing matters but the interests of the Shareholders," said the Water Rat quietly, and now his speech was much more measured. "The pursuit of profit on their behalf can be used to justify all and any actions by the Company."

"Yes!" said the Toad, half to himself, slapping his hand lightly on the table as he did so. "*And*—?"

"Nothing must stand in the way of the Growth of the Company. My own fate as employee is as nothing when compared to the future of the Company. I must be prepared to work for Growth at all times, but equally I can expect to be sacrificed at any time, if Growth demands it."

"And ...?" demanded Mr Wyvern-Toad, rising from his seat, putting his short arms behind his back, and walking towards one of the narrow windows.

"I must not question the ideal of Growth," said the Rat, speaking almost as impersonally now as a medium at a seance. "Growth is an Absolute, to be achieved by any means. For without continuous and uninterrupted Growth, the Company itself will wither and die."

"... Anything else?"

"I must never question the nature or contents of any of the Company's products, or how they may be used. I must not question the intentions of any client of the Company. To this end, I must act without seeing."

"Beautifully put! Anything else?"

"I have no personal responsibility for Company actions. The Company will be responsible in my place, where ... where ..." The Rat began to claw at his tie-knot, as if in renewed amazement at the words he found himself uttering.

Mr Wyvern-Toad turned from the window, his gaze flickering from rat to mole to rat. "... Yes, Gordon?" he said.

"... where it suits it. Only where it suits it. Ultimately ... in the last analysis ... when push comes to shove ... the Company itself is not responsible." The Water Rat looked down and said again quietly, "The Company itself is not responsible."

"Very *good*, Gordon! *Very* good! I couldn't have put that better myself, had I ever had to. All right—all right. Relax, please, my dear fellow! End of Question Time."

The Water Rat sat heavily back in his seat, breathing stertorously, and gripped his tail between his knees.

"Well, you have your meeting, don't you, Gordon?" said the Toad breezily. "I really mustn't keep you any longer. Perhaps you can call up to see me later—when you're free? Thank you, *so* much."

Mr Rette picked up his briefcase. He looked at the Mole, then at the Toad, then in a kind of blank and helpless amazement, back at the Mole.

"Leave him with me, leave him with me!" said Mr Wyvern-

Toad. You're not in any hurry, Mr Mole? No, good, good, excellent."

Immediately the drip-tailed rat had left, the Toad went on, "Hard things to say about one's Company, those. Very hard. But that is one of the problems, isn't it, one finds, with that thing called 'truth'—however we may like to debate the interpretation of that sticky little word. Don't you think so, Mr Mole? It's so much better when we manage to keep these things under our hats. Now ... that 'riverside' you said you're from. That is where, exactly?"

"O ... Ah ..." The Mole windmilled both arms in a spirited attempt at specificity. "Oxfordshire-Berkshire way, you know. Berkshire-Oxfordshire? A bit upstream from Toad Hall. I don't suppose you know it—?"

"Toad *Hall?*" repeated the Toad, frowning. "You don't mean Toad Towers?"

"No ...? Er ... No ...?"

"That's the *Oxfordshire* Toad Hall, you say? Not the one in the Peak District?"

The Mole was nearly floored by mention of the Peak District. But he persevered. "Um ... um ... Yes. Yes! On that bank of the river, I think."

"But you see, Mr Mole, the Oxfordshire Toad Hall was gutted by fire in 1924. It was rebuilt two years later as Toad Towers. I know this because, oddly enough, I happen to own the Towers."

"O! O my!—Well, then, Toad of Toad Hall is a relative of yours?"

"... *Was* a distant relative, I believe. He was—let me see— my grand uncle, twice removed. I never met him, of course. But I know he was an animal of some character."

"He certainly is!" replied the Mole, smiling warmly.

"Yes, ah ... Was?"

"O—er ... Was." The Mole looked down sadly. "Yes."

Mr Wyvern-Toad looked long and hard at this quaintly

attired visitor, much as if he had been a last hard line in a crossword puzzle. He opened his mouth to ask another question, but was kept from doing so by a gentle buzzing in the style of a bluebottle trapped inside a matchbox. He leaned forward—the Mole noticed that in profile his chin connected directly and fleshily with his collar, without evidence of neck—and pressed a small red square thing.

"W-T," he said.

Not another animal who talks to himself! thought the Mole. O, what poor, sad creatures they are here, after all!

"Stoatdegrave," said the curtly casual voice of an animal trapped inside the table-top. "Thought you'd like to know right away, W-T. It's come through. We have ImpAgrocon. It was a Board decision."

Very, very slowly, not wishing to cause a disturbance, the Mole bent down in his seat and looked underneath the table.

"Ha!" shouted the Toad, his face aflame with a triumphal blood-rush. "A Board decision! Of *course* it was. And how did the Board come by this decision, Stoatdegrave, do we need to ask? After year upon year of resistance? Nothing to do with one's having published the directors' home numbers on the cusp of the takeover, by any chance? Oh, *that* wasn't going to work, was it, Stoatdegrave, how often did we hear that? No, no, no—unheard of, can't have that! Good heavens, shareholders might start *ringing them up* when they're in the bath, and telling them to sell! No, no. Far too strategically brilliant, far too much of a stroke of near-clairvoyance on one's own part! And here they all are, you see, falling meekly on their swords like the Mouzeoletians on the field of Corinth. Good-good! Call a meeting, will you?"

"This afternoon?"

"Two this afternoon, yes. This has been a long one, Stoatdegrave. Thanks for chasing me up."

The Mole was still gingerly feeling and pressing around a

large area of wood beneath the table when Mr Wyvern-Toad spoke again. "It's mine," he said.

"It's mine!" he said again. "Six years of subtly snake-charming shareholders, six years of strategically precise fringe takeovers, six years of raising only the most slightly justifiable doubts on company efficiency—then, you see, a single, deft, surgically-specific, characteristically ruthless hammer-blow—the tiniest final push—and now it's mine—mine MINE!! ... That is, of course," (he went on in a very slightly humbler voice) "it is T.T.'s, and the shareholders of T.T.'s ... But great groaning galleons of gratuities, Mr Mole! We're going to go so far into profit now, the last three decades will look like the takings of a Bethnal Green whelk stall during a seafood scare!"

The Toad's glittering eyes bulbed out under pressure of mounting ecstasy. "Oh—hee, hee, hee, hee, hee, hee, hee!" he cried, and the Mole watched open-mouthed as the previously restrained, not to say mandarinic, animal did a nimble extended cartwheel—all the more remarkable for one of his rotund inclinations—for most of the length of the long beech table. "Pudding today. Pudding with pitchers of cream tomorrow!" he exclaimed, once righted. "What do you say to *that*, Mr Mole? You may not know it, but you have just been witness to a really quite significant event in the history of World Trade."

The Mole remained confused. After all, if there *was* no animal inside the table, then where could that voice have come from? It surely wasn't possible that Mr Wyvern-Toad was a ventriloquist? If he was, poor animal, then he must be a mad ventriloquist since, surely, no one who had all his wits would suddenly out of nowhere start up a conversation with a table-top?

"I'm—erm—very impressed," he replied circumspectly.

The Toad paused in mid-gloat. "You don't seem to be," he said, an eyebrow raised. "But perhaps that is because you don't quite follow. You're not in the world of business, Mr Mole, would one be right in assuming?"

The Mole did occasionally sell off some of his surplus runner-beans (and beetroots, when he grew them) by leaving them in a basket at the end of his tiny, hedged-in patch of garden, accompanied by an old biscuit tin to collect the farthings. Otherwise, though, he was not widely known for his business acumen.

"No—um—no," he replied.

"— Ah. Well then, I feel that perhaps I owe you an explanation," said Mr Wyvern-Toad. "Firstly, of course, because you happen to be here with me at this extraordinary moment—though to be frank, one doesn't yet know you from a Mindanao moonrat—and secondly because—interestingly, I must say—*most* interestingly—I do seem to be experiencing another of these uncomfortable urges to, ahh—for want of a more duplicitous way of putting it—tell the truth. You're not a journalist, of course—no, no! And a very good thing too in the circumstances. But first—do excuse me—" (and here the Toad clenched his neat small hands into fists and shook them exultingly over his head) "Hee-hee-hee-hee-hee-hee-HEE! It's MINE!!!—But Mr Mole," (he cleared his throat) "I do apologise."

"Perfectly all right," said the Mole, sitting on his paws.

The Toad walked briskly up to the wall and pressed another small red square thing, at which the colour somehow *withdrew* from all of the windows encircling the High Table; at which the Mole uttered a low moan of average audibility. "If you look out here—" said Mr Wyvern-Toad, gesturing.

"O-o-o!" responded the Mole, shrinking back into his seat. "I'd rather not." But even against this terror, manners proved irresistible, and he forced himself up towards the light in question.

"You see that embarrassingly old-fashioned little block to the north-east, over there?" asked the Toad, pointing at a sheer-sided sixty-storey over-towerer whose predominant colour (other than grey) was a stained jade-green. "That, at present, is the headquarters of ImpAgrocon, the Imperial Agrochemicals Conglomerate and, until this moment, one of our half dozen most vigorous competitors in the domestic and world fields. But from today, Mr Mole—from this very hour—like the inner workings of that block, there, and that, just beyond it, and that, with the amusing clock and the Art Ducko canopy, over the river beyond London Bridge—oh, and a dozen others dotted about the inner metropolis and beyond—it will be a mere department. A mere subsidiary of its parent company, a mere set of cogs in the intricate, earth-embracing machinery (or if you prefer a more up-to-date simile, of shards in the universal corporate wombweave)—of *Toad Transoceanic!*"

"My!" said the Mole, who felt he was expected to be impressed.

The Toad paused, turning to him. "You were about to say—your ...?"

"Um—no. Was I? No?"

"Ah. Perhaps not. You see, Mr. Mole, it was my relative, Thaddeus Toad, who founded Mollusk Oil in 1919—with some small help from a group of newly emergent weasel entre-preneurs—to work a single oil-field in the Saudi desert. And in little more than fifteen years Mollusk had grown to become one of the three most powerful oil-producers in this country. T-T the mal was himself, I have to say, the most capable of company beasts—"

"Was he?" asked the Mole in surprise. He could not imagine a toad nearer his own generation being capable in any field at all, if he was to be honest.

"Oh yes, he was. He was. It is intriguing, given his own reputed tendency towards wildness, but doesn't it sometimes happen that those who allow themselves a little licence to, well, *live* in their earlier years ... achieve, when the time comes?

Not least amongst the toad class, one might add! And it can't be denied, Mr Mole, Thaddeus Toad proved brilliant as an investor time and time again. Oh, he could quite happily have kept his wealth tied up in the family's modest West African cocoa plantations—never once in history a loss-making industry, cocoa! But T-T saw the future—he had that old Toad vision. He predicted the emergence of the mass-produced family car, long before it happened. He saw what was just about to become *the* most needed commodity, the commodity-of-commodities, without which this wonderful society of ours would grind down into ruin in a matter of years: *Petroleum Spirit*. He put up Mollusk petrol pumps all around the country—and not just on the trunk roads. You'd have seen a Mollusk pump up and working next to the Post Office in *Tobermory* by 1928! No, no. The T.T. empire would not be here today if it had not been for the efforts of my venerable grand uncle. Although, of course, those of us who came later have had *some* small influence on Company growth."

The Mole could not keep out of his mind images of the world he had been moving through for the past two days—of the great grey horror-route and its choking fumes, the apparently endless street-blocking cars and their choking fumes, and other things besides. "But if it harms the world," he said, unafraid to ask a simple question, "— and Nature, what then?"

One toad-eyebrow rose very, very slightly. "I have not the slightest doubt, Mr Mole, that you are a mal of the world." The Toad paused, meditating. "... And I must say, you know, I *like* an animal who can bowl a googly like that, right out of the sun! Trying to catch me by being completely straight about it, eh? Very good—oh yes, very good! There are few enough animals ready to risk *that* sort of approach! The answer, of course, and I'm sure you know it already, is that one has a Public Manipulations Department—I mean, ha ha, dear me, *dear* me—a Public *Relations* Department. One is permanently shielded from criticism by a phalanx of highly skilled Front Animals who are, to a rat, absolute masters of the art of presenting the favourable picture."

Onion-sauce, thought the Mole, but he did not say it.

"Yes, it is the Front Animals," said the Toad, "who smooth-serv one's products—wherever it can be made to fit—as 'Environment Friendly'—kind to nature, you see? It is they who—with the greatest ingenuity—generate all the advertising, posters, car-stickers and the like that reinforce the image of the Company as Caring, Responsible. A picture of some threatened species, say—one of the cuddlier creatures of the lower orders such as a panda (pandas always go down rather well) with some simple motif such as 'Mollusk CARES'? Circulate this around the world's infant schools and youth clubs, and hey presto—an unhealthy balance in the public perception of one's activities can be cut back, as it were, almost before it has begun to shoot."

Onion-*sauce!* thought the Mole again.

"It is our excellent Front Animals," went on the Director of Toad Transoceanic, "who bring in the kinds of experts who—ask not the reasons why—tend to reinforce the Company point of view. It is they who put spokesmals on air whenever there is some little problem such as an oil-spill, for example …"

"But—" said the Mole, struggling for words, "but—but this is all to do with, I don't know, just—*seeming.*"

"Seeming, Mr Mole! *Seeming!* That is exactly it—the name of the game: and we work very hard at it here at T.T. We are proud (though we are not normally heard to say so) of our capacity to *seem.* Oh, you know, we sponsor many, many 'environmental' projects each year—anything at all to do with trees tends to go down well, we've found. Tree-planting schemes, little woodland 'preservation' groups (so many of them are abjectly strapped for cash, they're more than willing to take ours). Then of course there are things like the Wyvern-Toad

Chair of Corporate Ethics at UIL, the Mollusk Lowland Bog Conservation Awards—oh ... one could go on for hours!"

"But, I don't understand," persevered the Mole, his voice deepening as he sought about for words. "All that—awful stuff in the air out there—it's still *there*, isn't it? It's just—there. And it's terrible to say this, but—you know—if what you do harms the world and Nature, well, it injures Pan."

A great weariness seemed to settle on the Toad's face like a weight, dragging down his jowls. He looked at the Mole now almost as if he doubted his presence in front of him—his very existence. "'Pan?'" he snorted. "Now *there's* a quaint concept! I'm afraid, Mr Mole, that 'Pan's' well-being is not very high on the Mollusk Prioritization-Paramountix-Profiles. No, no, not on the current PPPs, I'm afraid! Even if one does sometimes fear ... But what am I saying?"

The Toad paused, squeezing the centre of his dappled green forehead between thumb and forefinger. "Pressed as I am to go further, you know—for whatever bizarre reasons— it does seem that that is a sentence I am unable to complete at present. But really, Mr Mole! We must try to keep these things in proportion. We don't want to get in the habit of making mountains out of—" (He laughed, rather too loudly) "I do beg your pardon! But we are living in times of great—what should we say?—uncertainty? All figures are infinitely open to interpretation, given the right team. And a great transnational such as T.T. can move in only one direction—onward. Onward! Cutting its path like some vast ocean liner through the unresisting waves of—everything else out there, if I'm honest, towards Growth, Growth, Growth! Towards *absolute* dominion over world markets, towards *total* absorption (or quiet elimination) of competition!"

The Toad turned back towards the long window, rallying as he embroidered his argument. "— And 'Pan', you know, if he existed, would surely approve of the way we work here. After all, it is quite natural that T.T. should control that tower, and that, and that, and aim to take in that little enterprise near the horizon over there by the end of next year at latest. Isn't it the case *in nature* that territory must always be extended outward, outward, outward? Isn't it *natural*, too, to shed employees once their efforts prove superfluous, just as trees shed leaves—just as you (if you'll excuse me) shed fur at the right time of year? Companies do not exist for the purpose of maintaining animals in jobs! Or to benefit 'society' (whatever that may be). 'Society' (if it exists at all) is there as the merest set of adjuncts to the world's only worthwhile reality: the Great, Shining, Billion-Horsepower, Vastly-Cubic-Capacitied Economic Machine itself! 'Society' is nothing more than the trim—the optional accessory: the odd set of go-faster stripes, or low-level fog-lights, or stick-on blind-spot mirror-mirrors (if you must have 'em). No, no! If I could run my entire empire without the help of a single desk-mal, don't you think I wouldn't do it?"

The Mole had so many thoughts in his head now that he was completely at a loss for words.

"And now our agrochemicals are being used in most of the farming countries of any significance to World Trade," waxed the Toad, "isn't it wholly *natural* that we should try to sell them in places like China or Russia (when things have calmed down a little there), or in the Underworld, where so much farming is still done in the old idiotic Pre-Chemical way?"

"Well ..." said the Mole, scratching his head. "Blest if I know anything about it, really, but what if the elm tree grew everywhere, all across the world, in place of all the other trees? Would that be 'natural'?"

"A rather bad choice of example, Mr Mole, if I may say so, since there aren't any elm trees any more," retorted the Toad, not without a trace of smugness.

"— O! Aren't there?"

"I believe not. Where *have* you been, Mr Mole?"

"O—O.—But I mean, you know—if it did. If."

"First let it happen. Then I will give you a judgement."

The bluebottle buzzed again inside its matchbox, and Mr Wyvern-Toad responded. "W-T," he said.

"Sir!" squeaked a voice from inside, beneath, above and/or behind the table top. (Yet more bafflingly, if possible, it was a female voice this time.) "I've been looking for you everywhere! Ms Von Otter has arrived, W-T."

"Excellent, Alicia, excellent. Coup-de-grâce time once again; coup-de-out-to-grass time, ha ha! Three minutes." He turned to the still startled Mole. "Mr Mole," he said, "as you'll gather, I have another engagement. But I must say I have found it most interesting talking with you this morning. One didn't manage to glean your field ..." (the Mole found this phrase more than usually puzzling) "... but there will be time for that, no doubt. It—er—it might possibly interest you to know that there are going to be one or two really quite challenging openings on the executive here at T.T. over the next few months. The direction of flow here is not entirely controlled by Gordon's department! And I do think there may be one post that might rather suit an animal of your manifest abilities. You couldn't *possibly* find the time to come in again tomorrow?—Yes? After ten, say?"

The Mole was confused. Could so obviously powerful an animal really be offering him anything quite so humble as a spare fence post? And if so, what did he imagine he was going to do with it? But, had it existed, his own diary would not exactly have been overflowing, and he felt it would be rude to refuse an invitation even from an animal whom he had not (to be completely honest) wholly taken to. What could he do but accept?

So the Director-in-Chief, Chairmal and Principal Shareholder of Toad Transoceanic parted ways with the Mole. But before the Toad had quite got to the end of the long beech table, the Water Rat's intently careworn face appeared from behind the glide-apart doors. As the two animals met, the

Toad drew close and said in a very low voice, "Gordon! You brilliant, brilliant fellow! I don't know where you found him, but hang on to him like the Crown Jewels. A secret weapon, Rette, a secret weapon. Though one that is in danger of exploding in the user's hands, unless we can be a little bit ingenious …?" He walked briskly on, and the doors absorbed him.

Thus was the Mole's immediate destiny decided. A visit to the Company doctor confirmed he was bruised but not broken, and he spent the rest of the day in an anteroom of Mr Rette's personal office, and in an alcove of the staff restaurant, reading copies of pink newspapers left behind on seats. From these he learned several new things about the world in which he found himself, most of which he did not quite understand. (Those which he did understand he did not like).

Finally, at a quarter to six, both weary animals left the building by way of the great echoing lobby-cave. Set to one side of the floor here, the Mole noticed a black marble plinth bearing an unpretentious bronze of a small figure in driver's cap and goggles. His booted foot was raised to the running board of an artistically tapered segment of a 1928 Lambormuttoni *Gazelle*. Beneath was the inscription:

Our Founder

THADDEUS TOAD

The Mole paused just one moment by it, struck by the resemblance between the animal he saw there and another, known to him from earlier days.

CHAPTER FOUR

RAT WITHOUT A TALE

The journey out was, for the most part, much calmer than the journey in. Challenges to Mr Rette's equanimity came only at widely spaced intervals, whilst the Mole was developing a technique for issuing all moans of terror sub-aurally, through his solar plexus. Mr Rette said nothing at all, as they travelled, about the new footing for operations except to observe, rather gruffly, "It looks as if you'll be staying with us, then, for a bit." From his tone, the Mole guessed that this was neither a request nor exactly an offer of hospitality—more a statement of the inevitable.

After supper (Mrs Rette was out at a "Build Your Own Garden-Portcullis" class, the children already fed) the Rat quickly withdrew to his home office. Finding even the younger Rettes engaged—at their homework, he presumed, though if so, not very quietly—the Mole also started for his room with his now formally borrowed copy of *The Vole Who Mistook His Girlfriend For A Bidet*. Through the open door of the Water Rat's workplace he saw once more the slump-shouldered, bee-jumpered figure, already staring at his small grey screen and tapping urgently at the register of little letters. The Mole sighed, and shook his head, and went on by.

That night, even inside the relative darkness and security of his coat-hanger retreat, the Mole was not able to sleep. Great Thoughts kept drifting through his head like gale-blown icebergs, far too big and unwieldy for him to begin to make sense of them. It was quite unlike the Mole not to be able to sleep: in fact, he could not remember it happening before in his life. But there it was, and he tossed and turned, stretched and squirmed, wrinkled and then smoothed out his sheets, crumpled and re-plumped his pillows, twined and untwined his legs and then, by mistake, whomped the inside of the wardrobe with a foot. After nearly two hours of this, with a little grunt of annoyance, he got out again and switched on the light. By now the horrible glowing red-number-thing by the bed—which he had turned to the wall so that he did not have to look at it—read 1.45 a.m.

I don't know! he thought. Perhaps—if I could make a cup of cocoa? I'm sure Mrs Rette wouldn't mind—

So he tiptoed out of his room and let himself into the main living area by way of a small side room in which, amongst other items, there stood a semi-circular table with a glass top. A loose file of papers lay on this, and as he walked past, it caught on his dressing-gown and fell to the floor. He tried to gather up the fan of sheets in exactly the same order they would have occupied inside the file (despite the fact that this was boldly marked SCRAP), but in so doing—half asleep and half awake—he began to read what was printed on them.

None of it made sense, yet even so, some words and phrases slowly penetrated through to his awake-bit.

"Principal components," he saw, "4-iodo-2 propumyl-n-butyl morbamate (IPBM) ... Explosive threshold: 1—11% ... Natural impacts: not organo-degradable, persistent in soil ... Protective precautions: wear impervious garments and gloves; use full eye protection (goggles) ... In case of fire: call fire brigade quoting the Deadlichem Code No. XXX02 ... First

Aid: give artificial respiration IMMEDIATELY if patient is not breathing. Get immediate medical attention ... Disposal: DO NOT empty into drains or watercourses ..."

The file contained a full emporium-catalogue of substances made by Mollusk-Ratcaster (Wood Preservatives) U.K. Ltd., each of which had attached to it a variable litany of precautions against hazard and contamination, and colourful descriptions of what might happen to those unlucky enough to be exposed to them. No wonder, thought the Mole, that Mr Rette looked so tired: merely to know about such things, let alone to have to deal with them, would tire any animal beyond endurance.

Several times the Mole moved to put the papers away, but he paused every time as if waiting for a thought to surface. What is it that I'm looking at? he wondered.—No, but what? After all, he thought, how was it such things existed at all here? Had he, or any of the other Riversiders he knew, ever had need of 4-whatsito-2 thingumyl-n-buttill whatsitamate or any other such-like panoply of hyphens? Not that he knew. They had got on quite well without them (even if the gallery screen at Toad Hall did have a bit of woodworm in it).

And as he read on through the names (which he could see meant *something*), so he began to picture the way in which this ever-turning mill of production and use—from which he had now had his own first, unforgettable dusting-down—would, every month, every week, every day, every hour, be throwing out new forms of "substances hazardous to life"; chemicals that were (it did not sound wonderful) "not organo-degrad-able"; hyphenated-name-things that would be "persistent in soil".—*In soil!* If he had had any doubts about what he smelled on the air here—what he sensed—even deep inside a bedroom wardrobe in such a sealed-up house as this, they came to an end at that moment.

So troubled was the Mole by these ideas that he felt the need to sit down, and he groped his way towards the nearest of the mustard-coloured whales. Here he sat heavily, not seeing a small black device, decorated with yet more numbers, letters and hieroglyphs, that was wedged between two of the cushions. As he planted himself askew this object, so the very large black window-box facing him by the chimneyless mock-fireplace leapt into shocking and bizarre life. There were *moving pictures* in it now—of other animals, of animals' faces, a street, a shop that looked as if a bomb might have exploded by it, a police-*motor* with a flashing light, a crowd.

The Mole got up again, in equal parts frightened, mesmerised, and deeply curious. As he drew closer to the box he realised that there was a voice in it, or coming from it, but at a very, very low volume. This seemed—impossibly—to belong to a smartly dressed dormouse half of whom kept reappearing, seated, next to an object that looked like the title-page of a book, but made of glass. This floated somehow over a picture of the globe and read *ABC News.*

Once again the Mole was greeted by fragments of language, only just distinguishable to him above the sound of his own breathing. "… Now to war-torn eastern Europe …" he heard, then "… a new stage in the conf … as refugees continue on their hazardous and exhausting mountain journ … and the sole surviving enclave, now under continuous bombardme … stern politicians have once again warned Slav leader Skunkodan Mizelicevich that if …"

In place of the dormouse now appeared a picture of animals—foreigners, to judge by their dress—walking in a long column with here and there an open truck or tractor loaded with furniture. Then came a small group, perhaps a family, moving on along a boulder-strewn road with blank and hopeless faces.

"… ports have come in during the day of snipers firing on the refugees," said the speaker's tiny voice. "… been at least three deaths and a number of other, non-fatal injur …"

The Mole saw one figure with a bandage tied across his head so as to completely cover one of his eyes; and then several pictures of aged, exhausted animals in headscarves, staring ahead as if to take another ten steps might be the end of them. But after this came an image for which the poor Mole was completely unprepared, and it tore at his heart like nothing he had seen since he sat, desolate, at the former entrance to his home. It showed the arm and tiny paw of a baby—otherwise hidden under a drape of boldly patterned cloth—gripped in its mother's hand (the picture got somehow unsteadily wider) as she trudged and stumbled onward.

Tears rose burningly in the Mole's eyes, and he took two steps back from the terrible window, clutching together the lapels of his dressing-gown even in the warm, dry air, as if against the effect of some imaginary chill. It was quite beyond him to understand what he saw or the reason for its presence, at two in the morning, in this silent riverside home. One way or another, though, he still knew the most important thing about it: that what he had seen here was the work of something worse than brutish, some deep and unimaginable injustice—some thing that simply *should not be*.

"But I must help them," he whispered, moving back towards the dreadful window with one arm raised. Yet even as the words left his lips, mother and child were gone, the picture sliding sideways, and the dormouse speaker was there once more just as if someone had pushed him back into view.

"… ted Nations officials have today confirmed," said the tiny, tiny voice, "… rmy chief General Ratko Vladdich will be formally charged with war crimes as a result of eyewitness information on his role in … be brought before a War Crimes tribunal as soon as possible after peace … though this depends on …"

"Bit depressing really, isn't it?" said a voice from behind the sofa. The Mole jumped. It was the Water Rat. Seeing his visitor's tear-runnelled fur Mr Rette looked away at the window-box, then (as if he hoped his eyes would be dry by now) back at the Mole. "But we—can't allow it to get to us *too* much, can we?" he added grimly, stiff-lipped with embarrassment. "Uh—'scuse me. I was just going to fetch a drink."

He hurried through into the kitchen, returning a moment later with a glass of *Naiad Of The Churnet*. The Mole looked at him with (in terms relative to a mole) very large eyes indeed, and said querulously, "But what *is* that—there?—What is that window-box-thing?"

"What do you mean?" responded the Rat vaguely. "You mean the war in Jugoslavia? Surely even a mole such as yourself—I mean, do excuse me, I'm not trying to be rude, specially at this time in the morning. But you must *know* about it, surely?" He glanced away to the window-box again half expectantly, as if it might do him the favour of answering the Mole's question in his place.

"... to the most recent suggestions from scientists on methods of repairi ... ole in the Nozone Layer ..." pinpricked the box-mouse's tiny voice, "... include using a vast battery of laser-guns to ... damaging CMFs that have been released into the atmosphe ... sing military hardware to ... barrage of frozen Nozone into ... osphere where it would, in theory, melt to replenish nat ..."

Mr Rette's eyes fixed on the screen as if on the spinning watch of some master hypnotist. Then he blinked, and cleared his throat. Unfortunately, even now, quite large volumes of tears were still dripping off the end of the Mole's black-furred nose, and as the Rat looked back at him again it was as if the animal came into focus for a moment in his gaze.

"You can't afford to let it touch you like that, you know, Mole," he repeated, but in a different tone now. "You just can't. You'll go under if you do. We have to keep a distance on it all."

"Is that what you do?" asked the stricken burrower,

fumbling about in his pockets for a handkerchief but not finding one.

"Yes—Yes. Now you mention it."

"And you have to do it—all the time, then? I mean, all the time?—For life?"

The Water Rat looked back at his guest in deep unease. It was not a question to which there was any straightforward answer, apparently—not one that anyone was ever asked, perhaps. "Oh, here," he said, "— use one of these, please!" He rushed into the kitchen and came back with a box of paper tissues, from which the Mole gratefully pulled out a clump of eight at once.

"*Is* that what you have to do?" he persisted, snuffing. "Thank you."

"What else can you do?" replied the Rat. "Have you got any better suggestions?"

"But what happens if you can't do it, Mr Rette? If you don't have the—I don't know what. If you just can't do it?"

The Rat did not answer, and stared down at the carpet as if he might quite have liked to dive in. Then he looked back at his guest with what, for him (and all things are relative) was a glance of concern.

"How can you *be* so ...?" he asked. But then his voice tailed off, as did his tail.

"Born that way, I suppose," said the Mole helpfully, filling in the silence that followed.

Neither animal spoke for several moments.

"Well!" said Gordon Rette briskly. "Early start again tomorrow!"

"Have you been working until *now*?"

"No, no. I was in bed, but—" The Rat paused. It would have been far easier and more efficient for him to end the conversation there, but, when all is said and done, no rat is an island. "I had a nightmare, actually," he said.

"O, no."

"Yes.—Yes. It's one that keeps coming back—every few weeks or so, I suppose." Again the Water Rat paused, still hesitant about saying more, but also looking as if he would do so anyway.

"What happens in it?" prompted the Mole.

"Oh, I'm—" The Rat sat down on the sofa, which squawked as it part-enfolded him. He took a sip from his glass, pensively wiping the dampness from his whiskers. "I'm always driving. It's at night, you see. It's always night, and the car has no lights. *No* lights! I fumble around in front of me like a madmal, feeling all over the dashboard, trying to find the light switches, snapping things on and off. But nothing happens. My paws are trembling like jelly. There always seem to be a thousand switches—"

"There are, aren't there? O, sorry. Do go on."

"— Well, anyway, no matter what I get hold of, no lights will come on. And I feel the car swerving, and *swerving*—" (he held up his paws in front of him as if gripping an imaginary steering wheel) "—trying to avoid obstacles—if there are any, I don't know. I don't *know!*—Or at least, to stay on the road. If there is a road. And then even the movements of the steering wheel don't seem to connect up as they should with the movements of the car! It's terrible—" He sank down inside his dressing gown amidst the folds of mustard leather, looking for just one moment less adult than child.

"And then you wake up?" asked the Mole hopefully.

"No, no! It goes on: it's worse than that. I always see this lighted sign up ahead—a pub sign—on the roadside, I suppose. So the car swerves, and swerves, and I wind the steering wheel round and round, and the sign *creeps* . . . towards me. But eventually I get to it, and I climb out, and go into the pub—that part's O.K.—and I order a drink, and I sit down to calm myself. Then after a moment this other animal comes in—no one in particular you could say, some ferret—hedgehog? I can't tell you what he is, to be honest. I don't recognise him at all. But he sits at the bar, and when he turns around, he recognises me. He's already recognised me. And his face is very hard, and he comes over, and stands by my table— hovers over it until I look up at him. And he says, "You're Rette, aren't you? You're *Rette*! You *fired* me ..."

The Water Rat breathed out heavily, taking another sip of his *Naiad*. "And that's when I wake up. To get away from him. But it's as if he's always there, in the room afterwards, lingering. I can feel him, how much he'd like to—I don't know—get his revenge, I suppose. And the funniest thing of all is, I don't know him. I just don't know who he is."

"I should get another job," said the Mole bluffly, "That is, you know—if you have to have one."

"If I have to have one?! If I have to have one?!" exploded Mr Rette in an early-morning shout-whisper, his tail flailing like the arm of an industrious thespian. "Mr Mole, have you any idea of the size of my *overheads*?" (The Mole glanced uneasily at the ceiling.) "The *mortgage*? ... The children's *school fees*? ... The cottage in the *Dordogne*? ... The *cars*? ... The *boat*? ... The sit-upon *lawn-mowers*? ... The *holidays*?—*And* Janet's between jobs at the moment! The insurance alone—the insurance alone ..." (here he let out what might have been a small, strangulated sob) "I mean if I'm not paying the Getting-Fired-When-You're-Still-Quite-Young-Cover, then I'm paying the Getting-Fired-When-You're-No-Longer-So-Young-Cover. And *then* you have to double-insure every policy in case any of the companies turn out to be run by crooks (which is more than likely). You have to have *Life*-life Assurance for the life of the Life Assurance, and a Mortgage Protection-*Protection* Policy in case you lose the house before the first one's paid up! *Everything* has to be bolted down and then riveted in place on top of it! Every backup-circuit needs a backup-backup-circuit to back it up! Every copper-bottom has to have its bottom double-coppered!—Would you like a vitamin pill?"

"Um ...? I don't think so, thank you."

The Rat withdrew momentarily, returning with a small pot marked *Vita-Gluta-Supa-Lita-Life*. "I always take one of these each day," he said in a slightly less tortured voice—just in case, you know. Full of all the stuff you need. Plus a zinc pill, of course, for the immune system ... got to keep that working, all the bugs there are around these days! ... Where was I?"

"Copper-bottoms?" suggested the Mole hopefully, though he had not yet seen evidence of any such craft on the water outside.

"Yes—yes! And the *subscriptions*, you see—" Mr Rette clutched desolately at his ears. "The professional subs ... The golf course fees! One has to belong to so many courses now, to keep in touch with even *some* of the animals that count. And they keep building new ones all the time! *And* my membership of the Grand Order Of Water Rats, that keeps going up, too! It's endless, endless! To live according to one's expectations— I mean, you know, quite reasonable expectations—costs a vast amount of money nowadays. A *vast* amount!"

The Mole looked back at his host, deeply puzzled. But he did not speak.

"You see, Mr Mole," (and here some suggestion of a fanatic gleam seemed to creep into Mr Rette's bloodshot gaze) "I'm sure you understand—an animal *must live* according to his expectations. He cannot allow himself to slip back—not in any way, no, never! Even the thought makes me feel quite ... And believe me, it's not as if T.T. is exactly overpaying me. Comparatively—comparatively (and we don't even need to mention America!)—for only three-hundred-odd Gees per annum (plus a couple of little Nether-P consultancies on the side) T.T. is getting its Chief Axmal pretty cheap. Oh yes, G.R. Rette is bargain-basement stuff by today's standards, not much doubt about that. ... And I shall have to go on like this for years yet—*years*, if I'm lucky—ha, ha-ha—" (he tugged at his ears again, stretching them into something resembling small furred tent doorways) "before we're properly Secure."

All the Mole could do was ask another question, even if he did not really expect to understand the answer. "But—that is," he said, "well, what is '*secure*', Mr Rette?"

The Rat—oddly enough—took this query at face value, without even so much as a disdainful snort. "*When* you have *enough* invested," he replied patiently, "to *produce* the interest to *live* comfortably, and *pay* off *any*, and *all*, emergencies—illness, or earthquakes, or madness, or being carried off by a very large bird, or *whatever* it may be—for the *rest* of your *life*, then, you are *Secure*."

"And—um—well, how long does it usually take to earn all that?"

"All your life, apparently!" bawled the Rat, in a non-small-hours-of-the-morning voice. "Maybe you die first," he whispered acidly. "I don't know! It's a weasel-world we live in, Mr Mole. It's a weasel-world and a cockroach-race, and it's weasel values that have the upper hand—just everywhere, so far as I can see. They won, the weasels, they won a long, long time ago. Now all any of us can do is carry on regardless; keep the blinkers nice and tight. There's always another rat breathing over your shoulder, sniffing out your job with his delicately enquiring snout. There's nothing to bind us together here any more. Everything to keep us apart."

The Water Rat paused, looking away, then said very quietly, "Sometimes, you know, I feel awfully alone."

"— But your *family* ..." suggested the Mole urgingly.

"My family is a joy to me," responded the sunken rat, "when I get to see them for any time at all. But they are my *responsibility*. If I fail them, where will they be able to turn for help? And there's no time for friendship, even if (and believe me, it's a big 'if') there were any animals out here I'd specially choose to be friendly with. How can you have friends, real friends—when you spend your whole life on the treadmill? Watching the slats all day as they come towards you? Always putting your feet in the right place? Every time—*every* time—you have to get it right."

The Rat paused, running a paw heavily round the back of his neck. "Sometimes, you know, I do think, what does any of it matter? Maybe this civilization of ours has already reached its bin-by date. I mean, what do you think? Would it really make that much difference now if we did destroy the Nozone Layer—"

"... nose-own layer ...?"

"But of course, I forgot: in the remote and blissful depths of your mole-hole, the news has not quite yet reached you. You're better off not knowing, Mr Mole. Forget I mentioned it. Frankly, though—would it matter very much, d'you think, if the Animal Race just ceased to exist? Other things would go on the same without us. Much better, probably. Ants. Termites. Mushrooms. *Spirogyra. Protococcus viridis* ..."

"But don't you ever feel just a bit ... I don't know, excited by the world?—Despite everything, I mean?"

The Water Rat rose up a little from the dread mustardness and turned towards his guest. "I do—it's embarrassing to admit this, actually, but, well—I do write the odd bit of poetry now and then," he said. "It's usually around now, actually, in the early hours, that the inspiration comes upon me. Though I'm not sure you could call it being 'excited', exactly."

"How splendid!" responded the Mole warmly. "I'd love to read some!"

"You wouldn't," said the Rat. "— Would you?"

"Yes!—O, *please* let me!"

"Well ..." The Water Rat got up and walked over to an eighteenth century ivory-inlaid bureau. "This is one of my more recent efforts. Don't ask me to read it out, though: I'm terrible at that. Here. It's in free verse, of course."

The Mole read (silently and lengthily, and mouthing the occasional word or phrase) as follows:

SONG OF THE ROAD

Above the unclear car-clogged clearway
the kestrel clings to sky, its dark
flickering
6B-pencil squiggle
in pinioned poise, (*au point du jour*).
Remote smart-missile
primed thoughtless to
home in
upon
some minute creature of the lower orders.

What need YOU see, or know,
the war of minds that rages 'neath your fixity
of moving calm?
What need YOU judge the turmoil in the hearts
of rats as they thrust on
midst weasel-wilds of racing fury?

Oh lucky, lucky schedule-busting beastie,
whose only group
initiative
is the next swift sampling of micro-rodential
antipasto,
whose heart will never know imperatives of
firm or
equity adjustment,
nor perceive
nor witness
the naked Scampi of the Soul
as it makes its long last
clearway plunge
toward the Four-Pack of Infinity!

"I'm not *quite* sure what you mean by those last four lines," said the Mole (who was in fact singling these out from a majority of others).

"Oh, the ending's metaphorical," said the Rat with the abrupt dismissiveness of the seasoned versifier.

"But it is—er, um—very impressive," the Mole added encouragingly. "... For a poem that doesn't rhyme."

"I am still having trouble with that fifth line," said the Rat. "I didn't want '*au point du jour*' there, you see, even though it fits the meaning quite well—the poem is set at dawn. In my own mind anyway. But I wanted that phrase from ballet, meaning, 'Stuck up on the tips of your toes'. You don't happen to know it, by any chance?"

"'Fraid not," said the Mole. "But if I come across it I'll be sure to let you know."

"The problem is," said the Rat, the tip of his tail twitching pensively on the carpet, "I can never quite achieve the necessary degree of obscurity, and if you're too comprehensible no one will ever take you seriously. A reader should come away from a poem feeling ever so slightly frustrated—angry, ideally—and thinking, 'Even though there were moments when I nearly did, I do not honestly understand what that is about'. But it takes real technique to write like that. Because I mean, it's obvious, if you think about it—if you write what you *mean*, then you're stuck with something that means something. And then you have to do a whole lot of work to bury it all under metaphor and ambiguity. It's finding those words that nobody ever uses, like 'lineaments' and 'gyre' and 'plenitude' and so forth—that's the real challenge for us amateurs. We don't have the time to pore over dictionaries like real poets do."

"... May I ask you something, Mr Rette?" said the Mole after a moment.

"Go on," answered Mr Rette guardedly.

"Well—what does the 'R' in your name stand for?"

The Water Rat looked shamefaced and evasive. But then with a blush he answered, "Rathold, actually."

"O!—You weren't called Ratty when you were at school, by any chance?"

"That's a long time ago," answered the Rat. "But—um, yes, I suppose I was, a bit. Didn't encourage it of course."

"Well, well," said the Mole.

"Why do you ask?"

"Just my curiosity," replied the Mole. "I know one shouldn't pry."

"That's all right," said the Rat.

"And ... what you were saying about the weasels just now. Is it really true?—I mean, you weren't exaggerating?"

"A bit, perhaps. But only a bit. I mean, if you weren't who you were (whoever that is) you'd know all this just as well as I do. You do read the papers sometimes, don't you?"

"The back numbers, mostly," responded the Mole. "I'm a bit of a back number myself, I'm afraid."

"Well then, Mole," said the Water Rat sadly, and looking his guest directly in the eye for once, "welcome to Weaselworld."

CHAPTER FIVE

THE LAWS OF NATURE

The morning ritual on Tuesday was as the morning ritual on the day before. Again the two animals rose in darkness and, when he was ready, the Mole found his way along the unlit corridor clutching his unfinished mug of tea between both paws. Passing the just-open bedroom doors of the two smallest Rettes, he heard coming from the first the comfortable sounds of deep breathing, and out of the second wheezy coughing.

Twenty minutes later garage doors rose once more virtually in tandem and the two non-communicative commuters drove past one another in the road outside, setting off in opposite directions to cities ninety miles apart. In the village street—fog free, today—the thin stream of rail-bound animals was once more marching silently, briefcases in the "at ease" position, each figure effortlessly maintaining a similar distance from the next.

The Mole was prepared today for the journey up the Clearway—up to a point, at least. True, he still planted his paws tightly over his eyes five minutes before the Bedeutsam-PersonenWagen swooped down upon the great road. But at least now he knew what he was in for. Between bouts of subsonic moaning he even found it in him to manage a little conversation. Partly this was because he felt it to be letting the side down, rather, to travel *absolutely* all the way in tongue-tied terror: Moles From The Past had some dignity to maintain, after all. But he also spoke because he needed questions answered.

"It's coming from the *motors*, isn't it—a lot of what I can smell?" he asked, just as Mr Rette was in the middle of a particularly tense piece of overtaking.

There was a long pause. "— What?" said the Rat.

"The smell. It comes from the *motors*."

"*What* smell? You can't smell anything, can you?"

"Of course I can! O my, O my! It's dreadful!"

"But—in here? Not in the *car*?" Mr Rette sniffed loudly, his whiskers fibrillating with concentration. "You've got to be imagining it! I mean, I know such things probably don't have much meaning for you, but after all this car is a BPW *Blumenduft* IQ-Class. Amongst the *truly vast* range of luxury facilities with which the IQ-Class comes equipped," (and here a note of slightly bored superiority crept into Mr Rette's voice) "this car *happens* to possess Street-Sentient Air Conditioning, based on the world-famous BPW electro-equilibrial microcollandic dust filter. And (like every other part of the car) these devices *do not go wrong*. If any future archaeologist is ever lucky enough to dig one up, it will probably *still be working*."

"... But—"

"Additionally, of course," Mr Rette continued, "you do happen to be travelling in a machine that is equipped with what is almost certainly the world's *most* sophisticated Climate-Genesis Facility. If I wish, I can, at the touch of a button, simulate an Alaskan hoar frost whilst I am bumping along some swamp road in the middle of a tropical rainforest. At the other extreme, I can ask the car to emulate the midday heat of the Frying Pan Of Andalucia whilst I am stuck in freezing-fog in February in Farnham."

The Mole did dimly wonder whether this might explain why, after anything more than fifteen minutes travelling in Mr Rette's *motor*, he began to feel as if his eyeballs were being lightly simmered in cider vinegar while his fur crawled with a hundred thousand silverfish. Wisely, no doubt, he kept silent on this subject.

"— You have to believe it, you know," the Rat continued. "*Nothing* that comes out of the back of *this* car *ever* ends up inside it. The driver is completely protected from the pollution he is generating, *and*, of course—ha, ha—from everybody else's besides."

"But—well," said the Mole, in a very small voice, "that means you can't smell it, then?"

"Smell what?!" exploded the explosive Rat. "*Smell what*?! There *cannot* be anything *to* smell! At least ..." He fell silent, and sniffed again. "No ... No. Everything smells quite normal. I mean, it doesn't smell at all. Anyway, it would be at its worst just here—the air—wouldn't it? On the Clearway? Obviously."

"But it's not *just* here. *This* smell—I've been able to smell it everywhere, just about, ever since I—since the other day. But, O, there are a hundred others. Five hundred. I can't count them."

The Rat grunted.

"I suppose it's easier if you can't smell anything," said the Mole.

"Hm." The Rat sniffed, fibrillated, sniffed again. "'Spose it is."

"Why—um—why *do* you drive, Mr Rette—rather than catch the train?" said the Mole.

"Because I have a deep, perverse love of sitting in traffic jams!" re-exploded Mr Rette. "I get a *buzz* from the *congestion*! I love to exercise my Individual Freedom To Be Frustrated! ... *Get out of the Pandamned way*! Birdlouse! ... Any other questions?"

The Mole shook his head. He did have other questions, but saw that this was not the time to ask them.

There was a pause of twelve-to-thirteen-overtakings, after which the Rat asked in rather calmer tones, "But ... you smell things everywhere, you said? ... Not, I don't know—not in the garden, for example?"

"O!—The *river!*" replied the Mole definitively.

"Yes, I suppose it does have a ... But that's just sewage treatment chemicals. I'm quite certain of that. They had some problem with it getting into the riverbed silt or something, didn't they? Didn't I read that? But I don't think the stuff from the nuclear research place would smell, would it? It would kill you, but it wouldn't *smell*. That's all monitored now, of course, anyway. They have standards to work to nowadays."

The Mole did not quite know who "They" might be. "Do They?" he said dubiously.

Mr Rette fell silent. The Mole risked peering at him under the corner of a paw to find him deep in thought, or so it seemed.

Today, for whatever reasons of his own, the god of traffic had smiled on the capital's commuting animals. When Rat and Mole arrived at it, the raised grey ribbon-road ran on miraculously unblocked by any crash. Beyond it the streets of the centre were pulsing with sluggish life, so that every vehicle not held up at traffic lights was free to move at something nudging the speed of an arthritic cyclist. Not only did Mr Rette guide his BPW to the Toad Tower without any need to cry and scream, he was there ahead of time. As he parked in his own named bay in an apparently endless white-lit cellar-for-*motors* buried deep beneath the building, he and his whiskers were positively bristling with satisfaction.

"I shall be busy again all day, of course," he told the Mole rather brusquely. Then, as if collecting himself, he added, "But, well, er—good luck, then. I've no idea what W-T wants from you." He paused, looked away doubtfully, looked back under a brow of knotted fur. "I'm not sure, but—you may find he has some sort of proposal to make."

Mr Rette inhaled deeply, as if to charge himself up with city-basement vapours, and a look of sharp and, the Mole thought, not wholly pleasant intent settled on his face. He was, in fact, just on the verge of bolting off and abandoning his charge to his own devices in the cellar when he recollected that he might not quite be able to find his way to the Chairmal's suite unaided. So he accompanied him, and parted with him there.

Two hours later, after three cups of strong, perfumy coffee, the now slightly twitchy Mole was admitted by Mr Wyvern-Toad's secretary to his dazzling and expansive office. This—the Mole saw with dismay—enjoyed a sinkingly uninterrupted view through window-walls across the whole western and south-western tower-panorama of the metropolis. In accepting a seat, he tried to place himself as far from any view as he could possibly manage, not with much success.

"Mr Mole! I thought you might like to meet an acquaintance of mine this morning," said the seated magnate. "Young Gibbert Phangachs. A high flyer of promise, or so we hear. Though things being what they are, of course, he may have a while to wait yet before he scales his azimuth. You know the name, no doubt?"

"Fang-axe?" echoed the Mole apprehensively.

"Yes, yes! You don't know him? Oh, an excellent mal—insofar as one can ever say that of a politician!" The Toad giggled nudgingly. "At least we can rest assured he's a GOTWA mal to the marrow, eh?"

"Urm—uhr—got-warr?" echoed the Mole again, wringing his paws together in the hope that soon he would hear at least one word he understood.

Mr Wyvern-Toad turned to him at the start of an as-yet-unspoken sentence, and scrutinized him intently. "Mr Mole, for a mal with such a striking capacity for drawing out your fellow-beasts, you do seem to be—I don't wish to be rude, but—just a trifle under-briefed? ... GOTWA? ... Surely you must have heard of GOTWA, the Grand Old Toad And Weasel Alliance!"

"I've been—er—hum—out of the country, you know. For years and years."

"I see! You must tell me about that. All about yourself, in fact.—Ah, but here's Phangachs even as I speak! Come in, Gibbert, come in. I'd like you to meet Mr ... er ... Mole."

A tall, lean weasel strode into the office. He was dressed in a suit of charcoal grey some three per cent less charcoally then the Toad's, and his shirt was marked with stripes of very pale violet, blue and yellow. He might have been a year or two younger than Gordon Rette, and though still fresh-faced in a sleek-furred, feral way, he also had about him a forceful, slightly threatening air that suggested he was quite used to giving orders and being obeyed without demur—more than that, suggested he knew that in the game of life *he* was one of those who won. The Mole had, of course, never had a huge amount of time for weasels of any shirt-stripe, but he felt more than usually unsettled now by this individual's strangely staring, little-blinking gaze and slightly bulbous eyes.

"Ah—a mole—a mole!" exclaimed Mr Phangachs, as he turned with a show of suite-filling confidence to crush the Mole's paw and shake his arm. The shakee was just about to demand to know the reason why he was making use of the mole war-cry—reserved, as it was, for the use of moles alone—when he went on, "And what have we been leaking today, Mr Mole? Ha, ha!"

Mr Wyvern-Toad cackled with amusement at this remark, which the irritated Mole felt must be mildly insulting, even though he had no idea how. "So sorry," said Mr Phangachs creamily, with an arrogant smile. "A tired old joke at best, I'm afraid." He readjusted his protuberant gaze. "Were you at a party last night, by any chance?"

"No. I was reading a book about brain disorders," replied the Mole.

"Ah—"

"Phangachs," said the Toad. "Take a seat, please." He held out a box of cigars from which the weasel removed one gracefully. "I know you were expecting to find me alone, but I thought you might be interested to meet Mr Mole."

The Weasel returned a silent glance of enquiry.

"Cigar, Mr Mole?" asked the Toad. "Sit there, sit there— there, next to Mr Phangachs."

"O." The Mole sat, and gripped the seat he sat on. "Er— no, thank you. Not a smoker."

"— Yes, yes," continued the magnate blithely, "and not only interesting, Gibbert. Therapeutic as well, perhaps. For want of a better word. But tell me now—jog my memory, since you do seem to be moving around at such speed nowadays. What's your posting at present? You were moved, weren't you?"

"I was, W-T. I am now Under-Secretary For Development-Development." The Weasel glanced towards the Mole, then back at the Toad. He rubbed his snout in perplexity.

"… for Development-*Development*," repeated Mr Wyvern-Toad, in the most delicate and tapering tone.

"Oh. Ha, ha. That's just a little joke we have at the Department. Not, ah, generally for public consumption. As no doubt you'll guess, W-T, one's job is in effect to promote all forms of development one is being seen to regulate."

"Ah yes. There should be a word for it. Regumotion? … Promolation?" (The Mole frowned, not-not not-unconfused.)

"One assists the big boys—Pale Hole Cement, McVulpine, Tarworld—"

"… friends, all friends …"

"— gets them together to form the lobby groups they

need, at the very heart of things. Then, of course, helps the lobbyists who are lobbying me to remove the regulations I am meant to be using to stop them doing what we all agree unofficially they should be doing more of. It's intricate. There's a certain balance involved."

The Toad nodded. "Not everyone could do it, Gibbert. No doubt about it. Anything else new?"

"Oh, mostly Party work," said Mr Phangachs purringly. "I have secured helpful postings on a couple of the newest Pseudobongos. The National Nutritional Conservatory? That's one. Even as we speak we're leafleting out all the latest pieties about diet and exercise. Luckily, of course, most animals pay scant attention to that kind of thing, and thank Pan they do! Where would the sugar industry as a whole be, good heavens, if they took notice? No, no—the economy has need of fatties ... All those blob-like 'hog-brats—"

"Those obese otters!" said the Toad eyeingly.

"Those paunchy polecats! Those gut-bucket bunnies! Ha!" Mr Phangachs seemed to catch at himself in mid-guffaw. "... But I must say, W-T, one is not used to being quite so frank about it—at least, not so early in the morning. Especially," and here he turned to the Mole but kept his eyes fixed on Mr Wyvern-Toad, "with respect, in the company of those one does not know well."

"You're among friends here, Phangachs," said the Toad reassuringly.

The Weasel eyed the Mole as dubiously as his staring glance allowed.

"Mr Mole has been out of the country for some years," said Mr Wyvern-Toad. "Where was it, Mr Mole—?"

"Oh, the Belgian—um, the jungle.—Exploring, you know."

"Ah, an *explorer*," said Mr Phangachs, clamping his cigar between two rows of fine, white, pointed teeth. His gaze flickered up and down the Mole's dress as if now he almost understood it.

"... Well now, Gibbert, what do you think?" said the magnate casually, drifting into silhouette behind a blue-grey haze. "Life was so much simpler, wouldn't you agree, before you weasels got quite so well established. Wouldn't you say so, though?"

"Simpler? For the toads, you mean? Can't argue with that, W-T! But you cope with us pretty well nowadays, for the most part. And you have to admit, the toad order did have things all its own way for far longer than anyone could call reasonable."

"Oh, I don't know, I don't know! The Toad Party managed things well enough in its day. One-Nation Toadyism was a gloriously effective sales-pitch, if you'll excuse the professional vulgarism. And for a good many years longer than anything your mals have thought up! *Wouldn't* you say now, Gibbert? Come on!"

"One-Nation Toadyism?" said the Weasel, returning the Toad's bright, confident gaze with one of his own. "Meaning: 'we are the masters, but every so often we may graciously hand down little favours to you, to keep your resentment off the boil'? Less a sales-pitch than a conjuring trick, W-T, and you know it!"

For the Mole—alongside all other creatures he considered even half way sensible—politics was a subject quite beyond the pale. But he could hardly have been further from his home patch than he was now and, once again—like burps striving to crest the voice-box after a rather too indulgent picnic—he felt questions rising in him that demanded answers, if only he could get some he understood. "What—um—what happened to the Toad Party?" he asked after a moment. "If you'll pardon my ignorance."

"You see?" said the Toad, opening his green palms broadly. "It's still possible to be completely out of touch in this world. Amazing to think there may still be jungle out there extensive enough to allow it. One would have expected it all to be burned down by now! The Toad Party, Mr Mole, has in recent decades been transformed by (what shall we say, Gibbert?) the *force of argument* of certain rather effective Ferre-Weselo-Stoatist elements. It emerged renamed some twenty years ago as the GOTWA, the—as I said—Grand Old Toad And Weasel Alliance."

"— Although we don't often call it that nowadays, do we, W-T?" added Mr Phangachs, turning to the Mole for long enough to tell him, "We are now rather better known as the To-We Party."

"Tut-tut-tut-tut," said Mr Wyvern-Toad to himself through his cigar, shaking his head in mild mock-sorrow.

"You still haven't quite accepted us, have you, W-T?" observed the Weasel, grinning. "You're still a Toadite at heart, come on, admit it!"

"Phangachs, I willingly—gladly—accept the presence in power in this country of any Party that enables me and mine to carry on doing exactly what we damned well want. Just so long as it actually does so, you understand."

"You're not just a *little* nostalgic for the old days?"

"I am a bizz'mal a very long way before I am a toad, Gibbert, and it surprises me a little that I should have to remind you of that."

The Mole coughed wheezily, and grasped at the tip of an available straw. "So how was the party—well, um, changed?"

"A complicated story, Mr Mole," answered Mr Phangachs, his bulbous eyes a-glitter. "And, as with most things in politics, not easily summarised. Put at its simplest, it happened because over the years the Toad Party attracted increasing numbers of weasel candidates out of the spreading ranks of weaselry—"

"Couldn't keep them out—"

"Couldn't—sensibly—keep them out. And one candidate in particular ..."

"Ah! One in particular!" The Toad leaned back into his chair and shifting smoke-field.

"... who was, of course, eventually to become the Priestess. As some are in the habit of calling her."

"O—a *lady* weasel."

"Deep jungle!" said Mr Wyvern-Toad, his eyebrows high.

"Deep *jungle*! Good heavens!" Mr Phangachs paused a moment in amazement. "Is it possible anyone could not have heard of the Priestess? Even in a jungle? Well in any case, Mr Mole, it is thanks to the Priestess, and to her Vision, that the To-We Party can move forward into the twenty-first century bearing her creed and credo, as a force that will eventually make every process in animal affairs subservient" (here the politician's voice became tremulous) "to the Mystery ... the ineffable Mystery ... of the Market. For as the Priestess has taught us: from the Market all things in life must flow—"

"— And to the Market must all things in life return," added the Toad, beaming with pleasure. "Oh—with, perhaps, one or two small exceptions."

"And from the Market's all-embracing, ultimately inscrutable workings," went on the Weasel fervently, "there will in time arise the solution to *every* problem—*every* animal affliction worth the name. We need have the patience only to allow its Mystery to work itself through to its climax— driven, as it must be, solely by those two great engines of all animal endeavour: Greed, and Fear."

"O ..."

"You see," said Mr Wyvern-Toad, as Mr Phangachs was recovering himself and wiping a tear from the corner of one eye, "the trouble with some of these damned weasels is that they believe they can run things better than the toads did! But the truth—and I know you won't like this, Gibbert—the truth is that from the start the GOTWA has attracted a particular kind of weasel: one who had, how shall I put it, a certain sympathy with the old toad way of doing things? And some of these animals, coming at it from a slightly different direction—from their holes under trees and the like—"

"W-T! *Please!*" objected Mr Phangachs, still in the midst of blowing his snout on a finely-striped handkerchief.

"Isn't it the truth, Gibbert? You imagined yourselves as a new toad order. Come now! Toadery-without-the-toads! And some of you pass yourselves off as it, too. I name no names."

"What has become of—well, the other parties?" asked the Mole, who did at least know the identities of those flourishing in his own day from copies of newspapers he leafed through on his less-than-regular visits to the dentist.

"They are no longer relevant," answered Mr Phangachs sharply.

"Ahhh …" admonished Mr Wyvern-Toad, raising a finger. "There is such a thing as too much confidence, my boy."

"Oh, but you won't deny it, will you, W-T?" returned the politician, drawing in his chin and stiffening as if he felt himself under attack. "The Party's appeal to the bulk of the electorat today is unassailable. Unassailable! You must understand, Mr Mole, that in Weaselworld—"

"… As some of us now call it—"

"You included, W-T. Really!—In Weaselworld today, Mr Mole, an animal is defined by two things, and two things only: how much money he earns, and how much power he possesses. This is what matters, amongst animals who matter. And even amongst animals who do not matter but feel—ha, ha, wrongly, of course, in all but a few cases—that one day they may."

"Is that really how things are then?" said the Mole despondently, scratching his head as he struggled to make words out of thoughts. "Doesn't … O—sticking up for your friends matter any more? Or, looking out for them-as-is" (strength of emotion was threatening his grammar) "…um, for those-that-are-less-lucky-than-ourselves? And … and, what about everything else? I mean—what about *Nature*?"

The young politician swivelled smoothly on his swivel-chair and got a bead on the Mole with his pop-pop-eyes. A look of uncomprehending amusement waxed and waned on his snoutose visage, and he laughed in a clucking, supercilious, high-pitched tone. "Mr Mole!" he said. "If I didn't find you sitting in this office—really, of all places in the country—I'd almost think you weren't joking. Tell me—frankly now. What has been your own experience of the weasel species? I mean, how have you found us in general, weasel for weasel?"

"They are—I think—sometimes, rather over-fond of feathering their own nests," answered the Mole, candid as ever but, equally, hesitant to condemn outright. "And sometimes too at the expense of others," he added.

"Well there you have it!" said the politician. "In a nutshell, as it were. In Weaselworld, *nest-feathering* is of the very essence—an absolute, you might call it. And as this great weasel-imperative has bloomed—so that today it is found in the rudest of health in every order of animals that goes to the polls—it has become easier and easier for the Party to appeal with total confidence" (here he turned to the Toad) "to the prime mover in every electoral decision."

"— This being, Gibbert?" prompted Mr Wyvern-Toad, all smiles.

"Self-interest," responded the Weasel ecstatically. "Need one so much as say it, W-T? Pivotal—invaluable—*infallible* self-interest! Very short-term, very-very short-term, and very-very-*very* short-term self-interest! All animals—naturally, naturally—want to keep what they have—the more so, the more they have! And at every election they come back—more than enough of them to keep us in power and vote for us in the guise in which we have so skilfully marketed ourselves, as the very-living-embodiment-of-continued-prosperity-for-the-self-interested-mal. Policies, really—and this is strictly off the record but—policies are quite beside the point."

"O."

Mr Phangachs paused, wiped his brow, drew deeply on his second and rapidly shortening cigar, and blew another aromatic cloud over the small animal sitting next to him. "All any great political party needs, Mr Mole, is a marketable philosophy. Ours, now, is honed to perfection to fit the times we live in."

The politician got up and moved to stand between the Mole and the nearest expanse of window. He gazed down the length of his gun-barrel snout to the grid of streets below, with its pulsing throng of tiny points that were the heads and shoulders of rabbits, hedgehogs, stoats and weasels. "'All animals must have freedom to choose'," he said weightily. "'All animals must have Opportunity.' 'Every animal can and should participate in the Mystery of the Market.' In short, Mr Mole, *everyone* can join the club ... or at least, ha, ha, can imagine themselves doing so. What beast is there left—even in the depths of the Forest of Dean—who can resist such an invitation for very much longer?"

"*Do* some of them?" asked the Mole. "Resist, I mean?" He was wheezing audibly by now.

"This is the beauty of it, you see! Now, it's true we've been hearing a few things at the moment—in the opinion polls and so forth—about a supposed 'disenchantment' with the To-We Party, even—utterly nonsensical, of course!—with what we stand for. But then, when it comes to it, on election day, the fear that animals may be voting for *increased taxes*—and thus for, what shall we say, one new car less per year, or deferment of that new patio or conservatory or tennis court—oh, it stops them dead in their tracks every time!"

"You don't see any danger, Gibbert, do you," asked the Toad very casually, "that the electorat, or some parts of it, might be just a little put off by the knowledge that certain elements in the Party engage in what amounts to—what *should* I call it?—Priestess-worship?"

"Ha, ha, W-T. Ha, ha ... Difficult ground there, you know," said Mr Phangachs, resuming his swiveller.

Mr Wyvern-Toad raised an interrogative eyebrow. "... Go

on. Gibbert—say it. Say what you think, mal!"

"*W-T* ..." responded the young politician warningly, as if hoping to establish a mood only normally produced by the sounds of a dozen briefcases being snapped shut simultaneously.

"Say it, Phangachs!" cooed the Toad, his eye now hard upon the Mole.

The Weasel was sweating visibly, his chin pressed hard upon his tie-pin so that his nose was, in fact, almost in his pocket. "Granted, W-T ... there are many, many animals in the country who still hold the Priestess in the highest regard, and quite rightly so. Quite rightly so! But 'worship'? You astonish me ..."

Mr Wyvern-Toad sat behind his desk, eyes motionless and narrowed to slits, and said nothing.

"But, ah—well—dammit!" continued Mr Phangachs desperately. "Apart from—myself—and, ah, a small core of like-minded colleagues ... ha, ha ... there are very few left in the Party now who could be said to actually *worship* her!"

The young weasel fell silent. Mr Wyvern-Toad beamed him a smile of avuncular warmth and glanced at his watch. "I think it's almost time for the D.P.M. to go down, isn't it, Gibbert? Assuming they're on schedule."

"The D.P.M.?" echoed Mr Phangachs in a small voice, his eyes darting nervously around the room. "Oh.—Oh. Yes. They will have to be," he went on, as if relieved to find himself on a subject he could approach without embarrassment. "Have to get this kind of thing right—one heartily believes. Heartily—er—believes."

Both animals rose from their chairs and walked over to one of the western-facing window-walls. "Come and watch, Mr Mole," suggested the Toad.

"O-o-o-o, no-o-o-o," breathed the Mole, forcing himself to his feet.

"It's that tower—there—" said Mr Wyvern-Toad,

pointing to a triple block which from this distance resembled three vast dark bricks set on-end and in parallel to one another. They were partly cloaked in some way, like statues at an unveiling.

"Yes—thirty seconds. One very much hopes," said Mr Phangachs.

The Mole had not the faintest idea why they should be standing looking out towards one of so many tower-monsters. He was on the verge of framing a question along these lines when the triple-structure seemed to shake and crease in on itself and then, quite undeniably, it collapsed ground-wards in a hundred thousand pieces falling like avalanche boulders amongst a spreading cloud of dust.

"And we should feel it ..." said the Toad, "now!" He was just a little early in his estimate. One and a half heartbeats later there was a sound as if the air itself had been thumped with a hammer of Vulcanian dimensions, and his office's window-wall and everything attached to it moved visibly away from, and then back towards, the world around it.

"But ..." said the Mole. His mouth was circular, his hands planted deep inside his pockets. "But—um—but ... They don't just *blow up* like that, do they?"

"Would that they did!" replied the Weasel, smiling at what he took to be another joke. "It would save a lot of fuss, frankly. But, once these things have reached their bin-by date ..."

"So *this* one won't blow up—just like that?"

"Ha-ha! No ... No ..."

"What was the, um, the DeePeeEmm?"

"The D.P.M.? The Department of Pollution Mediation. Of course, it has gone to a new H.Q. But it would have been convenient to keep the place a little longer, in the best of all possible worlds."

"How many centuries old was it?" asked the Mole.

"How many centuries! Ha, ha, ha! The mal has razor wit!"

responded Mr Phangachs, briefly grooming his snout as he spoke. "It would have been—ahh—twenty-three years old this June, I'm told. I'm not *quite* sure the Government has yet paid off the loan it made itself to build it in the first place, in point of fact."

In the Mole's world-view any building, once built, was a permanent fixture, to be mended, shored-up, perhaps bodged a bit now and then, for the rest of time. The oldest parts of his own home dated back to the sixteenth century or even earlier, so Great Uncle Warpmold had once told him, and Toad Hall had had a central staircase in wonderfully carved wood of much the some date *and* a hidden spiral staircase that was at least two hundred years older. He was getting a little bit tired of being taken for a thick-head, so he did hesitate a moment before asking, "But why build *anything* to last for only twenty-three years?"

"Because it was cheap, of course," said Mr Phangachs. "At least, to put up. Reinforced concrete was—still is—very, very cheap. And no one is ever going to stop architects using it— they love the stuff. They have concrete in their blood! It's best to regard a building of that type in the same terms as, say, a milk carton." (A milk cart on what? wondered the Mole.) "Perfectly useful in the short term, but as soon as it starts to crumble and get dangerous, as they have a habit of doing, well, one simply throws it away."

"— Although of course in the case of a triple tower of some sixty storeys, sited in London SW1—" qualified the Toad.

"Quite, W-T. *And* housing a Government department nominally dedicated to minimising waste—"

"— Which needed to be blown up in a rather special and expensive way since it would, I believe, have flown apart if anyone had ever tried to dismantle it—"

"Yes, yes. I suppose there is a certain risk of political exposure at the moment one aims for the waste-paper basket."

"It's not like that here in the City, of course, Mr Mole," added the Toad beamingly. "Not with the right kind of company PPP in any case! Build 'em big, build 'em high, build 'em to last that little bit longer, then sell 'em off well before they become a problem! Let others worry about the demolition stage whilst those of us in the avant-garde—those of us who occupy the cutting edge of Corporate Destiny's ever-swinging blade—are out there building anew and thrusting, thrusting, thrusting," (here the Toad pumped his short arms in time to his words) "*thrusting* up into the sky! Up and up—upper and upper—uppermost and uppermaximost! So that as the sun swings round to cast its brilliance across the deft machinations—oh, the buyouts, the forced closures, the savagely efficient boardroom coups!—of each fresh day of trading, our towers—and of course, one great Tower in particular—cast ever longer and deeper shadows across the windows of our rivals! Such, Mr Mole, is the *lyric thrust* of capital! These are the true *cémentiques*, as it were, the *poésie concrète*, of every expanding business empire! Wouldn't you say so, Gibbert?"

Mr Phangachs smiled in concordance with this vision, relaxing back into the yielding button-bulges of his chair with eyes half closed.

"... Nothing more natural, eh, Phangachs? Nothing more natural!—But now I wonder, Gibbert—just in passing—*would* you mind if I were to hurl a couple of wonderfully naïve questions at you? Out of purest, purest curiosity?"

The politician's eyes snapped open, and for a single moment he regarded the Toad with the faintest suggestion of mistrust. "W-T," he said in an unguent voice, "I am at your disposal, as ever."

"Do sit down, Mr Mole—please," said the Toad. The Mole did so, coughing as quietly as he could manage, and oblivious to the fact that his host had gently nudged his chair a few inches closer to the Weasel's.

"All right, Gibbert. Now, tell me. Few could be more

familiar than I, could they, with the aims and imperatives of the GOTWA? As a—how can one put this, to preserve one's modesty?—not wholly insignificant contributor to Party funds in the past? And, needless to say, in the future too … all other things being equal." (Here weasel looked toad directly in the eye with a gaze of deepest interest.) "I have followed every stage in the evolution of the Party, and of course I continue to do so now even during its present little difficulties, ha, ha, if they can be called that."

Mr Phangachs drew in the claws of one paw, but otherwise did not move.

"Tell me, then, Gibbert—for my edification. What now, today, would you say are the *unofficial*—or, if you prefer, the *yet-to-be-publicised*—aims of the To-We Party? The Party of today—the Party of all tomorrows?"

More than ever now, Mr Phangachs looked uneasy. He turned to the Mole and stared at him almost as if he had never seen him before. "W-T," he said, "I really don't think you can ask me to …" But a long sigh took the place of any further words.

"*Relax*, Gibbert," coaxed the Toad. "Relax! Enjoy yourself …"

Mr Phangachs sat upright in his chair, smoothing the fur hard back along his snout. "Well of course, W-T, the first aim of the Party must always be to stay in power. No matter what the state of the country."

Mr Wyvern-Toad nodded, exhaled himself into silhouette, and turned his gaze thoughtfully towards the ceiling.

"To this end," said the politician, "we weasels have worked with persistence, foresight and determination over the years towards the elimination from society—"

"So-called …"

"So-called!—of all groups and organisations that could ever hope to oppose us. Long term, I believe our still perfectly realisable aim is an effective one-party Weasel State in which opposition (if it exists at all by then) will be so weakened that it can never be a threat to us."

The Mole did not like the sound of this one bit. But he was rather stumped for any useful comment.

"Of course you know, W-T, we still maintain much of our power informally," said the politico-weselian. "As has always been done in the past by the toads and their friends, through all those old lunch-tea-and-port-after-dinner networks: the Court circle, Grantaford, the public schools etcetera. Though, I am sorry to say, rather less through the judiciary nowadays, and not because judges have lost their taste for port! But, of course, we are also innovators, so that today the weaselry is able to keep a most effective grip on things through its glorious and ever-expanding network of Pseudobongos—"

"Um, excuse me," said the Mole recognising a word here. "If you don't mind me asking—what kind of house *is* a seyoodow-bongalow, exactly?"

"The jungle ..." sighed Mr Wyvern-Toad.

"The jungle," said Mr Phangachs. "With respect, Mr Mole, a Pseudobongo is not, in fact, a house, ha, ha—but, to give it in full: a PSEUDO-Autonomous (meaning in fact, covertly weasel-controlled) Bigenerously-Ordered (seemingly-) Non-Government-Organisation."

"O. Ah. O."

"— But to go on," said Mr Phangachs, "as it seems I must. There are (I believe) upwards of twenty thousand Pseudobongos now. I'm afraid I can't be too specific about that, since they are multiplying much too quickly for any one animal to keep track of them—even a Cabinet Minister such as myself. Their first job is the distribution of public money—really, quite large amounts of it—to any scheme the Weaselry approves. But their real purpose is rather subtler. You see, Mr Mole, we expect in time to be able to dispatch completely the weary—it should now probably be called extremist—notion that governments exist to 'govern'—ha, ha, what nonsense!"

This proposition did not seem like nonsense to the Mole, for all his ignorance of the subject, any more than the idea that fire-fighters, say, should exist to 'fight fires', or bakers exist to 'make iced buns'.

"— To pass 'Acts'?" expanded Mr Phangachs. "Make 'laws'? Help maintain 'social' (so-called, ha, ha) 'cohesion'? No, no! All of that is beginning to look very quaint now. Eventually one hopes to be able to drop the notion of 'government' by Government into history's big black bin-by bin-bag. At the same time, it is perfectly clear that if we are to achieve freedom for the force of the Market to enact its Mystery to the full, then we also need to have total control over counter-revolutionary forces—if any were foolish enough to surface. We must watch every move, block every inroad, monitor, log, maintain a cast-iron grip inside that velvet glove, that complex but invisible web of *Government organisations that do not seem to be Government organisations at all*— and surely, to date, the greatest masterpiece of Weasel Politics: the Pseudobongos!"

Mr Phangachs paused, carried away by his emotions. "It is the most natural, *natural* evolution imaginable. Wouldn't you say so, W-T?"

The Toad blithely smiled his assent, tapping some small grey keys as he did so.

"— And of course, Mr Mole," went on the politician. "in this we are doing no more than following faithfully in the steps of the doughty pioneers of that hardest-fought of all economic frontiers. Yes, yes. I mean the United States. Why, haven't we here in England revelled in the riches of U.S. culture—cinematic, linguistic, dress, food—some of it for the best part of six decades? Why, then! What could be more natural, now, than that we truly progressive politicians—we of the weasel vanguard—should be moving to embrace that great country's powerhouse economic doctrine as well?—And not only embrace it, Mr Mole, but make it entirely our own in the process so that, in the fullness of time, the way we do things *here* and the way we do things *there* will be indistinguishable? Oh yes! 'America in England!'—eh, W-T?"

The Toad raised an eyebrow. "'America in England!' Gibbert, 'America in England!' ... Oh, and vice versa every so often, you know? As and when conditions allow."

"— And when this process is complete, Mr Mole," said the Weasel, "why, *then*, the animals of this country will have approached the first great pinnacle of the Weaselworld Revolution. We will live then in a state in which *every* action implies a corresponding transaction; in which *every* mal who has it in him to fight *must*—from the cradle to redundancy— move forward from one success to the next; in which, effectively, there is no room for anything *but* success!"

The Mole felt for the purse in his pocket and squeezed it. Before he had emptied it to the homeless Vole, he had had some twopence three-farthings in it, and a penny stamp. "But um—what happens if you can't 'succeed', Mr Fang-acks? Or pay for what you want?"

"Then I'm afraid, Mr Mole, that in Weaselworld— Weaselworld in its fully-evolved state—you will have—ahh, well, no reality. No existence, in effect."

But—um, I thought ... Didn't you say earlier that you believed that all animals should have opportunities?

"All animals *do* have Opportunity," replied the politician primly. "But some animals have more Opportunity than others. As in nature, as in nature! Don't we see this, almost nightly, in the wildlife documentaries? If one is born a lion, naturally, one dines on gazelle. If one is born a gazelle, well, there it is, one dines on grass."

"And of course," added the Toad, "gets dined upon by lions. Every so often."

"Exactly, W-T, exactly! We of the GOTWA will remain

always, I believe—a one-nation Party. It is no more than a fact of life that not every animal can be conveniently included in the nation we envisionate."

"Then there will be homeless animals even when you have done everything you want," said the Mole sadly.

"Oh, I don't think you need worry too much about *them*," responded Mr Phangachs breezily. "The homeless of today are all for the most part quite able-bodied, and not at all badly fed. I don't imagine they are frightfully clean, when one thinks of where they sit, but you know, very few expire from homelessness. And most of them are perfectly happy, Mr Mole, just so long as they can busk enough for beer and cigarettes. No one in this country today is truly poor."

"But—not even if they have to spend their lives in shop doorways?!" asked the Mole, in whom puzzlement was rapidly being pushed aside by anger.

"... In the Working Party I happen to chair on this *very subject*, Mr Mole," responded the Weasel with silky confidence, "we have half a dozen really quite eminent academics, any one of whom would, I'm quite certain, be delighted to argue the case that 'poverty' is now purely a relativist term. It is such a damaging word, you know—so open to abuse—we should eventually find some way of removing it from the language altogether."

"But do *they* sleep in shop doorways?" persisted the Mole. "These acker-demmicks?"

Mr Phangachs tugged frustratedly at the ends of his short whiskers. "Ha, ha, no, I don't believe so!" he said. "But even if they did, I don't doubt for one moment they could demonstrate against all argument that a perfectly adequate life is to be had there. In any case, it will certainly be one of the crucial tasks of any future Non-Government to relieve the earning animal of this impossible-to-justify burden of supporting the 'poor'. It-doesn't-make-sense, and we-simply-can't-afford-it."

Mr Wyvern-Toad carried on tapping at the register of grey keys. "Do excuse me, Gibbert, doing this as you speak. A couple of little loose ends to tie up—transactions must be made in the moment, eh? Carry on, carry on—I can hear you. And ... er ... what *would* you see happening to them—the 'poor'—I hope you scented the apostrophes there, ha, ha! In the longer term? Just out of curiosity?"

Mr Phangachs' bright little eyes blazed with the righteous indignation of the theorist whose jackets have never been in holes. "To be poor is to fail, W-T. That is only common knowledge. Clearly the poor should not be rewarded for that failure, and I believe it only fair that they should be held up as an example to the rest, who will themselves succeed the more brilliantly—burn all the more brightly, as it were—in terror of the pit below."

"So ... you interest me. In a sense then, the homeless, being the most visible of the poor, do have a purpose of a kind? In the conditions you hope to make prevail?"

"Not quite so many of them, W-T!" glittered Mr Phangachs. "Ha! ha! Not quite so many of them! ... If they would only do us the great favour of reverting to creatures of the lower orders, then we—ah ... we, ah ... we could ..." Not unlike a driver scraping to a halt on a snowed-over hill using brake-pads long since down to their rivets, Mr Phangachs fell gradually silent.

"... Yes, Gibbert?" probed the Toad very gently, one eyebrow at full mast. "... What then?"

The Weasel stared out past nearby towers to the towers beyond. He appeared to be caught up in a massive effort of will. "I, ah," he said. "I, ah—W-T—we ... Oh! *Pandammit!* We will tidy them away into *hostels!*" he went on at last, with what looked like the most enormous relief. "Then at least they will not have to be seen! And as to the rest of them, who have accommodation, in the long run they will just have to learn to fend for themselves. A thriving Market-Mysterious Weasel

State will owe them nothing, since this is a state in which—it is almost too obvious to point out—in the fullness of time, all, even the poorest, will be able to fall back on the Mystery itself. The Mystery *itself* will support them—console them—reassure them. And even if, as some indirect result of our government-elimination policies, any of them did ... ah ... any of them did happen to d—ah—d—um—expire ..." Once again, and over much the same distance, the rivets squealed.

"... Even 'death' is a relative term—eh, Gibbert?" joshed Mr Wyvern-Toad amiably. "With a good logician in tow to help?"

"Onion-*sauce!*" breathed the Mole.

As if sensing opposition, Mr Phangachs turned to him. "Every Utopia has its flip-side, Mr Mole," he said glacially.

The Toad sat behind the black marble expanse of his desk, his reflected face appearing and disappearing amongst unwinding tendrils of smoke, and said nothing.

"At the other end of the scale," continued the politician, "—the end that matters—it will be the aim of the To-We Party in its purified state to further reduce, and in time entirely eliminate, taxation on the highest earners, whilst of course stimulating the spread of high pay for Top Animals into all feasible arenas of activity. Under us, a really rather small number of quite wealthy animals has already grown into a *rather larger* number of very, *very* wealthy animals. Under visionary weasel helmsmalship, a hypergyroscopic business-climate has evolved in which, I'm very pleased to say, the Mystery Standard for company directors' pay rises is now a very-modest-but-also-liberatingly-substantial *minimum* of twenty-five per cent per annum—"

"—thirty-seven per cent!" suggested the Toad Transoceanic Chairmal, beaming. "In certain quarters."

"Even forty-nine per cent, I believe, in some cases, W-T! Flexibly applied. And this—naturally—"

"Naturally …" sang the Toad.

"— is because the levels of pay are set *by the directors them-selves*, by way of a burgeoning network of Cross-Corporate Supramolumescing Committees—"

"All quite unimpeachable in their impartiality, of course …"

"— But equally, and again, naturally—"

"Naturally! …"

"— really rather keen to see a continuous, rapid rise in the Mystery Standard. Thus, one Top Mal from one Top Company will—out of the breadth of his knowledge and the depth of his wisdom—"

"The clarity, the diamantine perspicuity of his Vision …" crooned the Toad.

"— help to set the pay of the animal next to him—"

"And that Top Mal will, in the depth of *his* wisdom, sit on *another* Committee to set the pay of the animal next to *him* …"

"— whilst he, in turn, will sit on yet *another* wholly impartial and unimpeachable Committee that in its sagacity, and lucidity—"

"*And* of course with an eye to America, where H-TELs (that's Heap-Top Emolument Levels, of course, Mr Mole) are now some four hundred and eighty times the size at Heap-Bottom …"

"— helps to set the pay levels *of the first mal mentioned!*"

"Glorious! Moving! Stirring!" exclaimed the Toad, his eyes too now turned emotionally to the ceiling.

"*This* is Opportunity, Mr Mole," said Mr Phangachs, with the voice of dogma. "*This* is the kind of Opportunity that matters: opportunity for those at the top to climb higher, and again higher, in the brilliantined and diamond-studded Tree of Wealth! And, you see—when they are *very* lucky—for the occasional clawful of others to ascend from ground level into the Tree's lowest branches to keep them company."

"But—why?" asked the Mole. "Why do they want to? That is—I don't see, really, why anyone *needs* to be rich. Animals—

I mean, the animals *I* know—most of them—don't need much at all to be quite, quite happy."

"Long may they remain so, and they will be no trouble to the rest of us!" said Mr Phangachs in undisguised disgust. "I can't imagine what animals you do know, Mr Mole, to be frank." He exhaled a scout-cub's fire's-worth of smoke in the Mole's direction. "The fact remains that Weaselworld can only function as it should if those at the Top are paid—at the very minimum—two hundred and fifty times as much as those at the bottom. And under the Party in its purged state, that ratio is set to grow somewhat."

"But *why?*" said the Mole again, bouncing a little on his seat. "Is it because they don't enjoy their jobs, then—the top animals?"

"What? No, no. What do you mean? No! Most Top Animals *love* their jobs! Isn't that true, W-T?"

"It is, Gibbert! Oh, it is!"

"Every Top Job, Mr Mole, entails the holding of Power (with of course a corresponding Responsibility). And Top Jobs naturally—ha, ha, naturally!—attract animals who enjoy, and are capable of effectively wielding, such Power."

"So—um ..." The Mole scratched his head in another strenuous effort to draw forth the meaning of his thoughts. ... If these animals *enjoy* what they do, why can't they be paid the same as all the others? I mean—what is all that extra money *for?*"

The Weasel stared at the Mole in open-jawed disbelief and incomprehension. "*PAY THEM THE SAME?*" he squealed. "What is the money *FOR?*" But, again, mysteriously, in just a few seconds he had returned to his earlier unruffled state. "It is, of course, to reward them for Achieving. For without Achievement there is no Growth. And without Growth there is ..." (here his face became quite blank, as if he had opened a door on to a darkened void) "... nothing ..."

"And *wouldn't* it be a pity, Mr Mole, if we were all the

same?" said the Toad in airy amusement, coming to the assistance of the freshly pole-axed politician. "Wouldn't the world be a dull, dull place? Wealth does add that little splash of brilliance to life's drab panorama, don't you think? And it is a strange thing (and I say this as a—oh—moderately well-off mal myself), but that first acquisition of significant assets does have the effect of making an animal wish to repeat the experience on a grander scale. Ah yes! 'Appetite grows by what it feeds on'—as Wagtaile put it so succinctly in *Piglet*. And naturally so, eh, Gibbert? Naturally so?"

"Ha, ha—yes, W-T," agreed the Weasel weakly.

"— Well, Phangachs!" said the Toad in a newly brisk tone, and waving a freshly-lit cigar. "As I had always believed and hoped, there can be no doubt that you are a right-thinking animal. Well done! And thank you. With fellows like you at the helm—if only we can keep you there—I have high hopes for the future of this country. Very high hopes, Gibbert!"

The politician positively glowed through his fur with pleasure at this unexpected accolade. "Of course, we have to weather the current difficulties, W-T," he purred. "But even if we did—ha-ha, unthinkable as it is!—lose power for a term, we know from history that this is no more than a part of an inevitable, predetermined pattern of political evolution. Such lulls are necessary now and then, I suppose. Even *we* have to do a little spring-cleaning occasionally."

"I was doing some myself only the other day," said the Mole.

"— Yes, and for the best of reasons," said Mr Phangachs, ignoring this, "so that the Party's most creative and radical elements can regroup—retrench—and return with a yet clearer, yet more vigorous, expression of the enduring principles of the Weasel Mind."

"And the Toad Mind," added the magnate drily. "The *modern* Toad Mind."

"And the Toad Mind—yes, yes: our Party—the Party Of

The Self—is beyond all argument the only natural party of government. What could any opposition do except palely imitate the principles we already stand for? What else is there left to them? However it comes about, W-T, the Mystery must be allowed to bear down upon us in all its purity, and with all its force. *We are the future.*"

By now, the Mole had inhaled enough Havana cigar smoke to kipper a hundredweight of herrings. "I'm afraid—I think —ummmm—I'm—going to be unwell," he moaned, clutching his stomach through his waistcoat.

"Oh dear," said Mr Wyvern-Toad. "Through here— here ..." He threw open a shining black door and the Mole rushed through it.

He returned five minutes later feeling quite a lot better, if still a little shaky, to find that the rising young politician had already left (but had been "very glad to meet him"), as he was already late for a Sincerity-Skills Masterclass he was due to give at the Predation Studies Institute.

Mr Wyvern-Toad looked at the Mole in silence for just a moment. "Mr Mole," he said with *gravitas*, "you are an animal of quite remarkable abilities. And that is something I very, very rarely say to anyone."

"O—um—am I?" said the Mole.

"Quite remarkable, yes. And on the strength of them—if you happened to be remotely interested—I'd have no hesitation at all in offering you a Special Directorial Consultancy (Graded-Transitional, Vertically-Rated, of course) here at T.T. You may want to think about it. You're not off to the Okavango Swamp, or anything like that, in the next few days?"

"Um—no ..."

"No? Good. I'm sure you will be roughly familiar with the relevant Pinguific Indices for this class of work—which, incidentally, wouldn't be at all onerous!—and you need have *no* doubts in your mind that T.T. would be able to substantially—and I do mean *substantially*—improve on any

Agglomerized Emolumescencies (and, I hardly need add, Apocryphal Gorbelluities) you could possibly have in mind."

"O—"

"And, of *course*, if such things concern you even remotely, T.T. can also offer a unique Gilt-Tailed Preferential-Asylum Portmanteau, courtesy of our Global Sinkage-Advisorship, Tortitawa-Puddiphat."

"Um? ..."

"Think about it; think about it! I'm sure you'd find it a quite rewarding experience, being on board with us. Amusing ... amusing, should we say?"

Mr Wyvern-Toad walked the Mole to the door across an expanse of carpet that felt as velvety to the foot as his own fur, laughing at his side like the oldest of friends.

CHAPTER SIX

MIMESIS' DECEASES

The Mole spent much of the rest of his day at the Toad Tower in the staff restaurant on level thirty-nine. He was able to find a quiet seat in an internal 'corner' formed out of two curious panels resembling enormous bread-baskets that had been ironed flat and stained a lurid yellow-orange. Having thus minimised all views out to the windows and their drop to the distant earth, he kept his nose buried in his copy of *The Vole Who ... etc.*, only being distracted from it occasionally as the day wore on, when employees of the great firm took up seats nearby and talked between themselves.

One such exchange took place at about four o'clock in the afternoon, between two hollow-eyed mice whose fur had long since lost the sheen of youth. It ran, approximately, thus:

"No, but Norm! You *can't ingress* it on a ThrustFarq BasiScript! I know *that*. You don't have to tell me *that*."

"Well I just had to find that out for myself, didn't I, Norm? But look—here you have GLOT9, come on! GLOT9, a crucial—I mean, currucial, intit?—aheadhave restruct, one that's going to morph the morph for unimaginable tracts of time now. I mean, the next *two years*? Intit? At *least*. And you can't ingress it on what's meant to be *the* up-phase kompuroute-krackprod? It's ridiculous! Nor, Norm—and I'm talking from painful experience here, mate—can you do it on the Pneumaspek FoolprooTex—"

"No! ... What? What, you're telling me you can't i.g. it on the *Pneumaspek*? I don't believe that, Norm. I mean, are you quite sure of that? The FoolprooTex *is* what it *says*, Norm. I don't believe *that*."

"Norm, listen. Listen. I am *sure* about that. Didn't I spend three and a half hours on Tuesday night trying? I mean—three and a half hours, par for the course, no problem. But it was still a bit frustrating. All I wanted to do when I started was check I'd spelled 'saveloys' right. For me shopping list."

"Yeh, well. As you do."

"As you do, Norm. Right. As you do and as you must. But there it is, mate. We must not complain. The Emm is the Emm, when all is said and done."

"The Emm is the Emm, Norm, and never forget it. Never forget it! The Medial ..."

"... is the Message, mate, and that's the truth. But the point is, Norm, see—and I mean, you know, steady yourself, mate, before I tell you this. The horrible fact is, you can *not* ingress it *either* on the KompuThrall PeasiWrit! No—don't say it. This is serious. All you get on it is Gate One. Gate Two just sits there staring at you with the latchlift deader than the proverbial."

"No ... No. No ... No. Forward-*slash*-o-megalo-*mazing*."

The Mole was puzzled to note (amongst many other elements here) that these two mice sat, not facing one another as they might readily have done, but side by side, each staring ahead of him as if at some imaginary object placed two to three feet in front of their eyes. Every so often, one or the other would reach out to make small tapping motions as if at the surface of some receptive, but imaginary, surface.

"'Nother coffee, Norm?"

"No ta, mate. So come on then. You tell me. Since you

know all about it like you do. Where *did* I ingress it then? I mean, sit down, mate, 'cos this may just be too much for you. Where did I get i.g. finally? Eh? Not on my old Plumbrella Two, for example?"

"No … what? You're not telling me you've still got one of those! What, and it's still working? You should give that to a museum, Norm. I mean that. That's got to be a collector's item by now. That's four years old if it's a day intit?"

"But it *worked*, Norm! I mean—that is worth noting. Okay so the Plumbrella's an antique. So? So it gives me latchlift on GLOT9 where I can't do the same thing on a five-week-old BasiScript hardly out of its box yet. Ka-lunk. Open. That's all that interests me, mate. And I'm telling you, Norm, there aren't going to be many mals in labyvoid who know that yet."

"Not too surprising, is it, mate, what with you being the only known owner in labyvoid of a Plumbrella with a plug on it?"

"You may mock, Norm. You may mock. But I'm very sorry, brother. You either unlatch the gate, or you do not unlatch the gate. That's all I can say."

About half an hour later, the Mole was approached by a secretary from Mr Rette's department.

"Mr Moélle?" she said.

The Mole looked up, blinking. "… Um …?"

"You are Mr Moélle? I mean, *the* Mr Moélle? Mr Rette asked me to find you."

"I think I am. Mole.—Mole? I am *Mole*. Mole is who I am."

(The touch of fog in the Mole's response here can be explained by the fact that he had been in the midst of reading about an unfortunate shrew who kept forgetting not only where, but who, and even when, he was. This last aspect of his condition especially excited the Mole's sympathy. He had also been slightly thrown by the secretary's creativity with the vowels.)

"You do *know* Mr Rette?" the secretary asked him dubiously. "Mr Gordon *R.* Rette? The Head of Reasonabling?" She scanned the long vista of seated animals as if for sight of other, more likely moles.

"O.—Yes!"

"Oh, well then. You must be him, then, mustn't you? I do apologise. Always best to be on the safe side. Mr Rette has asked me to tell you" (and here the secretary's tone took on something of a sunset-gilded glow) "that Mr Wyvern-Toad has invited both of you to accompany him to a Private View tonight. If you happened to be free? He said he thought it might interest you."

"O. How nice of him," replied the Mole politely.

Having informed him of proposed timings the secretary departed, leaving the Mole to try to work out why the Toad might want to show him another view: did he think he especially enjoyed looking at great huge expanses of tower-things? And how could he tell him that he didn't, very much, without offending him?

In any case, at a quarter to six, the Mole puffed his way up another twenty-seven double flights of stairs to the Department of Degirthing, whose level he had by now clearly established in his own mind. During the latter stages of this ascent he began to pause at each new stratum to catch his breath, peering through big transparent doors to see repeated, from floor to floor, what looked to him like exactly the same dazzle-lit vista: at each of these he read out the floor number under his breath, to reassure himself that he hadn't climbed up to the floor he'd just left. There beyond the doors were the same parallel rows of desks in their hundreds, where animals sat gazing at window-boxes and tapping at keys, each row stretching away to doll-like tininess in far, far distances where the dazzle was no less intense.

On the Degirthing level the Mole approached Mr Rette's private office by way of the first hundred yards or so of such a perspective. Here some animals were now packing up to go home, secure in the knowledge, presumably, that their jobs in job-elimination would be there again next morning.

Five minutes later rat and mole entered another of the very small rooms with mirrors, rails and buttons that stood off the main ascent. The Degirthing Department dematerialized and, in little more than a flitter of a dog-bat's wing, another variant on the cellar-for-*motors* appeared in its place. The Mole made a mental note to ask Mr Rette how this disturbing miracle was accomplished: now, he saw from the drawn look on his companion's face, was not the time.

As they stepped through the slide-apart doors Mr Rette made a single comment, in a tone that might have mingled quiet exasperation and philosophical defeat. "I *do not* understand how you get me into these things," he said.

This cellar-for-*motors* was much smaller than the other. It was floored up its centre, almost as if carpeted, with narrow red bricks, and divided in the style of an old-fashioned stable, except that here the partitions were made of brick, topped elegantly by curves of some very dark wood. In each of the bays stood, not a horse, but a *motor*, all but three of which fell squarely into the blob denomination: super-squashed, projectile-nosed, rarely more than two-door.

The Mole did not recognise any of the variations here from what he had seen on the roads outside, though he did see the somehow familiar name BRAWSCHE repeated several times. In its glowing spotlit recess each machine gave off a palpable and, to the Mole, slightly wearying aura of exclusivity and very-much-its-own-thingness. Some seemed to preen, one or two grinned in a subtle, maniacal way, but the majority were distinctly snarling, their fronts like flattened and sheenfully-coloured versions of intimidating medieval helmets. They bore plates at the front lettered from WT 1 to WT 21, and were parked in numerical order.

A slightly stooping greyhound in chauffeur's uniform came up to them. "Good evening, sir. Good evening, sir," he said.

"Mr Wyvern-Toad is on his way down now, I believe."

And so he was. A door glid-slid apart at the far end of the range of *motors* to reveal that same animal's by no means tall, by no means slender outline.

"Delighted you could make it, gent'mals!" he said. "Thank you, Whipplewhitt—we won't be needing you tonight. Now … *what* shall it be?"

"Er … W-T … Might it be simpler if I brought my own car?" suggested the Rat, grinning slightly. The Mole noticed that he was clutching his briefcase very tightly in both paws.

"Great *torque*-curves, no!" answered the Toad emphatically, as he waddled along the row of machines. "Ride with me, ride with me, Gordon! You can train it in tomorrow, can't you? You can stand it for a day if you put your mind to it! I think …" (he paused, looking abstractedly from left to right) "I think it should be Number One tonight, you know. It's not every evening one has a passenger such as Mr Mole here!"

Did the Water Rat utter a very low moan at this suggestion—a moan such as might have been made by some manacled, despairing wretch in a remote island prison's subterranean cell? The Mole did think that he did; but he could not be quite certain.

The Toad led them on towards a *motor* rolled so very flat it seemed to the Mole's old-fashioned, vertically-attuned eyes that it would be necessary to inflate it before any one animal could get inside it.

"I call this beauty 'The Spirit Of Free Enterprise'," said the Toad. "She cuts corners like a butter-knife. Ha!"

The machine's two doors were hinged along its front-to-rear axis in the centre of the roof, and now rose slowly up rather like the stiffened ears of some metal-plated llama. The pale cream-gold back of the passenger seat slid forward with a hiss. The Mole jumped.

"Would you like to take up the rear, Mr Mole?" asked the Toad, gesturing, and the Mole got in, ducking low and then arranging himself on the tiny curve of the kidskin back seat. Clutching his briefcase to his chest, Mr Rette had little choice about where he sat, or more precisely, lay.

Mr Wyvern-Toad climbed in too, lay back in his seat, pressed half a dozen switches and fired up the engine. The Mole was conscious of a faint rumbling, as of a volcano erupting very close by. Almost lost in this sound, and no less elusive then before, came another low moan from Mr Rette's direction—the moan, perhaps, of some manacled wretch who hears beyond the prison walls the impending flow of lava.

"Hold on to your squirt-tails!" shouted the Toad, and the windscreen's virtually horizontal concave arc ate the perspective of the cellar. A wall-wide door opened up in front of them, and they were launched upon the city.

"The *Toadmobile!*" cried Mr Wyvern-Toad (in jest, apparently). "Hand-built to my own specifications by Jowlett and Son of Cowbag! Unique on the road, of course. Don't believe it, Mr Mole, when you hear it said that the field marshals of industry never enjoy their toys!"

The kind of deep silence that can be produced only by an animal gritting his teeth very hard was heard—or, depending on the reader's approach to semantics, not heard—to rise from that part of the tiny cockpit occupied by the semi-recumbent Rat. As to the Mole, since he hardly knew what he was looking at, and was quite incapable of registering so immediate a transition from "parked and stationary in building interior" to "moving at high speed along street outside", he had not yet had time to appreciate that he should be terrified.

In the streets outside the Toad Tower, thousands of T.T./Mollusk employees were now flooding out of the vast building and filling the pavements, as they started on their journeys home. It was not at all difficult for a practised eye such as that of Gordon Rette, insofar as it was in use at all just then, to pick out amongst them some of the most recent fruits of his Department's labours: animals whose pavement-speed was down to almost zero, their faces paralysed by wooden, entaxidermic stares, their knuckles grazing the pavements in despair. All around them the great torrent of still-in-work animals surged briskly onward, whilst here and there Unemployment Insurance-Insurance salesmals bawled their wares from little highly-coloured podiums decorated with blowing ribbons—far too late for some of these.

"The problem with these chauffeurs, you know," said the Toad, "is that none of the dogs will drive fast enough. They all want to sit there up front in the old states-wagons, ferrying one around as if one were royalty. On some occasions, of course, one has to put up with it. Otherwise, tedium—purest, purest tedium!"

Three *motors* were slowing down ahead in response to an amber traffic light. The Toad manipulated the lever next to him, stimulating the volcano, and the "Toadmobile" sliced ahead along the centre of the road to take the lights on red just as two two-lane streams of traffic were closing in on the crossing like the waters of the Red Sea, post Moses. A fanfare of hooters sounded behind them as if to celebrate their victorious passage, and as they did so Mr Rette moaned a low but, this time, entirely indisputable moan. It was as the moan of some apoplectic ancient, whose wheelchair has just rolled forward to the brink of a bottomless flight of steps. "*Don't worry*, Gordon!" said Mr Wyvern-Toad in exaggerated mock-surprise. "There's enough whump in this little beauty to shift us straight into the fourth dimension, not that we shall ever need it with yours-truly driving! ... Mr Mole? Where are you, Mr Mole?"

The Mole—now trembling like a slime-mould in a Force Nine Atlantic westerly—restored himself very slowly to an upright position, only to duck down again when he saw the windscreen filling with the view of another *motor's* rear: this time a very small item, in an older format rather evoking the shape of a tortoise-shell on which someone had unkindly dropped a stone.

Since there was now a high-kerbed traffic island solidly occupying his overtaking space, the Toad had no choice other then to slow down behind this obstacle, and thus to continue on at a mere five to ten miles per hour above the speed limit.

"Oh *really*," breathed the Chairmal of Toad Transoceanic, "I'm not travelling behind *that* underpowered little gruntmobile!" He trailed the offending vehicle for several hundred yards at a distance of some ten to ten and a half inches from its rear bumper, then—spotting a gap in the parked *motors* on the pavement side a few yards ahead—he volcanoed abruptly left. No more than three seconds later he volcanoed back to the right again, so placing the crushed reptilian and its now horn-playing driver behind them, if only by a matter of a few yards.

"One just had to show *that* horrid little car one's bottom," said the Toad. "Really, you know, it's a matter of principle! Since one's position in society (so-called) is Ahead, one *must have* vehicles that accurately—elegantly—reflect one's Aheadness. And it is only natural, surely, that we Creatures-Made-Vastly-Superior-By-The-CCs-Of-Our-Handcrafted-Block-Bores (not, you know, Mr Mole, that one would normally put it quite that way, but there it is) *must*, surely—out of self-respect alone, since one finds there, well, so very much *to* respect—*show* our superiority to the drivers of any matchbox-cars we find in front of us? What point is there otherwise in possessing a vehicle like this, in which the sealed bearings of a single rear wheel alone are worth the showroom price of an off-the-peg fish-can such as that we now see behind us?"

The Toad glanced in his mirror just in time to catch sight of a really quite expressive display of arm-waving by the crushed-tortoise driver. "And it has the delicious side-effect of annoying them so much, too! No, no, Mr Mole—hang in their rear view mirrors, hang in them! Fill them to overflowing with views of one's massive engine-case, one's panoramic sweep of tinted windscreen, and then, with a blast of cylinder-power such as their drivers are unable so much as to imagine—flash on, flash on by!"

A quiet moan of "No-o-oo ..." from Mr Rette (directed into his tie-knot) indicated that another changing traffic-light was looming nearer.

"In any case," the Toad went on blithely, "I have no idea why cars of that type are allowed on the road. Not only do they burn *far* too little fuel per mile, but they are generally driven by—does one need to say it?—Mr Phangachs' *insectes noires*. Those who will sit forever beneath the Tree."

"I want to go back to my hole!" groaned the Mole, his face now buried in the soft and yielding kidskin placed by the vehicle's makers to support him from beneath.

"*What* did the animal say?" asked the Toad in a shocked voice. "His *what?*"

The Water Rat made a super-mammalian effort. "M-mai Hôl," he said hoarsely. "The place in the ... jungle, where he had been—ah, heurhh—researching ... hah, um—South ... East Asia—you know—"

"Ah." The flattened projectile roared close along the edge of a pavement full of shrieking children, then swerved out and around the front of an accelerating bus. "Unstable part of the world, of course, South East Asia."

<hr />

The Mole saw nothing more of the journey between the Toad Tower and their destination. He was still adjusting to the idea that he was not yet dead whilst Mr Wyvern-Toad was parking the Jowlett in a reserved section of another cellar-for-*motors*. A de/rematerialization room was entered and swiftly aban-doned, and the three animals emerged into a high, lugubrious, misshapen hall whose smooth-but-not-smooth walls of streaked and blotched grey-matter were illuminated from a very high ceiling by a series of intense spotlights with narrow beams.

To his deep dismay the Mole saw that the place was filled with animals, virtually wall to wall. Many of these were of the weasel species—or at least, they appeared so at first sight. Most were moving slowly about—with difficulty, given the crush—and many held glasses of wine in their hands. Hanging on the walls, or standing in roped-off spaces, were a varied and extensive collection of objects whose purpose the Mole was quite unable to guess. It was clear that these objects were of interest to the animals present since they milled around them, looking at them, and here and there they gathered in small groups as if discussing them.

"You know, I think I'm in the mood to buy something," said Mr Wyvern-Toad, sweeping up a glass from a passing drinks tray. "I still have a space or two over here I need to fill. Don't suppose you've been exposed to much contemporary art down there in the jungle, Mr Mole?"

"… Art?" The Mole was rather more than averagely nonplussed, but thought it best to say something. "Er, no. Very art-free, the jungle, for the most part."

"Well if you want to catch up, you're in a good place here, or so we are led to believe!"

The three animals joined the ruminative crush along a section of wall housing a series of immense canvases. The first they came to was precisely that: an immense canvas. It was twenty feet high by ten feet wide and hung, unframed and unstretched, without the slightest evidence of having ever been touched by paw of beast. The Mole peered forward to read a small label, on which was written: *The Quest For The Picayune And Its Shadow In The Age Of Enlightenment.*

"Interesting …" said Mr Wyvern-Toad.

"Challenging …" said Mr Rette, and cleared his throat.

"Not quite the right size, though," said the Toad. "And with white walls, you know ..."

The Mole peered at another little label. This read: "Price: £58,500." He felt disappointed that such an obviously august (and augustly gloomy) institution as this could fail to check for misprints before opening its doors to the public. But this was a minor problem compared to that he had with the work itself, so he said nothing.

Behind them was a low grey-stuff block on which someone had left a paintbox. "Oh, look," said the Mole rather loudly, pointing at the box, which was full of half-squeezed tubes and eroded, paint-clogged brushes. "One of the artists has left their paints behind."

"I *think* you'll find that that is an exhibit," said Mr Rette, glancing about with a smile of embarrassment.

The Mole peered closer, and sure enough he found a label done in the same kind of lettering as the last. It read *Necronomiasis 3*.

The Mole (who did not have a glass) folded his arms behind him in attentive-professorial style. He thought he ought at least to make an effort, although it was quite obvious to him from the most cursory scan of the place that there was no art in it. Nevertheless—considerate as ever of the feelings of his fellow animals, however disturbed—he paused meditatingly before a red cylinder about three feet in height, at the top of which was fixed a complex-looking (and, he thought, rather well turned) brass device from which a long black rubber tube hung down. This time, he saw disgustedly, the gallery had forgotten even to put up a title.

"I think you'll *find*," said Mr Rette between his teeth, "that that is a fire-extinguisher." He spoke in a rather deeper voice than before and one or two nearby ferrets half turned to them as they walked on, looking down their long, narrow noses in what might have been amusement.

"Ah!" said Mr Wyvern-Toad, "I believe I see Aanthoony

Aardvaark over there. *Would* you excuse me? Find your way over to us! I would like a word in his ears." With that, gliding sinuously-but-with-dignity through the elegantly-to-grotesquely-and-often-both-at-once-dressed crowd, the Toad left his companions to their own devices.

"Don't s'pose there are any watercolours …?" said the Mole, largely to himself. He was peering at a deeply uninteresting arrangement of black horizontal slats set in a gleaming metal frame, which appeared (could it be that valuable?) to have been bolted into the wall itself.

"I *think* you'll find …" said Mr Rette through gritted teeth, and in a deeper tone still "… that that is an *air vent!*" Irritably he hustled the Mole on to what was—and the Mole was quite, quite sure about this—half a pound or so of kidneys (unchopped), painted silver and suspended individually from the ceiling on very long wires.

"Is *that* a piece of—er—'Art'?" he asked guardedly, in a very low voice.

"Yes," muttered the Rat. "You don't have to say anything about it."

"I like a nice portrait, myself. You know—of Garibaldi, or Queen Victoria. Or a nice picture of a river," said the Mole.

"Hm."

"— Early morning, dawn light. You know, the ducks flying over, a willow or two. A moored boat. Don't they do that kind of thing any more, artists?"

"Good grief, artists haven't been interested in landscape, or nature, for ages!" said the Water Rat very quietly, looking around him with a defensive eye as he did so. "Not that I know anything about it. But *nature* is so deeply defrosted (to use the jargon) you'd hardly dare mention it in a place like this."

"— Um …?" said the Mole, drawing a little closer to Mr Rette. "Mr Rette? Do you actually—well, er—you know—*like* any of these things?"

"No one *likes* them, Mr Mole," responded the Rat in a very tiny whisper. "That's not the *point.*"

The Mole was considering asking what the point was, in that case, when they reached a yet more thickly congregated area of the gallery. Here, two animals—a rather young hare dressed in something resembling a potato-sack and sporting what looked like a bulldog-clip on one of her ears (which bent over as a result), and a more conventionally dressed grey rat, also female—stood talking at the centre. Next to them was a slightly stooped, elderly pine marten with bags under his eyes. He was wearing what looked like earmuffs and pointing a long sausage-shaped object at the other two, and he stared down at a dial-rich device inside the lid of which two round things were rotating. There was an expression of the profoundest boredom on his face.

"Oh I think certainly, you know," the Hare was saying breathlessly, her nose atwitch with excitement, "if you compare London with the rest of the world—which of course means New York and San Fransisco (and, maybe, Tokyo), there is just no scene anywhere like the one here in London right now. There is a really happening, dynamic scene happening here now. I mean this scene is *really happening*, here in the London art-world right now. It's something we've not seen here probably for thirty years or more. I mean, Whiskielia, this kind of happening just doesn't happen very often. It's a real, contemporaneous, zip-a-dee-doo-dah on-the-button in-the-moment *now-thinger.* I've been doing gallery events for *so* long now—six months, virtually—and I can tell you, Whiskielia, I have *never seen* a scene like this. I've n—"

"Well, thank you very much," said the Grey Rat, "exhibition designer Gaenor Leverettski. Now we go on—in this special live relay for A.B.C. Radio Paw's *CurtainUp* (that's all one word) from the new *British is IT* show, here in London—to talk to the animal who has perhaps done more over the past two years to help put that scene on the world map. Hole

Hegginhoggom—your work has rarely been less than controversial—"

The Grey Rat turned here to a stocky, dark-prickled young
hedgehog who was dressed in a pinstripe suit not unlike Mr
Rette's—it could almost have been made by the same tailor.
The Mole noticed that on his feet the Hedgehog was wearing
a pair of just such exquisitely vile "sports" shoes (if that was
what they were)—covered in luridly coloured chevrons,
stripes, and letters—as he had seen gracing the feet of the
Hare derelict on his first journey into the capital. He mustn't
have left time to change after fives, he thought.

The Hedgehog looked about him, and in particular at his
interviewer, with a dully belligerent stare that seemed to say,
"You cross me? I break your nose."

"— and there's no doubt that it remains very much so in
this Right Bank show here today," continued the Rattess. "If
we could turn first, Hole, to what I think it's safe to say is one
of your less hotly-debated pieces, this—*The Passion Of The
Moloch In Free-Form Floating* (and here the interviewer pointed to
what was certainly a decapitated *motor* roof in the middle of
which lay a large, unpleasant two-tone stain) is, in fact, the
roof of a car—?"

"Yeh," said the Hedgehog. "My car."

"— which is marked in white rhetorically—histrionically,
some might say—with a great expanding, forceful, *moment-
specific* splash of colour, clearly thrown at it with enormous
force—"

"Yeh. By a seagull. Actually."

"— A seagull? Tell us more!"

"I was going out. The seagull came over, hundred foot up,
and splat. Bulls-eye."

"The result, Hole, is an enormously vital, energising,
expressive piece. Can you tell me, exactly, how you arrived *at*
the work itself?"

"I looked at the roof. There it was," responded the

Hedgehog in a morose voice. "It was strong. It was visual. It was on the car. You know. It was there. So I cut it off. Can't use the car when it rains—"

"Ha, ha—no!"

"You can. You get wet though."

"And would I be right in thinking that you applied the same broad visual strategy in this work? This is *Ulalume: The Question Answered*, where we see a long segment of patterned carpeting in the centre of which we find a comparable—you'd agree comparable, Hole, yes?—explosion of strongly coloured material—the result (and you'll probably have to help me here, Hole) of some chance incident?—Deliberate intent?"

"Yeh, chance, really," said Mr Hegginhoggom.

"— And this was …?"

"The girlfriend came in one night from the shops. Tripped over. Dropped a jar on the hall carpet. Chicken Tikka."

A unique, dramatic—one might say, *visceral*—impact."

"Visceral, yeh, visceral," agreed the Hedgehog mournfully. "An image. I looked at it. I said, 'Don't touch it.' She was just going to scrape it up. But I said, 'Leave it, Gretchen.' I knew I'd got one. You do, you know. You see it. Something strong enough to stand on its own two feet. When it was dry."

"And this pursuit of *images* in a world that is, some would say, already far too full of them …?"

"That's what it's about. That is what it's about."

"And so …" (here the Grey Rat moved again, towards what looked to the Mole very much like some kind of fish-tank) "… we come to what is certainly your most controversial work to date—and I am talking here to artist Hole Hegginhoggom at the opening of the *British Is IT* show on London's Right Bank—the piece known simply as *Fish Slice*, in which you defied, really, all possible viewer-expectations by dissecting the *actual carcass* of a haddock, longitudinally—mouth-to-tail, for listeners who can't see this—and suspending the two segments—really, quite spectacularly,

Hole—side by side in this tank of preserving fluid—"

The Mole's view of the work of art under discussion happened to be partly blocked by a female rabbit who was grinning at her companion with strangely stoat-like teeth. So he moved a little to his right, and what he saw made his heart sink. For here in place of anything created, or any effort to produce it, he found a borrowing made direct from Nature itself: the two halves of what had been a living fish, its organs and skeleton now exposed to view like pickled eggs on a bar-room shelf.

But then, the Mole thought to himself, No, this wasn't borrowing. This was *theft*. He clenched his fist. He would very much have liked to thump this Hedgehog.

"Looking at this construct as I am now doing, Hole," the interviewer continued, "it's impossible not to feel that you have really quite massive ideas—profound—unsettling—deeply—deeply challenging ideas about mortality, time, evanescence, animality's place in the greater scheme of things ...?"

"Yeh ... yeh," agreed the Hedgehog in the tones of a retiring senior undertaker. "Art is about *life*. Art is *about images. This is* an *image*."

"Absolutely, abso-absolutely!"

"Art should be visual," said Mr Hegginhoggom.

"Yes—Yes! Visual, and also, as you said before, visceral. And what could be *more* visceral, after all, than such a radical unprecedented exposure of, well, *viscera* themselves? I have to say, I'm strongly reminded of your much earlier work *For Whom The Bellboy Toils*, seen in New York—an intensely, to me, moving spectacle of a cheese and salami sandwich in an advanced stage of decomposition. And incidentally, Hole, if I can ask, was there anything else in it or *was* that, as it were, the formal totality?"

"A bit of lime pickle. Yeh. Sets off the salami, duntit? Sweet and sour."

"Yes—yes! I think that had evaporated by the time I got

there. In any case the work isn't on show here today at the Right Bank—"

"Nah. It dried out."

"I'm sure Radio Paw listeners will be very sorry to hear that."

"We sold it first though. Oh yeh. We always shift 'em."

"But that, too, Hole, just like your pointedly, probingly polysemantic haddock here, simply—what can I say?—grabbed one by the throat. It penetrated to the very heart of things. Lodged itself deep—*deep*—within the psyche."

Mr Hegginhoggom leaned wearily next to his demi-partite fish cadaver. "If it gets a reaction," he intoned, "any reaction, you know. That's it. Any reaction's a reaction. 'Cos it is *a* reaction. Art—" (and here he exhaled the long, slow sigh of the one-legged gravedigger for whom retirement is not an option) "*Art* is about *life*."

"Abso-absolutely, abso—ha, ha—lutely!" effused the Grey Rat. "So, thank you very much, Hole Hegginhoggom," ("Hey fridgerate," said the Hedgehog, wandering away) "— and I am joined now by Assistant Curator of the Haywain Gallery, Mark Weaselliard, on this opening night of the *British Is IT* exhibition at London's Right Bank. Mark, what *are* the implications *for* British art, would you say, in the works we see on show here tonight?"

"Oh, enormous!" replied the Curator, a nervy-looking loose-jacketed weasel with nicotine-yellowed claws. "Quite, quite enormous! Fundamental, in fact, Whiskielia. Since I think we can now at last begin to see that those old, tired and, one has to say, essentially nineteenth-century notions of 'pleasure' and indeed, 'meaning', in art are finally and definitively being broken down by the Craftless Arts movement as it is represented here."

"So 'pleasure' in art, so-called ...?"

"That notion did cling on, embarrassingly, and in what we can now see was an extraordinarily naive form, well into the seventies. It could still be seen, for example, in Slop Art, but has been courageously driven back by succeeding generations of artists since then. The, as it were, 'revulsion', the higher levels of bone-weary *'ennui'* I am able to register in myself *as* viewer *in* a show like this," (and here the Weasel, growing ever more excited, began to throw out his words so that a mist of spittle stood out in the spotlight beams) "these things *are* at the very heart of these works—their *raison-d'être.*"

"So—taking for example Hegginhoggom's *Sterna*-prizewinning haddock-cleavage—his, if I can say this, his Janus-plaice, ha, ha—"

"Ha, ha, yes! Well, there could hardly be a more perfect example, could there? But in just the same way—if we were to look here, for example, at Dearth Beanimink's most recent and I think, to date, most electrifying installation on the theme of used nappy-liners, whose complex conformations strangely resemble, what?—some parched volcanic landscape, dotted with active mud-geysers? In the past, in some extraordinarily primitive fashion, one might have found a display of this kind—what should I say?—'vulgar'?—'mindless'?—who knows, 'not art at all'?" (On each of the first syllables of these words the Assistant Curator thrust his pelvis dramatically forward. At the end of them he uttered a high-pitched laugh.)

"Abso—ha—lu ..."

"— But at this stage in the game, Whiskielia, there can no longer be any question that one is forced—*forced*—out of any such disjointed, jaundiced and *jejune* judgementalism. One is *forced* here to confront one's own perhaps quite inadequate responses to starkly universal issues: the containment of infant evacuations, waste collection, storage, disposal. And it is no less the case with Hegginhoggom's piece that one *must* confront, head-on, the feelings one would experience, inescapably, I think, were one to come across half a haddock out there in the field. The 'displeasure', the 'distaste' I am able to note in myself as I face up to the *idiomorphic event* of these nappy-liners—this in effect *essence of ur-nappylinerliness*—in which I think one simply *must* recognise Lacanard's seminal notion of the *brosse-pissoir de l'inconscient*—"

"Abso—Abso—"

"— These phenomena, Whiskielia, are the legitimate, the authentic, end-products of the making of art in its (to date) Hexapost-Modern—"

"— That's post-post-post-post-*post*-post—"

"— Modern, yes—Six-Ps-Modern manifestation. And thank Ppan—thank Ppan for that! Because what we have here on the Right Bank is nothing less than 'Meaning' (if one may be forgiven for making use of that word) in 'Futility'. 'Significance'—Within-And-By-Way-Of-Its-Fully-Accomplished-Absence'."

"... lutely, Mark ..."

"The quaintly antediluvian principle that art should in some manner 'interpret' the world—should pass through some quite arbitrary filter of consciousness lodged in a primitive, roughcast way within the personality of a single individual—the 'artist'—has been, as I said, finally and definitively exorcised here. There is, in fact, as I see it now, only one way forward for artists as a whole—"

"And this *is*, Mark ...?"

"The conclusion is inescapable, I think: that in the foreseeable future, artists should begin to stage exhibitions *sans operis.*"

"— You mean ...?"

"It has to be said. It *is* the next stage. Exhibitions" (the Weasel inhaled deeply here, drawing the next few sentences from himself with a series of epileptic judders)"—entirely, uncompromisingly, *without works*. Who knows, Whiskielia, we may arrive in time at the synoptically liberating stage at which artists will be relieved of the necessity of holding exhibitions *of any kind*. At that point, the viewing public will be able to contemplate contemporary art simply by remaining at home and meditating on its *absence.*"

During the last stage of this impassioned monologue, the Mole had been distracted by the sight of a greenish-brown stain on one arm of the curator's jacket. It rather resembled the shape of a duck in a watercolour, and so—having nothing better to do, and unnoticed by Mr Rette, who was by now in deep conversation with a fellow-toiler in degirthing—he moved forward a little to get a better look at it.

Mr Weaselliard drooped suddenly and turned away from the interviewer—so quickly, in fact, that the Pine Marten was only just able to follow him with his sausage. "Oh, but I'm so depressed!" he said, in a voice now completely drained of energy. "You know? Sick to the back fangs if you really want to know. Didn't I always mean to be an art historian of note? Wasn't it going to be *Weaselliard* who produced *the* definitive volume on Catoveggio's use of *civettasciuro*? *Years* of work— *years*, sitting in the V & A cafeteria—"

"Well, thank—"

"Years! Years! Utterly, utterly wasted! No one can publish books on painters who can *paint* any more! You'd be laughed out of court between here and Easter Island! No, no—"

"Well, th—"

"No, no, no! Instead one must slave on here, squandering one's not inconsiderable brilliance pirouetting on tinier and yet tinier pinheads in defence of ..." The Weasel looked about him now with startled, uncomprehending eyes. "In defence of ..." He let forth a strangled sob, terrible to hear. "Excuse me ... Excuse me. I think I'll just go and throw myself in the river. Obviously it's the best place for me."

So saying—and with his jacket flapping behind him like an un-guyed flysheet in a blizzard—Mr Weaselliard lurched away into the tight pack of animals in the general direction of a fire exit.

"— Well, er, thank you very much, Assistant Curator of

the Haywain Gallery, Mark Weaselliard," said the presenter swiftly. "And that's it for tonight from *CurtainUp* (that's all one word). Tomorrow night, Nigel Stoatson talks to playwright David Hare about the role of radical writers in an age where radicalism is out to lunch; novelist Miles Molesmiles discusses the latest fat volume in his *Ulf The Earwig* saga; and in an exclusive *CurtainUp* interview, visiting cult director Rintin Tarantulino examines the pitfalls and rewards of his own trademark 'Low Concept' brand of screenwriting. This is Whiskielia Ratrack, from the Haywain Gallery, returning you to the studio."

In a matter of a few seconds the pool of energy focused on the interview space had dissipated, and those in it had blended back into the crowd as if they had always been a part of it.

That poor Weasel, thought the Mole, gazing vaguely in the direction of his passing. "I hope he'll be all right."

But already Mr Rette had turned back to him. "I wonder if we can find W-T," he said in a rather hoarse voice. "I *must* go home and lie down soon!"

Spotting the animal in question talking to a tall, generously flap-eared individual of some species not yet known to him, the Mole acted upon the Water Rat's suggestion and began to squooze his way through the tight pack of bodies. He too felt an urgent need to leave: not only the weight of numbers but the heat in the place—even more intensely clinging, if possible, than inside the Rette home—had begun to make him feel a little faint. He felt elusively comforted, somehow, to learn that the Rat was oppressed in a similar way.

"... But when the chips are down, Toony," the Toad was saying, "what we must be sure of is that they are still going to agree it's art in five—ten—years' time!"

"The value of a work can be undermined by critical opinion, that's for sure," said the tall animal, who was dressed in black tie. His ears were very, very long and erect, like aspidistra leaves, and they flapped expressively as he spoke.

"But that doesn't alter the fact that every work is *sui generis* if only by virtue of it having been, well—produced. *That* arrangement of spots," (he pointed at a canvas) "is simply not ... *that* arrangement of spots—" (he pointed at another). "Although ..." (he squinted) "... er ... there's no doubt the differences are subtle ..."

"Ah! Mr Mole!" exclaimed the Toad with an enfolding sweep of his glass-free hand. "Do meet Aanthoony Aardvaark, of Aardvaark and Aardvaark. Mr ... er ... Mole ... Gordon R. Rette of T.T., I think you know already ..."

The Toad stepped back a little whilst paws were shaken, as if to get a better eyeline on his tall companion, next to whom the Mole had now been steered.

"So, Aanthoony," said Mr Wyvern-Toad, "tell me. Tell me! What would you say is your own deepest motivation as a collector nowadays? Be honest, now!"

"Well, I ... The Aardvaark paused, tugging down the full extent of an ear and scratching it. He looked at the Toad with what might have been some suggestion of resentment. "I ... Oh, you know that just as well as I do, W-T! It is what drives all collectors. I must have—really, you know, *must have*, when I think about it—things around me that are unique—quite unique—that have no duplicates anywhere in the world. This is, of course, to reinforce my sense of my own uniqueness—"

"Ah!" said the Toad. "Sorry, Aanthoony, your own sense of ...?" he added taperingly.

"Yes. Which is, I admit it, at best a rather fragile plant, and at worst, you know, virtually non-existent. I must, *must* have what others—and you in particular, actually, W-T, with your collections strewn about all over the globe—do *not* have, in order to be who I, er, think I am, damn it!"

"Ah-hah!" said the Toad again, ingenuousness writ large across his broad green face.

"... And if money can acquire this little badge of distinction for one—well, one has the money." The Aadvaark blinked and stared at one of the ceiling lights. "What did I just say?" he asked.

"As you said, nothing I didn't know already. But you see, Toony, you do bring out here the terrible dilemma of the committed art collector in today's world. Because if the work *is* to be pared down to the *purity* (you may have a better word) of that strip of canvas by Zero McCoypu as opposed to the work on the opposite wall by Nada Touphanclau (you have seen it?—yes) which is also near-as-dammit blank except for a single deep surface indentation made, as I understand it, by the artist's nose when she stumbled and fell against it—then doesn't that make every collector just that little bit too dependent on his brethren in the critical establishment to, what shall I say, hold the line, so far as demarcation of value is concerned? The point is, Toony, *can they keep it up?*"

"It's only the occasional rogue-opinioniser who ever makes any lasting trouble along those lines," replied the Aardvaark just a shade smugly. "And then only with isolated works. In any case, we already have the solution to the problem."

"Ah ... We do?" (The Toad guided the Mole back towards the Aardvaark art-lover's side, from which he had wandered somewhat.)

"Yes, yes. It's been obvious for years, frankly. Go only for *stunts of quality*—those that get into the papers. Their value is fixed in history. If it causes a stir, if large numbers of the great ungroomed can be heard objecting to it, there you have it. Buy it, and you own an *art moment*—something that stands above the scurrying tail-flicking tide of the beastly everyday. *And* above the butterfly-hops of critical opinion, if that's what worries you."

"Buy the moment," echoed the Toad. "*Compare diem.*"

"Yes, yes! The 'meaning' of the stunt is that it was noticed. There will not be another art-stunt this decade of the calibre of Hegginhoggom's Haddock, W-T, I guarantee it, and it is beneath me to remind you of the fact that *I* now own it, but something compels me to do so and I must say I quite enjoy doing it, too, to be honest."

"I could remind you that I own Wormhol's *Puddle*," responded Mr Wyvern-Toad, colouring slightly.

"Oh," said Mr Aardvaark, unconvincingly feigning boredom. "Hasn't that drained away yet? If anything was ever a risky investment! Of course you will certainly remember that I am the owner of Nullvole and Voll's *Optic-Fibre-Carrier In Yogurt?*"

"'A staggering symbol of the communications explosion', as one remembers it," said the Toad, feigning a deeper level of boredom. "— Come on, Toony! It's already as dated as a Polma-Tadema! In any case, for my sins, I am more than well equipped with N & Vs. At least six, at the last count. Use them to decorate the service areas, actually."

"Oh!" sputtered the Aardvaark, clutching momentarily at his bow-tie. "And name one that broke the media-barrier like the *Yogurt-Carrier!*"

"The *Telly-Jellyvision?*" responded the Toad with what was now a feline calm.

"— Damn you, have you got *that?!*"

"Toony, my dear fellow. I thought you knew."

"I hope it melts. I hope it's eaten by tiny creatures of the lower orders!" muttered Mr Aardvaark, who had now got bow-tie and one ear half-entangled.

"Neither has happened yet ... Ah yes, you know! I glance at it, occasionally, when I'm over here, and see deep into the heart of the Modern Dilemma every time I do so!"

"... You oleaginous little—!"

"Oh, I think one can afford to be a little bit oleaginous, Toony, don't you? I am an oil producer after all. And by the way," the Toad went on with easy confidentiality, "I did want you to be the first to know: only a couple of days ago, as it happens, I finalized a commission for Mr Hegginhoggom to build his next defining opus—an 11.11%-scale replica of *this gallery* (unhung, of course), to be made out of crushed filing cabinets, for the grounds of one of our Saudi division offices. One does have to dispose of these irritating little profit excesses somehow ..."

"May you enjoy it for all it is worth," responded the Aardvaark with a refrigerant stare. "... Excuse me. I see someone I have to talk to." And, without *punctilio*, he was gone.

"Oh, I do so relish these gatherings of the *cognoscenti* and the *anteanimali!*" murmured the Toad. "Particularly so in your company, Mr Mole!"

"O—thank you—"

"— But, now, are you fellows more or less ready for the journey west?" the Toad went on. "You've drunk your fill of Art?"

"I think *so*, W-T," said Mr Rette, with a weight and conviction worthy of office hours.

⚬⚬⚬⚬⚬⚬⚬

By the time they reached the Clearway it was already after ten o'clock, so that the great road was relatively empty, being occupied to only about seventy-five per cent of its standstill capacity. The Toad had followed a cross-town route of his own devising, by way of a selection of eminently jumpable back-street traffic lights, and now ascended the great ramp of exodus along a spur at competitive speed, headlights full on, pulling across the three well-populated lanes of traffic in a confident arc that carried the ground-hugging vehicle through a series of short spaces that had no doubt naively been reserved for braking-in-adversity by other road-users.

Reaching the outer lane, the Toad made an instant and seemingly unconscious shift into ballistic mode, accelerating towards the rear of the *motor* ahead (itself travelling at well over ninety miles per hour) as if he intended to drive through or over it. This machine quickly melted sideways into the anonymous wimplands of the middle and slow lanes, and the Toad's car surged ahead at a speed that left it standing.

Until now—for reasons that will not need to be explained—the Mole had been unable to very much enjoy Mr Wyvern-Toad's tactical flourishes, even the most brilliant of them, except by registering them as lurches in his stomach. For his part, Mr Rette was staring ahead through the windscreen with a glazed, imploring look on his face, his whiskers as limp as freshly rain-drenched grasses. It was almost as if he were urging the hideous doom he knew to be inevitable to come upon them sooner rather than later. His cybernian eyes were fixed on the ever unwinding tail of orange lights at the vanishing point from which the road ahead—breakdown phone box by breakdown phone box, sign by sign, clod-like over-bridge by clod-like over-bridge—moved towards them out of the night. Quietly, very quietly, wail of mole and moan of rat melded with the faint whispering of the atmosphere as it was split apart along the outside of the vehicle.

"... Yes, Gordon! One has to be the beast in front, eh?" said the driver, returning to a familiar theme. (He paused here long enough to unflash-reflash another slow mover ahead.) "Which is fine for those of us who are up to it, eh?"

Mr Rette nodded, though without blinking. "Y'ahh," he said.

"... Um ..." came a small, slightly muffled voice from the rear. "Um, well ... I just don't see how you get in front, if the road is always full. Isn't there always somebody else up ahead?"

The Toad considered this intermolation for a few seconds, then laughed until he shook. "The animal is a philosopher!" he shouted. "There's no arguing with that, Rette! Profound, don't you think? Perhaps, Mr Mole, this is what MOLE stands for—Meaning Of Life Explained—eh? Yes, yes! Such is the eternal challenge of the road. 'There is always another car up ahead'! But you see, Mr Mole, a car overtaken is still very much a car to the rear—another abject also-drove who has no choice but to view one's noble stern. One by one, one by one, each new overtakee must taste *our* grit, mizzle over with *our* spray-grease, gnash his fangs in futile frustration at the glorious and enviable sight of *our* rapidly dwindling poop! Really, it'd be a shame if there weren't other cars up front to do the same to!"

And sure enough, ahead of them now in the outermost lane a very large cream-white *motor* was visible. It was of the chauffeur-controlled, monarchy-mimicking, lumbering-stateswagon variety, and as the Toad got closer to it he read the number-plate, bearing as it did the denomination SAS 111.

"Well, well, you see, if it isn't Shrewsbury," he said. "Formerly of R.N.Z. and a small failed transnational outfit by the name of ImpAgrocon. We have got him out of the way more than once in the past, Mr Mole, and now, you see, here he is again, sitting smack bang in the middle of the fast lane as if he still had some right to be here!"

The crushed-flat Jowlett surged ahead at yet higher speed until it was only a few feet behind the huge pale *motor* with its broad, shallow gun-slot of a rear window. The Toad began his ritual of dipping and flashing, but the big machine carried on just as it had been doing, passing a long procession of crawlers doing less than ninety in the middle lane.

"... And we will get him out of the way *again*," said the magnate quietly. Next to him, the Water Rat had by now sunk into the profound silence of the soon-to-be-dead. His eyes, like the Mole's, were closed.

Mr Wyvern-Toad dipped, flashed, dipped, flashed, and drove almost near enough to the big *motor* to touch bumpers with it. As he did this for the third time a small, two-tone, needle-fanged face appeared briefly in the wide rear window. It stared, both at the vehicle behind it and (in the moments of dipping) at the silhouette of its driver, then retired from view again; and in a few seconds more the pale cream vehicle had increased its lead, if only by ten to twenty yards.

"Oh, we're not having *that*, son-of-a-Shroe," sputtered the Toad. "Who *do* you think you are, mal?" Another second or two and the Jowlett in all its ironed-out singularity was reattached to the pale lumberer's rear end, though by now both *motors* were travelling at upwards of thirty miles per hour faster then before. The Clearway tar sped under them as if unspooling from some vast machine hidden beyond the invisible horizon—a machine now revved up to a point where gearing differentials would soon begin to chew themselves apart, and bearings spray from their seatings into the black night sky.

But Mr Shrewsbury's humiliation was already scripted into the random placing of the machines flashing along that stretch of road. Ahead of his period *motor* was a banal fat-bottomed executive vehicle of the 99.3-pence-per-mile company-car-allowance type, moving at barely more than a hundred, and since Mr Shrewsbury's chauffeur was far too fastidious a driver to slip into the middle lane and pull past this machine on its inside flank, the only choice open to him was to slow down to the same speed.

The Toad, however, was hamstrung by no such scruple. Immediately the illegitimate overtaking-space became available he sliced leftwards, surging ahead with a deepening of the volcano-voice to a level resembling that of some vast underground explosion. In less time than it takes for a company to be bankrupted by a run on its shares he had passed both vehicles and restored himself, exultant once more, to his glorious reward: more than a quarter of a mile of metallically-unpopulated tar.

"Thus the Shroe is buried! ... I *come not* to bury Shroe! Merely to overtake him!" crooned the Toad, inhaling the sweet spring scents of his triumph, wallowing in the thickly ladled patisserie creams of self-delight. "Can't rely on *chauffeurs*, Shroes-nose—no, no, no! Have to do these things for ourselves, don't we, like big animals? And that, Shroe-features, is why *I*, Humfrey d'Etanguy de Buforchy Wyvern-Toad, have got ImpAgrocon, and *you* will be getting a transfer to the board of the Phoenowipe recycled-kitchen-towel company or the like!"

Mr Wyvern-Toad glanced at his somewhat plank-like front passenger. "Not anxious about anything, are we, Gordon?" he asked.

"I'm terrified—terrified—TERRIFIED—TERRIFIED —*TERRIFIED*!" blurted Mr Rette, in a voice blending tooth-less infant and querulous elderly dame in roughly equal parts.

The Toad looked at his passenger once, then again, and giggled, his giggle swiftly deepening into a full-blown belly-laugh. "The Mole Effect!" he cried. "Don't you feel *better* for that, Gordon? You do see how therapeutic it is, don't you? Though why you feel the need to be terrified in the hands of one of the world's most accomplished drivers is impossible to understand. Come on, animal—open your eyes for Pansake!"

"Vwill we be there thoon?" said the Mole.

"Very, very soon," answered the Toad. "... What? Not *another* oozing slugmobile in one's path! You know, Gordon, I don't have the slightest doubt where this country's Asphalt-Aggregation Programme should be going—do you? It's painfully clear we need a second, entirely separate Clearway network. So that we—what *shall* I say?—false modesty remains impossible, of course, in Mr Mole's presence—we Drivers of Significance can separate ourselves out completely from these silted riverbeds of the *hoi polloi*? You see, vehicles like *that* (he nodded to a dangerously slow-moving van, doing no more than sixty in the slow lane and decorated along one side with a crude painting of a tree with a sun behind it) which is no doubt crammed to the roof-weld with dropped-out, flea-bitten, mat-furred weirdites *driving* to some *anti-road* protest or other! What is *that* vehicle doing, sharing this road with ... *me*? It is one of the great truths of what we call

Democracy that *any* restriction on *my* freedom of movement (and yours too, Gordon, yours too) is an affront to the principle of Individual Liberty. I'm sure you'd agree?"

Hearing a slight slackening of volcanic intensity, Mr Rette had by now managed to half-open his eyes. "Oh, yuh—*ye*—" he said.

"And I'm sure you'd also agree," continued Mr Wyvern-Toad, "that the new network should be operated on a toll system, very prohibitively priced, so that all except Animals of Significance will be firmly deterred from using it. It's only fair, isn't it? One must have an open road (with, of course, the occasional overtakee up ahead) to go about one's affairs. We can't fly everywhere all the time!"

"*Ye—ye—*"

"In a Democracy, animals must be free to do as they please," waxed the Toad. "They must be free to drive their cars, and burn our products, to their hearts' delight. But we must also be free to get away from *them*, and really, you know, there should always be roads exactly where *I* happen to want them!"

Mr Rette cleared his throat as he fumbled with his tie-knot. "But as things are going at the moment—" he said.

"Oh! As things are going at the moment, Gordon, give it another ten to fifteen years and the place will have deteriorated to Underworld standards! The surfaces are well on the way in places already, I don't need to tell you. If the funds aren't pumped in soon we'll all end up slithering about in two-hundred-metre-wide-churned sloughs like something out of one of Mr Mole's rain-forests! *You'll* be at home in any case, Mr Mole! "

"… Mmm? …"

"It is appalling, of course," said Mr Rette, rallying. "Y-yes. Certainly it is. I suppose you've seen the latest figures from the Office of Congestion Planning?"

"Naturally, Gordon! What is it—permanent blockage on

upwards of forty per cent of the network except between two thirty and three forty-five a.m. by 2020? And after that? Good Pan, no! Something has got to give, and soon! What do you think about this, Mr Mole? As one who is seeing his country, I'd imagine, with the refreshed perceptions of the returnee?"

"I don't understand why they all have to travel about so much," mumbled the Mole. "Or at all, really. But if they do— have to, I mean—well, why can't they go by train?"

"Train? *Train!* My dear mal, the railways were put out of the picture decades ago!" replied the Toad. "Decades! How long have you been away? No one wanted *them*. There's no particularly useful symbol of individual liberty to be found in standing about every day on some grim windswept platform waiting for the delayed oh-seven-oh-eight with all the other sad grey flat-ears, and then sitting or standing in some crowded carriage that is *not one's own!* Great Dane! Even those at heap-bottom recognise the aristocratic distinction of being able to travel in a personalized machine, and let's not worry too much if its wings are about to drop off, or the doors are a different colour from the rest of it!"

"But there seem to be so many *motors*—"

"Of *course* there are! Of *course* there are! That is exactly as it should be! You do realise, I suppose, that vehicle manufacture and the allied trades—one's own included—now account for no less than one tenth of the working animals in this country?"

The Mole's heart sank a little. "O," he said.

"Yes, yes! One of the main *purposes* of roads is to let animals get about to make more cars! From which—obviously—the need for further roads arises. Do you know, there will be enough cars made here in the next six months to completely fill a new eight-lane Clearway between Milford Haven and the Moray Firth? Which is of course a perfect reason for building one instantly! And very good for business it is, too. The country's economy—the whole thing—is founded on—this."

The Toad gestured outward, grandiosely, with both hands (at which a very slightly manacled groan emerged from Mr Rette).

"But does it—" said the Mole, "O, I don't know! Does it make animals *happy*?"

"'Happy'!" The Toad almost wept with hilarity. "'Happy'! Mr Mole, you should be a satirist!"

"No, but I mean," the Mole persisted, "mightn't animals *be* happier if they were making other things? That they could use for something else than all this motoring about? I don't know—rowing boats?—rowlocks?—fishing rods?—carts?—horse-harnesses? —"

Mr Wyvern-Toad roared with laughter.

"— Wire baskets (to put ferns in)? Garden seats? Coal-scuttles? Skittles? Hoes? Biscuit-tins? Teapots, tea-cosies, teapot-stands, tea-caddies, teaspoons …?"

"Stop, Mr Mole—stop—stop!" implored the by now near-hysterical Toad, whose eyes were streaming so much that even as one of the world's most accomplished drivers he may have been in danger of losing control of his vehicle.

"I wathn't *being* thunny," muttered the Mole, almost inaudibly, returning to his seat-surface.

"What animals own is what makes them happy, Mr Mole," said the Toad after a moment, his calm restored. "Just that. Only that."

At this point they left the Clearway, and the Toad auto-matically geared himself down for the use of all those everyday techniques of the world-class driver on lesser roads: the Skilled Not-Seeing Of Vehicles Already Approaching On Roundabouts, the Expert Non-Use Of Signals (except of course for permanent main beam when to the rear of slow movers), the Dazzling Exploitation Of Long Blind Bends For Overtaking, and so on, and so forth. Rat and Mole both quickly retired again to their close-lidded, subliminally-moaning states, so that the former was at once startled and dismayed when eventually he heard the Toad say, "Damn! You know, I've forgotten to drop you off!"

Daring to open his eyes, the Rat saw that they had penetrated the upland to the north of his part of the valley, and were already very close to Mr Wyvern-Toad's residence.

"Enjoying myself too much, I suppose," said the Toad with uncharacteristic vagueness. "Never mind! Stay at my place tonight!"

The Water Rat considered this idea for the briefest interval, before recognising its single most important implication—a return journey with the Toad in the morning. "But—my wife! My children!" he said imploringly.

"They'll all be in bed by now anyway, won't they, Gordon? You'll just wake 'em up. Come on! You can phone through. Janet won't mind, will she?"

"That's very kind of you, W-T," truckled Mr Rette.

"Are we going to Toad Towers?" asked the Mole.

"No, no," responded the heavily-steering Toad. "Don't live *there* any more. That's all handled by one of our entertainments partnerships nowadays. My current U.K. residence is just up the road here. Temporary place, really. Much more modest. A lot less draughty, too!"

"O—so your real home is in Oxfordshire, then?"

"My real home ..." The Toad fell silent a moment as if ruminating. "Don't know about that, Mr Mole, to tell you the truth. One has—aahh—twenty-seven residences in all if you include the islands but not, of course, the yachts. L.A.? Saudi? The Glen Feshie Lodge? Japan? Antibes?—Oh, all over the place, you know. One is, you see, something of a Citizen of the World. One does not precisely *own* these places, you understand (and here, falteringly, the Toad's voice took on a note of piety), "it is more that one—ahm—looks after them, one has *stewardship* over them, *managing* them for the *benefit* of the generations to come." (There was a pause the length of a single abbreviated rat-moan before he continued.) "Although one does own them, of course! One *very much* owns them, one pandamned well owns every last one of them, and very nice it is, too, in one's own opinion! Ha, ha, ha! … The Mole Effect! The astonishing Mole Effect!"

"… But—" persisted the Mole once more, "where is *home*? 'Scuse my asking, but—there must be *one* place that you call *home*?"

Had the Mole allowed himself the freedom of sight just then, he might have been able to pick out a mirror reflection of the Toad's face as it grew weighty with weariness, much as it had done earlier, and became—if only briefly—the face of a far older animal. Instead, he waited, kid-blinkered, for the magnate's reply. Mole Effect or no Mole Effect, he did not get one.

CHAPTER SEVEN

THE BITER'S BIT

The Mole was wakened from his slumbers by the sound of voices—or rather, by the sound of one voice in particular. This was reverberating loudly enough to reach him even inside the copious depths of the empty, wall-length, mirror-covered wardrobe that had been his last night's resting place (for reasons that probably do not need to be explained).

He crawled slowly upward, scrabbling in momentary panic at the back of the nearest door until he remembered that it operated on a *sliding* principle. This released him into a paddock-sized bedroom done out entirely in shades of white and the palest blue-grey. As yet there was no sign of daylight visible in the uncomfortable crack between the long striped blinds and the thirty-foot-long dressed stone window frame.

A knock at the door revealed to his still-blurry vision the presence of an impeccably coiffurred, mascara'd young female rabbit dressed in a dark blue suit, plum-coloured silk shirt and matching scarf. She bore in front of her a fully laden break-fast tray, and stood wreathed about in the mingled scents of perfume and coffee, both of them of the highest quality.

"Mr Wyvern-Toad and Mr Rette will be leaving in five minutes, Mr Mole?" she said, in the brisk voice of the natural organiser. (Had he ever heard the relevant speech tones, the Mole might at this point have guessed her to originate from New Zealand.) "W-T hoped to have a word with you, if it isn't too early for you? Shall I leave this, or I can bring you something later if you prefer? Do you like kippers, by the way—we have kedgeree, if not?"

"O ... yes, ummm ... thank you. I'm very partial to a nice kipper," responded the Mole not ungratefully, though his stomach was as yet even less awake than the rest of him.

"Mr *Mole* ... Mr *Mole* ..." boomed the Toad's voice from somewhere round the corner of the open door. Then his broad green face appeared in it, followed by the rest of him, and the antipodean doe was briskly gone. "Ah good. You're conscious, I see! Excellent. I do hope this isn't too absurdly early for you. Busy day, you know—many nuts to crack, pips to squeak, shells to crush, so on and so forth! Have to be off, but I did just want to say—think about that little suggestion of mine, won't you? You might find it a bit of a change from the malarial mosquitoes, even if it was just for a while!"

"... Moss—Quay—Toes ...?"

"Yes and, oh, do stop over again tonight, by the way, unless you had any other plans. It's the first day of the To-We Party Conference tomorrow. You might be curious to come along with us—catch up on some of the latest and most radical developments in politics, such as we are told to expect."

"O, well, er—if Mr Rette doesn't mind."

"He doesn't mind! He doesn't mind! Just make yourself at home, my dear animal!"

With that the mogul was off on the breeze, leaving the Mole to enjoy the most luxurious breakfast he had ever tasted in his life—a breakfast he made last so long (in combination with a little essential grooming) that the day was quite well established before he had emerged from his room.

His previous night's sleepy first impressions of the house interior were confirmed by the briefest stroll around it. It was just like another 'art gallery', he thought, though this time done with proper plastered walls, all painted in an even and unbroken white, like cake icing, rather than that dreadful depressing blotchstuff.

All the walls and door-less arches had been modelled in a series of very odd and unpredictable geometric shapes, so that each room went off at a different angle. Many samplings of the art of the day were to be found here, either hanging, or set on plain stone pedestals. Interspersed amongst these objects—which to the Mole looked mostly like waste-tip escapees—were some things from earlier ages: large ornate cabinets of curving orange-gold wood made with scores of little drawers; dark swaths of tapestry and other old stuffs, some of them quaintly beaded and bearing images of animals, of which the majority were toads.

At the end of the main entrance hall stood a vast and gaudily painted urn whose many turns and decorative flourishes were covered in what looked like gold. To one side of this, built in as a partition, there stood a long section of a wonderfully carved wooden screen covered in strap-work decorations and odd little figures. In some vague way this seemed familiar.

In its severe simplicity, the long dining room beyond also looked to the Mole very much like another of those places where business was done. Here, in a backlit recess, he found a sculpture made in alabaster. It represented the short, podgily bulbous form of a toad in mottled armour and what may have been meant to be velvet pantaloons. The figure stood, one hand on his waist, his elbow pushed demonstratively forward, a sheathed dagger behind his thigh, looking up to the heavens in a peremptory, Pan-or-any-other-god-defying style that seemed to say, "Do what you will with me, Sir, but I am an Animal of Some Significance, and you will be well advised not to forget the fact." In his other hand this figure held forth a scroll, perhaps of pedigree, and his cravat-filling visage with its remote, intolerant gaze was decorated with a goatee beard of the most sharply-pointed type, and a moustache so full it resembled a pair of drooping black puddings. Beneath it, four clumsily-carved tragickal toad-cherubs (or were they frogs?) wept, lamented or stared in crazed disbelief as they emerged from pomegranates. An inscription identified this personage as Mountague d'Etanguy de Buforchy Wyvern-Toad (d. 1638).

The Mole could not help noticing that two of the chairs at the dining table were just out of line. Absent-mindedly, he wandered over to put them straight, and in so doing he realised that he had nothing else to do here now *except* to straighten chairs.

'Spose I can always go for another walk, he thought. The idea did not excite him, exactly, but his curious half was already thinking about the possibilities.

Eventually he stepped outside, to find that the house was much older (or at least, less modern) than he could possibly have guessed from within. It was huge, but not vast—a slightly rambling place with several steeply sloping roofs, and its walls were covered with a rough-looking stuff that had weathered down to a dull greenish grey, all very unostentatious. The Mole noticed that all of the windows away from the few rooms he had seen were blanked out with white shutters. He wandered through orderly but unexciting gardens to find a swimming pool, blaring turquoise under a cloudy sky, which he eventually saw had been made in the outline of a *motor*.

The gardens were walled on three out of four sides, and on the fourth the Mole came to a big, big view. It was of a kind that estate agents publishing in *The Riverbanker* might have described as being "across open fields" or "with a magnificent panorama of the Vale of Somewhere-Or-Other and the Downs of Somewhere-Or-Other-Else", but was in reality across *an* open "field" that spanned the entire mile-and-a-half drop from the ridge on which the house sat to the beginnings of the rolling country beneath it. This was marked with absolute symmetry by lines of young green wheat, and showed barely a hint of any other kind of plant-life. Even in March, the soil in it looked crumbling dry, as if it had been baked by the heat of an August sun. Both here and in the far distance—where shallow spurs intersected vaguely—the highest points of each great space had about them the whiteness of bleached bone.

The Mole recoiled from this void even as he saw it, finding his way back in the direction of an entrance gate. Here he encountered a tall Alsatian in peaked cap and black guard's uniform, sporting a pistol at his waist. His teeth were all his own and he looked to the Mole very much *not* the kind of animal to have a disagreement with, even over the price of a pound of runner-beans.

"Going out, sir?" said this animal deferentially. "Yes, of course. Just one moment, sir, if you don't mind. I must disarm the car-gun." He stepped into a small brick building at the side of the gate and pressed something.

"… *Car-gun?*" echoed the Mole, accurately for once.

"Oh—yes, sir," replied the Alsatian. "Shoots a projectile through the bottoms of visitors' cars. Only when they're not welcome, of course, ha, ha. Ha, ha!—Ha. State-of-the-art, you know, like everything always is with Mr Wyvern-Toad. Good practice to switch it off though, even if someone is just walking through. Shouldn't go off then anyway, of course!"

"O-o-o-o … good…" said the Mole not un-tremulously, stepping very gingerly around the outmost pencil-thin edge of the entrance grille. "Thank you." Pausing in the midst of his first stride in the direction of nowhere in particular, he added, "Could you tell me the name of this house? Just in case I—um got lost, or anything?"

"This is Darkwood Park, sir," replied the Alsatian, the faintest hint of surprise colouring his formal style.

"— O, and do you know, will I find Toad H … er—Toad *Towers* anywhere nearby?"

"Oh yes, sir—yes, you will. Down in the valley, couple of miles at most. Just follow that road (though of course it would be more advisable to drive, really)." Brightening a little, the big dog added, "You want to go on the Doom Tube, sir, if you're going down there. Blow your fur off, that will."

The Mole paused. He did not like the sound of this. But then, he thought, he didn't like the sound of *anything* very much. "Right you are," he said. "Mornin'." And off he went, as boldly as might any mole when time is no longer with him.

After walking for half an hour or so he began to descend a long hill. To the left of the road here he saw the beginnings of another barrier, in the shape of an approximately fifteen-mole-high wire fence discreetly topped with double-stranded barbed wire. What could be behind it? Some awesomely powerful military establishment? Some dread prison camp for the nation's most dangerous criminals? The "New-clear Research Place" Mr Rette had mentioned? The fence lost itself in rhododendrons and tall beeches, and then reappeared again further down the hill, continuing for as far as the eye could see. Beyond it—all but buried by ivy and mosses—he could just make out the line of a former wall marked as banks of brick rubble.

Continuing on down, the Mole began to hear strange sounds floating through the tree-branches—heavy whirrings and grindings, as of the working of devilish machines; over-lapping metallic tinklings and trumpetings, as of music-making, of a kind; wild tormented screamings and cackling laughter which came in waves then died away. In the road ahead there stood a virtually static queue of *motors*. On the side opposite the fence there was a high bank, topped with a rough footpath, which he duly climbed to get away from them.

Looking back towards the fence the Mole now saw a ghastly and, as so often, impossible sight: a miniature, open-topped train that was—yes!—impossible!—flying by *at treetop height.* This prodigy reared up into a space between the beech trees bearing a cargo of screaming hares and rabbits, all clutching at one another, their ears streaming out behind them in the wind, then dropped out of sight at another non-feasible angle. As the Mole stared open-mouthed at the high gap in the trees it was filled a second time by a flying train, again crammed with clutching hares and rabbits, and a quartet of quailing dormice.

"O but what awful place is this, now?" said the Mole, half out loud.

He followed the line of the *motor*-queue onwards down the hill until it turned into a boldly signed car park. Another hundred yards further on, the trees ended altogether and a great bare space opened on to a low building at which many animals had formed into a series of long queues. Fixed on this was a sign made out of shining spots of light in several colours, and this read:

TOAD TOWERS

YOU ARE ENTERING

THE ENTERTANEMENT ZONE!!!

Beyond building and sign stretched a landscape out of Hades itself. Here, in any one of a dozen different nightmarish enclosures, animals were being whirled about by great mechanical arms, or cannoned through watersplashes on log-shaped boats, or flung around in things that looked like gigantic cored apples, or spun upside down and back again in

gargantuan bananas, or whirled and spun in rotating transparent tubes. Yet, for all the horror of it, the Mole could not
fail to observe that the queues were forming, not on the far
side of the building, as if in hope of release, but the other way
round.

"'Entert-A-numment Zone'?" gulped the Mole. Even as he
read the words, he spotted what could only be Toad Towers
itself, partly hidden as it was by a great dome-thing
constructed of silvery hexagonal sheets. The house was
completely unfamiliar to him: a strange, bodged-together
fantasy of clock-tower, castellated turrets, spires and steeply
pitched roofs, the latter covered in tiles glazed in alternating
layers of peacock-green, gold and magenta, like the scales of
some exotic lizard skin.

Another sign to the right of the line of kiosks told him:

NEW THIS YEAR!
VISIT

TOAD TOWERS

THE HISTORIC HOUSE
STATELY-HERITAGE EXPERIENCE

AS IT BECKONS TO YOU FROM ACROSS THE CENTURIES

DRESS AS LORD OR LADY, AS BUTLER, HOUSE-
KEEPER, COACHMAN, NANNY (WE SUPPLY THE
COSTUMES!)

RE-ENACT THE LIFESTYLES OF YESTERYEAR —
YOU'LL LEAVE A COMPLETELY DIFFERENT ANIMAL!

Next to this stood a thrice-life-size drawing of a hedgehog
holding a feather duster and wearing a mob-cap of a style
instantly familiar to the Mole, whilst not far away yet another
sign announced:

OPENING HERE IN JULY!
THE WORLD PREMIERE
OF
ULF THE EARWIG
On Ice

The Mole stared, glassy-eyed. What was it that Mr Wyvern-Toad had said? Toad Hall had been burned down? And Toad Towers had been put up to replace it? And had all *this* been put up with it? No! Was that possible? He searched the expanse of whirlings, spinnings and plungings for any sign of the place he remembered. But there was nothing there—no hint—unless perhaps it was in the mix of colours in the beeches, yews and hollies that widely framed the windswept entrance, like a single lingering note of some long-forgotten tune.

From here, of course, the Mole knew exactly which way the river lay. But he did not want to go that way now. So he started back up the long hill, and after about three quarters of a mile he came to a junction where a much quieter road led off to his left. He turned along it, wandering on for another three miles—more, perhaps—following his own nose, taking in little or nothing of what he passed through.

He found himself walking along the wide mouth of a great empty downland combe. Though he was once more in a landscape of bare cultivation, with bits of hawthorn-dotted turf visible only on the steepest slopes, his view of the combe was obscured by fragments of a tall, outgrown thorn hedge. Half way along this—like some sad museum relic of a time when animals still used their legs to get about—he saw a dilapidated stile.

The Mole hesitated for just one moment, then clambered over the stile's rotting timbers and stood on one of the ridges of the deep-ploughed field beyond. From here, he could see that the steepest edges of the combe were fringed with solidly dark conifer plantations. At this distance they resembled fur that had been set with some vast wet comb, one diagonal row running parallel to the next. On the left hill flank though, a series of less predictable rounded shapes suggested the beginnings of older woodland near the hilltop.

It is probably true that the Mole had never quite lost his fear of the Wild Wood of his own home valley, in his own home time. But as he had come to know it over the years, familiarity had bred in him a guarded kind of love for the place, so that now—seeing something here that resembled it even faintly—he knew he would have to climb up to it. He staggered out across the corrugated field (there was no sign of a path) until he reached a hard-surfaced farm road. This led on into the combe, where it split into two. The right hand way curved off to join the hillside under the facing strip of woodland, where it became a rubble road of huge and ugly dimensions, resting on a new and staring-white bank of excavated chalk. As the Mole was looking at this—dismayed, as ever, by the bludgeoning crudity of the work—a group of roughly twenty riders descended on to it from some hidden channel in the trees, followed by a crawling, bumping and lurching chain of *motors*. All but one of these were made in the snouted-shoebox style, and even at a distance of nearly a mile the colour of the riders' costumes—blazing scarlet against the jetty greens of the trees—told the Mole he was in the presence of the hunt.

"How odd," said the Mole to himself. "—No, how *very* odd!" Here he was in The Future, where it seemed almost everything he had known and loved about the countryside had vanished. Yet here too, plain as plain amongst the greater blankness, was one of the old, old things—one that he had no love for, one of the last things he would have hoped to find here—carrying on just as if nothing else had changed.

For the animals of the Mole's day and circle, the hunt was one of those things that was simply not discussed. It did not run over their stretch of the Riverbank, and that was all they had needed to know. It was—had been—one of those activities that went on in the great elsewhere, and the less said about it the better. No question now that the Mole would walk in the opposite direction which, luckily, should also get him to his chosen destination.

A number of signs gleamed threateningly at him from the conifer-edge. One read: "This wood is managed by Outflow Forestry, a division of FrugoNatch TreeManagement Group P.L.C." Another admonished: AUTHORIZED ACCESS ONLY. Another advised: "Conservation Area: Please keep to the Pathmarked Ways". Another, twenty yards or so further up a sidetrack, shouted: "PRIVATE WOODLANDS! *No Path.*" (The Mole half expected to find another board demanding "Now: have you read all the signs? *And What Did They Say?*" but he did not spot one.)

"Conservation" area? he ruminated, as he continued on alongside the dry, leafless, suffocating depths of the plantation, whose rows of virtually branchless boles looked like nothing so much as the piers of a vast dark tomb. He could see no mosses, no flowers, and the one bird singing appeared to be singing from somewhere else entirely. And was it *really* possible that they made jam here?

From the other side of the combe—now well out of sight—he heard a distant babbling of hounds and the single, abbreviated sounding of a horn. He straightened his smoking-jacket: he was, after all, the most respectable kind of mole—known for it throughout his neighbourhood—and things like this had nothing to do with him. Yet again he quickened his pace, wanting nothing more now than to be as far away from this spot as possible. Deep in his mind, where he would not quite recognise it as such, there lurked a quite irrational fear that, respectable or not, this hunt might take it into its head to latch on to *him*—choose *him* as its quarry. How could he know for sure they did not have mole-hunts now? Even where the moles concerned were of the speech-making kind? His brow damp, he hurried on up the track with (so far as possible) ever-lengthening paces.

It was then he thought he heard the chink of horseshoes on hard metalling, somewhere down in the combe behind him, but much closer than the riders he had seen. Pausing, he listened, and heard the sound again, a little louder now.

"O-o-o-o-o . . ." he moaned, his earlier tolerably convincing Citizen-out-strolling strides transformed now into a panicky run. "O dear, O, dear!" he groaned. He just had to get off this track!

Another narrow, grassy division between conifer blocks was coming up on his right. Ignoring the PRIVATE WOOD-LANDS sign he scurried into it and followed it for many hundreds of yards until it ended, not with more Sitka-tombland but in an expanse of low hazel coppice whose pale leaning stems caught the colour of the sky in their bark. Pushing on through this—forcing aside the living hazels, and breaking his way through the still standing but papery dead ones—he emerged two or three minutes later into a steep clearing on the down-side, a place that might have been pasture once. It was smooth-grazed now by rabbits, though only in patches between encroaching scrub and brambles.

The Mole paused, panting, his heart thumping at the side of his chest and drumming its drumbeat hard inside his ears. Then those same ears pricked up again.

There was something in the hazel copse behind him—the copse from which he had just emerged. He could hear the faintest crackling of dessicated timber and the soft crish-crush, crish-crush of light paw-steps on the damp compost of last autumn's fallen leaves. Whatever it was, it was moving at great speed, and towards him. Even as he listened on, he saw its glistening eyes, its tapering snout and its auburn-and-white-furred face emerge beyond a clump of brambles. It was a fox.—It was *the* fox!

It ran out into the clearing, seeing him, yet far more in fear of what lay behind. And perhaps it did not fear the Mole at all. It ran on right by him, head dropped, tail drooped so low it brushed the rabbit-droppings off their makers' grassy perches. How small it was, thought the Mole—but then that was often the case, wasn't it, with the Unclothed animals? As it passed him the Fox made a low, barely audible crying-bark that seemed to say, *Get out of here, you fool! Get out! They're on to us!*

This was more than enough to remobilise the Mole. Terror now engraved as lines across his vision, his heart pumping as crazily as a derailed toy locomotive, he plunged after the hunted creature (even though in his reasoning mind he knew this made no sense), bursting into the clawing-tripping-brambled edge of another stand of trees at just the moment when two huntsmals came into sight on the ground above. That was where the track he had been following led to! These two—a toad and a weasel as flamboyantly attired on their steaming, panting, sheen-flanked steeds as ever they had been in olden days—caught sight of the Mole, the respectably if oddly dressed Citizen-Mole, as he flailed and struggled with restraining briars and then, freed, hurled himself on out of sight into the woodland.

"Was that a supporter?" demanded the one of the other in a Myrmidon's voice.

"Not sure! Didn't look like one: though he was wearing a shirt and tie of some sort!" replied the other to the one, as hero unto hero.

They galloped on along the track. Being high on the hill, this track separated the Fox and the Mole, in their refuge on the steep wooded slope beneath it, from any more secure retreat amongst the trees on the flat hill top above.

The Mole plunged after the hunted animal, tripping on roots, sliding sideways on damp pieces of fallen wood, dodging the squirls of honeysuckle that trailed against his face, crawling in places where he found no other way through the barriers before him. But moments later he found himself on a path of sorts—a deer trail out across a now open woodland floor of dog's mercury and ramsons, the latter not yet in flower but already filling the air with their hints and wafts of garlic. Here and there ancient ash pollards thrust themselves up under a canopy of sycamore, some resembling dancers with dropped heads and up-thrust arms, others gargoyle-faces, club nosed and thick lipped around their gaping rot-filled "mouths" and wearing pairs of madly twisted rabbit ears.

Perhaps aware of the dilemma facing them, the Fox was now trotting on slowly enough for the Mole to keep up, with an effort. Where to cut up across the track without being spotted by these two—evidently outriders from the rest—that was the problem. But the Fox made no pause, continuing on along the contours of the steep slope for what seemed, to the increasingly exhausted Mole, like miles.

Was the combe itself narrowing? And was that, now— could it be possible?—*another* great breathing-roar, as of *another* titanic road, he heard ahead of him? Or was it just the sound of a freshening wind in the treetops? Suddenly the Fox veered upward in the direction of the track, if track it still was. Again the Mole followed blindly as if the Fox might be able to lead him to some safe haven, some lair that could not be dug out with spades, or penetrated by trap-jawed terriers. But even as he emerged from the trees he heard behind him a shout of recognition and the thudding of approaching hooves.

What happened then took place too swiftly and confusingly for the Mole to make any real sense of it. He saw the Fox, momentarily stymied in the centre of the track to his right, but he also saw other figures—tall, grey-and-white-furred, combative, powerful-looking figures—emerging towards him out of the deep shade of a plantation of conifers on its far side. Two of these stepped out on to the track and threw something down over the ground where the Fox had been standing. Two others came out to his left, one armed with a rifle, the other with an ancient-looking cudgel. The former raised his weapon towards the riders. Then the Mole saw no more, his vision shockingly shut off in blackness by material pulled tight over his face and tied behind his head. Something that felt suspiciously like the butt of a gun was thrust into his back, and a growling voice said, "Come on animal—move!"

Guided on by the occasional thrust, or by an arm holding his own to steer him, and with muffled cries of protest coming from animals on both sides, the Mole walked, stumbled, and walked on again in deepening blackness. From the flatness of the ground he could tell that they were on the hilltop, whilst the continuous crackling of dry twigs and branches beneath his feet, coupled with the almost complete absence of light around his blindfold, suggested that they were walking across the woodland floor and that the woods here were once again plantations.

Eventually the group paused at a spot where the breathing-roar was strong. He heard a sound as of dead branches being pulled back, and the heavy scraping of a timber door-brace, and then found himself being guided down steps—scores, perhaps hundreds of them—to a place where the ground levelled out once more and the air was warm and pungent with the presence of animals.

"Give that Mole his sight back first," said a rough-throated, slightly threatening voice from somewhere behind him. "Leave those others."

"This is outrageous!" exclaimed a much lighter voice. "This is *broodnap*-with-use-of-force-of-arms! A most *indictable* criminal offence!"

Sharp-clawed paws fumbled irritably with the material of the Mole's blindfold and there was a muttering and a cursing and a "Which hamfisted clot tied *this* damned knot?" After a low growl of frustration the cloth was tugged free over the Mole's nose, which proved just pliable enough to let it by.

The captive found himself in a place that was at once familiar and very strange. It was a big sett-chamber whose furnishings, all of them threadbare, made it look like some curious hybrid of a none-too-clean kitchen and a war-room. Unwashed mugs and a big chipped brown teapot stood on a tea-and-otherwise-stained deal table, and on the straighter pieces of wall hung maps and charts marked out with pins and tape crosses. In one of several dark and looming passage entrances stood a rack for guns. But it was the place's occupants that drew the Mole's gaze. These included five large young badgers, each of them dressed in variegated combat gear, a tough-looking scarred otter, and an immense, elderly hare sporting an eye-patch and wearing a bullet-belt across his chest. Two of these animals were carrying guns that had obviously seen many years of use, and two of the young badgers each gripped the arm of a blindfolded huntsmal. A pheasant with a bandaged wing was also picking along the edge of one wall, and beneath the table the Mole could see the white tip of the Fox's brush just protruding into sight.

"Well, Mole! So you like to follow the hunt in your spare time, do you?" demanded the hoarse voice. "Or support it anyway? Unusual interest for a mole. Bit on the violent side, wouldn't you say?"

"I do *not* follow it!" retorted the Mole angrily, turning to the voice's source, a yet larger and older badger, whose markings instantly suggested him to be father to the rest. "I thought *it* was following me!"

There was unbridled, snarling laughter throughout the chamber at this remark, not least from the one-eyed hare, whose visible eye streamed with tears of amusement. But then the Fox emerged a few inches from beneath the table, cowering back momentarily at the sight of the blindfolded hunters. It made its crying-bark and again the Mole thought that he could almost understand it, though no words of the civilised language had been spoken.

He is speaking the truth, it seemed to say. *He ran with me.*

"Well, well, well!" responded the badger-elder. "Now that's not what you normally expect of the Clothed and Worded, is it? Not even moles!"

He walked slowly towards the Mole, scrutinising him, and a look of puzzlement briefly clouded his expression. "You don't set hounds on your fellow-citizens now as well, do you? I'm talking to you, Toad! Pay attention!"

"We most certainly do not," replied the huntsmal in a clipped, impersonal tone worthy of a prisoner-of-war.

"Good. Take off their blindfolds. And a warning, you two of the 'pink'. We are well armed here."

"— Oh, *really*," breathed the Weasel in haughty dismay when he saw the nature of his surroundings. "Really—this cannot be possible!"

"So, Mr Toad," said the Badger elder. "Take a seat, if you like."

"I prefer to stand," replied the Toad, eyeing chairs and table with disgust. "*Major* Tode," he added peremptorily. "Major F.T. Curfieu-Tode (Retired), Master of the Oxfordshire and Berkshire Borders Foxhounds."

"Well, boys," said the Badger. "We are honoured with the presence of a Master here. Show respect, now. So, tell me, Major—"

"Is this an interrogation?" demanded the Toad.

"It is!"

"On whose authority?"

"I don't think you need ask us that, Major."

"In that case, I refuse to participate."

"All right then," said the Badger, taking two steps towards the defiant amphibian, his shadow falling from a height across the dismayed green face. "... The authority is mine. So, tell me, Major Toad—"

"Tode," interrupted the Toad, though in a cracking voice. "Curfieu-Tode."

"I see. Well then, tell me, Major—you're not troubled by any personal doubts, I suppose, about hunting your fellow-animals?"

"A fox is not a fellow-animal!" replied the Toad, spitting out the words as if it disgusted him to speak them.

"Oh? I see. In what way is he different?"

"That is a ludicrous question! *It* is a creature of the lower orders. *It* is a member of the great Unclothed. It lacks words. And amongst the furred, as we all know, it is a sub-animal, the lowest of the low. What is more, it is a cunning, vicious creature. It will kill simply for pleasure, and not because it needs to eat—ask anyone who keeps a hen-run. And if we did not control them, they would be everywhere. Only scruffnecks who live in holes beneath the ground could possibly fail to know this."

"... And when toads and weasels and others of the Clothed and Worded ride to hounds, as you put it, in pursuit of the fox, would you say they are killing because *they* need to eat, or, who can say now—for some other reason perhaps? Do we know any recipes for fox, boys? Fox-and-ham pie—no? Fox soufflé? *Filet-de-Renard-aux-prunes*?" (Here the Fox cowered back into the shadows, a confused expression on his face, and the Badger added, "I do beg your pardon, Fox. Very insensitive of me.")

"Oh, dear, dear, dear," mewled the Weasel derisively. "He's *talking* to it now!"

The Badger cast a baleful glance in the Weasel's direction.

"You don't look underfed, Major," he went on. "Needy? I don't think so."

"Foxes must be controlled for the good of the country-side!" sputtered the Toad. "And the hunt is by far the most efficient way of controlling them. And it is good for the animals themselves. It is both necessary *and animale*. That is all I have to say on the subject."

"Would you agree with that now, Weasel?" The Badger stepped towards the other animal, one pace only, towering over him. "Answer, please."

"Wordsel—" said the Weasel, in a pallid attempt to assert his status. "— *Mr* Wordselwese if you don't mind. Weselwerd P. Wordselwese, L.L.B. (Hons). And as a solicitor, I should warn you—"

"— Good for the countryside?" insisted the Badger.

"It is an excellent way to defend the environment," answered Mr Wordselwese with a well-oiled swiftness, much as if he had spoken this phrase many times before. "And as a sol—"

"Ah! The '*environment*'!" repeated the Badger with stony irony. "And what parts of the 'environment' do you defend so nobly, sir, in killing foxes?"

"The hunt helps to keep the fox population in balance," said the Weasel smoothly. "If it weren't for the hunt, it is quite obvious that these animals would take over the whole of the countryside eventually. There would be plagues of foxes. You would hardly be able to move for them. The lamb population would be decimated, and there wouldn't be a chicken left alive on any farm not protected by high-voltage electric fences."

"Quite correct," said Major Curfieu-Tode. "And since by and large we only catch the weak, or the sick, this does of course help to keep the fox population healthy, happy and sane. It is a very, very natural process."

"So, you see, boys," said the Badger, addressing the gathering of young badgers much as if he had shifted gear for a moment and was now in the process of delivering a lecture, "they hunt the sick and the weak. These toads, who were, we remember from our school lessons, the founders of that once-common great ideal of ours, Animal Fair Play. Tell me, Mr Wordselwese, how exactly was hunting 'good' for the lynx, the beaver, or the wolf, in earlier days? How did hunting them to extinction improve your 'environment', I wonder?"

"It improved it by getting rid of them!" barked the Toad in the Weasel's place. They were pestilential! They were dispensable! They destroyed farm stocks, they attacked children, and the blasted beavers created serious flooding every winter! We have a far better world here without them."

"So this 'environment' of Mr Wordselwese's is simply what *you choose* from amongst the unclothed to leave alive here?" breathed the Badger, his hoarse voice deepening. "Much as that twenty-odd square miles of plantation wood up there is now—for you see, don't be too shocked, Major, we can all read here—a 'Conservation Area'?"

The Toad's green face took on something of the hue of the jacket he was wearing. "An animal of your sort cannot possibly understand," he said, "that we toads, and those who work with us, *are* the Countryside. *We are* the living embodiment of everything worth *calling* Countryside. No one is better equipped then we to act as stewards over it—to manage it—to care for it . . . to cherish it. Who better to decide what lives, what dies, which trees are felled and which are planted, than those who have always done these things?"

"I can think of some."

"No doubt you can."

"And is there any room in this grand plan for the choices of Nature herself?"

"We are a part of nature!" shouted the Toad. "The decisions we make are a part of nature! The only nature worth having. The hunt is the most natural thing you could hope to find!"

"An interesting argument," responded the Badger gravely,

looking away. "But perhaps I can ask the opinion of your quarry-of-the-day on that?—Come out, Fox. You're quite safe with us."

The Fox barked and whined briefly and the Mole thought he understood him to say, *Thank you, but I know my place.* After a moment though, he crept forward into the light.

"Oh, this is ridiculous," said the Weasel, an expression of jeering disgust on his face much as if he were in some way personally offended by the Fox's presence. "Great Pan, what are you doing, animal, talking to *that*?"

The Badger did not respond. Instead he looked balefully about the sett, catching the eye of more than one of his fellows as he did so. "'*Natural*' ..." he repeated. "Tell me, Fox, do you know of any animal in Nature—any amongst the Unworded and the Unclothed, I mean—that hunts its quarry by gathering into mounted groups and sending out packs of trained dogs to do the tracking?"

The Fox gave a single coughing yip.

"Never heard of one then? No ... you're sure about that now? Oddly enough, I haven't myself, as it happens. Nature is never 'fair' exactly, is she, Fox? No, no. But so far as any of us here happen to know, does Nature *actively organise* unfairness? Does she set an organising, methodical intelligence to work in pursuit of single victims? As if," (here he half-turned to the Toad) "as if in some kind of off-kilter military exercise, in which a small army is pitched against a single, all-but-defenceless enemy? Not exactly Nature's way, is it? But you see, our toad friend here—"

"I am not your friend!" said the Toad in a strangled voice, blenching.

"... Brother Toad—he thinks rather differently. He thinks he and his hounds are as much a part of Nature as a posy of primroses."

"It is *Sport!*" blared Major Curfiew-Tode. "It is *Tradition!* It is the way in which *civilized* animalkind relates to nature!"

"So, Mr Fox," continued the Badger calmly, the Major's way of 'relating' to you as a representative of Nature—if he didn't happen to be here now in, what is this, a kind of conversation with you?—his way of 'relating' to you would be to have you pursued and mauled by two-score of kennel-hounds trained to no other purpose."

"That is the only way to treat creatures of the lower orders!" snarled the Toad, staring at the earth floor. "Kill 'em! Blast 'em! Cook the ones that can be cooked, and stuff the rest! Any bits that are left over, give 'em to the kiddies!"

"I wonder how you would feel if any of them ever took up similar ways of 'relating' to you, Major Tode."

"Don't be ludicrous, animal! What—who are you, anyway? Some breed of sentimental loony-animalist, pretending that foxes can talk and slugs can fly and hoping—and you may hope!—to bring the world crashing down about our ears? I demand to know, *why are you doing this?*"

The Badger stretched to his full height, and the Major took a quarter-step backwards. "Calm yourself now," growled the former quietly, a great weight of dangerous emotion held in check behind that quietness. "We of the burrows are no great respecters of rank, *Toad*. We are doing this because it is the only course left open to us. If we could fight you in the courts—through parliament—don't you think we would do it? But you control the game there just as you try to do here in these downs. You are abjectly feared by those few politicians who do not love you."

The Toad looked at the big animal with a sneering defiance that suggested he did not disagree with this. "But eventually, Major," the Badger continued, "we shall find out why that is. And put a stop to it. "

"*Will* you, holedigger!" responded the Toad in a strangled voice.

"In any case, you know," put in Mr Wordselwese, in another stab at an authoritative tone, "these creatures enjoy the chase.

Oh, yes, I assure you they *do*," he continued into the resulting barrage of ugly laughter. "We have commissioned several scientific studies that prove this beyond a shadow of a doubt."

A chair crashed over, as the Otter flung himself bodily at the Weasel, his face a tortured mask of rage. He was within a split second of burying his teeth in the other animal's neck when the Badger and two of his sons pulled him back.

"Easy, Otter, easy!" said the big animal. "Hold off now! We know how you feel … Easy! Let the Fox speak. Let's hear his voice now. "

The Otter—still under partial restraint—glared at the now trembling and speechless solicitor with eyes that might have burned holes through fur and bones with only the slightest adjustment in the wiring. Then he turned away silently and walked back to his place beyond the table.

"You see, Major Tode …" said the Badger quietly. "You do have to understand, you know, how much you have made yourselves hated." He held the Toad's gaze until the smaller animal, after a struggle, dropped his eyes. "— So, Fox … 'Enjoyment'. You *enjoy* it, we're told. It's all just a lot of fun and games then, being hunted to the death?"

The Fox barked, snarled, growled and whined, taking a couple of snaps in the direction of the Weasel's leather-booted calves. "For any of you who don't quite understand the lingo," said the Badger, "… you of the pink do not, I suppose?"

"There *is* no 'lingo'!" fumed the Major, pinkening-in-the-pink as he spoke. "You self-deluding troglodyte mustelid!"

"… Hear it, boys!" The Badger gestured broadly towards the Toad. Listen to what this animal is saying. Think, now— think about it, please. *There is no lingo*. Isn't it strange then, that we should be able to understand? This is essential, you see. The first thing you must do, when selecting a victim for your 'sport', is deny him a language. If he has no language, he has no identity, and thus no rights. He is no longer 'he' but 'it', or 'that', as the Weasel put it. Could you understand what the Fox said, Mole, by any chance?"

"Um—yes, a bit," replied the Mole, moving a few feet closer. "I think I could."

"What did he say, if you don't mind? 'Translate' for us."

"He said—um—well, it wasn't very nice."

"Go on anyway. If you don't mind."

"He said, 'Yes, wonderful, better than a trip to the seaside, and I always specially like the bit where you get torn into pieces and the dogs pull out your innards. Nothing like it—er, mal'."

"... Father?" said one of the burly young badgers earnestly. "I think that's an example of 'irony', isn't it, Father?"

"Quite correct, Roger, yes," replied the elder.

"Of course, you can get the right scientist to say virtually anything if you pay him enough," said Mr Wordselwese.

The Badger's eyes widened and he turned slowly back towards the speaker. "... Excuse me, Mr Wordselwese? Would you mind repeating that?"

"I said you can get the right scientist to say anything if you pay him enough. And we had to pay an awful lot for those reports, or so I heard. Well over the odds, I'd say, for what we ended up with."

The Badger's black eyes narrowed, and he walked back towards the Weasel. "... Boys," he said, "I do believe we are witness to a very strange phenomenon here ... Very strange—who knows, perhaps unprecedented. We have just heard a weasel voluntarily speaking what may well be the truth!"

"Yes, I'm afraid I did," said Mr Wordselwese, now quite aghast, his open lower jaw revealing not only his fangs but the pink of his gums. "Why did I say that?"

The Badger's gaze fell for one moment on the Mole, who had walked over to the table at the invitation of one of the badgers-junior to pick up a mug of tea and was now sitting next to the soothsayer in question. The Toad, meanwhile, had fallen back from his colleague-in-pursuit, his large mouth agape with disbelief.

"Of course, one of my own main reasons for following the hunt," continued the solicitor chattily, "is because I am such a snob. Yes, Yes! A desperate, desperate, inveterate, hopeless snob! And I do love every minute of it, you know. So good to mix with the animals who count—such as the Major here, of course." (He turned fawningly to the Toad.) "One does worry sometimes that the firm is not quite, ah, well, influential enough to impress. But one knows in one's heart of hearts that one is of a superior type, and it is crucial, obviously, to associate oneself with the hunt for just that reason. I can tell you though, I don't enjoy the riding much any more. It's murder on my piles, if you must know."

The Otter and Hare stared at one another in uncomprehending disbelief.

"... Why am I saying this, why am I *saying* this?" quavered the stricken Weasel. "The ditches are the worst, of course. Oh! The ditches! But even that is worthwhile, I firmly believe, to enable one to reinforce one's sense of one's own sup ... one's own sup ..."

Here the Weasel's voice trailed off altogether, and in the silence that followed, the Badger studied him long and hard. "Let me ask you again," he said eventually, "— just out of curiosity. Would you admit, now, Mr Wordselwese, that it might be unpleasant—very unpleasant, in fact—to be a fox pursued by hounds? Not 'enjoyable', as you claimed just a few minutes ago?"

The Weasel's jaw worked, and foam appeared along both rows of shining fangs. He let out a little choking snarl of frustration. "— Yes, yes—yes!!" he gasped, wholly despite himself. "But what you don't see, you burrowers, what you simply do not see," he went on, a staring conviction settling upon him, "is that these creatures (he indicated the Fox with a toss of his head, spitting out the last word as if it sickened him), "are *vermin.* They are *pests.* It is right and proper, normal and natural that we of the Upper Orders should do just as we wish with them."

"And what is this word, '*vermin*', Mr Wordselwese?" demanded the Badger, rage in his voice now like the rumblings of a storm in the distance. "If I take off this shirt," (he clawed at it furiously, breaking off one of the buttons as he did so and exposing a part of his black-furred chest) "— if I abandon words, and bark and growl at you in the old style instead, am *I* then a candidate for inclusion? Am *I* then '*vermin*'? Would you dare call *me* '*vermin*'? Would you, animal? *What is this word?*"

The Weasel cowered, speechless with conflicting stresses. "Vermin is less than animal," said the Toad in his place. His voice was cold, restrained, and full of hatred. "And it applies to *anything that we choose.* Anything that becomes a nuisance. Anything that we decide needs to be controlled. You grossly misrepresent that creature by inventing words for it. I tell you, it is beneath understanding."

"Not beneath my understanding, *Toad!*" roared the Badger. "No more than you are yourself, though there is no understanding your way of thinking!"

"With vermin, we do as we like and as is necessary," said the Major. "That is all there is to be said on the matter."

"So this fox is your plaything, for the game with dogs? Your ball of blood. So the Pheasant here," (he nodded to the motionless bird, caught in mid-peck by the mention of her name) "is your plaything for the game with guns? As simple as that?"

"It is far more than that," came the Toad's reply. "This is a *Sport*—a Sport of great, great seriousness."

"And what is 'sport', however serious, except a game—a diversion—an amusement? We do not play games with the lives of other animals, Major Curfieu-Tode. Civilised animals do not do so. It is you who have yet to see this. It is you who have yet to achieve ..." (the Badger paused, snorting out his breath as if he despaired of being heard) "... maturity."

"How dare you patronize *me*!" bawled the Toad. "You will be telling us next that vermin have rights! Oh yes, I know how your mind works! And I tell you, holedigger, foxes may have rights just so soon as they take on responsibilities to match, and demonstrate the first ability to deal with them!"

"Babies have no responsibilities, Major, so far as I know," snarled the Badger. "Perhaps you should hunt them too. Follow your pack around the infant-school playground?— You see, boys," he said, "here is our enemy—one of our enemies, one of our enemies! Here he stands before us, as rigid and unchangeable as the roots of an old tree grown around a rock. Here they are—toad and weasel: reasoning, apparently civilised animals who use their reason only to brand others of the animal race as vermin. How can any thinking creature do this? You already have the answer: they do it by twisting thought. They begin with what they want to prove—believing it, you see, wholeheartedly believing it—and drag the bare edges of every argument up to meet the claim. All right, Major—"

"I refuse to answer any more questions!" hissed the Toad in implosive fury.

"— may I ask, now," continued the Badger as if the other had not spoken, "what of the *pleasures* of the hunt?"

The Toad remained silent, and then the Hare stepped towards him, rubbing the tip of his own nose lightly with the butt of a pistol. "This is our course, Major," he said quietly. "Just for a change, eh? Sorry."

"But let me ask this Weasel here," said the Badger. "Since it seems he doesn't refuse to answer. What would you say are the pleasures of the hunt, Mr Wordselwese? ... Assuming there are any, of course, and that you don't perform the whole operation out of a spirit of civic duty?"

Sweating profusely, his eyes darting about the room, the

Weasel choked out, "It's … a … fine … way … to-see-the-countryside."

"To see the *countryside*," repeated the Badger, "To see the *countryside*! But hasn't the Major here already told us, he *is* the countryside. You don't need to get on your horse to look at him!"

"The—countryside—" said the Weasel, gesturing and choking again, as if to indicate something of slightly wider dimensions than his co-rider.

"Ah!" roared the Badger. "*That* countryside! I do beg your pardon! Yes, yes—I like to see that countryside myself, now and then. I often go out and poison a lake, or set fire to a wood. Sometimes I will take a whole family of weasels with me to some quiet spot, at gunpoint, and throttle them one by one before I make myself a daisy chain and sit down to admire the view—"

"Uh—Father?" asked one of the lumbering young badgers, scratching behind an ear as he did so. "Is that another example of 'irony', Father?"

"Yes, Melos. Yes, that *was* a slightly less subtle example of irony. Try again, Mr Wordselwese, if you don't mind."

The Weasel's jaw worked, his bright little eyes stared feverishly and his claws extended and retracted as if to rip at the bowels of the air itself. "Yes, damn you—*damn* you, why shouldn't I say it?—it is the chase, the chase, the *chase*! It is the glory of the kill, the kill, the *kill*! Oh, we spend far too much of our lives trapped inside clothes," (he scratched at the robust cloth of his scarlet jacket, and his eyes rolled until the whites were visible) "in shirts, in ties, in suits, in Harris Tweeds, in perma-press Cavalry Twills! In the chase you can become truly animal again—claw down the long, dark, windy tunnel to your never-satisfied inner being, your true, your ferocious weasel-heart! You can destroy for the sheer bloody joy of destroying, yes, and the longer it lasts the better!—Don't you understand? We *need* to kill! We *need* the sight of blood, we need that ravening joy, that rag-doll death, those staring death-masks lying in the long green grass, that ritual, that sacrifice, and the wild, cruel laughter that always follows on! You don't know, you don't *know*—oh, it is so *good* to laugh like that!"

The Mole had edged a few inches to his left in the midst of this tirade, moving his mug carefully out of the path of the Weasel's arm-flailings. It did not stem the flow. "When the hounds sink their teeth in, oh, it is so urgently satisfying, one could almost fall into the fray with them! That fox there—I could tear it apart now, yes, even as I look at it! I could ... *dah!* ... I could ... *damn!* ... I ... could ... ah ..."

The solicitor dragged himself to a halt, staring about in stricken embarrassment at the group of silent faces as he did so. Even now, though, he remained prone to rapid-fire bursts of snarling at nothing in particular. Silently, the Hare held out a small brown cushion, which the Weasel grabbed and gnawed at hungrily, growling through it in a high-pitched tone as he did so.

Major Curfieu-Tode regarded his co-rider with what was now undisguised contempt. "I have to say," he observed with a curl of the lip, "we toads are quite above such emotions. Have been for centuries."

"'Destroy for the sheer bloody joy of destroying' ..." said the Badger. "For the 'joy' of destroying? In the old times, when we killed animals ourselves" (here again he looked around the room, from one pair of eyes to the next)"—and I know this is a difficult subject, but it must be faced. When our predecessors killed other animals, they—we—did it in order that we could live. We—they—respected their prey in death."

Here the Otter made a single sharp movement of a forearm, tapping his paw lightly against the butt of his gun in a gesture that did not go unnoticed by his leader.

"Yes, Otter—the old debate," said the Badger. "The old debate! And it may well be you have a point—even when" (the big animal's eyes shone for one brief moment) "you are good enough not to make it. I won't presume to speak for other species, then. Some behaved in other ways? ... Well. Perhaps they did. But when we badgers killed, we offered respect. It was a law amongst us."

The Mole stared hard into his mug of tea, more deeply disturbed than he could say. For even he was unable to resist the call of ancient race-memories of the days when moles too still killed their own earthworms, snakes and lizards for breakfast and supper, instead of going to the village grocers for their cold tongue, and ham, and cinnamon oatcakes.

"Did we hear any suggestion of *respect* in Mr Wordselwese's words?" asked the Badger.

"Of course not!" snapped the Toad, as if the fact should be quite self-evident.

"— Just the opposite, in fact," said the Badger patiently. "Yet if the purpose of the hunt is to (how did you put it, Weasel? Rather well, I thought) 're-enter the windy tunnel to your inner animal being'?—your *animal* self—your unclothed, unworded self?—then what right is this you claim to hunt this animal here, this fox, who by the logic of the thing must be your blood-brother? You destroy him, as viciously as your ingenuity knows how, in order to be *like* him?"

"It is Sport, it is *Sport!*" fumed the Toad, his eyes blank with self-righteous rage. "It is the Tradition of the Countryside! We do what we have always done, we will go on doing what we have always done, and that is that!"

A silence followed, in which the Badger nodded. "So there it is," he said, exhaling heavily. "We have made great headway today with you, Major, haven't we? Not that we should expect any different. Those who feed their own blindness will never change, and change ..." He sighed again. "*Change* will have to come about in other ways. So we had better end this, hadn't we? All right, boys—time for some 'sport'? What about a little game of hunt-the-toad? And hunt-the weasel too, since he's here to play?"

"You would not dare!" wailed the Weasel, his thin knees knocking.

"Oh, we won't be doing any hunting, Mr Wordselwese. Harepeace—do we have the Essence Of Fox?"

"Here," said the big Hare. "Vigour of pungency guaranteed to ... December 31st this year. Should do."

"Take them back up," ordered the Badger. "We won't ask you to do this without your clothes, yet, Major. You may not be ready for that. Take them to where there are one or two climbable trees—they may be in need of them. Then—the fragrance." He turned back to the Toad. "Not our way, you see, Toad, to do this without giving you half a chance. You might throw the Fox to the dogs, stunned with the butt of a crop, but we won't do the same with you today." The Toad opened his mouth as if to speak. "Don't deny it, will you? We know it happens. You see, Major, you cannot do such things—you cannot *ever* do such things—without it becoming known. ... Fox, you stay here with us for now. And welcome. Stay as long as you need or want. You too, Mole. But of course you are both free to go whenever you want.—All right. Blindfolds on!"

The Mole, who had sat through most of this debate with open mouth—even to the point of letting his tea go cold— was in no state to make decisions. "Um—O yes—Um— Thank you—yes," he replied, in roughly that order.

"We will come back, you know!" yelled the Toad, from inside his hood of black. "We will come back and find this place with some of our lads—and believe me, *holedigger*, we've got some good tough lads with us these days—and we'll take it and every one of you apart! You will be nothing but well-bruised badger-steak by the time we've finished with you!"

"First you'll have to find us, Major," replied the Badger quietly.

"Oh, we're good at that!"

"You'll need to be. Though you won't necessarily find us in.

We do have other *pieds-à-terre* in the region. And out of it. But if you come here again, remember, please: we will defend ourselves by every means available, and to the death if necessary. I think your idea of a fight is still one in which the other animal is unarmed and outnumbered, isn't it?"

The Toad—a short figure in scarlet and black—stayed silent. Then both he and the Weasel were led out in the direction of another snaking tunnel and stair-flight than the one down which they had first entered.

CHAPTER EIGHT

MOLE THE MOLE?

"Something very unusual happened earlier today," said the Badger, wiping his mouth with the corner of an old cotton handkerchief. "Very unusual. And it could be of great use to us to know what caused it."

The Mole and the Fox had been invited to an early supper at the sett. This, they learned, was one of a loose network of underground outposts of an organisation of unclear shape and extent, known as the Animale Restoration Front. The Badger had been one of the organisation's three original founders: the names of the others were not given. When the Mole asked what it did, the big animal told him that it was "dedicated to direct action aimed at undermining the processes of Weaselmind at every possible point of contact". He said this very quickly, as if he had said it ten thousand times before, and the Mole should know the answer anyway without being told.

The Fox had a certain difficulty with cutlery, about which everyone was most understanding, and dined rather messily straight from the bowl. For his own part the Mole had found the main dish of green lentil and tomato soup flavoured with garlic and cumin distinctly odd, yet more delicious the more of it he ate, and the bread—a wonderfully damp, brown, springy, sweetish, pungent-smelling stuff—was so good he eventually dared to ask for the recipe from its creator, the taciturn scarred Otter, whose face lit up at the compliment.

The Otter had, in fact, just been quietly explaining his trick of only putting half the necessary flour into the first rising when the Badger spoke, and in such a way as to prepare the gathering for discussion. The table was cleared and mugs of flower-scented tea brought to it. Then the Badger rose, lit partly by candlelight and partly by the beam from a generator-powered angle-poise turned on to charts on the wall behind him.

"... What happened?" he said, looking round him. "What happened was that, without warning, at exactly the kind of moment when he was least likely to, our weasel guest began to speak the truth. And he revealed more of himself to us in a few sentences than we could ever have extracted from most of them in a year of interrogation. What he said confirms once again—as if we didn't know it already!—that the denizens of Weaselworld are lost to Nature in every worthwhile sense."

"Good thing there are still a few burrow-dwellers left, Father," chipped in one of the large young badgers brightly, as if to offset some impending gloom.

"They are there. They are there," responded the Badger with a ponderous thoughtfulness. "But until communications improve—exist, in most places—we will never know exactly how many remain to keep the flame alight. We tend to keep ourselves to ourselves, we burrowers, and it has proved a weakness. We survive in self-isolated pockets, more often than not. But don't despair, William: you know the A.R.F. can change that, given time."

"Yes—by joining Weaselworld!" snarled the Otter in disgust, turning in his chair.

"We know your feelings on that, Otter," said the big animal. "I understand your point of view, but I think you're wrong. That isn't the point here. What we have to keep before us, to carry out our work at all, is that it is we burrow-dwellers—we alone—who have evaded the change, the trans-formation, that has made the weaselry and Weaselmind the force it is in the world today. We have to accept as fact that the majority of animals are elsewhere now. Yes, yes—very much elsewhere! Isn't this one of the most interesting things about the 'confession', if that was what it was, of that posturing little legal-weasel? He hunts in pursuit of his 'true, ferocious weasel-heart'—his words, correct? I suppose it is only to be expected that a weasel should go out in search of the very worst of his old self, but what's striking, surely, is that even a weasel can feel an inner need for some—thing—that is absent in his everyday life."

"— And if a *weasel* can do it ..." said the Hare.

"Exactly, Harepeace!—Then what latent—who knows, possibly massive—force for renewal may be out there, hidden amongst the docile hordes of Weaselworld?"

"But they are no longer *creaturely!*" growled the Otter. "They are no longer *animale!* What is going to start this change?"

The Badger nodded, but in such a way as to stem the flow.

"I heard another of them this morning," put in Son Number Four. "On the radio. Claiming it all like they do as 'part of Nature's plan'."

"It and they are as much a part of Nature's plan as the filth they pump into the watercourses!" responded his father heat-edly. "You see how they twist thought itself? This is what we are up against. Pan's Mistake, Bert—*Pan's Mistake!* Remember what we call them whenever you hear that kind of propa-ganda! And Weaselmind—as we see it in operation every-where—"

"Weaselmind, which has no boundaries," added the Otter.

"— which admits of no boundaries, is a force that *mimics* Nature, manipulating what it finds there, reproducing it in ever more grotesque and destructive shapes, moving ever onward towards a single end—"

The Badger left this sentence uncompleted, and no one spoke. But for the Mole, there was very probably not an animal present who could not have finished it for him; and even the Mole might have made a fair stab at it by now.

"This is our enemy," said the A.R.F. founder a moment later. "A state of mind? Yes, a state of mind. The 'profit-motive'—what is that in Weaselworld if not a universal sacred axiom? Yet look at it a little harder. What do we see there if not some strange, unnatural hybrid of the old collective instinct to survive? When a weasel-run company expands its territory, isn't it driven by just that instinct in the Unworded that causes them to take over and hold new territory? When it absorbs others of its kind, isn't this too a form of 'kill'? In Nature there are limits, but for a weasel organisation with any power behind it, the very idea of limits is out of the question."

"Um—" said the Mole quietly into his collar; then he thought better of it.

"In Nature too there is colonization," went on the Badger, who was warming to his theme. "But it happens slowly, slowly, slowly, *slowly*, and always there is the most delicately-set balance between the competitors. Can't we see it, even now, in any old wood that has been left alone to behave as it wishes? Those damp alder-gullies to the south—in the low lands west of the Aldermaston Bomb Factory, and south of Greenham Common, where the streams wind their way on over gravel beds, and ironstone leaks rust into the water—how is it the alders grow just there? Because the ground is soaking there, and because the alders can stand it—like it, for all I know—where the oaks and birches can't. The elders are that wet land's destiny, like the plants growing under them—the reeds, and those feather-leafed mosses of the orange, boggy ground where your feet sink inches in. And on the higher slopes, where it's drier and you can make a path? There, only there, grows the herb paris—the wild daffodils—the patches of buckler-fern. A 'bargain' has been struck in such a wood—yes, as weasel thought might have it! But this is a bargain that will hold for centuries, longer, if only it is left alone. Where in Weaselworld do you find anything to compare with it?"

"NO-where!" snarled the Otter, slapping the table emphatically with the flat of his paw.

"Nowhere," repeated the Badger blackly.

"— Um—?" said the Mole again.

"Yes, Mole? Yes—you wanted to say something?"

"Well—O, I just wonder why they do it. I mean, why don't they just go fishing a bit more? Or rowing, for example? Or having picnics by the river?"

Three of the large badger-youths turned to the Mole with half-open mouths, not sure if he was serious, but also startled as if by the possible radicalism of his thought. One of them, who had a pencil and a jotter pad, scribbled down a note.

"They do it because they can no longer help themselves, Mole. They have murdered conscience, wherever they can find it. As Otter said, they are no longer animale. They have become detached from the meaning of Nature's gentleness-in-violence. They have come to love power for its own sake. And they have lost all ability to be gentle *in* Nature. They have brought their great machines, and their explosives, and their chemicals, and piece by piece they are voiding the world into a bare factory floor in their own exclusive service. One by one, one by one, they invade each last remnant of Pan's domain—"

"— But we are going to stop them, Mole!" snarled the Otter, the rage in his voice only just masking the underlying bleakness.

"The weaselry have placed themselves at the centre of everything we know and value," continued the Badger gravely. "They are like greedy children, stuffing their lairs with Nature's riches, taking out, taking out, taking out—never,

never putting back! If we of the burrows get in their way—
well, of course, if we are not worded they simply kill us. If we
are worded, then they do their best to block what we say at
every exit and paint us as other than we are."

"They know how to do *that*," said the Hare.

"But even if we don't get in the way, they still kill us indi-
rectly, since they have now so poisoned the earth in pursuit of
the 'perfect' weasel-support-system that many of us die merely
as a side-effect. Here is the great, mad paradox (I'll explain
'paradox' later, Bill, if you don't mind). In pursuing survival in
their own unique, inanimale way, they are turning our world
into a vast field of animal-traps that will destroy them as
surely as it does everyone else. Only give it time. They can't
wall themselves in forever."

"But, Pan—" said the Mole.

"Pan can do *nothing!*" broke in the Badger savagely, and there
was a look in his eyes then such as the Mole had never known
possible—an unseeing blankness that spoke of loss beyond
the power of words to express it. "Pan is dying alongside the
rest of us!" But then—seeing a look of profound shock pass
over the Mole's own face—the big animal added more gently,
"You know, Mole, I'm not exactly noted for my optimism.
Who knows? Perhaps it's just that he has withdrawn from us.
For as long as it takes. But if he goes from us entirely, then
that will also be the day of his revenge, yes, and the end of
Weaselworld. It may be the only way that Nature can fight
back: by going to the very brink, where these uncreaturely
creatures themselves can no longer survive."

"But if it did all get so bad—" began the Mole.

"— Then what could live on here afterwards? What
indeed? Not any of us, that's for sure. But if life itself could
go on—perhaps, finally, that is all that matters. If at least
there are *some* plants and insects clinging on in the world—
then it may be that Nature can repair herself. Though it's
beyond me to imagine how. Let's hope it's not quite so bad as

that yet, Mole. In any case, before we come to that pass, there is one choice still left open to us."

"To fight!" said the Otter.

"To fight," said the Badger. "As best we may. There is nothing, you see, Mole—nothing, we believe—of which this Weaselmind is not capable since it cast off the counterbalance of inner Nature. And so very many other animals are deeply drawn to it: it magnetises them; it tells them how to live. And sometimes I fear it does worse than that. Weaselmind *infects* other animals. Any animal can lie. Any animal can (with an effort) hold opinions without thought, convince himself that what he does is 'in truth' all for the good. And you see, in the long run they do believe it. It's how they carry on—by believing that in some way all of this is good. It's the first, the last, the most necessary lie."

Another pause followed in which gloom seemed to be wrestling with defiance in the shadows, and no animal looked at any other. For all that, the Mole felt a question bubbling in him. "What—um—well—"

"Go on, Mole, please."

"What would you put in its place, Badger?"

"Oh!" The Badger stretched his great grey arms and brought them together behind his head, growling pleasurably as did so. "That has been debated, and debated! There are so many ideas. I doubt that I can offer much, as a burrower of strictly limited horizons. But I can still imagine a world in which we lived again by the most ancient of understandings: where every animal—*every* animal—had gone back to his first relationship with soil and sward, river and forest—knew the limits on what he may do here, in his blood. Yes, and I can picture a future in which that great road up there is cracked into a million pieces, and cornflowers and chicory are growing up between them, and the only things that move on it are the shadows of larks and lapwings. Don't ask me to do more."

"I can imagine it," said the Mole in a low voice. "... The other world."

"Tell us, then!"

But before he could speak, the Mole's heart was pierced by the most desperate, aching sadness. He stared hard into his mug of strange-scented tea, grasping it hard to fend off tears, which would have embarrassed him in this tough new company. "I ... I don't think I can, just now, if you don't mind," he said at last.

"Some other time. Some other time," said the Badger kindly, his gaze resting on him. "— Well," he said briskly, "I'm going for a little stroll, I think, before the night's work begins. Perhaps you'd care to join me, Mole? A breath of freshly polluted air?"

Five minutes later, the two animals (one of them armed, the other not) emerged into the murk of the conifer plantation by way of a pair of stout wooden doors set at an angle rather like those of a coal-cellar. These the Badger carefully camouflaged with brushwood once they were secured.

"Always err on the side of caution," he said. "Essential rule for anyone trying to make change from the bottom up!"

Another great road did run very close by here. The sett-exit rose a few yards from a boundary fence, in a spot well shaded by trees: it was a part of the plantation not reached by vehicle tracks. And even as the two moved away from it, in the direction of a narrow ride, they heard the long wailing-blare of *motor* horns.

"Always a bit on the short-tempered side, trapped animals," said the Badger, grimacing.

They walked a few hundred yards along the ride in silence. Then the Badger paused, laughing a low, hoarse laugh. "You see this little tree?" he said. "Know what it is?"

The tree was still in bud, so that the telltale shape of its leaves was not yet visible. But the Mole squinted at its outline and the emergent pattern of the bark and said, "Is it a Service?"

"It is! They were all over the place in these woods when I was a cub, the Service trees. This wood here hadn't been clear-cut in centuries—*centuries*, I'd say. Just a few trees out here, a few more there, and the coppicing of course. Then the weaselry arrived in earnest, with their clever new plan to replant every wood in England, it seemed, with these—" (He waved a disapproving paw at the Corsican pines and the Sitka spruces.) "And what did they do here, Mole? Make a guess."

"Um—I imagine it wasn't very nice, possibly?"

"They *bombed* it! No, you see. I'm not joking. They *bombed* this wood from helicopters—"

"Hell-ee-koptaz?"

"They bombed it with their chemicals and their petrol sprays, because they knew *these* trees," (and here the Badger grasped the firm stem of a healthy young tree) "— *these* trees in particular were difficult to kill, and would still keep coming up from seed. Clumsy, arrogant, stupid …!" The Badger shook the little tree in a growling rage, as a substitute perhaps for some absentee weasel-forester bomber-pilot's throat. "They killed everything. Or they thought they had," he said, calming himself. "But then what? They plant their cash-crop, profit-column pulping-conifers and they go away for a few years, and lo and behold, here and there in those places where the light can get in, along these rides and in gaps in the planting, what comes up? Correct. The Service trees come up—just like these are here. They couldn't kill them, you see! Not if they were going to keep this as woodland. They *couldn't kill them*, damn them!" He shook the tree again.

"Oh, but you should have seen this wood, Mole, after the weasels had been at it with their chainsaws and their spray-bombs. Armageddon Common, that's the name the burrow-dwellers gave it. And the deeply, *deeply* mad thing is, you see, down at the southern end, where one little shut-off patch of the old wood survives, it's now 'Designated' as a 'Nature Reserve', because a few of the butterflies that once lived *everywhere* round here still manage somehow to cling on there. You'd be designated yourself if you lived down there. Just take your clothes off, frolic about a bit. And the rest of it—this great nothingness—well, you can't have missed the signs. A 'Conservation Area'? Meaning, 'Keep Out, Because We Shoot Here'! The slimy, weedy, snag-tailed little *hypocrites!!*"

"Careful, Badger," said the Mole, "or you'll be doing the weasels' job for 'em!"

"Oh—yes," said the big animal, releasing his grip on the sapling. "Yes. I do sometimes forget myself." He turned to the Mole and looked at him steadily. "... Where are you from, Mole? If you don't mind my asking."

"O, I'm from—" The Mole paused, seized again by a powerful emotion. He did so want to tell someone everything about himself. He needed to say it and be believed, if only so that he could begin to believe it himself. "I'm from the Riverbank, you know. Direction of Toad H- Toad Towers. But ..."

"Go on ..." The Badger stared, standing there in front of him like a great boulder. "There's more to it than that, isn't there?"

"How did you know?!" spluttered the Mole. "I mean—did you? You did?"

"I don't know anything," said the Badger carefully. "Just the old animal-intuition working away there. Just picked up some scent of something, you know, very faint."

"Do you ... Do you know anything about, I mean, have you ever heard of, well, time tunnels?"

"Ah!" The Badger smote a large fist into a larger paw-pad. "*I knew* there was something about you that was odd!"

"You have, then! You know about them?"

"I've often wondered if I might recognise someone who'd been along one," said the Badger. "For one thing, I suppose, their clothes would rather tend to give them away!" He laughed an expansive, growling laugh, then caught himself, looking about cautiously. "How late are you, then, Mole? Now, let me see ... Let me guess ... Eighty, eighty-five years, or thereabouts?"

"Yes, but—you mean, you believe me, then? You think it really happened?"

"Knowledge of these things is passed on from generation to generation, isn't it? You learn about them as a cub. I did. You hear things. Sometimes an animal disappears—you know. I've always kept an open mind. There was something about you—picked it up straight away. But my dear Mole! You must be in a state of deep, deep shock at ... all this. At everything."

"At everything! Yes," echoed the Mole dolorously. "S'pose I am."

"But—courage, eh?—Courage! You moles are resilient creatures," said the Badger as if searching about for words. "You get through, for the most part, don't you? Come what may?"

The Mole choked, on the very cusp of a sob. " Y—y—" he said.

"That's the spirit! You can do it, eh? And, er, did you just 'arrive' here, earlier on?"

"No—no. I've been here several days. Lost count now. I've been staying with Mr Rette of, um, Toad Transoceanic, who's been very kind, and last night I stayed with Mr Wyvern-Toad, at—O, um—Darkwood Park. I am meant to be back there tonight, you know."

"You—wh ..." The Badger raised a paw to his forehead, and held one eye open as if to see the Mole through it more clearly. "You've been staying with *Wyvern-Toad*? *The* Wyvern-Toad? The inimitable director of *Toad Transoceanic*?"

"Yes."

"One of the most criminally-minded exponents of the art and craft of world despoliation on either side of the Atlantic—*you're staying* with *him*?"

"Um—yes. If you mean Mr Wyvern-Toad, I mean. Yes, I am. In one of his wardrobes, in fact."

"Great jumping-mice ..." muttered the Badger in a deep, low voice, "great bandicoots ... great Schomburgk's leaf-fishes ..."

"I don't underst—um—wh ...?"

"Great bare-headed rockfowl!" the big animal went on, his voice growing rapidly louder. "Great bonteboks! Great hairy-tailed *moles*! But what an opportunity, Mole! What an opportunity. The Badger paused, trying to collect himself, and squinting at the much smaller animal. "Are you, Mole—are you ... how shall I put this, er ... *particularly friendly* with Mr Wyvern-Toad?"

The Mole hesitated. He had to be frank, of course. "Well, no, not very," he said. "Although he has been very nice, I s'pose. Hospitable—you know. He even offered me a post from Toad Transoceanic, though I don't have any idea what I should do with it, things being what they are."

"*He has offered him a post!*" cried the Badger, smiting his great striped forehead with a rhetorician's hammer-blow. With some effort he took control of himself once more, and stood for several moments in the silence of concentration. "I'd like you to see a bit of what we do, Mole," he said quietly. "If you can find the time.—Tonight, I mean. We are just about to go off on a little campaign—something that may bring modest results, we hope. Join us—why not? I'm sure you can take it, can't you? It won't be pleasant, of course."

"But I am expected back ..."

"Where? Darkwood Park? I know where that is! That will be no problem; we can get you back up there later on. What we have to do won't take very long—an hour, an hour and a half at most. And we should be away to it by six-thirty."

"O—well—"

"Good! You're agreed, then? You see, Mole, what I'm thinking, in a rather loose way at present, admittedly, is that with just a bit of persuasion you could become a mole for us. I mean—you understand—at Toad Transoceanic." The Badger fell silent, and looked about as if he suspected some weasel had beamed a magical ray on him. "— What?! That's astounding. I certainly didn't mean to say that!"

The Mole meantime was no less nonplussed, if in a different style. "A ... mole," he repeated carefully.

"Yes, a mole—even though I have no desire to go on with this now, and had hoped to win you over to our cause much, much more gradually (as is always best practice in such situations), I do seem to have blurted it out, so there it is. You *could* ... only if you sympathise with the aims of the A.R.F., of course, and we will put no pressure on you, you must understand that ... but you could, if you chose to, become a mole for us. We need every bit of information we can get about the activities of organisations such as T.T.—You see? You are so very well placed! *You could be our mole there.*"

"But I am—" (the Mole coughed here in slight embarrassment at stating a fact he thought might be obvious, and of which, indeed, he believed the Badger had already taken cognisance) "- I am a mole."

"Yes, but I mean, a *mole*. An *underground animal!*"

"Ah. O." The Mole hesitated, thinking very hard. "Surely, surely, the *Badger* could not be mad, too? Were they all mad here, after all? Was it the poisons in the air that had driven these poor animals distracted?

"You do see what I mean?" said the Badger in a low, conspiratorial voice, bending towards him. "*A mole.*"

"Um ...?" said the Mole, as so often hitting a rather higher note than he had intended.

"Look, this is obviously difficult for you, and I have

mentioned it far, far too soon," said the Badger. "Why don't we forget the subject for now? Let me just say, Mole, that given who you are, and where you're going to be going, you *would make* a truly wonderful, no, an incomparable, a quite unique mole. Imperceptible—flawless!"

"I ... *am Mole*," temporized the Mole, though striking an unmistakeable diminished fourth of doubt.

"You are, indeed you are, and indeed you could be!" cried the Badger, all encouragement.

"Glad you think so," said the Mole. "Um ... nice, um, grass here, isn't it?"

"Grass? ... Grass.—Oh. No, it isn't, really. I don't want to disappoint you, but not when you compare it with what grew here before. You must remember—Great Pan, you must *know* how the woods were hereabouts in the old days. You're from them, aren't you—the old days?"

"I am," replied the Mole. "Yes. I am." Of that he was still certain. But he wanted to move the subject away from himself. "Have you been doing—what you do, for very long, Badger?" he asked.

"You mean the A.R.F.? No, no. It is all quite recent, though the ideas behind it have been around for at least three decades now, in one shape or another. The A.R.F. is not just us, you see. It is in several places. It has its equivalents abroad. It is an expression of so many burrowers' ideas—so much anger, so much of a desire for change."

The Badger exhaled deeply. "I had other sons, once," he said. "Yes, and even a daughter. But they were all of them too clever, without being intelligent. They got sucked away, joined the weasel merry-go-round. I never see any of them now. A couple of them used to come and visit me regularly—not here, of course—drive up as close as they could in their glossy this-month's-model cars, tell me off for being *retro*, if that was the word, and brag about how well they were getting on and how I 'didn't know how to live'. And I don't!

Thank Pan—not that way, Mole. I pray I never shall!"

As the Badger was talking, the Mole looked at him as if to see him a little better, observing the wear and tear (though it wasn't exactly shabby) of the heavy military-style overcoat he wore, the two pieces of quite skilful stitching in his scarf, the few grey hairs amongst the black of his stripes, and the care-worn, dreaming, weary-but-defiant look that came and went behind his large dark eyes.

"Who knows what we may achieve, Mole," he continued, "given time. Surely to Pan, if there's to be change it will come first from the burrows! If we can begin to spread the first few seeds of doubt, touch the consciences of some of the other animals—the rabbits may hear us, some of them, and the hedgehogs, those who remain, and the otters, of course. The weaselites will try to stop us at every step, and they have all the power in the world on their side. But we have to begin some-where. You've timed your arrival well, Mole. The battle is just about to be joined in earnest. Weaselworld has barely heard of the Animale Restoration Front. It will. Believe me, it will!"

"But—well—" said the Mole, scratching his nose and straightening a couple of zigzag whiskers, "what are you going to *do* exactly?"

"For the time being, we're agreed that we focus only on the obvious. And we've started, as you've seen, with the weaselry's abuses against what they like to call 'creatures of the lower orders'. Working as we must at present, it is the only way forward: we burrowers have no representation in the galleries of power. It isn't us who write the newspapers. We don't make the television programmes! You're not a vegetarian, Mole, by any chance?"

"O! No, not really. I do buy the occasional half a pound of sausages, or a bit of bone to make a soup. And when I go on one of Ratty's picnics, of course, I eat all sorts of lovely things—cold tongue, cold ham, cold beef, potted meat, O, all sorts of things."

"Shame on you!—Although, of course, I apologise. I should not say that. You are from the Past, after all."

"But is it wrong? To eat meat?" The Mole was astounded.

"I can't tell you that. We all have to make that decision for ourselves. What I can tell you is that it is wrong—it must be wrong—to eat certain kinds of meat, when the animals from whom it has been made have lived their lives treated as nothing more than ..." (here a look mingling disgust and incendiary rage darkened the Badger's face) "lumps of meat on legs. You don't know about the chicken batteries, of course." (He paused again, regarding the Mole with his penetrating gaze.) "But if you join us tonight, Mole, you will. And perhaps it wouldn't do you too much harm. You see, in most of these places they are kept inside for the whole of their lives, from the moment the shell breaks to the moment when— well, we need not go into that. And they must live these lives in semi-darkness. Gr*ahhh*!! If Pan had any strength at all he would rip the roofs off those places with a great wind and drop them on those who run them!"

The Badger roved about as he spoke, anger pulsing visibly through him. He went on: "And there is worse—"

"Oh, stop, stop, stop!" cried the Mole, covering his ears with his hands.

But the Badger waited, and when the Mole had uncovered his ears he took a stick and scratched a small rectangular shape on a bank of moss. "You see this," he said in a controlled but slightly trembling voice. "In the worst places of all, this is what each bird is given by way of space. This—*this much*. For its *whole life*. And those who control these death camps, in their deep weaseline concern for their prisoners' welfare, have argued 'officially' that to make their system completely acceptable for the future all that will be needed is to extend the space to ... this." (He scratched a very small extra space alongside the first.) "This, they say—yes they say it, you see, in so many words, just as if it was the truth, and for some reason the

words do not burn their mouths like acid as they come out!—
this will be 'acceptable' (oh, they love words like 'acceptable'!)
for all future prisons. And they dare—they *dare*—use the word
animale—"

The Badger flung aside the stick and, growling again,
hammered a great fist so hard against one of the young spruce
trees that it shook to its crown, dropping dead needles all
about them. "I could kill them all!" he roared. "Happily,
happily, I could kill them all!"

"I want to go home," said the Mole in a low plaintive voice.

"Self-pity will get you nowhere, animal!" snapped the
Badger, fury still spiralling in his system. He stepped away
from the Mole, leapt at another equally inoffensive conifer
and shook it, growling continuously as he did so for a good
half minute, biting his way along one branch so that it was
stripped of foliage. Then he breathed out, long and hard.
"That's better," he said. "I'm sorry. I have behaved very badly.
After all, we have only just met, and even if we hadn't ... I'm
sorry, Mole. But you see, these things—if you think about
them every day, as I do—these things are hard to bear."

The Mole stared at the grass at his feet. "Yes," he said.

"But you must see too, we have to bear them, and think
about them, if anything is to change. You do see that?"

"... Yes."

The Badger walked gently up to the Mole and put a big
arm firmly around his shoulders. And as he did so, the tears
began to flood down the Mole's face, running in tiny rivulets
on to the velvet of his jacket where they sank down into the
material.

"... You could go back, you know," said the Badger, after a
long and pensive silence. "Time tunnels run two ways. Or so
my mother taught me."

"M—m—m—" said the Mole. "M-m-mine is all b-built
over. They're putting up a great b-b-big—I don't know—
THING—on it. A *thing*. A b-building-g."

"… Ah. That may present a little problem, then," responded the Badger. He studied the same area of grass that was currently of such great interest to the Mole. Then he opened his mouth as if to speak, inhaled as if to speak, but did not do so.

"No. I shall have to stay here now," said the Mole, recovering something of his composure. "You're right, Badger. I know that, really. I shall have to learn how to … *be* … here. I shall have to—" (he wiped his eyes with his paws and then began to rub down his jacket with his handkerchief in as businesslike a way as he could manage) "—I shall have to toughen up, won't I? I shall have to."

"As I said before, Mole, you get through, your breed," said the Badger, patting the small animal on his back perhaps just a little harder than he intended. "You don't look as if you should—not exactly—but you do, don't you, for the most part? Make the old mole war cry? Soldier on?"

The hint of a smile hovered on the Mole's still stricken face.

"S'pose so," he said. "— S'pose so."

"… *So*," said the Badger decisively, rising up to his full height as he spoke. "Will you join us tonight, Mole? Take one small exploratory step for creaturekind?"

The Mole did not speak but he did, a second or two later, nod.

"I'm very pleased—honoured, I mean that—to have you with us. All right, back to base, double quick now. They will be getting impatient!"

***

Back inside the sett, the small gathering of animals was well on its way to readiness for the night's action. (The Fox was gone.) Routes to and from the target chicken-prison, and alternative escape routes, had all been mapped out on the ground well in advance. That the place was left unguarded at night had long ago been established. Old hand-pump garden sprayers filled with misleading scents were being packed by the Otter and two of the badgers-junior for use in the event of pursuit by dogs (the Mole heard with some dismay.) And hoods were to be worn at the point of attack, since an attendance by the Press was expected.

"We have a *guarantee* of that, this time?" asked the Badger as the last elements of the plan were discussed.

"Yes," said the Hare. "We had confirmation this morning—it's definite. Mr Alfred Highodge of the *Berks and Oxon Amalgamated Chronicle* will be in the area (in the back bar of the Miller of Malsfield, to be precise) *with* a photographer, and he will be 'called out' to the site by we don't need to know who, at the right time. We'll get some coverage."

"He'd better be there."

"Don't worry, Badger!"

"Fine, but we have to understand, there is no point in doing this if it's like the last time and they fix the place up and clean off all the slogans and forty-eight hours later it looks as if it never happened. Is there, Harepeace?"

"Point taken, sir!" replied the Hare, as he completed the cleaning of the firing mechanism on his fifty-year-old weapon.

Dusk had already settled by the time they emerged under the solid spruce canopy, where there was little more light now than at the bottom of a bottle of black ink. The Otter took the lead, and the Mole and the others stumbled on behind him across an obstacle course of brash and broken branches until they reached a firebreak-channel. Fifteen minutes later they left the trees at the head of the big combe, from which they climbed quickly on to an open expanse of cultivation at the hilltop. Here there was no cover at all and they crept on, keeping in low profile until they began to descend again into another combe, narrower than the first but, it seemed to the Mole, just as long. They moved for some time along a kind of miniature terrace-path, trodden down by the weight of cattle into the turf and dotted with thorns and juniper.

The Mole was impressed by the skill with which this band of reformers tracked the terrain, which they seemed to know intimately. And when eventually they left the downland slopes altogether for a lower-lying country, he was even more impressed by how they kept themselves invisible, travelling inside the lengths of isolated belts of trees and thorns that had perhaps once been hedges, and making use of low banks and shallow open ditches.

After about half an hour the Otter paused, raised an arm against the risen moon and jerked his hand twice at the dark mass that lay ahead of them. This looked to the Mole suspiciously like the edge of another conifer plantation, and so it proved to be, except that here—screened by a single row of trees on their right—there also stood a cluster of long sheds not dissimilar to those he had seen on his first emergence. They were very long—perhaps 150 yards each—but a fraction of the height and width of those first prodigies. There was a curious thrumming in the air, rather like the sound a child will make by rubbing a digit round a wetted glass, but a thousand times more intense. The Mole realised that this must come from the sheds themselves, and as they cautiously drew nearer to the first of these he could also make out a low, muffled gabbling sound and choruses of long, thin squeeings punctuated by the occasional high-pitched squawk.

Harepeace and one of the young Badgers went on ahead to double-check that the site was clear of unwanted company, whilst the rest waited, partly unpacking their few small items of equipment as they did so. The Mole was by now holding his handkerchief over his well-masked nose, since there was another smell here that was quite new to him—a powerful, clinging, ammoniac stench that seemed to possess the very air itself. As he stood enduring this, so he began to pick out details in the moonlight. There were no windows in these buildings, only wooden elements resembling long covers of some kind, with gaps at the bottom. Many areas of the timber were discoloured by damp-loving plants, and mosses formed lumps like little berets in the regular corrugations of the roofs. Things that might have been baby-bottles—but for use only by babies of unimaginable dimensions—were fixed to the sides of each building. And there was everywhere, he realised, a pale, powdery, adhesive dust that coated not only the ground along the 'window'-gaps but, more thinly, the grasses and bushes beyond, and even the lowest branches of the plantation trees beside him. These, as a result, had the look of foliage as shown in old engravings.

On the ground by his feet the Mole spotted a fragment of paper, partly buried under debris. Having nothing better to do, he picked it up and squinted at it in the moonlight. At its top left were printed the initials M.P., large and bold, and peering around them was a cartoon-chicken, grinning at him with teeth. Under this were the words, "MULTI-POUL-TOMETE LTD. Bringing Broilers Economically To The Nation's Supermarkets. 'Efficiency' is our middle name! M.P. bridges the broiler-gap from its 200-million-strong flocks of pampered poulets and cossetted capons, living the life of luxury from Argyll to Corn …" Here, fortunately or unfortunately, the paper ended.

Hare and badger-youths returned within five minutes, confirming the all clear.

"Remember, all of you," whispered the Badger, "many of them will be mad, or not far off it. We must go gently." With a small breast-drill he rapidly opened four holes in the wall of the nearest shed, set roughly five feet apart from one another, and a narrow-nosed saw was inserted into each. But immediately the sawing began there was little further need for silence: a wave of squawking terror seemed to flood through the inside of the building from where they stood to its furthest end, lapping back again at a very slightly lower volume. After this, every chicken in the place was singing.

Those animals who were not sawing were now busy painting, and in four separate places the letters 'A.R.F.' appeared at speed, whilst the Badger unrolled a piece of rough paper on which was blocked out the following message in large green letters:

THESE ARE ALSO ANIMALS
REMEMBER
A.R.F.

This he nailed up next to the newly-created hole. The smell rising out of this was now so overwhelming that the Mole thought he might pass out altogether if he stayed there very much longer. But after what the Badger had told him earlier, his desire to know once more had the upper hand. He took one step towards the hole, and the Badger saw this.

"Well done," he said. "Go on—take a look. Move very slowly."

And so he did, though gulping for air through his handkerchief as he did so. Inside the shed he found what must have been several thousand chickens, stretching away into an invisibly gloomy distance in light so dusty-yellow-dim it made the moonlight bright by comparison. Most of the chickens had shrunk *en masse* from the sounds of the break-in, and were now congregated at some distance from the hole in a vast press of feathered bodies. Some weaker individuals were still trying to find cover amongst the many, only to be repulsed with pecks by those at the edges, whilst out of the throng itself rose a continuous, low-level, frightened clucking the Mole interpreted as *Pardon me. Excuse me. Pardon me. Excuse me. So sorry. Pardon me* ... with the occasional burst of *Get out of the way!* or *Get off, get off, get off, get off!*

"What do you see, Mole?" growled the Badger from behind him. "Is Nature in this place? It's all right, you don't need to answer. These are not birds, to those who run these hell-holes. They are a *stuff*, like this timber here," (he slapped a plank) "or this piece of concrete. They are things, matter, units in a process. They spend their whole lives in these places. They can't walk about like any self-respecting animal. They can't live in families. They can't dust-bathe—there isn't any ground to scratch. There is no sunlight. They are packed in so close they can't even stretch their wings." A note of sorrowing pity intruded on the Badger's tone of cool urgency as he spoke this last phrase. He paused, then went on as before. "Even our puffed-up hunting-toad respects the fox that can escape him. But here—you understand—they are not *seen*. Those who do this *do not see*. In Weaselworld, blindness is a professional necessity."

"But the other animals," said the Mole, turning. "*Other* animals must be up in arms!"

"What, you mean those who queue to buy the chicken dinners? 'Fraid not. Mole. 'Fraid not. Oh, they know well enough these places exist. They know it, but they also manage to forget it. They are very clever at forgetting, the mass of animals—at knowing and forgetting, both at once. All right, let me come in now."

The Mole retreated, and as the two animals passed, the Badger placed a big paw on his shoulder. "We will change this," he said. "We will change it by changing weasel thought. Surely, it can be done." He leaned forward into the extemporized doorway, shouting, "Silence!! Silence, please!" However, his distinctly large—not to say predatory—animal form did nothing to reassure the inmates, whose squawkings, cacklings and squeeings rose to yet higher volume before dropping back sufficiently to let him renew his request. Gradually, though, the noise began to die back to a level low enough for his voice to be heard, and some of the chickens at the edge of the throng nearest the Badger took a curious, hesitant step or two in his direction.

"We are the Animale Restoration Front!" he said, when he could be heard. "We are your friends! We are the friends of all the animal-oppressed! We are here to help you. Answer me, please: *do you know where you are?*"

Some of the birds began to make a low, even sound more like a dove's cooing than a squawk. The undulations of this the Mole began to understand to mean, *Home ... This is home ...*

"This is your PRISON!" shouted the Badger. "You must know this! You are prisoners here, and the way you are made to live here is an affront to the dignity of animalkind!"

This is home ... squooed the chickens. *This is the world.*

"Do any of you know how to stretch your wings?!" demanded the Badger, against the flow of bird-voices.

He was answered by a series of distressed cluckings that did not say either *yes* or *no*, or, if they did, were not clear enough to be intelligible.

"If you step through here—through this doorway that leads to freedom—you will be able to stretch your wings whenever you like!"

Gabblings, cluckettings, squeeings and cackles came from all directions. The Mole heard cries that seemed to say, *There is nothing through there, don't believe that animal, it is a door to nowhere! It is emptiness! It is the void! It is full of glare and brightness!*

Others repeated the call: *This is home ... This is the only safe place ... This is The World, this is The World ...*

Then, over to the Badger's left, a more focused squawking and clacketting seemed to be claiming, *They will eat us! He is lying! They only want to eat us! It's a trick! Don't go, don't go, don't go, don't go!*

"Blast it!" muttered the Badger, more irascibly than diplomacy might have wished. Then a paw was placed firmly on his arm. "The Press is here. Better move soon." It was the Otter.

Beyond him a gruff little voice said, "Oh, *Pawn*, that unbelievable *powng!* Dearie, dearie me! I hope I don't get anything on my shoes—only cleaned em' this mawning!"

You want to eat us! You're a big chicken-eater! You're a liar! came the fowls' accusations once again.

"We're *vegetarians*, dammit!" shouted the Badger, though to himself he added, "Apart from the Mole here."

Unfortunately, some of the nearest fowls must have heard this. *The **Mole** wants to eat us! The **Mole** wants to eat us!* came the babbling chorus. Hearing this, the Mole felt very, very guilty. If he had suddenly been lit up from inside so that he glowed in the dark he could hardly have felt more the centre of attention. He swore to himself that he would never eat chicken-paste sandwiches again, even if they had been made mostly with watercress.

With an effort, the Badger controlled his annoyance. "All right, birds!" he called. "It's up to you! I repeat—and it is the truth—you are *prisoners* here! Beyond this door we have made for you lies the wide world—the *real* world. I understand your fears! Yes, it can be a dangerous place. Yes, there are foxes and other beasts here that may attack you if you're unlucky. But these woods stretch out a long way, and there are others beyond, to the west—that way—that way!—and there is food in them. There is seed; the spring grass is just coming up sweet and green. That's a far, far better food than you have tasted—believe me! Free yourselves, if you so choose. Out there you can begin to live with dignity, as every chicken should!"

A series of contradictory currents became apparent in the crowd-voice, some of which still claimed, *No, no, it's dangerous! Don't trust them! It's warm in here, we're fed here, there is always food and water, this is home! We know where we are here, we know who we are, we know what's what! This is The World!*

Other, more isolated strands could be heard to echo some of the Badger's words: *Freedom? Dignity? Stretch our wings? Stretch our wings?*

Very slowly indeed, a handful of the bigger birds moved a few feet closer to the opening. As they did so the Mole saw that many of them had lost feathers, especially from their tails. One of these birds clucked out, *We want to see, we want to go. But we're afraid! Afraid! Afraid!*

"No need," said the Badger, his voice glowing with encouragement. "No need. It's up to you. It's your choice. We're leaving now. The way is open!"

He stepped back through the opening and a couple of the chickens came up to it, moving nervously up and down the threshold. Then one of them hopped out, falling over as she did so. But with a struggle she found her ground-legs, and then the next joined her, and the next.

A bright light flashed. (The Mole jumped. Amazingly, the chickens did not.) "Nice one!" said a voice. "Er ... can we 'ave a few more chickens in the background there, please? A few more chickens ...? Yeah, great ... No ... Er ... could you ... Just get them a *little* ... yeah ... up ... back ... Nice ... Nice! Egg-squizit, ge' it? Oh, yeah, this is wot choo *call* a photo opporchooni'iy! *Nice!* ... yeah ... just try one from this angle, yeah, great, great ... nice! Beeyoootiful, darlings ... *Nice ...*"

One of the chickens paused near the Badger's feet. *You said foxes*, it clucked. *We know about foxes. Word goes round, foxes are what is Out Here. They'll kill us. We know that.*

"It's the risk you have to take," said the Badger. "Tell them you were freed by the A.R.F. I can't guarantee it will help. I'm sorry. Try it, anyway. If you have to; you may never meet one."

Through the hole came the oceanic gabblings of the multitude. *Here, here is home! Warm, safe, food, know what's what, stay inside here, danger, danger!*

Mr Alfred Highodge of the *Berks and Oxon Amalgamated Chronicle* presented himself. "So, er——" he said, in his gruff little voice, "that's the Animale *Restoration* Front? Rest ... urr ... ay-shun. Right ..."

The Badger proceeded to give a swift "exclusive" interview

to this journalist, who in a down-at-mouth way seemed almost interested in what he had to tell him: it appeared genuinely new to him, and eccentric too. He duly noted down that the A.R.F. was fighting to restore '*animale*' practices and values in farming, and in the wider field of animal activity; that weasel values must be questioned and opposed ("That's important," said the Badger) where they did not lead to common benefits ("Don't know how we'll be able to get that one through, though," said Mr Highodge, chewing on his filter tip, "and of course, so far as the paper goes, I haven't seen you, not down 'ere"); that the chicken prison camps presented an unacceptable affront to animal dignity and to Nature itself ("Naychah itself, yeh"); that there was now a great tide of protest rising from what was, and would be again, the wellsprings of animal conscience—the burrow animals. ("The burrow animals—izzat right?" said Mr Highodge dubiously.)

"... Bit of a storm in a teacup though, intit?" Mr Highodge was heard to say as he and the photographer departed in the direction of their *motor*. "I mean, after all, they're only chickens when-all-is-said-and-done."

The Badger turned back to both Mole and Otter, the irony in his expression grey-shaded by moonlight but legible even so. Several of the escaped chickens were now standing at the woodland edge and one of these had found an area of loose dry soil. Driven by some knowledge that had survived through generations of shed-floor life, she was just beginning to make a shallow depression here in preparation for a dust-bath. A few feet away another bird stretched her wings out, drew them together again, and then flapped vigorously.

"*Good,*" said the Badger. "We've done all we can. Back to base! The Mole and I will go another way. I must get him back to his... hosts. Give me two to three hours."

So saying, the big animal led the Mole away in the general direction of the ridge on the top of which sat Darkwood

Park, this time making use of perfectly legitimate (though silent and unused) rights of way across the night-time fields. Over the whole distance, they spent not much more than five minutes walking on the tar of *motor*-roads.

They reached a point some two hundred yards from the brightly illuminated entrance gate, and its patient night-shift attendant, at five-to-nine exactly.

"Thank you, Badger," said the Mole. "Couldn't have got back here without you."

"A pleasure," said the Badger.

"I'd ask you in, but—"

The Badger laughed softly. "I think I might not be the most welcome guest."

"Well—"

"Think about what I suggested, won't you, Mole? You could help. No doubt about it."

The Mole scratched his nose. "All right," he said, though he still had no real idea what there was to think about.

"If ever you need to reach me, come to the plantation. You can find your way there?"

"Yes."

"You'll always be welcome. Remember that. And ... even if it looks as if no one is there, just hang about. Someone will spot you—get a message through."

"All right.—Thank you."

The two animals clasped in a swift creaturely embrace and the Badger stepped away into the shadows of the trees, where only the white stripes of his face-fur were visible. The Mole could just hear the sound of his steps at first as he followed the path away down the hill in the direction of the valley beyond.

CHAPTER NINE

TO-WE, OR NOT TO-WE?

At half past twelve on the following day the Mole found himself sitting on, under and amongst the low-lit red and gilt plush of the Riverside Restaurant at the Charolay Hotel in London's Strand. This—Mr Rette had explained to him warningly and in a low whisper as they entered—was a *world-famous* and *exclusive-beyond-all-other-imaginable-notions-of-exclusivity* restaurant, from which the Mole naturally assumed that for some reason or other it did not want customers.

The Mole sat on, under and amongst this low-lit plush—in a confusion that did at least by now feel middlingly familiar—at the right paw of one Mr Probity Stote, leader of what he had been told was the only opposition party worth the mention—the New Animalists. Mr Stote had quickly shown himself to be an animal possessed of energetic, even fervent, eloquence, and was, it seemed, "young" in terms of the politics of the day, which meant at best (to the Mole's eye in any case) not yet in need of a walking-stick.

On the Mole's other side sat a colleague of Mr Stote, Mr Nosepoak Catpole, whom the politician had introduced as his Shadow Minister: what he might shadow, or what shadow he might be under, was not clear. Mr Catpole was a European polecat, very well groomed and quietly spoken, whose eye-masks of charcoal fur seemed only to intensify the roseate glooms around him. Facing these three sat T.T.'s top axemal (as he had not long since been presented) Mr Gordon R. Rette, and Mr Humphrey Wyvern-Toad, whose reputation went before him.

As of nine-fifteen that morning the Mole—or, as he should no doubt better be known in the circumstances, Mr Mole—was fully and formally within the employ of the global-oligarchal-über-corps known as Toad Transoceanic, in the post of "Special Directorial Consultant". The fact that he did not know this—or, for that matter, have the first idea why he should be sitting amongst all this rather oppressive finery now—was quite beside the point, at least as far as his new boss was concerned.

The intricacies of ordering had already been dealt with. Mr Rette was to have *Coq-au-Champagne-en-Papillotes*, Mr Stote and Mr Catpole shared a like taste for *Poule-au-Pot Richard III*, whilst Mr Wyvern-Toad had ordered *Pintadeau Brochetté, Balafré, Pietiné et Flambé a la Riche*. Mr Mole, much to Mr Rette's ongoing embarrassment, had ordered nothing except *sautéed* spinach (it was one of the very few words on the menu in English), crossing his fingers that *sautéed* did not translate to mean 'with chicken' or, for that matter, any other kind of fowl.

"... But let's just be clear about this," Mr Stote was saying. "I am a realist! I am nothing *if not* a realist! I'm quite sure you know already, Mr Wyvern-Toad, I would be the very first to agree that any modern political party that is also serious about being in power *must* accept the realities of today's world. I have gone on record as saying as much, more than once, and in more than one country; and indeed, in more than one language in several of the countries concerned."

"Granted, Probity," replied the Toad, pushing back his seat until he was six inches further from the table. "But you see, I am just a tad curious to know what exactly you mean when you say, 'realities'. To be blunt: if any of my friends in the business sector *were* to think of running with your party—and you know of course that that is by no means certain——"

Mr Stote glanced casually towards the world-famous view of the river—banked, bordered and bridged as it was by a variety of large horizontal-rectilinear structures made of drab blotched grey-stuff, or grey-green stuff, with a diminishing perspective of towers beyond—as if to catch at an argument he had just spotted flying past the window. "Look, er——" he said, "if I may dare state the obvious …?"

"Please!" responded the Toad smiling and opening his small green hands.

"—— The Mystery Of The Market, Mr Wyvern-Toad. The Mystery Of The Market!"

"… is … er …?"

"There is not an animal left in politics, not a sane one, in any case, who does not now see and accept that society— national, global, society—has no other frame of reference— no principle of operation, if you like—*except* the Mystery. There is no other Great Idea left. There is no other Great Idea!"

The Toad raised an appreciative eyebrow and took a sip from his very long-stemmed wine glass.

"The Mystery is, I believe," went on Mr Stote, "in my heart of hearts, our first and last guiding principle. Although to call it a 'principle' is slightly to confuse matters, since, of course, it can never be understood, even less controlled or regulated. Such is the wonder of the thing. Ha, ha, it would hardly be a Mystery otherwise!"

"Ha, ha," said Mr Rette, and coughed.

"It could be said—I really do believe this—" the youth-lessly-youthful Stoat went on, "that we have now come to the end of political philosophy. In the face of a Global Marketplace, where funds vast enough to cripple or re-float entire Nations-of-Significance—why it's absurd to be saying this to you, of all animals, but—*enigmadillions* of dollars, *arcanatillions* of pounds sterling, *crypticrillions* of deutschmarks, *obfuscatillions* of yen—when such volumes of cash can be shifted electronically at the whim of the investor in less then the flicker of a Gila monster's eyelid ... Why, then, in the face of this new world order—this Mercantocracy, as Milton Trappratt terms it—where so many of the processes of commerce and job-creation are underpinned by great multi-territorial corporations such as ... well ..."

"Don't embarrass me, now!" said the Toad, grinning expansively.

"Oh, perish the thought! But in those circumstances, Mr Wyvern-Toad, it quite inevitably follows, doesn't it, that all fundamental 'decisions'—if I can use that word for convenience' sake—for any nation's well-being are already being reached in advance by something higher. Something that is, as it were, far more abstract, far wiser than the mere wills of individual governments: the *Global Cash-Flow Consciousness*, the *Planetary Psyche Of Profit-And-Loss* in all its ineffable randomness and inscrutability!"

"Ah yes ..." said the Toad pleasurably, taking a sip from a very slightly shorter glass. Mr Rette nodded sagely, frowning as he did so. The Mole suppressed an impulse to scratch his nose, frowning also.

"No government—really—" went on Mr Stote just as brightly, "*no* government can promise to work *too* hard for the social well-being of its animals any more. Look at what happened to Sweden, only last year! They tried it on, didn't they? And what happened? Why, the Market-Mystery simply—disapprovingly—pulled the plug, and all their painstaking, idealistic social programmes drained away in minutes down the P.E.D: The Plughole—"

"— of Economic Destiny, yes, yes! It's true enough. So what would you say, now, Probity (oh, and do call me W-T, by the way. Everyone else does!)," said the Toad, angling gently, "What would you say, then? Is there really no remnant of old ... principles? ... that you and your party would even *think* of trying to apply? Were you to find yourselves in power? In this modern, modern world of ours?"

Mr Stote opened his arms as if to embrace that world. "Put it this way, W-T," he said. "We of the New Animalists concede—I concede it myself, quite openly: your animals control the game. And the price of the tickets. It is and always was, I suppose, inevitable that that would happen. All that is left for we politicians to do now is to manage the pitch as best we may—"

"Maintain the stands—control the crowds ...?"

"You, and the Mystery, are global, vast, intrinsically out of reach. Present-day governments are little more than parish councils by comparison. Their first purpose today can only be—I'm sure I can put it this way, between friends—"

The Toad inclined his head slightly, warmth writ bright across his visage.

"— can *only* be to serve as the handmaidens of enterprise. Enterprise! Enterprise! Enterprise! *This* is the core agenda. And the bigger the enterprise, W-T, the more pliant must be the handmaids! We *must move* towards a fairer distribution of influence. Directly we take up office—and I can guarantee this to you now—we shall be working far harder than this present shambolic crew have ever done to eliminate whatever powers remain to government to block the aims—let's be clear, the Market-Mysterious, the unquestionable aims—of Business Strictly Of The Larger Kind."

"So—what?—'Environmental' laws ... animal rights laws ... consumer health-protection laws ...?"

"Oh, out of the window, W-T! Out of the window! 'Precautionary-principle' consumer protection? That has to go. Far too costly to Business! The right of Business (Strictly Of The Larger Kind) to sell what it makes—*however* and *when-*

ever it wishes to do so—must be seen as the standard by which every other is set."

The Toad raised an eyebrow. "... Even if ... not of course that it would happen, Probity ... but even if, say, some animals got a tiny bit under the weather now and then?"

"Ah—hah, hah. One wouldn't want to put it in quite those terms, perhaps."

"Not that it would matter, of course. Our researchers would still confirm the products in question to be perfectly harmless."

"And our review panels would agree with them, I'm sure!"

"— Not least. Probity, one hopes, because *our* representatives would continue to sit on them just as they do now? We do like to keep our fingers on the pulse, you know."

"Oh, more of them. W-T! More, and more, and more of them, yes, as a matter of fundamental principle! And not simply *on* our committees: your mals should *lead* our committees—whenever they can make the time, of course. Your decisions must be our decisions—I really do believe that. Politicians must always defer to the superior knowledge—the *savoir faire*—yes, if I can say this, the beguiling *savoir-faire*—of the world of business! Say, for example, we were to have a committee to look into the subject of fuel taxes on corporations—"

"Please, Probity! You will put me off my *pintadeau*."

"But if it did prove necessary for public manip ... er ... ah, public relations purposes, W-T, why then, who better to chair it than Lord Greaswesall of Aerobrit—?"

"... Ah! Ah yes. I catch your drift. Lord Greaswesall, whose views on the subject of aviation fuel taxes have always been healthily negative? As one should jolly well expect of a mal in his position!"

"Don't quote me yet on this—we are still pre-launch—but I can tell you that one of the pillars of the marketing strategy for New Animalism will be our original-concept Virtuous Foreign Policy—"

"It has wide appeal," suggested Mr Catpole. "Up to 57 per cent of those who do not know better think they want it."

"Exactly!" went on Mr Stote. "And who better to help implement it, in committee terms, than the directors of companies such as Arsenalspace UK and Obliviontia, without whose expertise in weapons manufacture no such policy could ever be enforced? The New Towns Agency? Who more capable of overseeing it than the head of our largest construction company, Greenfield Stoat himself? Competition policy? No doubt there either. We'll have Lord Ferrebury of Retco in on that one! As the chair of the country's most gigantic hyper-market chain, this is a mal who *knows* a thing or two about competition! The 'Environment' Commission?"

"Dear, dear, dear—"

"Well, of course, W-T, at this stage we have to keep it. But we're seriously thinking of putting Lord de Toadzie in to chair. His is a long and tireless record in the battle against futile 'environmental' legislation. And again, W-T—it goes absolutely without saying—if you yourself had any time free …"

"Always willing to help where one can, Probity."

"Well, for example, we had thought of you as a possible candidate for the important new post of Minister For Entrepreneurialism. With your background …?"

"I do spend *so* much time on the far side of the Atlantic. And, indeed, the Pacific. It is a problem. But, ah, don't rule me out yet."

"You might consider it?"

"I shall certainly consult my diary, Probity. That much I can promise you. But just to change tack here slightly for a moment, what is the position of the New Animalists on the financing of Chairs and Professorships and research units and so forth in the universities by little outfits such as mine? We do seem to have a need for more and more specialised gradu-ates these days—"

"And you will get them. W-T! Under us, I can guarantee you, British universities will finally break free from their time-warp as mere playgrounds of the intellect, pursuing (forgive me) 'knowledge for knowledge's sake'. Yes indeed! They will emerge gleaming into the light as the most sophisticated skills-factories on earth, customizing labour specifically to the needs of corporations such as Toad Transoceanic. Handmaidens of enterprise, W-T. Handmaidens of The Mystery—the universities as much as any!"

"Well said, Probity. Well said!"

"But the point is this, W-T. It's not just that we of the New Animalists comprehend this issue fully. I have to tell you: what we are actively working towards now—even as I speak—is a thoroughly revised, pure, high and radical state of modern political awareness—"

"— a *clarified* state," put in Mr Catpole quietly.

"— a clarified state, a *clarified* state!" echoed Mr Stote. "— In which it will be possible to make *every* decision without contamination by intermediary 'values', 'principles'—"

"— 'ideology'," said Mr Catpole, more quietly still.

"That above all," said Mr Stote. "Yes, yes. That above all!"

The Mole had just spotted a small platoon of waiters approaching with a miscellany of dimly gleaming platters, and tucked his napkin into his collar in readiness. Seeing this, the dismayed Rat kicked him beneath the table, signalling as subtly as he could that he should remove it again forthwith. Unfortunately, the Rat's signals proved so subtle that the napkin-wearer did not understand them, thinking instead that Mr Rette had come down with some possibly fatal constriction of the windpipe (he had been eating a kind of bean-stick made out of very old, dry bread.)

Gallant as ever, the Mole rose immediately to slap the sufferer on the back. In so doing he placed himself directly in the flight-path of a salver on which there sat a rather small fowl, which was also quite flat, skewered, and in flames. He

was saved from otherwise inevitable immolation only by the
nimblest last-second footwork of the waiter, who danced
around him even as the Mole was dancing aghast in the opposite direction, whence he glided on around the table, not
unballetically, in a state of extreme shock. As he drew close to
Mr Rette—whose grey face now wore the expression of one
just woken from, or into, a recurring nightmare—he heard
him hiss, "Sit *down!!*—Er, Mr Mole.—Please!" At the same
time, the Rat plucked the square of heavy white linen from its
offending location and stuffed it beneath his tail.

The Mole returned to his seat, dodging another bird-
bearing waiter on the way. He felt quite naked now without
his napkin, and slightly upset as well. After all, why had Mr
Rette stolen it? He already had one of his own.

"— So, er ... thank you, thank you ..." said the Toad, as
five waiters began to flit around him, spoons, ladles and
bottles murkily aglitter like sucker-footed bats around a
minaret in Madagascar. "— Should we take another example
not a thousand miles away from one's own field of endeavour,
Probity? The, ah, 'Right To Pollute'—as some wits have been
in the habit of calling it—which of course the To-We Party
has defended pretty staunchly through its long term in office?
A phase-out for top-end Deadlichem discharges, say? They
have been under a little pressure recently, at least to be seen to
consider it ..."

"You need have no worries on that score, W-T! We will
evade the issue in just the same way. Really, it goes without
saying.—Yes ... thank you, thank you. On the PM ... er, *PR*
front, I suppose there may be a case for a *little* more by way of
self-regulation ..."

"Senna pods!" said the Mole brightly, though to no one in
particular. "Never fail." He looked enquiringly at the corner
of the tablecloth: it might just do, he thought, in place of a
napkin.

"There has been a certain problem of style, hasn't there,

W-T, in recent years?" went on the Stoat. "Oil platforms dumped at sea, that kind of thing? It's very sad, but the electorat is still a little inclined to bouts of hysteria on issues of that sort."

"Point taken, Probity. Point taken. We have had such thoughts ourselves. Though of course we shall always have to weigh any practical changes against the tailline-of-taillines—"

Mr Stote gazed back at the magnate admiringly, to be sure he had grasped his meaning. "— The interests of the shareholders. W-T?"

"The interests of the shareholders, Probity. Nothing more sacrosanct!"

Feeling his boss's jocular elbow in his ribs here, Mr Rette paused. He had been in the act of lifting a piece of limp steamed courgette to his lips, and carefully avoided the eyes of the other animals. The courgette slid limply from his fork.

"But none of this alters the fact, does it, Probity," continued the Toad, "that your Party is still encumbered with more than its fair share of, how shall I put it, insistently over-principled animals? Old-style 'redistribution'-merchants and the like, still haunting your ranks? Ron Rabbett, say, or the wonderful Rodney Frogtrey? They *will* keep getting up and making those quaintly historic calls to arms. Some more of this excellent Beaune?—Waiter?" (The Mole looked sideways: surely, he thought, Mr Wyvern-Toad couldn't really be offering Mr Stoat a bone from his horribly scorched bit of bird?)

"Oh, we will have them damped down soon enough, W-T," responded the Prime-Minister-in-the-wings. "I guarantee it. But for the time being—up until the election, in any case—I think it might be an idea if we keep a few of the old-style Animalists about us. How else, after all, will the electorat be able to distinguish us from, hah-hah, the party we intend to drive from power?"

Eyebrows momentarily at full mast, the Toad nodded. "A point," he said.

Again Mr Catpole leaned forward, the dark foci of his tiny eyes almost lost amongst the gloaming of his fur-mask. "Our researches have shown," he said in his low, calm voice, "that the ethical style can be marketed successfully."

"That's at the heart of the thing, you see!" said Mr Stote, his nostrils positively quivering with enthusiasm. "But that aside, I don't need to tell you, W-T: there is a great weariness with the To-Wes now, after all this time. The same old voices. The same old faces. Really, you know, all those long orange snouts! Yet in the very same breath I have to speak the never-spoken truth: a modern electorat will never support anything except another form of Weaselry. Isn't that the case? That is why what we of the New Animalists offer them instead is ..." Mr Stote opened his paws.

"... The To-We Party at prayer," said Mr Catpole, rather as if he had just unveiled a small plaque in a shopping mall, and echoed his colleague's gesture. "... Give or take a few minor details."

Mr Stote sat back, tapped the end of his long orange snout, and beamed. "Let's take an example," he said. "'Open Government'? Yes, we can offer that. Of course we can. Entirely feasible."

"Market-proven," said Mr Catpole. "Wide consumership appeal."

The Toad looked momentarily perplexed. "— But you wouldn't want to do anything so foolish as, say, passing a Freedom Of Enquiry Act? Surely!"

Did Mr. Stote's breathing become a hair's-breadth heavier at that moment? He did look sharply at Mr Catpole, and crumbled the end of the biscuit-stick he had been using as a pointer. "Well, er, we may need to be seen to be interested in it," he said.

"— as an aspect of the New Elegance," added Mr Catpole quickly. "The New And More Fecund Seeming." (The Toad held up his glass in appreciation of this phrase.)

"But I am completely certain," continued Mr Stote, "that if we set the right mals to the task it will be possible to build in all manner of clauses, and sub-clauses, and riders, and qualifications, so that whilst we may seem to be making changes, we can in fact arrive at a state of affairs in which no one is the wiser about anything. Who knows, we may even be able to improve on what the To-Wes have been pretending to offer, in that *passé* style of theirs!"

"We do have plans for a 'Right Of Enquiry'," said Mr Catpole, "by which any member of the public who dares to try to find out how things are done is *guaranteed* to end up knowing less than they did when they began."

"The American style, W-T!" grinned Mr Stote. "The grand old American style!"

"'America-in-England' then, Probity?" said the Toad, holding up his glass.

The Stoat gazed back at the Toad as if entranced by his choice of words. "Oh!" he said, raising crystal to crystal, "'America in England', W-T! Wherever—whenever—whatever—*whoever*! '*America in England*'!"

Mr Stote and Mr Wyvern-Toad laughed together affably; Mr Catpole and Mr Rette grinned thinly; and Mr Mole struggled on with his stringy *sautéed* spinach (which, he thought—and he didn't want to be churlish but—which really didn't taste anything like so good as the succulent, bite-worthy stuff he had once been able to grow in his own small garden).

Gliding away from this summit half an hour later in one of his statelier limousines, Mr Wyvern-Toad leaned forward in his seat and touched the Mole on the sleeve. "Very intriguing!" he said. "Wouldn't you agree, Mr Mole? Did we need you there, I wonder, or did we not? I have a strong suspicion that Mr Stote might have said almost exactly the same things even if you hadn't been sitting there right next to him."

The Mole did not find this idea so very surprising, and was therefore rather stumped for a useful reply. "O," he said. "Ah. S'pose he would."

The limousine was chauffeur-driven today, and for the very best of reasons, viz. that Mr. Wyvern-Toad and his two companions were now travelling in it to attend the second part of the opening day of the To-We Party Conference which—this being March—was being held at the salubrious and popular south-coast holiday resort of Hove. The Toad might just have been lunching with the Leader of the Opposition, but he had by no means yet severed those ties of affection and friendship that attached him, however opaquely, to the party still in power.

The sea-front at Hove was noted (Mr. Rette explained, when asked) for its several-mile-long display of lights and illuminated flashing signs, many of them attached to buildings housing funfairs, amusement arcades, and other covered entertainments. Normally these would have been switched on only at dusk, but during Conference Week the To-We-supporting premises—still the majority, it seemed—put their lights on during the day as well. Mr. Rette was just trying to explain the meaning of the word "neon" to the Mole when the long black car with its smoked-glass windows slowed to a halt in the approaches to a huge building that might have been some kind of theatre. On the front of this hung what must have been the largest illuminated sign on the whole sea-front. It was made in the shape of a Union Jack whose component elements—the Cross of St. George and the national emblems of those other, hilly countries bordering on England—each lit up individually, flashed several times over, then united in a glorious blaze of red, white and blue before blacking out to begin the cycle all over again.

But the limousine was not able to complete its journey to the striped awning that covered the way from celebrity drop-off-point to entrance, since the area of road in question was already occupied by a large group of animals. These were chanting and waving banners, one of which the Mole saw to read UNITE AGAINST SPECIESISM! Another long fabric banner held up by a line of animals read **NO** TO THE KEEP-'EM OUT BILL! At the far side of this group, however, a second and larger line of animals was swiftly advancing. These the Mole took to be soldiers, since they wore curious shiny visors over their faces and carried weapons resembling staves. But Mr Rette explained, when asked, that they were policemals.

"Perhaps we should park somewhere else, sir?" suggested Whipplewhitt, the driver, who (the Mole noted) had cleverly learned how to project his voice through inch-thick glass. The Toad agreed, and the big car swayed around and ran up into a quiet alley at the side of the Conference Hall.

The Toad threw open a door and leapt out nimbly over the prostrate form of a semi-conscious derelict, who lay on a narrow strip of pavement between the alley's cobbled gutter and the wall. This figure—an aged frog, as it happened—had not been spotted by Whipplewhitt, whose eye was on the demonstration in his rear-view mirror. "Great Dane, these animals are everywhere!" said Mr Wyvern-Toad absent-mindedly, already scanning the building's long wall for sight of some other way in.

"O!" said the Mole, hurrying round the back of the car. "But we must help him!"

"I have already helped him, Mr Mole," said the Toad, still squinting. "I help him every day, as it happens, by generating a not insubstantial slice of this country's wealth. This drops down through a series of filters and sifters to end—some small part of it, I am perfectly sure—in *his* doss-house."

"Yes, but—"

"In any case, you know, Mr Mole, you must catch up! Everyone in this country is an *individual* now. We go our way, he goes his, all of us pursuing our individual destinies and, well, there you have it. Keep things simple, my dear animal!"

"But—but—" said the Mole, who was by now tugging at Mr Rette's over-extended sleeve and pointing in a hopeless way at the inert slab-dweller.

"Come on, gent'mals, hurry now, or we'll miss Mr Nuttmutch's speech!" urged the Toad. "And I'm sure he has a lot to tell us."

"Oh—!!" gritted Mr Rette, frenetically fumbling through his pockets as he did so. "Here! Give him this!"

The Mole pushed the money into one of the supine animal's tattered pockets, thinking as he did so that he would have been a lot better off with a bowl of soup and some warmth from a nice fire, and a friendly word or two. But he had no chance to dwell on such details, and no more than ninety-five seconds later he found himself walking up a flight of thickly carpeted steps into the Conference Chamber itself. This was an auditorium of such breadth, cavernous height, and multi-spotlit brilliance that for one moment the Mole fell back, unable to force himself on into its lofty spaciousness, or to face the great frozen tidal wave of animal faces it contained. Seeing him hesitate, the Rat turned back, putting a hand under his arm and encouraging him on.

"I want my hole!" moaned the Mole in a tiny voice.

"That's just what you'll get if you don't come on!" gravelled the Rat in a comparably tiny whisper, as both of them were hurried on in turn by ushers. "… Mr Mole," he added, in respect to the Mole's new status within the company.

Once inside the auditorium, the Mole could see that at least two thirds of the gathering was made up of weasels, stoats or ferrets. Every few seats or so there was a toad or two, easily distinguishable even at a distance thanks to a certain innate verdancy. But the other animals …! The other animals were recognisable as hedgehogs, rabbits, squirrels, rats, shrews—yes, and even the occasional mole—only at a second or third glance. For over their own, relatively much shorter noses each one of them was wearing a long, false weasel-snout, held on with elastic rather like a party mask. Yet stranger still, on most of the faces which the Mole could see closely, the wearing of these masks was pretty superfluous. For in each he seemed to see the same bright-button-eyed rapacity—the same snarling, weaselesque ferocity—barely concealed under a veneer of civilised behaviour. The toads, he also noticed, went unsnouted.

"We don't have to wear those noses, do we?" he whispered urgently.

"No!!" snowled Mr Rette. "Never mind!!—Forget it! *Don't look!*"

Thanks to the earlier good offices of Mr Gibbert Phangachs and others, Mr Wyvern-Toad and his colleagues were immediately taken to seats allowing them the most uninterrupted view possible of the proceedings, in the very middle of the front row. This was a great relief to the Mole since it meant that the tilting multitude of animals now rose up out of sight behind him. Sitting to his left he found an immaculately be-suited fellow mole, sporting an extra-long weasel snout—it appeared to be making his own nose itch—and a pair of socks that looked as if they had been stitched together out of four small Union Jacks. The same design was also to be found on his breast-pocket handkerchief, his tie (in elongated form) and his cufflinks (very small, in enamel). On the far right of the group, beyond the Rat and the Toad, sat Mr Phangachs himself.

Almost as soon as they were settled, the auditorium began to crackle with applause and an animal—the Prime Minister himself, the Mole presumed—stepped forward from a row of be-seated others to a rostrum at the middle of a broad stage decorated in shades of the party's emblematic colour, Portland grey. This creature was not a weasel, nor for that matter spurio-weselo-proboscate. He was a bespectacled squirrel of middle years: anything further from the musteline would have been difficult to imagine. From close to, his mild-mannered, slightly diffident stance suggested (to the Mole, at least) that he might have preferred to be doing something entirely different—playing shove-halfpenny in a tap-room, for example.

The Squirrel began his speech immediately, before all the applause had died away, and was listened to thereafter in an attentive silence—except perhaps, it is shameful to relate, by the Mole himself, who found it very difficult to concentrate after the first few minutes. This was partly due to the sopo-rific drone of the Squirrel's voice, whose verbal emphases seemed to die in his throat even while singing the praises of his government's *sloops of policies* and *dreadnought bills*. But it may also have been due to the fact that the Mole had not the first idea what he was talking about.

The Mole's thoughts began to wander in the direction of the prodigious architectural gulf above and around him. He gazed up at the ceiling with its nebulae of spotlights—half a mile away, or so it seemed—wondering what kinds of stepladders they could possibly use when they had to repaint it, and how anyone could hold them steady. And who would ever be brave enough to go up there? He shuddered. When his mind did drift back to the Prime Minister, it settled on the odd shape of his spectacles—a shape that was echoed across the faces of hundreds of seated animals. To the Mole these resembled nothing so much as two window-boxes set side by side, so that it seemed there was a programme (a word he had learned two mornings previously) on in each, the rather unvarying subject of which was a large, tired eye. He noticed too how stiffly the Squirrel held his great bush of a tail, as if he feared it might otherwise drop off into the auditorium.

"... There can be no doubt, therefore," the Prime Minister was intoning, "that this Government has been responsible for a *sustained recovery*—yes, year on year, year on *year*, and year on year on *year* on year—a recovery always soundly based on *Investment, Enterprise, Exports,* and the timeless faith of our great Party in the ever-rejuvenating force of *Private Ownership* ..."

In what looked like a no more than twenty-times-rehearsed moment of spontaneity, the Squirrel stepped neatly to one side of the rostrum, leaving his speech notes conspicuously behind him, to a tiny ripple of appreciative applause. "This weasel—this toad—yes, this great *mixed-animal* family has come together here with me today to renew its deep family links with the whole of British malhood ..."

He began to walk towards the front of the stage. "And I know we shall all be working together now, with gritty resolution, yes, and with that buccaneering spirit that has always driven the To-We Party onward from one great triumph to the next. ..Yes, I say—" (and by now the Prime Minister had moved to the very centre of the stage and thus, as it happened, closer to the Mole than to any other person present) "— Yes, I tell you!—With all the bloody, ruthless me-firstism of which those pioneering gay-blade piratical rovers, the buccaneers, were capable!"

A light hail of 'Ohs' that might have expressed confusion, or even shock, were heard from various points in an otherwise silent hall. "Now let's be honest with ourselves," said Mr Nuttmutch, a new energy suddenly apparent in his voice and bearing. "If the opinion polls are to be believed, fellow To-Wes, then this Government has already lost favour with a much, much larger section of the electorat than we'd like to imagine—let alone, ha, ha—admit in public!" (He paused for just one moment here, his rag-weary eyes staring in panic behind his window-boxes.) "We—ah—hah!—all know that Mr Probity Stote and his so-called 'New' Animalist party have only got as far as they have because they have stolen the mantle of To-Weism from us. What *is* 'New' Animalism but weaselry-and-water? Weaselry-without-the-fangs? Yes, Conference—weaselry-without-the-Snout?!" (Applause, some laughter.)

"Probity Stote says he has embraced me-firstism ... though, of course, ah, hum, we never call it that in public." (The boxed-in eyes stared hard once more.) "Oh yes. *Oh* yes! We're all Priestessites now!" (After a disturbed pause there came heavy applause from isolated pairs of paws.)

"He likes to pretend that any government he led would make 'virtuous' changes. Yet what could be more virtuous, fellow To-Wes, what could be more ethical—than the society that exists already, which *we* have created? Do we not already have in this country a legislative, a cultural, a moral framework in which all the decent, ordinary working animals who fight hardest to clear a space in the jungle—yes, like the buccaneers who infested the Americas' Spanish coasts, ever ready to work at slash-and-burn and destroy the occasional village where they had to—can guarantee good livings—very good livings—for themselves and their families? This is the modern self-help society! Yes, Conference, the self-help-by-helping-yourself society—a society in which the staunchest will always say, 'My need is greater than thine'!"

If the Squirrel's glass-veiled eyes had been bulbous earlier, they nudged the telescopic now. But he paused only long enough to allow a couple of fulsome cries of "Wo!" and "Wo-yo-wo!" from younger audience members to break the silence. Mr Phangachs, meantime, had leaned forward in his seat, horror engraved upon his features, and was staring past both toad and rat towards the Mole in what looked like the deepest suspicion.

"Let's face it, Conference," said the Prime Minister. "Maybe the polls are accurate. Maybe they are, yes! But think, fellow To-Wes, isn't the answer already there in front of us, staring us hard in the face?—The *weasel heart*, Conference! The *hidden weasel-heart*! Hidden as it may be, I do believe—with every fibre of my being, I do believe—there is a weasel-heart beating in every animal in this country! It is not just you, my friends, who have donned the Snout here today." (There was laughter—affable, or nervous—from a handful of spurio-proboscites and others near them.) "It is not just *you* who have found the flame of weaselry burning in your innermost being! There are millions out there—tens of millions!—not just those who support us, but those who do not yet know what it is to support us! It is to these animals that we must appeal now, to secure the continuance of this great Party in power. The vast majority are, I believe, *always* ready to condemn what they do not understand, *always* graced with the ability to form hard-and-fast opinions without consideration of the subject—yes, Conference! No less than any one of you fine animals, seated here today—ahh ..."

Noble conviction and abject, gelatigenous funk were now mingled together in the Prime Minister's face in roughly equal measures. He tugged despairingly at a triangle of material in his breast pocket, wiping first his damp tawny brow and then his spectacles (actions he might have been better off performing the other way round.)

"... And I say to you again," he went on in a strangling *falsetto* that deepened in moments to *soprano orotundo*, "it is to exactly that fine-tuned British readiness to condemn others at the drop of a hat that the GOTWA must make its primary appeal today! We must work harder, my friends, than we have ever worked before, to bring down the high dudgeon of the nation on all those who live at the shadowy outer fringes of the Mystery.—Yes, I *mean* the unemployed! I *mean* the homeless! I *mean* all of those who choose to lurk, hidden away from sight in that regressive dropout order, the burrowers! What are these animals? Decipher my incisors, Conference. They are *feckless!* What else are they? They are *bone idle!* These are the self-made *sofa-parsnips* of our time—where they own sofas, and do not simply sit on the bare earth!" (Cries of "Hear, hear!" rose from a number of aged female throats.) "These are animals who are *simply not prepared to work.* They are *a drain on the State*; they are a constant, rock-heavy *burden* on that noblest and longest-suffering of creatures, *the Taxpayer!*" (Here applause began loudly at hall-top-right and spread slowly across the entire gathering, gaining volume before it died.)

"We must *breed* and *bleed* this tendency to condemn!" shouted Mr Nuttmutch, in whom a glassy-eyed conviction seemed now to have triumphed over any earlier conflicts of feeling. "Yes, I say, bleed it—bleed it, and breed it—in so doing uniting all honest, decent British citizens by touching their innermost spirit of mean mindedness where it is most tender! What are the single mothers? Lenticulate my labia, Conference! They are an *outrage!* They are *an insult to the scruples of every decent mammal!* They are *shiftless!* They are *irresponsible,* many of them barely older than children themselves!" (Heavy applause.) "What do they do? Why, I hardly need tell you what they do. They plot—they scheme—to get themselves pregnant, so that they can spend the most productive years of their lives *living at leisure at the Taxpayer's expense!*"

This sparked off another round of applause, with shouts of "Hey, Carrol! Say it, Carrol!" and "Wo!" "Yo!" and "Wo!-Yo!-Wo!" For one moment Mr Nuttmutch basked like a sun-dappled basking shark in the warmth of the response. "Let us not—let us not *ever,*" he said, "for one moment contemplate the possibility that any of these loafers are living as they do as some side-effect of the Market Mystery. No. Absolutely, categorically—no! Remember, Conference, *they are* our working stock of plausible scapelice. To be poor *is* to be blameworthy. To be homeless *is* to be damnable, to the hidden weasel-heart, and as we look about us today, why, isn't there fuel on every side with which we may continue to kindle the fires of condemnation in it?" (The uneasy quietness returned, though again broken by cooings of assent from aged female voices.)

"— The asylum seekers," said Mr Nuttmutch. "What are they? Fixate my dentures, Conference! Yes, yes: they are *bogus!* We need not say as much of them, of course. We need only imply it, to touch that ever-sensitive nerve—that ever-flowing wellspring of intransigent xenophobia—pulsing through the breast of every decent indigenous mammal. *Think the worst*: it might be our motto."

The Mole, frowning and muttering to himself, had just discovered a small humbug—a humbug from the Past, no less—lurking in the deepest corner of his watch-pocket. Brushing from it a little watch-pocket pocket-dust, he put it in his mouth, hoping vaguely that it might do something to relieve the distaste he was feeling at having to listen to this (it did seem) really very disagreeable display of humbug from the Present.

The Prime Minister half-turned to the row of animals behind him on the stage, several of whose faces had by now taken on the fixed and sub-pellicularly pallid look of corpses. "My most valued colleague the Home Secretary," (here one of the row, an especially vicious looking, gimlet-fanged and bespectacled ferret, twitched slightly) "is—and rightly so— most highly regarded in the Government for the bold, unflinching line he has taken on the punishment of crime. And yes, Conference! It is *criminals* who cause crime, not social conditions!" (Vigorous applause in two sectors, kindling again to high volume as the complexity of the idea was absorbed.) "And it is *punishment* that deters criminals, not any feather-brained 'animale' pursuit of understanding of the hypothetical background to criminality in so-called 'deprived childhoods'!" (Faster applause, with swifter ignition, and cries of "Wo-yo Carrol! Tell them, Carrol!" from a number of the younger sources, modulating—rather as if the utterers had just had their tails slowly run over by a bus—into long high-pitched wails of "Woooooo!" and "Yoooooo!")

"Yes—yes!" shouted Mr Nuttmutch into the penultimate "Yoooooo!" with a couple of dynamic sideswipes of his long grey tail. "The decent-honest citizens of this country *all need something to hate!* This is the truth, fellow To-Wes: the country *needs* its criminals!" (The hall fell rather too quiet again.) "Our young thugs! Yes! Our dear young thugs! We need them no less than we need the asylum seekers, the feckless, idle unemployed. They too are lynch-pins in this broad British landscape of condemnation, that will, I believe—once just a little more work has been done—serve to reunite the honest-decent majority behind us in a triumphant display of that steel-eroding vitriol on which this great Party of ours must always thrive!" (Again here there were brief outbreaks of applause, Yo-yoings and Woo-wooings.)

"We *must learn*, females and gent'mals—British society as a whole *must learn*—" said Mr Nuttmutch, with all the weight of which he was capable, "to *condemn* a little *more*. To *understand* a little *less*."

This reverberant precept had been launched on the ocean of faces with what proved impeccable timing. "*Condemn* a little *more!*" shrieked one crone-vole at the rear of the hall, her synthetic weasel-snout wobbling crazily over her whiskers. "*Understand* a little *less!*" bawled a sweating, suede-furred weaselkin in a silk Paisley waistcoat. —"Wo!—Yo!—Wo!"

"*Condemn more!*" sang a trio of dowager ferrets. "*Understand less!*" yelled others near them in hideous polyphony. "*Loathe* a little *more!*" screamed a bevy of plump male stoats of a certain age. "*Love* a little *less!*"

"No quarter!" shouted the invisibly-flushed Prime Minister, stirring the emotion that rose up amongst the still-growing tide of voices, as if it were the contents of some great pudding-basin of phobias. "No mercy! No hiding-place!"

"*CONDEMN* A LITTLE *MORE!*" came the baying and/or squealing cry from a good half of the audience. "*UNDERSTAND* A LITTLE *LESS!*"

Glitter-eyed elderly female weasels, strings of pearls a-dance upon their bosoms, their crocheted hats falling from them in the mêlée; rotund, balding little business-rabbits; flat-topped young ferrets moist-eyed with malice; grim-jawed, jowly old dormice and shrews in ill-fitting suits; even some of the (to this point) self-restrained toads—all now rose from the floor in unison to the rhythmically-delivered chant, "CONDEMN-MORE! UNDERSTAND-LESS! CONDEMN-MORE! UNDERSTAND-LESS!" whilst through and against this gradually emerged the grim antiphon, "PUNISH! PUNISH! PUNISH! PUNISH!" Gibbert Phangachs was on his hind legs with the rest now, his pop-eyes more than popping in rude musteline ecstasy as he screamed out, "*Hang*-them! *Hang*-them! *Hang*-them! *Hang*-them!"

Mr Wyvern-Toad, still seated next to him, looked about him in what might for all the world have been quiet amusement.

<hr />

After such a high point, the rest of the afternoon's proceedings could only have seemed an anticlimax. The Prime Minister stood at the edge of the stage—exulting, in a subliminally anxious kind of a way—in what proved to be the longest standing ovation given to any To-We leader in office since the War. Then he yielded the platform to various of his Ministers who stood in turn to make rather more conventional speeches. (None of these left the safety of the rostrum.)

So it was that, some two hours of mostly uneasy dozing later, the Mole found himself standing, yawning, in the theatre's Marine Lounge with its uninterrupted and to him—since this was his very first view of it—unsettling panorama of the flat grey waters of a southern ocean. He stood now with a cranberry-jelly and passion-fruit *canapé* in one hand, a clam *paté* and paw-paw *vol-au-vent* and a glass of queer-tasting stuff called "Pimmpps" insecurely gripped in the other. Mr Rette was also not unresentfully holding in reserve for him a nibble combining *gaffelbieter* and olives stuffed with pine kernels. The Rat himself was not eating and drank only mineral water since, as he had just confided to the Mole, he had started to feel a bit queasy during the speeches. "Just one of those things," he said. "Comes and goes—you know."

"You ought to boil up some nice fresh mint," the Mole advised. "Stand it for an hour, that's what you do. Then drink it down. That'll set you right. Where do you keep the mint in your garden?"

"Mint? I've no idea. Do we have mint? ... Mint ... mint ... Can you get it in capsule form?"

"Kap—seyool—?"

"— Oh, but who am I *asking*?"

The Mole and the Rat stood crammed into a tight huddle (the seemingly endless room was, seemingly endlessly, packed), still in the company of the Toad but also now in the presence of Mr Hejj Hogsquatch, the Minister for Road Promotions. Also present were (to Mole's left) Mr Nigel P. Doggesbotham, Junior Minister For Invisibly Subsidised Exports, and (to the Mole's right) Mr David Selweaze-Todd, who held the important post of Minister For Munitions Panderage. Rather in the background stood a Mr Lori van Feretaar, President of the Road Lumberers' Association.

The Mole was disturbed (it goes almost without saying— the Mole was always disturbed) by the appearance of the third of the four just-mentioned. He was a tall, imposing and perhaps, in weasel terms, darkly handsome animal, yet he seemed also to have about him some faint hint—some bizarre, sketchy implication—of the toad.

At first everyone in this circle had been rather stiffly agreed that the *ex tempore* sections of the Prime Minister's speech had been "extraordinarily successful", if at times "a trifle risky".

"When it comes down to it," said Mr Hogsquatch, "all that matters is how it plays in Swindon. If it went down okay in Swindon—"

"— Particularly in Swindon East, of course," ventured Mr Doggesbotham.

"Yes, and above all with those crucial residents in Numbers 1 to 53a, Meadowside Close—then we may still be in with a chance."

"They'll like it," said Mr Doggesbotham, stroking the silky curls of his short spaniel-snout in a manner worthy of a Restoration princeling. "The animalist press will pillory him, of course. But what *is* the animalist press these days? And who reads it? And they were always going to pillory him anyway, so where was the risk? And the PM's completely right, of course. We must appeal to the hidden weasel-heart!"

"Just give 'em more roads," said Mr Wyvern-Toad provokingly, one eye on the relevant minister. "Just give 'em more roads! That'll keep them happy. You'll have to find the money, Hejj. Sooner or later!"

"Oh, you don't need to worry yourself about that, W-T," responded Mr Hogsquatch, a thin-lipped animal whose deep permanent fur-frown qualified even his least insincere attempts at a smile. "The Treasury will come our way eventually. By the time we're finished every Clearway in the country will be at least twice its present width.—Not that we ever will be finished, of course."

"Dear, dear—only *twice*?" responded the Toad in stagy mock-disappointment.

"*At least* twice is what I said! Ha, ha, can't catch me there, W-T. No, no!"

"Just so long as we have the blacktop, Hejj. The roads must go on rolling, eh?"

"They will," responded Mr Hogsquatch with earnest ardour. "They will! After all, W-T, no one knows better than you how much I love roads. Big roads—yes, great big roads! Concatenations of contiguous Clearway concrete! And bypasses—yes, yes!—and bypass-bypasses! And then—why not?—bypass-bypass-bypasses to by-bypass them!" A mystic gleam had risen in the Minister's blackcurrant little eyes and shone there now like moonlight on two tiny duckponds, though the Mole was shocked to see that Mr Van Feretaar—who stood very close behind him—had a tight grip on his tail, and appeared to be squeezing it even tighter as he spoke. "Oh, run straight on through all those dank, wet water-meadows! Bulldoze a path through the fringes of all those boring temple closes! Slice right though those 'historic' parks and all those piffling little Polka Dots Of Scientific Concern! Flyover-flyovers? Yes! And flyover-*flyover*-flyovers to over-fly their lovely, lovely fly-flyoverliness!"

"That's the spirit, Hogsquatch," said the Toad. "That's what we want to hear!"

"... And *cars*, W-T!—*Oh!* Oh, *W-T!* I *love* cars! You know it—you know it. I have *always* loved cars! I love their engines! I love their carburettors! It's true—I'm perfectly *crazy* about carburettors! I'm *mad* about manifolds! *Potty* about pistons! Just helplessly *beside myself* about big e—"

The Toad held up a wineglass-hand with the greatest delicacy. "And we're very glad to hear it, Hejj," he said, in a way that confirmed he had heard it more than once before. "But you know," he went on, addressing himself to all three politicians at once now, "you fellows really ought to try to do something about all these beggars and homeless about the place. They don't exactly help the image, do they? As someone I was talking to recently might have put it—it's not the best marketing strategy. Damn near tripped over one myself just now, right outside the hall here."

"The beggars, oh, the beggars," volunteered Mr Selweaze-Todd with weary *hauteur*. "It's quite true of course, W-T. They are a serious embarrassment. Absurdly too many of them on the streets. And what is so appalling about it is that most of them seem to come from *Glasgow*."

"We should jolly well send them back there, then!" said Mr Doggesbotham, laughing. (As he spoke, Mr Hogsquatch was approached by an animal with a clipboard and apologised himself away into the crowd, closely followed by his ferret friend.) "... So, David. What have you been up to of late?" There was a certain fraternal chattiness in the Spaniel's tone, perhaps hinting at expectations—justified or otherwise—for his own career. "Haven't seen much of you in the House."

"No, Nigel," said Mr Selweaze-Todd, who, as these things happen, was now standing so close to the Mole that he was virtually standing on him. "You wouldn't have done, no. Very busy elsewhere actually ... In point of fact, I have just yesterday finally brokered what is certainly the most phenomenal private arms deal of the past ten years. The Omanians, you know. All absolutely top secret and off the record, of course—not *quite* mainstream, ha, ha—but—ah— with not a bad little percentage for oneself, all things considered."

The Minister's formerly complacent large black eyes were now staring much as if their owner had swallowed an avocado-stone—as did the eyes of all politicians who chanced to rub shoulders with the Mole or, as here, rub elbows with the Mole's shoulders.

Mr Selweaze-Todd looked sharply behind him, then beside him (on both sides), then beneath him, as if urgently checking the floor for the presence of animals with jotter-pads or microphones. "Wha—?" he said. "Who—? Whi—?"

"Ah-haaah!" responded Mr Doggesbotham, nudging his colleague conspiratorially in the waistcoat. "*Secret arms deals*, eh? Big potatoes, David! Capacious croquettes! No, Minister, I have to say it: bubble-and-squeak of bulgiform proportions! Pan knows, David, *any* percentage of an arms deal short of a percentage of a percentage of a percent is some percentage! Eh? (And even a percentage of a percentage of a percent would be well worth sniffing at.)"

"Be quiet, you fool!"

"But—*arms* deals?" repeated Mr Doggesbotham, just a little more quietly, envy deep-etched upon his tone. "Great

Crested Grebes! I wish I could report anything on that kind of scale. *Eheu*, Minister, for one's own part one does still seem to be stuck with all the usual humble little scams. Opinions sales—naturally, it goes without saying. But ARMS SALES? That's right down at the other end of the pool, I'm afraid!"

"Shut up, shut up!" hissed the toadesque Weasel through gritted fangs, still staring about him for signs that anyone had overheard. "Shut *up!*"

"Life being what it is, though," continued the Spaniel breezily, and almost as if he had not heard these warnings, "I suppose it is still quite pleasant to get the occasional little liquid reward for questions in the House.—Such as one does *not* remember to declare in the Prestigious Members' Register Of Interests, David, we barely need to ... ahh ..." (A hoarsely-harrowed note had entered Mr Doggesbotham's tone as well by now, and anguish and self-regard were blending in his face like vinegar and cocoa thrown carelessly together by some bungling cook's assistant.) "... We barely need to ... mention ...?"

For just one moment the Toad caught the eye of Mr Rette, responding amusedly to the million-word gaze he found there.

"Ubbh ... hbbh ..." said the Junior Minister For Subsidised Exports, grasping at one of his own, crumplable ears and staring at some imaginary point of infinity with eyes no less large than those of his distinguished colleague. "I did not say that!—Yes, I did!—*No*, I didn't! I did *not* say that, and I will sign a sworn testimony to that precise and substantive effect, on this instant! Put it before me—come on, come on! Elaborate it—put it on House Of Commons headed notepaper—give me witnesses—make copies on vellum in quintuplicate—stamp it with the Seal Privy—where is it? I'll sign. I'll sign! I did say it. I did—I did say—I did say exactly what I said. What I said was ... what I said. Nothing other, and it's ..." (he uttered a low whine) "... it's ..."

"... 'true'? ..." suggested Mr Wyvern-Toad.

"*That is not a word one uses!*" snapped Mr Doggesbotham, baring his teeth to the gums as he did so. "I do beg your pardon—I do—er—beg your pardon, Mr Wyvern-Toad. Ha, ha. Ha."

"Think nothing of it. Been up to—ahhh, anything else much, recently?"

"Oh, just the usual sorts of trade, you know. Badgering one or two of my senior colleagues to get them into talks with— well, ah—some of the mals from your end of town, actually, Mr Wyvern-Toad.—That pays pretty well, David, as it happens. Not up to *arms sales* standards, but it covers the time-share in Tossa del Mar, eh? With a bit left over for the odd crate of Rioja!"

"… My end of town, Mr Dogsbotham? You said …?" nudged the Toad gently. "Not, oh, I don't know … Toadenholl, for example?"

"Yes, him!"

"And, let me see … Owlsuit?"

"Yes, yes!"

"Nathajacques?"

"Er … no. Not him. Not yet!"

"Bankvole?"

"Yes—*oh*, yes!"

"How *very* interesting. You must send me a list …

"I'd be—ah—hah, delighted. Would I?" The Spaniel gulped deeply enough to cause serious concern for the coupling on his uvula. "Ahhhh—ha, ha. D—D— Doggésbothàm, by the way."

"Apologies—apologies. First time we've met, isn't it? Doggésbothàm—of course."

"Dog—Ezz—Boat—Arm," mouthed the Mole under his breath, practising against the moment when he might have to speak the name.

His face-fur now bristling with suspicion, much as if it had been roughed the wrong way with a suede-brush, Mr

Selweaze-Todd stared at his drink and then laid it and a piece of half-eaten canapé on to the tray of a passing waiter. He looked as if he were on the verge of departing, but lingered even so. "What, er—what, Nigel—I think you mentioned ... 'liquid' rewards, just now?" he said carefully. "They don't *arrive* in alcoholic form, one presumes?"

"Don't want to talk about it!" snarled the Junior Minister, pulling petulantly at another ear. "I don't! I won't! But since you ask, David, of course—all I meant was the occasional wad."

Mr Selweaze-Todd looked very thoughtful. "A—wad?" he asked. "Of ... tobacco?"

"No, blast it, David! *Cash!* Moolah! Readies! Wampum! Fiduciary Pandamned Currency! 'Liquid', David—'liquid' in the sense of 'immediately exchangeable for goods and services' (particularly services), and 'not in any way requiring the inter-mediary attentions of one's accountant', nor, of course, 'discernible to the prying eyes of H.M. Peruser Of Taxes'! ... Delivered surreptitiously to one's paw—and—ha, ha—and ..." By now, the Spaniel seemed genuinely quite close to tears. "And ..."

"Delivered—surreptitiously?" prompted the Panderage Minister almost cruelly.

"The usual way David! The usual way! In a Pandamned sealed brown envelope! We don't *talk* about this? *Do* we? I mean, everyone else is doing it, aren't they? It's the normal thing, isn't it? Standard practice! Part of the job! We just don't *talk* about it!"

Noticing that foam had gathered along Mr Dogges-botham's bright pink gums (and how these animals did foam about all the time, he thought) the Mole took a pace or two away from him. But the Toad guided him gently back again, passing him another zykolafruit and peewee tartlet as he did so.

"We certainly don't, Nigel," agreed the tall Weasel. "But one does seem to be talking about it now, doesn't one? Almost, one might say—odd, isn't it?—almost as if one couldn't help it. I wonder why. I do wonder why. You—er—don't happen to know why, do you, W-T, by any chance?"

The Toad met Mr Selweaze-Todd's challenging and (for the moment) coolly humorous gaze with unblinking eyes. Just the tiniest speck of perspiration might have been visible on his forehead (but then, the air was very hot.) "Could it be … something … in the room?" he answered, successfully disguising any effort this reply may have cost him.

The Minister was unimpressed. "Or in the drinks?" he said, still staring. "I wouldn't drink any more of that, Nigel, if I were you. Not unless you want to spend the rest of the afternoon afflicted by untoward candour."

But … ah … but …" muttered the *distrait* Dog, who seemed to have recovered very little of his earlier composure. "I mean … What has happened to me? What has happened to—I don't know what to call it. All that? I was always so—you know—so *good* at lying … I had a certain poise, a certain—*je ne sais quoi*. It couldn't just vanish, surely?"

"You will be good at it again. Nigel! *We* will be good at it again," stated Mr Selweaze-Todd as if he had been making a policy statement in the Commons, though keeping his voice focused well within the circle. "After all, it is quite right for us to … lie … for want of a better word. And particularly, I am sure you gent'mals will agree, it is right for *me* to lie—and I see I must continue to use that vulgar term—since I am an animal of quite exceptional talent and importance. If I choose to lie, then, in my judgement, this can only be correct since *I* am the one who so chooses. It is no business of lesser beasts whether one tells the truth or not! Let them obey the rules as capricious, scurrying little creatures must and should. Such rules were not made to apply to mals of my calibre. No, nor perhaps to you, Nigel."

"That's most kind of you, David," said the Spaniel, brightening a little.

"Yes," proclaimed the Weasel, though a touch patronisingly, "I do think you may eventually deserve to be counted, Nigel. As *One Of Us*. You've clearly been working long and hard at it."

"I have! Oh yes, I have!"

"You obviously have some idea how to go about putting yourself on the winning side."

"One does hope so."

"And it is quite clear that the widest sphere of political influence is always achieved by those most skilled at ... blunting the edges of whatever may inconveniently be the case. Yes. *We* are a small and select group, Nigel. But *We* are the future of politics."

"Yes! Yes!"

"So ... Hm!" said the Minister, thinking deeply. "There is no doubt that a certain strategy will be necessary. It seems one must make a tactical retreat to, as it were, re-mass one's troops at some other position on the semantic battlefield. And then advance once more—just as soon as one's earlier words have been forgotten—brandishing the *Gleaming Falchion Of Veracity*—"

"... Yes, David. Yes! Marching under the time-honoured banner of *Honesty, Decency, Integrity*—"

"Standing, ever-courageous, ever-firm, behind the *Glittering Hauberk Of Fair Play!*"

"... in the securest knowledge that An *Englishmal's Word is His Bond?*"

"Ah, yes! And that *We Always Say What We Mean!*"

"... And, contrariwise, David, that when we say what we mean, *We Very, Very Much Mean What We Say!*"

"And that, whatever we do, or say, *It Just Jolly Well Has To Be Cricket!*"

"... And that, whatever we say or do, *We Will Never— Never!—Beat Around The Bush!*"

(Onion-sauce! thought the Mole. *And* roasted parsnips!)

"… Yes, Nigel, and in the securest knowledge," said Mr Selweaze-Todd, "that even if anyone did discover the truth about what one did, one would simply take them to court and—with the sterling assistance of barristers fully conversant with the plain unvarnished plausibility of one's case—sue them for libel into the millions and tens of millions! Not that one *would* be found out, thank Pan! Under normal circumstances, at least."

"No, no. The Government does still seem to know how to carry out enquiries into these things so that conclusions can be averted. But even if the truth did come out, David—"

"As a result of some horrible error—"

"Some horrible, *horrible* error—well, even then one would simply be moved to a posting on some low-key (though of course highly influential) Pseudobongo and then, after six months or so …"

"Bingo!"

"Bongo!"

"And off again, just as before!"

By now the eyes of both politicians—the gleaming and the pink-rimmed—were moistened equally with emotion. Even so, in the pause that followed, a single small voice rose up with a query. "But—um—" said the Mole. "Well, how can you say all that and still—if you don't mind me saying so—tell fibs?"

Mr Selweaze-Todd looked down from his height to the source of this prickly little bagatelle. He snorted with disdain and irritation, both of them of the most genteel kind. "It is really quite simple," he replied, "Mr—er … Mole … Quite straightforward. Though to be frank one doesn't really see why one should have to waste one's time explaining it to someone like *you*. In any case: one has to lie to oneself about it, too."

"Aaaaaahh!!" whined the Junior Minister For Invisibly-Subsidized Exports, jamming the ends of both paws hard between his teeth. "You *shouldn't* have said that, David! No, no—no! That is just too close to the bone! That is just too much; that is positive profligacy with the dinkum, David! That is *wilful over-generosity*; that is *crassly irresponsible management of the available sooth-resource!*"

(Celery-and-giblet stuffing! thought the Mole in consternation. With gravy on it!)

"Well, of course, Nigel," responded the Weasel, "one doesn't normally *admit* that one lies to oneself. Even *to* oneself. Q.E.D.—Q.E.D."

"No, no," added the Spaniel, in ghastly tones, "one doesn't even *know* one *is* lying, *because* one doesn't admit it, even and *especially* to oneself. Q.E.D.—Q.E.D., and *ipso-ipso-facto*."

"No—no—no, no! One doesn't admit it *because* one doesn't know it, and *vice-vice-vice-versa*."

"And one is, therefore—definitively, and without ambiguity—utterly innocent of wrong?" concluded Mr. Doggesbotham with a wan hopefulness.

"I would say so, Nigel, yes. That is my firm and considered opinion on this subject. The problem, of course, is that though I hold this opinion—firmly, decisively, and with all due prior consideration—I do not in fact believe it. Oh! Ruddy ruddy-ducks! Hell fire and Pan's little pickled gherkins!!" The tall weasel, snarled and foamed in a sudden and most unstatesmanlike fury, then pulled at his short tail as if, had he been able to reach it, he might have bitten it off and eaten it on the spot.

"... and I don't suppose," said Mr Doggesbotham, in a now deeply depressed voice—I mean, one can't possibly lie to oneself about *whether* one *believes* the considered opinion one holds, even when one already *knows* one doesn't?"

"That would obviously be the next step," grunted Mr. Selweaze-Todd, breathing hard. "That would certainly be next ..."

"But it's just not *p-o-o-o-s-ssibl-e!*" howled the Spaniel, much as if he had been trodden on by something very large. "It's just no good! It's useless! Useless! Oh, I'm so miserable! I hate myself! I *hate* myself! Don't you find me nauseating? You do, don't you? You *do*! That is what I am, isn't it? *Nauseating!* Say it—say it—say—"

"Control yourself, Nigel!" whispered the Panderage Minister, aghast at this display of inchoate emotion.

"I hate myself!" ranted the Spaniel. "I hate everybody! I hate being a politician! I hate the Government! I wish I was dead! *And* my name is really Dogsbottom!"

"Nigel, even under present circumstances—"

"Dogsbottom! Yes! Yes!" wept the ministerial hound. "I had it changed by Weed Poll. Dogsbottom, *Dog's Bottom!* The great family secret. I mean, how could anyone ever have hoped for a career in politics with a name like that? Even if it does, actually, mean something other than you think? (It was actually 'Dog's *Botten*'—E. N.—if you go back far enough. Meaning either, 'latrine of the dog-fox' or, 'spraint-place of the dog-otter'. According to which authority you believe.)"

"You have clearly gone into this in some detail."

"So there you have it," said the Spaniel limply, all energy drained from him now. "There one is. A probable historic otter's toilet. And a no more than averagely compromised animal, I believe, in the current state of the political market-place. If ever you did need any questions asked, Mr Wyvern-Toad—nudge, nudge, nudgetty-nudge, you know—remember, won't you, Dogsbottom is your mal? Dogsbottom is willing! Ha, ha. Ha. One's rates are genuinely competitive. Half-a-swimming-pool-per-question, par for the course. And if you ever needed to meet anyone—"

"I already know them all."

"Well—you know—if anyone new ever came along. We can often guarantee meetings even with inner Cabinet personnel for little more than the price of one of those nice Victorian-style plastic conservatories with the pipe-radiators and the fiddly ornamental imitation-woodwork.—Oh, and perhaps a SqueegeeStone-sett patio on the side, where negotiations prove more difficult?"

The Spaniel's red-rimmed stare had intensified by now to the point where it seemed that some kind of complete mental collapse might be imminent. "Uh—excuse ... er ... me," he rambled. "Ah ... someone I, ah, need to urgent, urgent, must, er, ha, ha—someone I ..."

And so—clutching together a half-empty glass and one of his ears as if he believed they were all of a piece—the Junior Minister For Subsidised Exports turned and walked erratically away into the noisy, guffawing, controversy-avoiding crowd.

"Well, well, well," said Mr Wyvern-Toad.

"W-T, I must part ways too, I'm afraid," said Mr Selweaze-Todd, any earlier ruffles vanished now from his calm surface. "I do—er—trust that none of this rather curious conversation will go further?" His eyes wandered briefly to the Mole, and the Rat, and back to the Toad, who raised his hand consolingly. "Don't even suggest it, David! *Far* too odd to be taken at face value!"

"Yes. And in any case, one would deny every word. I have already forgotten it. (Although, of course, I haven't.)"

"*I* have already forgotten it, David! (Although, of course, I haven't either.) *We* have forgotten it! (Though we have not.) Until our paths cross again!"

The Minister For Munitions Panderage cast one last brief, supercilious glance at the Mole, and moved off with all the stately dignity of a fully equipped battleship cleaving the waters of a calm and moonlit southern ocean.

"Glorious, fellows, don't you think?" cried the Toad, rubbing his hands together almost hard enough to light a fire with them, as he and his colleagues found their way out of the

Conference Hall. "Oh yes, quite wonderful! Stirring! I have always relished the cut-and-thrust of politics. Observing it, at least. They are so awfully, awfully useful, these politicians. Balancing up there on their verbal trapezes, forever drawing the eyes of the crowd from the places where the game that matters is being played! But you know, Mr Mole—entertaining as all this is—we must try to put your gifts to more practical use at some point. We *must* get him on the plane with McMinc next month, Gordon. Vital! Wouldn't you agree?"

"Ahhh—y—"

"Vital—*vital*. I must say I'm in an excellent mood! And Whipplewhitt's looking terribly overworked, don't you think?"

"Ahhh—Wha -? Nu—N—"

"Yes, yes! Done *quite* enough for today. I know we're stuck with the Molls Moyce, but I suppose I can bear it. I'll drive!"

CHAPTER TEN

EYE AND EYOT

Another fortnight passed, and on some days the Mole was summoned to the Toad Tower, and on others he was not. But by the end of the second week he had made the early-morning journey along the dread grey road often enough for its face-less features and macrometric curving lengths to have grown dimly familiar. Recognising them now gave him the same kind of satisfaction he might have found, in his earlier life, from being able to pick out the patterns of flaky paint in the end wall of a barn.

But he did not get used to the travelling—in some ways quite the opposite. Each day he spent on the road he grew more dizzily aware of the sheer, blank unnaturalness of being whisked along at sixty or seventy times the speed he could walk across a field. He did gradually begin to grasp that the danger of death that rushed upon him in every passing roar and whisper—death of the most distinctly *non* reversible-with-a-nice-cup-of-tea variety—must be postponable, if only by dint of it not having happened yet. But that did not help him very much, because after each first half hour watching the daylight claw its way above a *grisaille* horizon through the oil-spray film that coated and recoated the windscreen, everything outside seemed charged with faint threat. Even the small, lonely oaks the Mole could see dotted along hedgerows, in the gaps between the towns, looked wrong somehow. No trees should ever flash by an animal as rapidly as *that!*

The Mole stared out at the shifting flux of animals in ever-rekindling amazement. As he saw it, no less than a third of them at any one time seemed to be in the midst of holding up the little talking-to-animals-who-weren't-there boxes (the things Mr Rette called 'deracitels'), as a result of which, moan-inducingly, they had but one paw left for steering. He reasoned with himself that they too must be on the great road each morning because they had to be—that they too must be slaves of the towers, each roaring along his or her inexorable path to the window-box at the desk at the point in the row in the grid on the floor of the tower that was his or hers alone. Deep down, though, he could not help feeling it was other-wise—that in reality all were lost as in some nightmare limbo of perpetually frustrated escape, searching and searching for a place of rest they would never arrive at. They were like a vast flight of crows, he thought, feverishly circling over winter fields on which—for whatever reasons—none could ever settle.

Poor, poor animals, thought the Mole, in his moments of *motor*-borne reflection. When would *they* ever be able to stop and marvel at the sight of the moon as they walked home? If they saw the moon—even the new moon—it would always be through glass. They would *never be* walking home, and they would go on seeing all that remained of the only world that mattered through grease-grime and hatefully squashed insects. When would *they* ever scent the evening air, and brighten, and freshen as they rediscovered its mystery and beauty? What they smelled instead would always be this clingingly-scented fug of dusty upholstery, hot metal and shiny-stuffs, and what-ever got in to join it from outside.

And yet, he thought, if Mr Rette was anything to go by,

many of these animals must be *proud* of their instruments of self-torment! Even the Mole himself could sometimes detect a kind of hideous, stomach-lurching beauty in the things, as the sun pierce-glanced off some high-gloss window shapes in the moment before the boxes in question went into shadow under a bridge hulk. There was something about the way their windscreens glazed the absence-of-view ahead with curving reflections of sky, the way their sheened metal forms blocked perspectives down the streets of the city, that emptied his own mind, glazed his own eyes. So it was that on the great grey road one Wednesday morning, a few hundred yards from the Maidenhead Turnoff, the Mole conjured his first collective noun-of-the-future, one that was practical, he thought, for use across the length and breadth of Weaselworld: a *horror* of cars.

Now that he was an established employee of Toad Transoceanic (and it must be borne in mind that this was a fact the Mole himself still had not grasped—showed no sign of ever grasping), Mr Rette treated conversations with him rather more cautiously, so that their exchanges on the road tended towards the monosyllabic end of the range. It was only the Rat's broader relations with his fellow sufferers in travel that threw much light on his inner state. The Mole noticed that in between the cries of "Thrusting young tailcrusher!" and "Black-kneed bagworm!", one in particular seemed to grow more insistent on each journey: "Pan help us! They are ALL my enemies!!"

Every so often, though, in the very late evening, the Mole might pause hoveringly by Mr Rette's study-door, cocoa-mug in paw, and so spark off a talk with the room's sugarless-blooded inmate. One night he even ventured to wonder what the Rat might be doing so very late at night—still staring, as he was, with rectangular eyes, at his little grey screen, and tapping away at his register of little square keys with similarly proportioned fingers.

"Answering my wizzrites," retorted Mr Rette tappingly, as

if this was the most obvious thing on earth.

The Mole had also worked out for himself by now—with perhaps just a little prompting from Justin—that a "whizz-right" was some kind of fast letter, that arrived (somehow) without assistance from anything so lowly or physically encumbered as a post-animal.

"... Do you always have to do that, then—at night?" he wondered.

"Yours ... sincerely ... G.R ... Yesss ... Rette ..."

The Mole said nothing.

The Rat paused. "Yes! Obviously! *Yes*, yes. *Yes*, yes, yes. Crucial. *Crucial*. Answering one's wizzrites? Can't not do *that*! *Suicide*, not to do that! Madness. Crucial!"

"But—" The Mole hesitated, acutely aware that he might need to pose any more searching question from just the right angle.

He hesitated a little too long. "... 'But'?" demanded the Rat hydrochlorically. "Did I hear a 'But' then? Is that possible?"

"— Well, I mean, why can't you do it in the morning?"

"Because it has to Have Been Done by morning! It has to be In The Bag by morning! It has to be Plopped In The Pot, and Slapped On The Table, and Plumping Up All The Furry Little Tummies by morning! Because by morning, there will be a lot MORE wizzrites—a LOT more wizzrites—sitting there, staring at me, waiting to be answered!!"

"O," said the Mole. "So it rather—never stops, then? I suppose?"

Mr Rette tapped on, his fingers small intemperate flamenco dancers. The Mole was just turning to go, his cocoa barely drunk, when the Rat relaxed a little, and said, "No. It never stops. It never stops! It is another of the great leaps forward of modern times." He sighed, and sat back in his chair. "In the Dark Ages, you know, three years ago, we still had 'meetings'—gatherings (yes, I can remember them) of living, breathing animals, held around 'tables', in 'rooms' allocated to the purpose. Ideas could be exchanged, problems could be solved—sometimes, anyway—through the pooling of effort, the meeting of, well, minds. All the animals, pulling together—"

The Mole nodded understandingly.

"But nowadays there's no longer *time* for anyone to meet. And now, in any case, we have wizzrites, don't we? So we send wizzrites instead. And because everyone feels so out on a limb all the time (what with there being so few meetings), animals are *forever* sending wizzrites. They report every detail—they check over every detail—and then they write to make sure *you've read* what they wrote, and taken it in. And *I* have to write back to confirm that I have actually done so, to avoid *them* being able to claim, at some point in future, that I haven't, or didn't. Then they have to write back again to let me know that they know I have read what they wrote, because *they're* afraid I might otherwise claim, at some point in future, that I told them, but *they* didn't take it in. Meantime, no one ever speaks to anyone, and even a close colleague from the old, dark and primitive days three years ago begins to seem as if he might have turned into a gap-fanged back-stabber haunting the corridors, and wizzways, waiting for you!"

"... But, how do you ever get any work done?"

"That *is* the work! It is a new kind of work! Don't you see?"

The Rat pointed at his little grey screen with a histrionic finger. At his fingertip, the number '14' had changed to '15'. "Look, you see?! The next one! The next one! And the next!" ('15' was now '17'.) "Two! You see? It goes on growing, and growing, like mushrooms in a tunnel—like aphids in a gardening programme—endlessly churning out more, and more, and—hahahaha—*more* of its kind!"

"But, that is ..." said the Mole gropingly, "... *couldn't* you all talk? Couldn't you all decide just to stop, and sit down, and, you know—*talk*?"

"We don't have *time* to decide to stop! We're all far too busy already, checking our wizzrites! And in any case, deciding to stop would involve—well, stopping. And then—actually holding a *meeting* about it? *No*, no! Far too difficult!" The Rat paused and sighed again. "This is how we live, Mole, now. Always at the edge. Always pushed right up against it. A permanent war-footing, you see? You do rather tend to lose your sense of gaiety. Never mind! Give it five years, and G.R. Rette's job will be done by a robot anyway."

"— A *rowboat?*" said the Mole, open-mouthed.

"... Yes, but there's the rub, you see," went on the Water Rat, "(as Wagtails said in *Piglet*). Because if, sooner or later, most of the jobs on the planet have been taken over by machines, what will the six or so billion animals of eminently employable age and ability (who face quite considerable over-heads, not least their golf course fees), have *left to do?*"

Here the words "riverbank", "picnics", "fishing" and "lounging lazily" drifted through the Mole's head like traces of some ancient but hopelessly defunct tradition.

"Some nights, you know," said the Water Rat exhaling deeply, "my tail feels positively leaden with *angst*. No, no! This is not the airborne, free-flowing, sinuous thing that once it was, this tail, back in my glory-days of youth! Far from it. Far, far from it."

"You haven't ever tried Syrup of F—"

But the Rat went on (still, it seemed, talking mostly to himself), "Best not to notice these things, I suppose. Best not to talk about them either, really. It's only when you start putting things into words that they get out of proportion. Steer clear of 'em if you can, that's the best way. We are British, after all." He hesitated. "— Or English, anyway. Whatever that means. I am from Dorking, in any case. That much is certain."

The Mole gazed at the rings inside his cocoa-mug. "I don't know why animals in this world can't just be happy," he said.

The Water Rat lifted his tail and let it thump back on to the carpet, flaccid as a superannuated draught-excluder. It was all he had to offer by way of a reply, apparently.

In the moments before he fell asleep that night, the Mole was filled with a sudden, unexpected rush of compassion for his host at 'Kennylands'—and for the Badger and his fellow-idealists too; so much so that for a moment he paused in his breathing, staring into the inky darkness of his wardrobe-bed in the hope of catching a glimpse of his own two feet in the narrow black yonder. Quite why he wanted that, then, he had no idea. Just checking he still had them, he supposed.

As it turned out, the Mole's feet were to be very useful to him in the weeks that followed. Thursday was one of those days when—for whatever reasons—he was not invited in to the T.T. nerve-centre; and it poured, and he stayed inside the house, writing and musing and even making a half-hearted stab at a couplet or two, on a pad he had found on the desk in the room in the Tower where Mr Rette sometimes abandoned him. Mrs Rette was busily packing cases, ready to leave later in the day with her soul-mate, Erminia Minkwell, on a shopping-tour of three European capitals.

"— Well, I won't be able to do it once I start my new job!" she said to him more than once as she rushed past, a study in scarlet and black.

In the afternoon there was a telephone call (the Mole was used to phones ringing by now and often stood, fascinated, watching them do it). It was Mr Rette, using the most abbreviated form of panic-telegraphese to tell his wife that "the thing had come up" and that he had to be on a plane to Abu Dhabi in forty-seven minutes, and wouldn't be back for several days.

"Oh well, Mr Mole," said Mrs Rette, breezing away again.

"Looks as if you'll have to depend on Solveig for a day or two.—She's awfully good, though," she added, disappearing through a door. "So efficient! Can't not be, being Scandinavian!"

If any wider implications of this change did succeed in attaching themselves to the Mole's cerebral pin-board, they very soon dropped off again. But by the next morning—with Mrs Rette gone, and Solveig out purchasing medicines, and Justin apparently mouldering in bed with a temperature—it was clear to the Mole that he really did not have *very* much to do.

In any case he was increasingly restless. And the sight of clear spring sunlight pinkening the tips of the garden shrub-blots under the edge of a retreating cloud was enough to decide him: this morning, he thought, he would go for another little walk, and never mind what he might find in the course of it! He had long since worked out just which meadows the Rettes' and the other, packing-crate houses had been planted in, so it was a simple matter now for him to orient himself on the lie of the land this side of the water. That said, he did not want to go too far from the river, for fear he might lose his bearings. (He had never known this hilly country well, and that was *then*).

After five minutes' strolling, he was pleased to see a signed footpath pointing up a steep chalk bank in the exact direction he wanted to go. Up there, he thought, he would be on the hill ridge but, with luck, still able to look down into the valley. And so it was. At the top (a three-and-a-half-minute puff, at the outside) he found himself at first among yews, with the river down below to his right positively blazing in the morning sunlight, a narrow water-pavement seen through the hard edged blackness of their foliage. Then the yews gave way to a broad and openly curving hilltop mostly covered with beeches and ash. None were trees of any great age, but this was a pleasant, expansive woodland even so, strange to the Mole only in that for the whole of its length he had neither sight nor sound of anyone working—or walking, for that matter.

After another fifteen minutes or so he found himself approaching a stile in a fence at the woodland edge. This led him out under the branches of a big oak on to the steeply sloping flank of a long downland pasture that dropped away with the end of the hill as it tapered eastwards. He looked down towards the river and the view beyond, squinting as he tried to work out which of the fields and woods he saw in front of him had had these same outlines—or something roughly resembling them—in the time he could almost now refer to as 'the past'.

It was during this *reconnoitre* that his eye fell upon a shape in the river, opaquely visible beyond the still bare outlines of riparian trees. The shape was short, and narrow, and dotted here and there along its length with pollard willows: it was an eyot—one of the many tiny islands that stood midstream, or sometimes to one side of the flow, like shards of the riverbank that had somehow become detached from their moorings and deposited wherever the current wished.

The Mole scanned the reach of the river, looking for other recognisable landmarks, and a little further downstream he spotted a weir. It had far bigger, more clumping, uglier metalwork mazed around it than he remembered, and great banks of greystuff too. But even so, he knew it—it could be nowhere else on the river—and in so doing he also knew the island. He studied its sliver form through the trees, squinting against the sunlight, and as he did so he said, "O!" and then a minute later, "O! But no!" and a minute more again, and very quietly, "O my—O my—O my!"

Without further pause he set off down the big hill pasture in the direction of a stile at the bottom end and so, too, in the general direction of the island, the memory of which was drawing him to it now as unswervingly as if some animal he knew and loved had been standing there on it calling him by name.

The stile let him out on to a bridleway hemmed in on both sides by tall banks of bramble, so that he had to backtrack a little and then cut down riverward along the edge of a vastly-too-huge expanse of ploughland. This was traversed by another of the wonders of the future-present (he knew their shape by now, if not their purpose): a row of sky-puncturing, four-footed, tapering metal skeletons bearing cables high above the fields on things like giant concertinas attached to sets of stuck-out scarecrow arms. When he got closer to them he could hear the cables sizzling in a quietly threatening way, and as he walked hesitantly beneath, he felt an obscure twisting in his head, as if some washerwoman of the skies had been busy wringing out his brain. The cables plunged earthward a little further on, taking to the ground inside a metal compound only to re-emerge and continue on as before on the far side of the river.

So the Mole reached the riverbank and found his way along its unkempt, pathless edge towards his goal. There were the willow pollards, as proud and blunt as a row of freshly banged thumbs, and very much as he remembered them. There were a couple of alders too, but otherwise the eyot seemed much smaller than he remembered it, and far less covered in trees and shelter.

But it had been here ... It had been *here* ...

The Mole sat down very gently, feeling behind him for a tree-bole for support and never once taking his eye from the island, as if he feared it might drift off downstream if he did. Because, after all, he had forgotten all about it: he had forgotten all about it until now—until this very moment! It had been *here*, on *this island*, that Ratty and he had seen ...

"O my, O my, O my," said the Mole. "O my—O my—O my—O *my!*"

They had been searching for Portly, one of the otter-young. The lad was forever wandering off and then being found again, belly-up and happy as a water boatman, hidden away behind this little patch of yellow flags or that old hollow tree. But Portly had vanished more thoroughly than usual on that occasion, and so they had been rowing, all through the night—on and on into the scented, mist-veiled dawn of the most glorious midsummer morning, awake before the earliest birds because *they* had never been to bed! And a little breeze had sprung up and set the reeds and bulrushes a-rustle, and suddenly—the Mole could see it as if it were happening right before him now—Ratty had sat bolt upright, every whisker taut with concentration, and asked him if he had "heard it".

And he didn't hear it, not at first. But Ratty had, and Ratty was already in an ecstasy. He was at his most poetical, waxing on about the sweetness and the beauty of the sounds he heard. The Mole could picture him now, transported by quite inexplicable raptures whilst he, the Mole, carried on rowing downriver, his gaze on this bank, then on that, on the lookout for a plump pup-shape.

But as they drew closer to the island—that mysterious, tree-shaded little island whose centre was, then, like a clearing in a tiny wood of crab apples and wild cherries, screened off from the water's edge by them, and by banks of tangling dog roses and purple loosestrife whose colours had never seemed so vivid—then he too had heard it.

The piping.

"O my, O my, O my," said the Mole. "O my, O—"

The piping! Which had led them straight to Portly—round, contented little Portly—fast asleep in a place where every awakening bird had fallen silent, and cradled at the very feet, the very hooves . . .

"We saw him," breathed the Mole to this empty, modern, not-quite-clean river water, and to anyone else who might be listening; to himself above all, perhaps. "We *saw* him, and I had—O—I had forgotten!" But how could that be possible? "Unless he . . . unless *he made* us forget? There, on that island . . . Did we? *Did* we? O! Certainly we did: Ratty and I saw PAN!"

The Mole looked hard about him. Wasn't there even a nuthatch pecking about up the back of this tree, whom he could waylay and tell about his memory? Didn't he *deserve* a witness for something—he had no words for it—something as *awesome* as this? "He led us to the lost child—his piping led us there. His piping—this *was* what Ratty heard. Surely I remember that ... Don't I? And I have thought once or twice since that I heard it—yes!—around a bend of the River, when the breeze was in the reeds, or ruffling the water into little waves, or making that roar in the tops of the trees in November when the wind is in the west and coming up over the Wild Wood from the back!" The Mole looked at the river flowing past. "Yes. I thought I heard it. Then."

Yet for all his ardour, gazing at this eyot now, the Mole found that he was beginning to lose the thread of his memory in the very moments he was struggling to reconstruct it. For—what had he looked like? What had he *looked* like—Pan, the defender of Nature, the guardian of all animals? And what did he do to show them ... How had he ...? But no. Now even the questions themselves were going, fading into calm.

"But we did see him," said the Mole with conviction—a conviction strong as an Edwardian gentleman's billiard table, that would keep its place in a room even during an earthquake. "I know we did. That's all that matters, isn't it, Mole? And you won't forget it again, now, will you? No—not now!"

He stared on across the water at the row of willow pollards. A part of him was ready now to go and wander on, or back— it hardly mattered which. But he did not budge, and instead sat on beneath his alder tree, a frown in dark velvet deepening across his forehead. It was as if this slip of an island still had something to tell him, a message to pass on—one the Mole did not want to receive, yet must hear even so. What *was* it, there, in that row of blunt-headed willows? What did he seem to see in them?

"Nothing," said the Mole out loud, after a long pause. "Just—nothing. And that is why ... That is why I shall have to go. Isn't it, Mole? That's the truth. You have to go. You have to move on. You are not *right* here. Not now. You have to look, to try to find—O I don't know what! Somewhere, perhaps, there may be another valley that is ... that is ..."

He did not dare to complete the sentence, but the words he might have said (and thought, instead) were: *more like the world you remember.*

He pictured the Badger and his little band, and their grim, hard-fought battles against 'weasel-mind' on whatever back-woods fronts they could find to stage the battle. And a part of him, the doughty, unbeaten part, the warrior Mole, rallied at the thought that he might yet join them and play some kind of a part in ... what, though? Making it all as it had been before? Surely not! How could that be possible? The very idea made him feel out of his depth, floundering even for a first position, a peg, an argument within himself. Yet sitting there by his islet, the Mole did think long and hard about the Badger and the A.R.F., as much drawn to them by his memory of the big animal's strength and conviction as he was put off by the madness—so it seemed to him—of any attempt to unravel the threads of an entire civilisation.

Finally, the quietest inner voice was strongest. "You must go, Mole," said the Mole out loud, repeating what it told him. And for what it might be worth, the pollard willows on the little eyot seemed to stick up now like thumbs, sore or other-wise, raised in some mute signal of approbation.

Having decided, of course, there was no going back on it, and with such skills as he had as a field tactician the Mole began to consider his options. After all, he thought, there were always two choices in the world—to go down into the nearest available hole and stay there till the storms had blown over; or to put on one's neckscarf and get out and about and *see* a little of life, and never mind the weather. He could not fail to learn by travelling, that much was certain. And he was curious. Yes, he thought, he was still positively abristle with unanswered questions! So he would travel, and learn, and make himself stronger by so doing—or, if the worst came to the worst, fail molefully in the attempt.

But then, O, how would he go about it? Justin had—very kindly, thought the Mole—offered to lend him his bicycle, if ever he had a need for it. Justin never rode this bicycle himself, or so he said. And if that really was the case, thought the Mole, then perhaps he might borrow it, though it would have to be for a very less-than-certain period. If not, though, well, he could always do as he had always done, and put one foot before the other.

Finally the Mole got up. And now, lo and behold, there *was* a nuthatch up there, pecking and picking its silent way along the cracks in the alder bark. "I am moving on," the Mole told it. He got little by way of a reply.

<hr />

Justin Rette may have been off school with a cold, but it had not kept him in bed for very long. The Mole found him much as he had come to expect to find him, planted solidly and concentratedly in front of one of his many window-boxes, tapping keys and moving and pressing the little flicker-thing he called a 'bug'.

"I've just been for a walk," said the Mole brightly, a comment that called up on the young rat's face a look mingling solicitous pity with creeping horror. "Do hope I'm not in the way—?"

"No, Mole, that's glacial, come right in," responded Water Rat Junior through a slightly bunged-up nose.

"'Course you're not well now, so I don't s'pose you'd be much wanting to be out there yourself, perhaps—today—" prodded the Mole gently.

"Sunny *day*," said Justin guardedly. "Sunny day today! Don't want to be out there in the sun, do you, Mole? Might get cancer of the fur! All that UV blasting down on you?" (Yew-vee? thought the Mole echoingly. Could there be some fault in the yew trees, too?) "It's worse at this time of year, too—"

"But it is fine outside today," said the Mole. "In a—um—manner of speaking. And anyway, it's ..." He windmilled a half-bent arm, already knowing he was on a losing wicket. "It's—well, you know—'real' ..."

"Well there it is, Mole," responded Justin Rette in a pear-shaped voice. "Real life is just another kasement." He turned back to gaze wonderingly at the largely blank latency of his current screen. "I'm setting up a labycamp," he said, and clicked. "Several of them, actually, when I've finished. See, Mole—I mean—you probably don't know this, but this is so, *so* glacial it's positively *cryogenated*: we're starting to see the first toddlers coming into TK now. *Babies*, more or less! They cry when their mothers lift them off their tapperboards, apparently! Like, I thought *I* was an aheadhave, but I didn't get in there until I was a squeaky old dodderer compared to them."

"How dread ..." began the Mole, then thought better of it.

"Yeah," continued the young rat reflectively. "It's a race against time now, I reckon. I mean, any animal can get in there now—you could do it yourself, if I showed you! All you need is the most basic TK skills, get your labycamp set up and—I mean, *cubic*, mal!—go out there and conquer the world without ever leaving your bedroom! We're all going to be doing business on the Lab—that's coming, Mole. It's here right now. So it'll only be a matter of time before some of those babies start to turn themselves into infant millionaires, right? That's what I plan to do, anyway. Start small; think big! I can still beat some of them to it, I reckon. You've got to be retired by the time you grow up."

"Um—"

"Hang on," said Justin, getting up. "'Scuse me. Mum said I

had to do this. I forgot." He picked up a long blue-and-silver can with the word GLAIDE printed sweepingly around it, and pressed. The room was at once engulfed in a mist of sweet-acrid, eye-needling, lung-clinging vapours that left the Mole wheezing like a pair of punctured bellows and clawing at the half-open door to escape.

"So as I—Oh …" said Justin, turning to note his absence.

"… Sorry, er … Mole? Oh, there you are. Yes, it is a bit— I don't know. A bit strong, I suppose? Don't notice it much myself, apart from the fact that it's disgusting. Mum says it makes the air smell better. Compulsory, see?"

After his sixth urgent intake of the relative purity of corridor-air, the Mole was able to respond with "… Does … she?" But he had to wait until the smell did nothing worse than call up mental pictures of mercury-beaded snowdrops gleaming amongst banks of electro-plated nickel silver aconites before he could venture back into the room.

"I just wonder," he said at last, ruddering hard towards what he still felt was the only worthwhile question, "I mean, all I wonder is, will you be *happy* doing what you said? (Whatever it is.)"

Justin looked at him quizzically, his whiskers sheened by the light from his bendy-lamp, very much as if he were trying to work out if the Mole could be serious. "'*Course* I'll be happy!" he exploded. "I mean, this is IT, Mole. This isn't just refrigerated, mal, what you're looking at here, this is *Antarctica*! Po-siti-vely! This is the Permafrost, this is the Beardmore, this is *the* big Ice Lolly. This is ba-a-a-a-a-a-ad!"

"… bad …?" echoed the Mole, smally, confusion levels peaking into the red again.

Justin took a breath and looked at him. "Oh," he said. "— The jungle—right? I mean, you know. I like it. I *like* it! See, a lot of these animals, they're just amateurs. All they want to do is play, really." He clicked and tapped a little and the box-window came alive, in a sense, with a display that read:

"HI, folks! And howdy-doody you-all Happy Laby-Campers everywhere! WELCOME to the Laby-Summer-Camp of Mr and Mrs Ron and Eff Rat of Number 3, The Shrubberies, Worpledon. Well, have we got news for you today! We want to share with all you good folks out there—an' shucks, we sure ain't shy about it!—our latest EXCITING DISCOVERY— how to make long-lasting fruit bowls, pen-holders, drawing-pin-pots, and any number of other useful *small household containers* out of *your* old compressed grass-cuttings and wood-shavings!! Interested? OKAY! —"

"That's no use, right?" said Justin, eyeing the display with the bristling eyebrow-arch of the emergent professional. "They just want to give it away. And of course, what they've got to give away is … um. No comment. No, the trick is, obviously, to start to trade. Me, I don't know yet. I may just start with old tecton parts. Got enough of them, if anyone wants them! But I have been thinking, actually, you know—if I could find a supplier—maybe I could branch out into something like Cubic-end Tee Shirts? Everybody wants them. All you've got to do is get your logo right.—See?" He plucked lightly at the shift he was wearing, indistinguishable as it was to the Mole's eye from any of his other top-apparel. "This is a *Melvin Schwein*, obviously. You get the name right, like he did, I reckon you've done it. Or these jeans, of course." Here the young rat indicated a sewed-on label bearing the stitched imprimatur *Phulandis Muni*. "They cost Dad an ear and a tail, these jeans. And you can see why, can't you, with that label on them!"

"— Um—Can I? —"

"Oh, YES! They're *Phulandis Muni*! You take that label off them, Mole, and you wouldn't want to be seen dead in them, especially not on my school playground! Clothes that can't be bothered to logocast they're special? Forget it. No, I'm serious. It's no go with no logo, Mole, a nono, a nogo, you've got to have a *logo*, a *logo*, Moleogo, a logo is a *gogo*! LO-GO-WO! LO-GO-YO! Baa-arp! Baa-arp! Baa-arp! Baa-arp!" To the Mole's great consternation, Justin began to beat rhythmically on his knees with the flats of his paws, hunching down as he did so, then spreading his attentions out towards the table top and a convenient chair-back. "... Whole different *calibre*, see?" he continued, gradually reining himself in again. "No, Mole, I reckon all I have to do is get my logo right and I'll be in there too. Something like—RET? Big bold letters, of course. Just R-E-T—boxed in, maybe? Or how about 'J. P. Rette'? That's got a kind of homey feel to it, doesn't it? 'JRett'? Modernistic? 'Jrike'? Or how about," (he spread the word across the horizon) "'*Retitas*'?"

"... But you wouldn't want to—I don't know—" The Mole moved his paws in front of him as if trying to bring into being an imaginary something. "— You wouldn't want to, sort of, *make* things? I mean—you know—in, um, person—?"

Justin looked back at him blankly. The Mole continued moving his paws around the imaginary something like an amateur conjuror in a deepening panic, until he realised the blankness was permanent.

"I don't understand!" said Justin. "I mean—like what?"

The words 'fishing-rod' and 'picnic-basket' drifted downstream on the Mole's thoughts, unspoken.

"No, I reckon that's a bit of a terminal emulator," said Justin glumly. "*Making* something. Deeply unglacial. Entreprup—um—EntrepreNURRealism is it today, Mole. What you make today is *money*, right? Somebody else does the thing-making bit."

"Does anybody still ...?" The Mole paused. He had been hoping to change the subject, but realised even as he formed the question that it would probably take him into deeper waters still. "Does anybody still make books, now? Much? For old-fashioned fellows like myself?"

The young prophet of tectonometry gazed at the Mole with compassionate eyes. "Well, they do," he said. "I suppose. In one or two places. For the time being."

"I do rather like a book myself," continued the Mole plaintively. "When I can find one. It's nice to nuzzle what you read. When you don't own spectacles."

"Yes, but you don't want to *trust* them, Mole! Not if you've got the choice! Not even in the jungle, really. There's a whole different quality of stuff here on the Labyrinth. I wouldn't go for books if you can help it. They're just—I don't know what they are. Bits and pieces. Little snippets of this and that. Faded print, on crumbly old paper. If it's here in the Labyrinth, see, it *has* to be *more right*. Books are just things they put on shelves in pubs now, really."

"... pubs ...?"

"All round the places where you eat? Haven't you been into a pub yet? It's what books mean: 'You Can Eat In This Bit'. Where they don't have books, it means, 'This Is Where The Serious Boozing's Done! Take Your Plaice Elsewhere'."

"I haven't been into an inn for—O—a long, long time," said the Mole wistfully.

It was at this point—at the end of one of those unfillable pauses—that the Mole raised the subject of his decision to travel, and the use he might possibly have for a bicycle, if one happened to be still available. Justin seemed surprised—even a little confused—by this news, and the Mole felt he ought to explain a little more to him, difficult though that was in the circumstances. After all, he didn't know himself quite what he wanted to do—not really. "I would like to see a bit more of the world," he said, "— um, the world away from the jungly bits; you know. And I'm, I suppose ... eventually, I'd like to look for a place to dig my hole. A fit bit of turf."

Justin's mouth made an 'O'. "... Your *hole?*"

"O, ah. Yes. Just another of those fossilly old expressions of mine. Bless me, I do keep coming up with them, don't I?—Um—settle down? In a manner of speaking?"

"Well, Mole, you're very welcome to the bike. I mean, honest, if you want it you can keep it. No, really! Dad gave it to me when he was trying to find new ways to trick me—errr ... 'encourage' me—to exercise. But he sort of lost interest when he realised he'd have to pedal everywhere with me too if I was ever going to use it. Clever, that. He never got his enthusiasm for it back, somehow. Can't imagine why."

They found the bicycle in the northern third of the triple garage, in an area given over to things other than *motors*, behind a pile of empty tecton crates and in between the sit-upon mowers. Neglected the bike may have been, but, to the Mole at least, it was a thing of speech-bereavingly daunting high technology, clompingly massive and robust even to eyes accustomed to the great black frames and springing leather seats of an earlier age. Yet at the same time it was also absurdly light-weight—so light, in fact, that when the Mole first lifted it, he pulled it up from the floor with a jerk.

Once the saddle was adjusted (to the bottom) it didn't take him too long to learn to keep his balance on it: that principle transferred unaltered. And after falling no more than eight times into the dark embrace of the conifers, he also understood how he should grip the brake levers. The main problem he had was with the things Justin called 'the gears', of which this bicycle (being, apparently, a very special model) had twenty-seven (or twenty-nine, Justin added, depending on how you counted them). The young rat did explain, to the best of his ability—limited, in this field—what the gears were meant for and why it might be worthwhile, in theory—if you absolutely *had* to ride a bike—to try to use them. But the Mole could see in front of him only an arcane assembly of little black levers and wires and cogs, more opaquely complex in construction even than the workings of a steam-roller, and all scaled and squeezed down into a tiny expanse of metalwork. All he wanted to know was that if he turned the pedals the thing would go, and if he pressed the handles, there, the thing would stop. And if it was difficult on the hills, well then: he would just have to get off and walk.

So keen had Mr Rette been to see his son adapted to the outdoor life—on occasional days of the year, at least—that he had acquired a comprehensive range of other items which might now prove very useful indeed to any mole planning to set off towards the far horizon in search of plots and paddocks new. One by one Justin pulled things out from dusty shelves—a one-mal tent that resembled a large olive-green ladybird once erected (this took some effort), a primus stove, utensils, a set of four copious panniers. He was even able to find a small portable radio ("Really out of date design," he said. "Unglacial. Sad. No headphones, see? But it does still work, with a battery in it.") and trumped all these discoveries by producing an entire cyclist's wardrobe in what was, or had recently been, the apogee of spindle-voguishness: fur-clinging 'trousers' in an outstandingly nasty, shiny, stretchy black-stuff ("That's Flykrasoft," said Justin weightily, twanging them. "Hey—re-frig-er-A-ted."); a large sky-blue tee-shirt with MOLLUSK CARES emblazoned large and pink across the chest; a "helmet" also tending to the subcoccinellidan in shape, but ridged and colour-striped and made with curious teardrop-shaped gashes in it as if better to let the rain in; and then—the final touch—a pair of wire-framed, quite perfectly ovoid, hideously gleaming "Reflekta-Shaydes", in which the Mole, now holding them, saw himself, and young Master Rette, and the whole of the garage, weirdly emblobbed in miniature.

"Unfortunately those don't fit me," said Justin. "Keep slipping off the snout. *You* could wear them, though, probably. You've got solider fur. Hey, you'll be *such* an on-road icebox, Mole, if you go out there wearing this lot!"

The Mole was dubious. The Mole was, in fact, very deeply dubious, not to say more-than-a-little-profoundly-aghast at the thought of wearing any of these items in the seclusion of his wardrobe, let alone out *there*, in *public*. But he responded warmly to the young rat's enthusiasm (odd, he thought, how

Justin almost seemed to enjoy setting up the tent in the garden), and decided that if he had to wear this uniform to make his departure from 'Kennylands' to please the lad, then so he would. He did, of course, protest long and loud at Justin's feverish over-generosity, but the truth was that the junior Rette was positively relieved to have found a use for all this lifestyle-threatening stuff, and couldn't wait to see the back of it. "I'll *loan* it to you, then!" he cried. "A loan, but just for life! (Two lives if you've got another handy). Come and haunt me when you've finished with it. Woooooo! Justiiiiin! Here's your trooooousers! Soooorry about the hooooooooles!"

"You're the best of fellows," said the Mole with feeling.

"'The best of fellows'," echoed the young water rat gruffly, grinning.

The Mole's old burrower's skills in packing things away neatly into confined spaces served him well as he began to compress his equipment into first this front pannier and then that back one.

"Which way d'you think you'll go, Mole?" asked Justin, his tail sine-waving in what might have been the mildest curiosity.

The Mole paused in mid-push. Had he thought about that? But even as he asked himself the question, he recognised that he had done, somewhere deep inside his head. "I think I shall be heading east," he said. West, he knew, was probably prettier, even today—and hillier, too. But there was some-thing—some magnetizing of his inner compass—that spelled out 'East', or at least 'East First'. He pictured low, broad valleys, threads of water, reed-beds, clumps of woodland, networks of small fields smooth and velvety under fine old pasture, with the cowslips dancing across them in the breeze—somewhere that might feel as familiar to him when he came upon it as once had this river-country here.

"Don't know if this'll be any use," said Justin, returning from the house with a map. It was a *Hollowmew's Motorist's Map Of The South East Of England, Scale: One Third Of An Inch To The Mile*

(Price: 3/9½d). "*Totally* out of date," said the young rat. "Cars still had running-boards when they printed that! Split windscreens, good grief! I found it in DecrepitAid. But the roads'll probably mostly be the same. Possibly. Apart from the Clearways of course. And bypasses. You don't have to have it.—Oh! Another thing I forgot!"

He went back into the house, returning a moment later (the Mole held his nose). But in Justin's hand now was a solid-looking padded brown envelope marked boldly FOR THE ATTN. OF MR M. MOLE. "Dad said I had to make sure you had this if he didn't get back to give it you himself. *Very important,*" he said. "*Very—very—very* important!"

No more than middlingly puzzled as yet, the Mole opened the envelope only to find it stuffed bubble to bubble with fifty-pound notes, tightly held together by large rubber bands. ("Fifty pounds!" breathed the Mole at the sight of the very first of them.) Also enclosed he found a note on Toad Transoceanic headed notepaper. This read:

From: G.R. RETTE, Degirthing. <g.rette@tt.co.uk>
To: M. Mole Esq., S.D.C. (T.T.) <rette@kennyla.co.uk>
Subject: Confidential. *Do not stak.*

Regarding your initial Agglom. Emol./Annex. Gorbel. (currently rated as per post-Transitional V-Scale Pinguific Index/further review) and covering the period of One (Nominal) Calendar Month in S.D.C., minus deductions, Accounts have insisted I withdraw on your behalf *in CASH*—enclosed in full—pending the establishment (as per our discussion of Monday morning last, which I hope you will remember?) of a Bank Account in your name (as is in fact the normal procedure for animals in all professional positions throughout the whole of the Western World). (As I believe I pointed out to you more than once at the time.)

"He said to tell you, if you didn't understand, 'It's yours'," said Justin.

"M—mine?"

"That's what he said!"

"But this is a—O, there must have been a huge, dreadful mistake!" said the Mole querulously, gripping the seeming-prince's-ransom hard between his paws. "I shall have to ... But what *shall* I do? When will Mr Rette be back? The end of next week! O dear, O dear, O dear! O my!"

"You don't have to do anything," said Justin. "Except, maybe, spend it."

"But—who is it from? Who sent it?"

"Well—Mr Wyvern-Toad, I guess. Sort of. Him, and the Great Firm of course. Dad did say, I'm afraid, you *had* to get it. He'll be in trouble if you don't."

"In trouble?—O! ... O ... But I haven't done anything to deserve it."

"Who does? Don't ask me, Mole! It's what Dad said. You have to have it, and that's that. Sorry about that!"

What was the Mole to do? Had Mr Rette been coming back as usual that evening, he could have spoken to him then and there. But he wasn't coming back, and the problem now was that the Mole's inner decision had been made, and made quite firmly and tuggingly. He simply could not wait another week: he had to go. He *had* to go. "... Mr Wyvern-Toad wants me to have it? ..." he repeated to himself under his breath, as he pushed the envelope hard down into the back of one of his panniers. Could he, in all honesty, treat this too as a kind of loan, one that he might at some impossible to imagine point in the future repay, or simply give back as it was? Well, the fact was that he could not leave it with young Justin: he had to make himself responsible for it, one way or another. "M—mine ..." he repeated almost silently, no less disturbed than he had been at first.

Later on, the Mole wrote a letter to Mr and Mrs Rette. It

gave him a lot of trouble. He stumbled and hovered over the choice of words for more than an hour, because after all, he thought, he *was* leaving next morning—he certainly was, and never mind the weather—and in his heart of hearts he could not say for sure if he would ever find his way back here. And then at the very end he gave himself a brand new problem by putting in a P.S. after his signature. This began "Have gone in search of ...", but there he paused. In search of what, exactly? The thing (the things) the Mole might go in search of, deep down—he could not put that into words. It was too difficult. So once again he sat with his pencil poised, looking for a single word that might do instead.

He did sleep well that night, and in the morning—so beside himself with embarrassment that he might as well have had a double walking at his side—he came downstairs resplendent in fur-clinging Flykrasoft and clinking zip-clip cycling shoes, with MOLLUSK CARES writ large and pink across his chest. Solveig stood, mouth open, her whiskers atwist with curiosity, but Justin rose beaming from his cereal bowl with a triumphant cry of "Frig-o-riff-i-CO! Hey, Mole, mal! Icicle down, mal! See that, Solveig? That's a real glacial, antarcticacial pedaller-mole there! He's going to be the icebox of the blacktop, is Mole!"

On any other day this would have been enough to project the Mole at speed straight back inside his wardrobe. Instead, though, he took the young water rat's warm approval of the quite-staggeringly-dreadful at face value. After all, he thought, that *was* why he was dressed like this.

Breakfast over—and now with a full sandwich-box and a glucose-charged, logo-spattered drinking bottle—the Mole did his final bit of packing. (His more normal attire was carefully squeezed down into the top of his rear-right pannier.) The magic fortress-gates of 'Kennylands' swung open for the very last time to let him pass, chivalric and luridly aglow, though with his chain slipping horribly on the cogs.

Justin followed him out on to the road. "… Mole?" he said, as he put the gears back into middle range. "There was one thing I wanted to ask you, actually. It's just—Dad said you used to live round here a long time ago, or something?"

The Mole nodded.

"No, it's just I was wondering where it was, exactly."

"O …" said the Mole, as if to answer. But he said no more, since in that short moment his eyes had filled to the brims with tears. But this was not the style of a heroic exit, or anything resembling it! "Dear me," he said, with a throat as tight as a guy-rope in a gale. "O dear … Bit of grit in my eye. 'Scuse me." He blew his nose, and dabbed, and blinked. "There. That's it. Got it out now." There was another silence as he collected himself. "It was … O, it was a very long time ago. But it was—I lived—He waved imprecisely cross-river and up-river, both at the same time. "'Bout three miles on up the valley, and over a bit? *That* sort of direction—"

"And was it—" said Justin, pausing himself. "Was it, like— you know—in a *hole*?"

"Yes," said the Mole, troubled again by grit.

"Gosh," said Justin, archaic himself for the length of a word. He mused for a moment. "Wow. That's glacial, Mole. That's glacial. Major. Well—um—see you, then."

"Over the hills and far away!" said the Mole, aspiring to brightness. Perhaps it was something about his choice of words that caused the young rat to look at him then just a little more intently, as if he might be wondering now, and curious, and even—so very, very slightly he did not know it himself—envious as well?

"Would you like to come with me?" said the Mole.

Justin stared blankly at the hill beyond the hedge. "You must be JOKING!" he responded, in a doubt-free voice. "Good luck, Mole! Icicle down, mal! Lolly-lolly-lolly! Send us a wizzrite! Or a—or a postcard, I suppose. If you absolutely must!—Bye!"

At the top of the first long hill there was just one point in the road—the Mole remembered from long-gone experience—when it was possible to stand and look back down the bending, dimpling combe and around the edge of a thin beech copse to catch a last glimpse of the river. He pushed his bike up the length of the hill (in this he had no choice) and didn't hurry. But when he got to the top he did not look back.

<hr/>

Decency and propriety demand in equal measure that we pass over all mention here of the by no means concise nor temperate reactions of Mr G.R. Rette on his return, seven days later, and his attendant discovery of Special Directorial Consultant Mr M. Mole's non-presence at—or more precisely, permanent migration from—his home. It must be enough to report on the contents of the letter, delivered to him by his dutiful but puzzled son, and addressed in very small (in fact, quite pin-prickingly tiny) handwriting to himself and his wife—a letter that was carried some distance around the rooms of 'Kennylands', and more than once waved rhetorically to the air in a paw that was less than steady. This read as follows:

Dear Mr. and Mrs. Rette

I hope you will get this soon. It is Friday now.

It must seem very odd for you to come back and find me gone—but I have thought about it hard—and it must be all for the best. All things considered. As it must have been a dreadful ~~news~~ nuisance for you to put me up for so long. Though of course you have been very kind.

I do not know if I can ever make it up to you. But I hope you will think of me as forever grateful. What ever happens.

I shall try very hard to give the money back to Mr ~~Wivur~~ Toad.
And clear up that mistake if I can.
I shall not forget you.

Most truly yours

Mole

P.S. Have gone in search of

　　　　　　　　　　　　England

ENDNOTE

With the exception of a few imaginary details and link passages, the descriptions of landscapes, both rural and urban, in this novel are based on direct observation. But anyone looking for such locations on the ground in the order in which they are described would be quickly frustrated, since the England of Weaselworld resembles nothing so much as a patchwork quilt whose source elements have been cut up, reshaped and transposed in shameless pursuit of narrative convenience. This said, the general trajectory of the Mole's journey east (in Volume II) could be traced without too much difficulty.

It may also be worth noting that the inspiration for the setting for the Mole's first emergence into Weaselworld does not lie in the Thames Valley, as might be expected. However, it can be found very near to it, and is in a river valley.

G.L.J.

Will the Mole find 'England' on his journey east? Whom will he meet and what adventures will he have on the way? Will he find a place resembling the world he remembers, or is he doomed to roam the devastated countryside of Weaselworld as a lonely drifter? Will he ever see Mr Rette and his family again? Or the Badger and his small group of freedom fighters? And can the Badger ever hope to make headway against the massed forces of the weaselry and Weaselmind?

Why was Mr Wyvern-Toad so keen to get the Mole "on the plane with McMinc"? Who is he and what is McMinc Inc, the Re-Mind Agency, Globobank and the World Mystery Consortium? What are their plans for the future of the planet. . . . . and can the planet's animal and plant populations survive them?

FIND OUT in the second and concluding volume of *The Wind In The Pylons* by Gareth Lovett Jones, which incorporates

PART TWO — MOLE THE WANDERER
PART THREE — IN FARAWAYSIA

For news of the publication of Volume II, please visit the web-site <u>www.hilltoppublishing.co.uk</u> and leave your address and/or e-mail address. Alternatively, send a request to Hilltop Publishing Limited, PO Box 429, Aylesbury, Bucks. HP18 9XY.

Also published by Hilltop

Libidan

By P.J. Goddard

Bill Kennedy develops medicines for rare hormonal disorders. His life at Asper Pharmaceuticals is completely uneventful – until the freak laboratory accident that turns his humdrum world on its head. *Libidan*. A psycho-sexual stimulant of awesome potency. A once-in-a-lifetime discovery to make him wealthy beyond his wildest dreams... if only he can find a way to perfect the formula.

hearted and calculating men in white coats, then read *Libidan*
– it is closer to the truth than you might think.'

'A clever and highly enjoyable work.'

'It is imaginative, well written and in parts side-splittingly
funny. I thoroughly enjoyed it…'

'*Libidan* is a challenge. As the story unfolds it improves with
every chapter, and becomes more enjoyable with each twist.
Here philosophy meets quantum physics, genetic engineering,
and the future of mankind. Read it – you will never think or
perceive the same way again.'

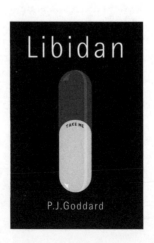